That didn't [...]
pulled by f[...]
control. Sh[...]
his kiss and [...]
pressed her soft flesh to his. His hot mouth found
hers and his kiss was so hard it hurt for a moment
before she inwardly fought him for a second, then
yielded like a drowning woman needing, begging
him to rescue her. Where kisses were concerned,
she thought, this was as good as it got.

And Adam was as good as gold for the rescue. His
big hands went up and down her back, stroking
gently when he wanted to press her hard. She
smelled of light jasmine, of natural pheromones
and wanting him. Her skin was summer peaches
plucked at their prime. And he was flaming with
deeper desire than he had ever known. He had
loved a young woman with all the intensity of a
young man's love. Now he was beginning to feel
the wild power of a man's love lick his heels.

Adam groaned inside himself. He wanted to take
her now, envelop her in his arms, go deep into
that pulsing, luscious body and stay there a lovely
while.

With the tip of his tongue he traced her warm,
sweet lips as one big hand cupped the back
of her head. Her lips parted and his tongue
slipped inside her mouth, pleading, begging, yet
ravishing, slaking passion even as it aroused it.

She felt herself nearly fainting with desire that
began in her brain and traveled in dizzying waves
to her toes. And the fear she felt of her stalker
was no greater than her fear of the heartbreak
Adam Steele could bring.

FRANCINE CRAFT

PASSION'S FOOL

ARABESQUE®

PASSION'S FOOL

An Arabesque novel

ISBN 1-58314-728-4

© 2006 by Marjorie Holtzclaw

www.kimanipress.com

Printed in U.S.A.

To Saundra M. Woodard
who has the heart of a lioness
and the soul of a dove.

Acknowledgments

As always, I want to acknowledge
the truly magnificent help given me by
Charlie Kanno and June M. Bennett.

Others remind me never to forget
that it all begins with God and His glory.

The Eighth District
in the Metropolitan D.C.'s Police Department
exists only in my imagination and is put there for
smooth-functioning story purposes.

—Francine Craft

Chapter 1

Raven McCloud walked along New Jersey Avenue in northwest Washington, D.C., in the still-hot mid-September evening, to her car parked two blocks away. She had meant to leave the house where she had conducted an interview before it became this dark. But the information she was getting from a woman who lived a few doors back had been too useful to cut the conversation short.

Her breath caught as she realized there were heavy footsteps behind her. A small chill ran the length of her spine and she quickened her step. She was in a shabby, largely deserted residential section of the city and the streets were nearly empty. Gentrification was well underway with some houses having beautifully finished exteriors and some woefully dilapidated. The luminous dial on her watch read 7:30 P.M. She began to turn and thought better of it. She had been robbed twice before, once at gunpoint, but that had been some time ago. She had been carjacked once, too, but she wasn't going to think about that. Not now.

Raven turned her head. She wasn't a fearful woman, but there were so many things to consider here. The man be-

hind her to her left could have many things on his mind.
She refused to think about rape; she was pretty good at
jujitsu. She hurried and the footsteps hurried, slackened
her steps a bit and the other footsteps slowed. She
clenched her hands, holding her tote and her purse close
to her side. A woman had been assaulted in broad daylight
four blocks from this spot two weeks ago. The culprit had
been a junkie. A trickle of sweat ran down her back.

The footsteps were overtaking hers. Why in hell hadn't
she asked someone in the house to walk her to her car?
The woman she had interviewed had a brother and an
uncle in the house, but they had been in the basement
shooting pool.

Suddenly she knew it was fish or cut bait because whoever the footsteps belonged to was at her side. She could
hear heavy breathing and out of the corner of her eye,
she saw a man a half foot taller than her five-feet-eight-
inches. The man laughed softly, evilly and reached out.
"It's about time. Give it up," he said in a deep bass voice.
"No use fighting it, mama."

What the hell did he intend to do? Raven wondered,
as ugly pictures flooded her mind. Fury filled her and she
braced her legs to fight, but her knees threatened to
give way and his hard knees struck the side of her thigh,
throwing her off balance. He snatched her purse, but
couldn't take her tote, to which she stubbornly held on.

"Stop! Police!"

There were pounding footsteps then as the man who
owned the welcomed voice came to her side. Her assail-
ant dropped her purse, vaulted over a nearby gate and
ran down an alley.

"Are you all right, ma'am?" a baritone voice asked softly.
Then, as she turned, he exclaimed, "Ms. McCloud!"

Her voice shook with outrage. "You came just in time. God only knows what that creep had in mind."

She was getting lightheaded and he reached out, steadied her. "I'm glad I was nearby." He picked up her purse and handed it to her.

The dizzy wave subsided and she saw him now in the streetlights as her eyesight steadied. "Detective Steele. Oh, am I glad you were nearby too."

"This isn't a great neighborhood for you to be out in at this time of evening. If you're driving, where's your car parked?"

"About two blocks away. I was interviewing someone and I badly needed the information."

He drew a deep breath, then expelled it hard. "Investigative reporters. Look, you're shaking and that was one big, bad *hombre*. I parked a block or so back since I was coming up this way to see someone. I could have chased him, but I needed to see after you."

"Just walk me to my car please and I'll be fine."

He shook his head. "No, I don't think so. You're dazed. Walk back to my car with me and I'll take you somewhere for a cup of coffee to steady your nerves. Then I'll have one of my men pick up your car and take it home for you. I'll take you home afterward. I'm worried about you."

She laughed shakily. "No need to be worried, detective. I'm okay."

"I don't think so," he said evenly. "You've been investigating a big case for your TV station for months and there are people who'd like you out of the way, or at least to stop you somehow. You don't deny that, do you?"

She shook her head. "We all have jobs to do. I haven't had too much trouble." She paused. "Except for heavy breathing calls, footsteps like the ones tonight that turned out to be a little dangerous. I still have my tote and I think he always intended to run."

She didn't believe her own words and he looked at her hard.

"The creep tonight was right on you and it wasn't to wish you good evening. God knows what was on his mind. Junkies are known to act and never think."

"Yes. Well…" She told him briefly what the man had said. "I think he just goes with the territory. I could smell marijuana. He wanted my money and maybe my credit cards."

"Please. Let me take you for coffee and something to settle your stomach. You're more upset than you know."

She thought a moment. "Okay. I certainly need something. Fortunately my little girl is with my friend and her husband, so I don't have to get right home."

"Good! Let me make a quick report on my cell phone and we'll go over to Chinatown to a restaurant I think you'll like."

Inside the cozy restaurant, Raven felt cold, not so much from the air conditioning as from continuing fear. As the detective looked for desirable seating, she wondered. Had it been plain robbery or something worse? Detective Steele looked at her as he cupped her elbow in his palm. "Once we get some coffee in you, you'll feel better."

Lord, she was still trembling, he thought. She wasn't telling him everything. He guided her to a corner table. There weren't too many people in the restaurant and service was swift. A waitress brought the coffee and the aroma immediately began to clear Raven's head. She used plenty of cream and sugar and found herself gulping the coffee as Adam Steele watched her, his eyes slightly narrowed.

His heart was acting up like a teenager's. She was really attractive close up, but he already knew this because he'd held her in his arms at the CCG Ball the past spring for all of a hot ten minutes before the man she'd been with had claimed her.

With the last swallow of the strong brew, she leaned back, taking deep breaths.

"Feel better?"

She nodded.

"What do you think that man's attempting to assault you means?"

She laughed shakily. "Who knows. My boss insisted that I take jujitsu training, so I'm not as afraid as some women need to be. I've been robbed before. You never get used to it, but I've managed to keep my wits about me every time."

"D'you think the CCG investigation has anything to do with this? Tom Carr has become a powerful man and you're part of an outfit that's trying to take him down."

She thought about the investigation she worked on. Tom Carr, chief executive officer of the Citizens' Charity Group, was being accused of fraud and embezzlement at the nonprofit group he had helped to found and now headed. Tom was a proud man and he had come to hate Raven and her boss as the investigation continued. Tom was known as a charming but vindictive man who boasted about destroying his enemies.

She looked thoughtful. "He's hurt a lot of people who can't defend themselves."

"I know."

"And he might have had Cree Hawkins killed. Cree was my first cousin and we were very close. We were the children of brothers." Her face clouded as she said it.

"I know that, too. Cree was my friend. You and I met so briefly and you were married. Carr's outfit is in my jurisdiction. That's our case and I've kept up with it."

She smiled softly. "You don't look old enough to have a jurisdiction." Then looking more closely at him, she realized that while he looked young, he also looked ageless. He could have been a very well-taken-care-of forty. There had been sadness in his life; she had read about it. God knows he was good looking enough, but she had thought that when they danced at the ball in April.

The Citizen's Charity Ball was one of D.C.'s most illustrious events. Tom Carr went all out to see that all the right people were there. Entertainers sometimes donated their services, and they always raised a lot of money. Some of the city's most illustrious and wealthy members were on the CCG board of directors.

He half closed his eyes. "When did the heavy-breathing calls start?"

She thought a moment. "A little before Cree was killed. Tom Carr knew very well that I knew most of what Cree knew. I've been wary, but I've just watched my step."

"You were scared tonight. You're still scared."

"I can take it."

"Are you sure you're okay now?"

"Getting better all the time. I can't thank you enough."

His grin was lopsided, infectious. "I could say it's a part of my job, but with you, it's an outrageously welcome part. I run into you once in a while, but not often enough, and we've never had another chance to talk, even briefly."

She put an elbow on the table, musing. "I remember you best from the CCG Ball. You looked so dashing in your tux, the way a man ought to look in a tuxedo. You ld me you had a teenage son, then the dance ended..."

"And your Black knight claimed you at the edge of the dance floor. I was afraid you'd be married by now."

He liked the musical sound of her laughter. "Oh, that was Ken. He's my boss and we're not an item."

"He'd like you to be."

She glanced at him obliquely. "He's a very good friend. Nothing more."

"I'm glad."

"Why?"

"Because I've got designs on you that I'm going to be honest about."

She drew a sharp breath and said nothing, but her heart beat faster.

"Let me order you something to eat. I haven't had dinner. Have you?"

"No. I was just going to throw something together. My daughter, Merla, will be coming home later...."

"And my son's visiting his beloved grandparents. It looks like we're free. What would you like? Or would you prefer going to some place fancier?"

She took a menu from the table rack and studied it a few moments. "I like it here and I'd love sweet and sour shrimp."

"I've got an idea. How about sharing that and a beef and broccoli and some other dishes if you'd like."

"Sounds really good. I'm hungrier than I thought."

He studied her closely, then looked away, closing his eyes. Her body had lots of deep curves, covered by amber skin the color of beautiful black tea—a blend of orange, brown, yellow, cream and tan. Her hair was off-black and hung to her shoulders in chemically straightened curls. The pale blue linen sheath she wore was discreet, but a gunnysack couldn't hide the woman. Her eyes crinkled mischievously at the corners as she did her own studying.

He ordered and as they waited she said, "You mentioned your son. I read in that recent *Post* interview with you that your wife died."

His eyes were suddenly bleak and narrowed as he said tersely, "My wife died five years ago in a plane accident. She was returning from England where she was taking further training in economics in London. Ricky was nine." Tears stood in back of his eyes.

His big hand lay on the table. For a moment, he looked helpless. She placed a long slender hand on each side of his and squeezed lightly. "I'm so sorry," she said softly.

It was such a simple gesture, he thought, but it brought up all the fierce hungers he'd battled since Kitty died. Lord, he missed a woman's touch. There'd been a few women in his life, but they hadn't caught fire. He was raised not to take advantage of women. If you didn't care deeply, you didn't bed them, didn't take up too much of their time. Sex may or may not be a need, but it linked with a lot of other things.

"Thanks," he told her. "Let your hands stay against mine at least a little longer. I don't mind telling you it feels good. I'd like to see you again, Raven. Would you like that?"

His knee brushed hers under the table and her lips parted a little. She looked down to hide the sudden heat that suffused her.

"Sorry," he said.

"It's all right."

"Okay. I'm going to push it. How quickly can you arrange for us to see each other again?"

She closed her eyes for a moment. "Oh look, don't

read anything into my saying I can arrange to see you again. I'm the well-known forty, detective, and happen to be turning forty-one on—"

He finished her statement, "October fifteenth."

"How'd you know that?"

"I'm a cop and cops make it their business to know things. I'm interested in you, lady. The next day after the ball, I had an assistant find out your birth date. WMRY is a newsgathering institution and they're open to disseminating information too."

"Touché. And how old are you? I'm afraid I don't know your birthday."

"It was July eighteenth, and I'd be happy to tell you anything you want to know about me. I'm thirty-three."

His leg brushed hers again. "Oh, look, really," he said, momentarily taken aback. "I'm not hitting on you."

She was usually a reticent woman but Adam Steele brought out all the joy in her. "Why aren't you hitting on me?" she teased him. "Oh, I'll bet you have plenty of women hitting on you."

"I'll answer your first question first. The only reason I'm not hitting on you is I don't want to frighten you away." He leaned forward. "I haven't run across anyone like you since Kitty died. You two are so much alike it scares me. And yeah, I never want to suffer like that again, but I'll risk it. I would have pursued you after the CCG Ball, but Ricky got sick. The doctors thought he had rheumatic fever. Thank God he doesn't, so I'm free."

"Adam."

"Yes."

"Run for your life. We haven't *got* a future, you and I."

"Don't bad-mouth us. We're drawn to each other. I know I am to you."

His resonant baritone was getting to her. His eyes on her were very warm and very interested.

Her cell phone rang and she dug into her tote to answer it. It was Viveca Sloan, her best friend since childhood. Viveca and Carey, her husband, had picked Merla up from school and taken her home with them. Mrs. Reuben, the woman who took care of Merla, was down with the flu. Now Viveca laughed. "I'm afraid your kid got homesick a half hour or so ago, so we brought her home, but listen, you don't have to rush. We're going to a late-night movie and having dinner before, so we've got time to kill. Whatever you're up to, enjoy. How's Mrs. Reuben doing?"

"Much better. Listen, if Merla wanted to come home, she wants to talk with me. Can you put her on?"

"Oh, she's in dreamland. Carey had to bring her in. We're at your house. Don't worry. She's fine, but don't stay out too late. Remember our dinner before the movies."

"You know you're welcome to anything we have there and we've got frozen tacos, pot pies, a lot of stuff."

"Thanks, but I've got a yen for some killer fast food. Come home when you can, sweetie. May I be nosy and ask who you're with?"

Raven's smile was wider than she knew as she looked at Adam. "Detective Adam Steele. You met him at the CCG Ball."

"Hear me swallowing hard. Next to Carey, he's da bomb. Hm-m-m. Don't get carried away and forget to come home."

Raven hung up chuckling and explained to Adam that he had met Viveca at the ball.

"I remember. A very attractive woman, almost as beautiful as you are."

"You're kind. Few people have accused me of being beautiful."

"Oh? This gives me a chance to look you over without seeming too fresh." For a few moments he was silent as his eyes went over her voluptuous figure. The heart-shaped face and the almond eyes were dark and dreamy with long black lashes. Her expression was both strong and tender and he had to fight fantasies of holding her and making slow, feverish love until they both were sated.

His expression carried and she looked down as he asked, "You look at me, then away. Why?"

She smiled. "Who knows why?" But she knew that he was turning her on sky high and she was loving it. And she didn't like loving it because after Kevin, it would be a long time before she wanted anything deep with another man. Her shattered heart held back when a man sought to get closer to her. She had tried all she knew to make a go of her marriage to Kevin and it hurt to fail so badly.

"I know Viveca's husband, Carey," he said, changing the subject. "We work together with a youth group as tutors."

"Carey's a nice guy. The two of you are a lot alike."

"Some women go for the rougher types. I'm hoping you like my type."

She answered him very slowly. "Right now it's almost impossible for me to like *any* man more than a little. I'm running scared. I hate being hurt."

"We all get hurt at some point."

"Okay. I hate being coldly savaged."

"That wouldn't happen with me."

Their dinner came and she was spared responding to him.

The food was superb. The beef and broccoli and sweet and sour shrimp were just right, done far better than in the average restaurant. The carrots, onions, and baby corn were among her favorite vegetables.

She stopped eating and broke open a fortune cookie.

"Haven't you got the cart before the horse?" he asked.

She laughed. "I always do this. I can never wait until the end of the meal." Eagerly she drew out the slender strip of paper. "Lead with your heart," she read aloud.

Adam threw back his head, laughing. "Confucius could do no better."

They ate for a short while in companionable silence. Then he told her, "I want to know all about you. Is there time?"

She shrugged. "There isn't too much to know. I'm divorced with a precious little girl who's too smart for her own good." She stopped then, frowning. "Someone seems to be after me. You already know I'm an investigative reporter for WMRY-TV and we have a fire-hot case on our hands. Tom Carr hates my guts the way I'd probably hate his if the shoe were on the other foot. Glen Thompson of Special Investigations tells me an indictment is certain for fraud, racketeering and embezzlement. Tom's held on for a long time, but this time his number may be up."

"You think he's behind the trouble you're having? The heavy-breathing calls, the feeling that someone's following you? Anything else?"

"That's about it and for a month or so it's happened often."

She paused a long moment. There was something else, but she didn't tell him and she wondered why. She only said, "I get the idea they're playing a game to wear me down...."

"You think then they'll strike with something more drastic and you'll be less able to defend yourself? Or being jittery will make you careless?"

"Yes." She paused for a long while. "Adam, it's not myself I worry so much about. I do believe you make your own fate sometimes, but I'm worried sick about Merla. We're bonded as tight as two people can be and she'd be devastated if something happened to me."

"I'm making this my business, of course, and it isn't, but have you thought of another line of work? You said at the CCG Ball that you loved kids. How about something safe, like teaching?"

She shook her head. "You're sweet and thank you for trying to help, but reporting is in my blood. I'd feel like half a person without it. This is the first time it's proved dangerous and I think I'll see that it's the last. Tom Carr values his hide and his reputation; he isn't going to do anything too dastardly."

"So you keep telling yourself," Adam said softly. "In many ways I'm older than you are. My job puts me in contact with people you'll never see the backside of. And I've known reasonable people to turn into monsters when they're threatened, do unbelievable things, even murder. They're horrified at themselves when their deeds are done. You went out for Tom Carr and if Ken Courtland, your boss, has any security to offer, demand it. Demand it anyway. You're playing with dynamite."

"I know that now, and Ken knows it too." For a moment she looked thoughtful. "There's something else, Adam. My ex-husband, Kevin, hates me too…"

"*Dr.* Kevin McCloud?"

"You know him?"

"Let's say we've met. He roughed up his girlfriend one night and was arrested. He came to me to plead that I not make a case…"

"Well…"

"I refused. I detest men who mistreat women. The woman dropped the charges. I understand they're still together."

"Miriam Delaney, or do you remember the name?"

"I remember the name. And yes, I found out he has quite a few women."

"That's useful information. Kevin will never stop trying to take Merla from me. I long ago came to the conclusion that he's incapable of loving anyone, but he wants to be loved and he showers Merla with gifts that I can't give her, lets her have her way. But then he turns and punishes her unfairly and she resents it. He's mixing her up and if it continues, I'm going to take her to a psychologist. I won't have her mixed up. I love her too much for that."

"You don't think he'd hurt you?"

"Yes, I do. I know far more about Kevin than I know about Tom Carr. Kevin's devious and he's malicious, vicious even. I know about a man, a former partner, that he destroyed. This man was brilliant, but emotionally ill and Kevin befriended him, then slowly drove him mad. It was deliberate and it was one of the reasons I filed for divorce. The man's wife sued Kevin for malicious emotional wounding and of course, she lost, but it's stayed with me. I don't think Kevin would hesitate to have me killed if it suited his purpose, and that purpose is to take Merla. He's pushed me around a couple of times. I fought back and that's yet another reason I left."

The thought of anybody hurting the woman before him enraged Adam and made him want to hold her closely.

"So he never really hurt you physically?"

She thought a moment. "I'm not being truthful, and I want to be to you. He slapped me once so hard it twisted my neck. We were arguing about Merla. I felt she should be disciplined for something and he didn't. I insisted and when she left with Viveca, Kevin and I began arguing again and that's when it happened. I defended myself well enough, got medical help and I went to see a lawyer right away. I began divorce proceedings immediately."

Adam didn't try to stop himself from saying it. "If I were physically close to you, I'd hold you. You need that."

And she surprised herself by answering with a quaver in her voice, "I'd *let* you hold me. You're a nice man, Detective. I wish I'd met you first. But then you'd still be too young."

"That's nonsense and you know it. You're nearly forty-one and I'm thirty-three. We're both ancient in wisdom learned from life's hard knocks. It's settled then that we'll at least see each other, weave ourselves into the fabric of each other's lives?"

She smiled, then looked somber. "Maybe it's not the smartest thing I've ever done for myself. I swore I'd never get entangled with another man, not for a long time anyway, but I'm lonely and you're so..."

Her smile was steady, warm.

"So?" he said after a long moment.

"Compelling. But Kevin was a compelling man too."

He shook his head, leaned toward her. "Don't compare me to Kevin McCloud. I could never stop kissing and holding you long enough to yell at you even, let alone hit you."

"And I'm grateful. But I can't have a physical relationship with you, Adam. I'm too old for you and I'm just not ready for one."

"Listen, you may not be ready, but you're not too old for me." He took her hand. "We'll go ahead at *your* pace. You call the shots because I want you on any terms."

"But is that fair to you?"

"You're being more than fair when you agree to see me. Let me take it from there."

Chapter 2

"Carey! How's it going, man?"

"Great, Adam. How're things with you?"

At Raven's big three-bedroom townhouse in southwest Washington, Adam and Carey Sloan greeted each other.

Adam shook hands with Viveca who flirted a bit, but not enough to make him or her husband uncomfortable.

"Lord, when I think of the times I've wanted to introduce you two to each other," Carey said, "but I knew Raven was aching and not yet ready for romance…"

"And here she's fooled us both," Viveca chortled.

Raven threw her head back. "Stop it, you two. There's no romance here. Detective Steele was simply good enough to rescue me when somebody robbed me and he took me for a cup of coffee to settle my nerves."

Viveca's hand went to her chest and Carey frowned. "What the hell?" Carey grated. Husband and wife looked deeply disturbed.

"Tell me what happened," Viveca demanded, her cocoa-in-milk skin blanching. "And don't rush over it. Details. I knew you should get off this damned case…."

Viveca was a couple of years younger than Raven, but they had similar minds.

"It's not that easy," Raven began to get up. "Look, I've got to see about Merla."

"Merla's fine," Viveca said impatiently. "I looked in on her just before you got here and she's deep in slumberland. Don't wake her up. Tell us what happened, love."

Raven sat back and drew a deep breath, nodding. She gave them a good depiction of what had happened, and Viveca frowned deeply. "Oh honey. There must be someone else Ken can put on this case."

"No, it's my baby and I've got to see it through. Anyway, the robbery may very well not be connected with the Carr case. I've been robbed before and Carr was nowhere in sight. I'm the one who's got the whole thing staked out. I'm fast finding out where all the bodies are buried. It's a matter of getting the rest of the proof. We're nearing the end of this."

"And the beginning of a long court battle that Carr intends to win," Viveca argued. "You'll be in more danger than ever."

Raven's eyes met Adam's and held for a moment. "Tom Carr's a charismatic man. Even with the evidence and my testifying against him, he can win. He's one of a kind."

The Sloans both sat back on the sofa, mulling over Raven's information. Carey's dark brown curly hair, olive skin and light blue eyes contrasted with his wife's. They were almost even height, so in heels she was taller, but his well-exercised, muscular body was a good match for hers. Both families had been great about their mixed marriage, so they were comfortable with it, but had found they had individual problems they were intent on working through.

Raven looked at them fondly and thought she loved

them both to pieces. Viveca worked with Raven as an ad executive at WMRY-TV.

"Well," Raven said. "Did you two work up an appetite?"

"Yeah," Carey said, laughing. "We saw a tray of pre-fried shrimp in your fridge and you said we were welcome, so we sampled some and we're ordering mixed seafood."

"What're you going to see?" Adam asked.

"An old movie, but a goodie, *The Bodyguard.* I liked it the first time around and Carey's never seen it."

"I liked it," Raven offered.

"So did I." Adam looked at Raven again with his eyes half closed. She looked more relaxed, but was still tense.

They had settled into quietness when a door opened and a little form came down the stairs. "Mommy!"

"Sweetheart! I thought you were asleep. I was coming to see you."

"I heard voices," the eight-year-old, black-haired Merla murmured. "I wanted to see you."

Her dark brown skin smooth as satin, Merla stood in the middle of the room in her flower-print pajamas, rubbing her sleepy brown eyes.

Raven held out her arms. "Come here, baby." And as the child came to her to be enfolded in her arms, she asked, "Don't you feel well?"

"Um-hum. I just didn't want to wait until morning to see you. I had a bad dream that you had gone away and I was crying."

"Oh dear. Trust me. I'm never leaving you. *Never.*" She hugged the child tightly and rocked her.

After a few minutes, Merla sat up and turned around. "Hello," Merla said to Adam who looked at her with bemused eyes. He loved kids and had an engaging way with them.

"Hello yourself," Adam said. "How are you?"

"Okay, I guess. Who're you?"

"Sweetheart," Raven said. "Let me introduce you to Detective Adam Steele of the Eighth District Police. Detective, Merla. My pride and joy. The light of my life."

"I can certainly see why. I'm delighted to meet you, Merla." He sat now in a chair and stuck out a big hand.

Merla's thin shoulders hunched. Then she got up and walked to him, shook his hand. "And I'm delighted to meet *you*. D'you read good bedtime stories?" She liked this man. "Uncle Carey was reading me one, but I fell asleep. Now can you? They've got to go to a late-night movie."

"Sure," Adam said quickly, "I can do that. But do you like music?"

"Yes, but what kind of music?"

"Harmonica?"

"Oh, yes. My favorite boy at school has a harmonica and he plays it for me once in a while." Merla wriggled her little body with delight.

"My, my," Raven murmured as she looked at Adam. "You do make easy conquests. She doesn't take to just anybody."

Adam grinned and took out his harmonica before he said, "Tell you want, Merla. Why don't we give them all a treat?"

"That's neat!" Merla came alive with glee. She sat on the edge of Adam's chair.

Adam warmed his silver harmonica with riffs and sailed into a lively melody he had picked up in his travels in Sierra Leone, Africa.

When he had finished everybody applauded and Merla said shyly, "I don't want to be greedy, but would you play one more?"

"Of course I will. Anything for an appreciative audience."

He played another tune and slid into yet another one. Then he played the old Irish tune "Danny Boy." Merla looked at him with her little mouth slightly open and Raven sat thinking that he really was quite good with children.

Merla said gravely, "That's so pretty. Thank you." Merla hugged her mother as Adam put his harmonica back into his jacket pocket. "Mommy, I'm sleepy again and I'm going back to bed. Give me a kiss."

"Anytime." She kissed Merla.

"Let me give you a kiss because you played your harmonica for me," the child said as she planted a big kiss on Adam's cheek. "Come again, anytime."

He thought she was so sweet. Like mother, like child.

A short while later, after they had all looked in on a sleeping Merla, Carey and Viveca prepared to leave.

"I ran into Allyson today and we talked about special plans for fall tutoring. She's got great ideas, Adam. You're lucky to have her on your team." He turned to Raven. "Allyson is Adam's sergeant. A real winner and easy on the eyes."

Raven was dismayed to feel a ridiculous twinge of jealousy over a woman she didn't know and a man she barely knew.

The Sloans left and Raven turned to Adam. "Thank you again for rescuing me earlier. Why don't you slip off your jacket? It was thoughtless of me not to ask you before. Would you like more coffee?" Then she blushed. She was alone with him and she was nervous and twittering. She slowed herself, sat down and leaned back. "Thank you for playing for Merla."

"She's a precious little girl. I want to introduce you to my kid who's growing like the proverbial weed."

"I'd like that. Give me a little time and come when it's convenient."

He looked at her, smiling slowly. "Can I sit with you on the sofa. I need to talk with you."

"Okay."

He got up, walked over and stood before her and she felt her breath coming faster, but she found she could focus on him at last. And yes, he was just as drop-dead handsome as she had remembered from the CCG Ball. Earlier, she had been too dizzy with fear and surprise to focus. He was black walnut-colored with shiny, black, close-cropped hair, a long, finely shaped head and masculine, even features. The heavy silken black eyebrows lay over light brown eyes with gold flecks. Those eyes were kind to the world he looked at. His features were masculine, rough-hewn and his mouth was everything she'd ever dreamed of kissing.

Oh God, she thought, he might as well have been kissing her, the way she felt. She guessed it made a difference that he had declared his interest. She told herself that she was only responding from simple physical need. He moved slightly toward her and she moaned to herself, *No, don't come any closer*, then told herself sharply that she was going backward. All the way back to her sad-sack days when she daydreamed all the time.

He grinned, realizing that he was getting to her as he reached out and put a hand on each of her shoulders, began to lean toward her. She was conscious of his wide shoulders, slim hips and his sinewy, muscular body. She was certain this man worked out with a vengeance.

"No," she said, "why borrow trouble?"

"Why run from happiness?"

Touché! she thought. Would she ever be happy again?

"Tell me about your marriage," she said. "Come sit down."

He talked and for a moment she couldn't listen. Her eyes were on his mouth that was wide and mobile and curved over big, white, perfect teeth. She could imagine his mouth on hers, flaming. His skin was smooth and beautiful, but it was his eyes that held her. Probing, intelligent, tender, those eyes had known deepest happiness and shattering pain.

He drew a deep breath and began. "We married at nineteen when we were both at the University of Maryland and no, we weren't too young to marry. We were both older than our years, and simply knew what we wanted and went for it. And we were never sorry. Her name was Arlis Marie. She was so fond of cats—we had six—that I called her Kitty." He paused for just a moment before he continued. "Neither Ricky nor I cared all that much about cats and after she died, it was just too painful to watch them. I gave them all to friends.

"Our son, Ricky, came the first year and she dropped out of school for two years to care for him. My parents and her parents helped us. I majored in criminal justice and she majored in economics.

"We couldn't have been happier." He pulled out his wallet and showed her a photo of a dark-skinned, absolutely beautiful young woman standing on a beach with him and holding a baby in her arms. All three seemed suffused with joy.

"Was I ever that happy?" she asked wistfully. "You were lucky."

"Yes, until my luck ran out."

"You were devastated."

"Yeah. I wanted to die but I had Ricky and he was part

of Kitty, so we've held on to each other. Lord, he misses her as much as I do. You've got to meet him. You know, not until I met you at the ball did I feel there could be someone else for me. She was so beautiful and you're like her, except you're *you*. And I thought you were taken. Life can be kind; you're *not* taken."

She took his hand. "Adam, be kind to *yourself*. I don't want any more hurt in my life ever again, that I can help, that is. The age thing is between us. I've never been attracted to younger men."

"You're attracted to me and I'm not really a younger man. I've been through the mill. Doesn't being attracted, drawn to me, mean anything?"

"Of course it does. Can we be friends?"

"Lovers is what I want for us," he muttered to himself so she couldn't hear him.

"What?"

"I'll tell you sometime. Even when I was in my teens, my parents called me an old soul. I hung out with older kids. My brother Damien, who is a twin to my sister, Dosha, is thirty-four and Marty, my oldest brother, is thirty-six. Marty was always my buddy."

Adam looked at her steadily, his mouth curving into a smile. "Let me tell you a bit about my family. We're a close bunch. My dad married early, had just one kid, Frank, who in turn had three kids, Whit and Ashley, both famous gospel singers, and Annice, a noted psychologist. My dad's first wife, Lillian, left him for another man, but Frank wanted to stay with her and he let him.

"Dad married my mom a couple of years later and they had Marty, the twins, Dosha and Damien, and me. Both sets of kids are very close. We don't really consider Frank a half sib, but a whole sib and that's how he sees us. We've got so much love for each other."

She smiled. "Your expression is to tender and loving when you talk about them all."

"Look," he said, "I'm pleading my cause. Be kind to yourself *and* me. I just sense something between us that couldn't be better. Give us a chance."

"Friends," she said stubbornly. "I'd like that because I sense that you'd be the best. We both like kids, take part in our worlds, are happy in our jobs…"

"Why don't you tell me about your marriage to Kevin? What was that like?"

She thought a moment. "Take hell and multiply it by ten and you've got our marriage."

"Were you in love when you married him?"

"It's funny you should ask because that's goaded me. I looked up to him, admired him. He comes from an old-line D.C. family and inherited money. He was a big-time professor at Howard, had a doctorate in biology from Canada's McGill University and is a brilliant man. He can be charismatic, but Kevin can also be a monster…"

"Did he batter you in the beginning?"

"No, that came later when he knew I had a mind of my own. At first, I was his minion. Whatever he said, that's what I did. He even wanted to think for me. You'll meet my maternal grandfather, Macklin. I call him Papa Mac. He saw through Kevin and warned me about him, but I was thirty and couldn't find what I thought I was looking for. I'm—passionate, Adam, and I dreamed of even higher passion and never found it the way I wanted it. You'd never think of me as being passionate, would you?"

"I would. I feel it in you, but you hold it tightly bound up."

"Oh, bless you. I've always been so afraid of my feelings. So, I thought Kevin was like me, holding it in, only there wasn't much to hold. Kevin is a cold man and he despises... Oh, Lord, Adam, I just can't talk about all this now. I will sometime..."

He took both her hands in his and held them tightly before he brought them to his lips. "I'll wait for anything you need to wait for."

She closed her eyes as hot tears lay behind her eyelids and a sharp thrill went the length of her body.

"Thank you."

The voluptuousness of her was getting to him and the lilting cadence of her voice was music to his ears. And it wasn't just her body—she was so responsive, so tender. Yet you sensed steel in her when she needed it.

"So you're a passionate woman and you're terrified of where it'll lead you. Am I right?"

She nodded. "I *feel* so much; I always have. I avoided boys my own age. I didn't want us to be two fools together. Papa Mac made a great parent. My own parents were away in Africa working for the U.S. Government. Papa Mac talked with me a lot and kept me on an even keel, but I know now I missed my parents and felt they'd abandoned me and that hurt. I felt that if I loved them enough, they wouldn't have left, or if they'd loved me enough."

"Children and what they go through." Adam shifted slightly. "Listen, about passion. I was your counterpart. My dad used to tell me, 'Son, don't ever be afraid to be passion's fool. It can bring you glory you'll never have otherwise. Find a woman you can trust and believe in and just let go. *Feel* everything you feel for her. Love her body and her spirit and yes, her soul, and you'll find happiness beyond anything you could dream.'"

"That's beautiful, Adam."

"Be passion's fool with me, Raven. There's so much we could have together."

To her surprise, she lifted his hand and lightly kissed it. "You're so great. I've never known anyone like you, but fate isn't always kind. I do think we can be the best of friends."

"I'm going to press for more because I think we can work as a team. I want you to meet my son, Ricky. Like his dad, he's got great taste in women. My whole family will love you."

"Won't they object to our age difference?"

"Nope, not at all. They'll know we're *right* for each other."

"Be careful, Adam. You deserve someone who can give you more children if you decide you want them."

"If *we* decide."

"You're not listening to me."

"I'm listening to both our hearts."

Sadly, she knew that he spoke the truth, but hearts were known for betraying people.

Adam glanced at his watch. "Hey, I don't want to go home, but you need your beauty sleep. But then again, you *don't* need beauty sleep. You're already beautiful without it."

She laughed. "Thank you, but I'm not, you know. Attractive perhaps, but far from beautiful."

"It's in the eye of the beholder, but it goes beyond that with you. You have an inner beauty that feels so damned good. It's like Kitty's beauty was. Do you mind my talking about her so much?"

"No, I asked you to and I love it that you do. You've known a great love and I admire that."

"Then help me to have another great love—with you."

"You said you'd hold back, and I'm holding you to that if we're to go on seeing each other."

"I'll do the best I can, but if you're hungry and a buffet is set before you, it's hard not to quickly reach for the food you need."

She smiled slightly. "You're a buffet too. Do you know how gorgeous you are, body and spirit?"

"No, but I'm glad you think so."

The quiet fear began to set in and she whispered to herself, *Go before I make a fool of myself.*

She sat thinking to herself that she had loved her parents and they had left her, only to die of fever in a far-off country. Lord, that was so long ago, but the pain still lingered. She had married Kevin, a man she didn't love because she was afraid of love, especially afraid of passion. Her cell phone rang. She picked it up from the end table by the sofa.

It was the heavy breather again and she moved to hang up, but tonight he had an old message for her that he had partially given many times before: "*There's gonna be a killing—soon!*" The voice was guttural, ugly. Deadly.

Her face went ashen and her hands trembled. Adam came closer as she hung up.

"What's wrong, Raven?" he demanded.

Her eyes looked haunted and her breath came faster. "It was…" she began, then stopped.

"You told me about heavy breathing and the threatening calls. He said something else this time. What did he say?"

She hesitated for only a moment. Not telling Adam didn't stop it from having been said. "That there's going to be a killing *soon*." Her own voice was rasped with fear.

"Has he said this before?"

She hesitated a moment. "He's always said that *one* day there'll be a killing. This time he said *soon*." An edge of hysteria was in her voice as she said, "I call him the hellhound."

"I don't wonder. I'll have a tracer put on your phone."

"Ken has tried to have the calls traced. They come from a pay phone and cannot be traced."

He swore and pulled her to him. "You're shaking again. It's all too much for one night. Has this kind of thing been happening often?"

"No. Sometimes a couple of weeks pass and there's nothing. Maybe a low whistle like one in a horror movie and that could be just a coincidence." She began to laugh softly and it came out a whimper. "I'm beginning to believe there *are* no coincidences. Damn it! I have a job to do and I'm going to do it."

"You're scared and you should be. I want to spend the night, sleep on your sofa."

She had never felt fear the way she was beginning to feel it now. "No, it's all right. I'll be all right."

She began to shake harder, uncontrollably and he shook his head. "No, it's *not* all right. I'm going to camp here. You need someone here and tomorrow we can make plans. Please don't argue."

She drew a deep breath. "Okay. I really appreciate this."

"Have you got a sleeping pill you could take?"

"Yes, I have some left over from when I had a virus last spring."

"Good. Take one and I'll let down the sofa."

"No. I have three bedrooms. You'll be comfortable. Adam, I'm sorry to inconvenience you like this."

He grinned crookedly as he looked at her with tender concern. "If I were a romance writer, I couldn't have written a better scenario."

But with the fear still chilling her down to her bone marrow, she went up to check on the room where he would sleep and she wondered which was the deeper fear, the evil voice on the phone and everything that had happened lately, or the threat Adam Steele posed to her heart?

What the hell is going on?

Around two that morning, Adam came sharply awake. There was a strange, harsh sound of something cracking, as if someone might be trying to break in. His trained mind knew immediately that he was in Raven's house. In a couple of seconds he was on his feet, listening intently. The sound came from downstairs. He pulled on the big all-purpose terry cloth robe Raven had left on the bed and got his Glock gun from the night table. He had slept in his underwear and lost no time in getting down the stairs from the third floor. He moved stealthily to the second, then the first floor where the sound was louder. Over near the kitchen door it was loudest and he crept along, gun at the ready. Then he nearly burst out laughing with relief. The refrigerator was cutting up, probably going bad.

Opening the door to the avocado-green appliance, he admired the spaciousness. There was enough food stocked in it to feed an army. He selected a lager beer and pried the cap off with a bottle opener he found in the drawer. Good, he liked his beer in bottles. He drank up and looked around him as he went into the living room. The woman had taste. She had shown him around and he really liked her décor of golden oak woods, a lot of heavy glass, many bookcases, and electronic equipment. There were green, growing plants hanging from the ceiling and setting about and a thirty-gallon tank of big goldfish stood in a shady corner.

The second floor was given over to a physical fitness room, a small room with a movie projector, office space, and a playroom for Merla. The third floor held the spacious bedrooms. Yeah, he thought, he could live here quite comfortably, but he and Ricky loved their house in upper northwest on Seventeenth Street near the Maryland line.

"Adam."

He was at the foot of the stairs when he looked up and saw her coming down the spiral staircase. His heart caught in his throat and went dry. His whole body tensed. She was wearing a dusty-rose tricot robe that wrapped around her voluptuous form and her eyes were frightened and bright.

"I heard something and came to check it out," he said. "Go back to bed. You need all the sleep you can get."

"I know. What was it?"

"I think your fridge is going bad. It was cutting up big time."

She shook her head as she came on down the stairs. "We just sleep through the shenanigans of that appliance. It started last week. The repairman says it may be a lemon. When Mrs. Reuben is well, we'll take the time to file a formal complaint." She reached him and touched his arm. "I'm glad you stayed over. I'm grateful."

He narrowed his eyes. Her touch had been so soft, very tender, and it told him what a deeper touch would be like and how he would respond. He didn't want to *wait* for what they could know. They had wasted too much time already. If Ricky hadn't gotten sick, he'd have pursued her after the CCG Ball. He was rough now because he wanted to kiss her so badly.

"Go back to bed. It's going to be hell on you tomorrow."

"What about you?"

"I'm used to it. Cops lead a hard life."

She smiled a little, teased him. "Oh, I hear that it's not as tough as it's held to be. I like the cop shows—the pretty, lustful broads, the chases in which nobody ever really gets hurt except the bad guys. You guys love every minute of it."

He grinned. "You're easily persuaded. There's enough in being a cop to satisfy me, but I've yet to know what you see on TV."

His big frame in the dark blue robe was getting to her. He smelled of the woods and a hint of a good man's cologne, blended with his own special male smell that drew her, turned her on in deeper places than she'd ever known. Good Lord, she had met him, had been so attracted she had pretended an attraction to Ken that she didn't feel. All just to hold Adam Steele away. He was too young for her. Why yield to hopelessness?

But that didn't stop her from going closer to him, pulled by forces she couldn't or didn't want to control. She only knew that she lifted her face for his kiss and his muscular arms went around her, pressed her soft flesh to his. His hot mouth found hers and his kiss was so hard it hurt for a moment before she inwardly fought him for a second, then yielded like a drowning woman needing, begging him to rescue her. Where kisses were concerned, she thought, this was as good as it got.

And Adam was as good as gold for the rescue. His big hands went up and down her back, stroking gently when he wanted to press her hard. She smelled of light jasmine, of natural pheromones and wanting him. Her skin was summer peaches plucked at their prime. And he was flaming with deeper desire than he had ever known. He had loved a young woman with all the intensity of a young man's love. Now he was beginning to feel the wild power of a man's love lick his heels.

Adam groaned inside himself. He wanted to take her

now, envelop her in his arms, go deep into that pulsing, luscious body and stay there a lovely while.

With the tip of his tongue he traced her warm, sweet lips as one big hand cupped the back of her head. Her lips parted and his tongue slipped inside her mouth, pleading, begging, yet ravishing, slaking passion even as it aroused it.

She felt herself nearly fainting with desire that began in her brain and traveled in dizzying waves to her toes. And the fear she felt of her stalker was no greater than her fear of the heartbreak Adam Steele could bring.

Then suddenly he stepped back a bit, still holding her, laughing shakily. "End of the line," he told her. "If this goes on a second longer, I won't be *able* to let you go."

She could have cried with frustration. What was happening to her deep reserve and the control she had learned to exercise relentlessly? Did he think she was easy?

"Okay," she said softly. "You're proving to be wiser than I am."

He expelled a harsh breath. "No, I just know how I feel about you and I want you to always feel safe with me. I want you to know I'll never hurt you, never ask for more than you can or want to give."

Everything in her still yearned for him and she told him, "I hate the circumstances that keep us apart."

"Nothing keeps us apart—except you're not seeing straight."

"I think ahead; you live in the present. You'll come to think ahead, when you're older."

He shook her gently. "I'm thirty-three. Stop treating me as if I'm *twenty*-three. I'm raising a kid and I think I'm doing a pretty good job at it. I can't do that without thinking plenty ahead. Give me a break, Raven. Will you?"

"I don't want to have you grow tired of me, decide you've made a mistake...."

He kissed the side of her throat. "I know my own mind. Ask my parents and my sibs, and you'll come to know I do."

"You're nice, Adam. Really nice. I know that much."

"Thank you. You're someone special and I warn you I'm going to move heaven and earth to have you for my own."

"We'd better get upstairs, get some more sleep."

He nodded and thought he didn't need sleep. He couldn't remember when he'd felt so wide awake. "I checked your security system. It's the same as mine, but individualized."

"It can't help me where I have to go," she said ruefully.

He spread a big hand on the side of each shoulder. "I'm going to get more security directly from the police department for you. I'll start on it no later than I get in this morning." Then fiercely, "I won't have you hurt, Raven."

She didn't even try to stop herself from lifting her mouth for his kiss which came as a feathery touch on her lips. Everything in her ached for him then and she was helpless against the onslaught of her feelings. She knew she could better control herself if he didn't represent much of the safety she needed now. He kissed the side of her throat and held her away from him. "Be merciful to me, lady. I wish I had better words to tell you how much I want you for myself. We've got to stay friends so I can press my case."

Standing in the circle of his arms she silently fought a hunger she couldn't subdue, but he was toning his pressure down, making it easier and she was grateful.

"I'm sorry," she finally said and when she would have stammered something else he put a finger across her lips, then lightly, teasingly traced her bottom lip.

"If you're really sorry, be my sweetheart."

"If only I could. Adam, you're right, we have to get to bed. I've got a crushing day ahead tomorrow—no, today."

"If we were lovers, I'd carry you up."

"I'd break your back."

"Then you could nurse me."

"You're a nut case."

"No, I'm a man who's falling in love."

She hesitated. "You said you wouldn't press me, but how can you help it when I act like a giddy teenager? I do apologize for my behavior. I'm drawn to you and I'll just have to accept the fact that this cannot be."

"Tell that to your heart."

She did not look at him as they climbed the stairs and both stood at Merla's door.

"My heart hates being broken," she said.

"Trust me," he responded.

He stood just outside the door while she looked at Merla in the glow of the hall light. When she came out and closed the door, they walked to her room and he touched her face, aching to kiss her again.

"Good night," she murmured and he nodded thoughtfully and walked the few steps to the room he slept in. He was as tense as a strung-out guy wire; he knew he wouldn't sleep much for the rest of the night. Already sweet dreams of Raven had begun to crowd his mind.

Raven closed her door and leaned against it. Had he kissed her like that, filling her veins with hot honey, or had she imagined it? She smiled a little, thinking she didn't want to get into *her* bed, but his. Too bad they couldn't be the team he thought they could be. But they could be friends and perhaps one day he and she would find someone who was age appropriate.

Chapter 3

In spite of little sleep, Raven felt fairly good the next morning at WMRY-TV. Her nicely appointed office had posters of Diana Ross and Nancy Wilson, Billy Dee Williams and Seal. There were also flower prints. She got up and walked over to her African violets which were in full glory on a table near her window sill.

"The plant mama," a deep voice said behind her and she turned to face Ken Courtland, her boss. Tall, attractive, dark brown-skinned, he was in his element this morning in a tan linen suit with a dark blue shirt and color-coordinated tie.

"How are you, Raven? Now me, I'd like to go back to bed."

"I'm fine when I forget about something that happened last evening. I hate telling you about this, Ken, because I know you'll worry." She told him about the incidents, but not about Adam spending the night.

"I called you and left a message," she told him, "and you were talking with the noon anchors when I came in this morning."

He looked concerned. "It was nearly dawn when I got in and I called, but you didn't answer."

"I must have been in the shower and I didn't hear. I guess I was so rattled, I forgot to check for messages."

He frowned deeply. "I'm worried about you, Raven. What does Detective Steele say?"

"He's concerned too. You know there are two people who could be behind this: Tom Carr and my ex, Kevin. Tom's running scared and he'll do anything to keep out of prison and protect his good name. Kevin hates me, too, just as Tom does. Neither man would hesitate to kill me if it would save their hides. But they're going to be very careful and they know they're being watched."

Ken looked haggard. He came and squeezed her shoulders. "You make damned sure you keep me posted."

"The first woman I know and interviewed worked for CCG. She says she overheard Cree and Tom quarreling shortly before he was killed."

"Well, well. Did she go to the police?"

"No, she was—and is—too scared. I'm afraid she hasn't got a lot of self-esteem." She couldn't tell Ken the woman was Desi Howe who'd once worked as an administrative assistant at WMRY. He'd insist that Desi talk to police and she was too frightened. But Raven *did* tell him about other talks she'd had with Desi.

"You pointed out to her, of course, that she could call anonymously?"

"Certainly, but she says her boyfriend had once been involved in drugs and doesn't want her to have any part of this."

Ken rubbed his jaw with one finger.

"Let's see. She talked to you. She wasn't too scared to do that."

"What she's seen is worrying her and she has to get it off her chest. I had to promise not to use her name if I went to the police."

"Hm-m. Sounds ripe to me. And you did give Steele this info?"

"I haven't yet. I have to mull it over. I wanted to talk with you first."

He came closer, looked pleased, but bothered. "Lord, I'm so sorry. Good thing a policeman came along, *and* you got a chance to talk about the mugging he helped you with."

"Yes." And she thought ruefully, to her own private policeman.

"I know Steele. He's good. I'm glad he got to you."

"So am I."

"At that CCG Ball, I got the idea he was getting sweet on you."

"He's just a friendly person."

"Sure," he said cryptically. "I need to talk with you in my office in a half hour or so. What do you have going on?"

"I'll be there. I'm going to talk with Blaine and Will. I'm meeting Desi Howe for lunch."

"I miss Desi. Damn Carr for luring her away."

"I agree. I miss her too."

"Oh yeah, how'd the first interview go yesterday? You knocked it out of my mind when you told me about the creep who mugged you."

"Ken, that interview was pure gold. On my second interview, the woman has a story to tell about a grandson who died because a promised grant from CCG to the clinic didn't go through. I was going to call you, but I remembered you had a dinner engagement."

"That good, huh? I'll need to hear more, but I don't

have the time right now. You know you can call me at any time." His eyes lingered on her. Why couldn't she understand how great they'd be together? "Hey kid, you look really good having gone through what you did."

"Thank you." Her navy crepe sheath always got compliments.

He glanced at his watch, frowning. "I've got a conference call to get in on, but…have you had breakfast?"

"Ah—yes." She and Adam and Merla had had waffles with blueberry syrup and Canadian bacon with eggs scrambled with scallions and sharp cheese. She didn't know how she looked, but she surely felt good.

A tap sounded on the door and a florist's deliveryman came in. "The lady at the desk said to just bring these back."

A dozen red roses artfully arranged with broadleaf fern in a crystal vase made her heart beat faster. She loved roses. Kevin had never sent her roses and that made her love them even more. "Thank you so much," she said to the deliveryman. "Just a minute and I have something for you."

He smiled broadly and shook his head. "No, that's all taken care of. You just enjoy them."

He left and Raven found Ken looking at her speculatively. "Admirers at such an early hour? All a part of Adam Steele rescuing a damsel in distress?"

She nodded. "He really is a nice man."

"A nice *young* man."

"Yes, that too."

He bit his bottom lip. "Maybe it's nothing, but Steele is a hunk and a lot of women are after him. Be careful. The kind of hurt your ex dealt you is enough to last a lifetime."

"I'll try to remember that."

"Good. Remember, too, that I'm free and only a few women are after me and none of them matter except you," he hinted playfully.

"And you're also a hunk. So much for decisions." She was getting flippant, but his remark had stung her. Not that she hadn't constantly thought about Adam being younger. The kiss they had shared had been youthful in its quick wildness, yet ageless. A man of eighty deeply in love might kiss as well.

"You do my poor old heart good with your compliments," Ken said. He was forty-eight and well preserved. "But enough small talk. Detective Steele is going to want to talk with you. He's known as thorough. Everybody wants him to investigate. His solve rate is way above the city average. I don't want anything to happen to you, Raven. You mean so damned much to me."

"Thank you. I'll be sure to be careful."

When he had left, Raven sat reflecting that he had said he didn't _want_ anything to happen to her; Adam had said he wasn't going to _let_ anything happen to her. She leaned back in her chair. Young men thought they had the world on a string and could handle whatever came their way; older men knew better.

She got the ringing cell phone out of her tote bag to be greeted by the lively, loving voice of her grandfather.

"Papa Mac," she said joyfully, "how are you?"

"Better now that I'm talking with you. I've got a bit of a head cold, but you know I'm never sick and I don't intend to be now. I eat right, exercise, live right. Now tell me what's with you?"

She didn't intend to upset her grandfather by telling him about the creep yesterday. "I'm doing rather well, I'd say. I met a man…" She paused a few moments. "He's so nice. Too bad he's too young."

"What do you consider too young, baby?"

"He's thirty-three and he's too young."

"Does he seem to really like you?"

Remembering Adam's kiss, she murmured, "Yes, he does. I actually met him some time back, but I didn't want to be involved. I'm forty-one in a little over a month. Not a very romantic time of life."

"That depends on you. Your grandmother and I had romance going until she died. She whispered that love poem "How Do I Love Thee" to me when she was dying. I wanted and want that for you, sweetheart. Too bad you wound up with Kevin."

"The world has changed, Papa Mac. We just did a segment on the night news about how much romance has changed. Didn't you watch it?"

"I did indeed, but it's only partially true. This world will always have romance in it. Too many of us don't intend to survive without it. Tell me more about the young man you met some time ago and let slip through your fingers until recently. I'm pitching for romance for you and don't you forget it."

Raven could picture Papa Mac as he talked. Bright silver hair cut in a close, curly cap, loving blue-gray eyes in parchment colored skin. Papa Mac still cut the wood for his fireplace, loved to run, walk, bicycle and to sing in his church choir. He was seventy-nine and vibrant, had the tiger of the world by its tail and wasn't about to let go.

"I'll try to remember." She replied, "I'm afraid Kevin left me a legacy of doubt and anger."

"God heals everything and time heals all wounds. In

Kevin's case, I think it'll be time wounds all heels. Has he given you anymore trouble?"

"I'm not sure. He'll always be trying to get Merla and he wants to talk with me as soon as possible. I don't know what about. Papa Mac, I'm afraid of Kevin. I think he's crazy. You know what they say about the thin line between genius and insanity."

"That fits Kevin to a T. Well, I've got to get ready for my church choir tonight. I'm giving a barbecue." Papa Mac's voice got somber. "You watch out for Kevin, and that new case you're onto is one I don't much like. A man like Tom Carr is a rat even when his back isn't against the wall. You will be careful?"

"You know I will."

After she hung up, Raven held the receiver with the open line buzzing until the automated operator curtly asked that she hang up.

She glanced at her daily calendar. Desi. She really looked forward to talking with her former coworker again and Desi had said she thought she had more helpful information. They had been close, but Desi had drifted away. When should she tell Kevin she could see him for a few moments? Raven propped her elbows on her desktop. She still missed her frequent talks with her cousin Cree. He had been dead since early May, murdered in cold blood, and God, it hurt so much to think about it. A certified public accountant with CCG, he hadn't been particularly fond of his boss, Tom Carr, and was looking around for another job. She needed support. She was sorry Viveca was off today; she wanted to talk with her and would call later.

Blaine Woodland, the other investigative reporter, tapped on the door and came in. "You busy?"

"I'm going in to see Ken in a few minutes. What's up?"

Blaine ran a hand over his dark brown semi-Afro. "I wish I knew." He sighed. "You said something about talking with Carr. Is that going to be anytime soon?"

"Tomorrow, in fact. Do you want to tag along?"

He smiled ruefully. "I've got my own fish to fry. I've been talking a lot to your cousin Cree's wife. I'm trying to jog her memory of everything she noticed and heard about her husband before he was killed. I know she was out of town, but there might have been something before she left. After that, Ken has put me on another case. He thinks you can handle Carr's case alone."

"I imagine the detectives have thoroughly gone along that avenue. I'm talking about Glen who's with Special Investigations for the city." She thought about it being Adam's case and felt certain he had covered all the angles.

Blaine's cinnamon-brown face looked thoughtful. "Cops sometimes don't get it all. Besides, they're pushed to the wall with low manpower ceilings and short budgets."

She couldn't deny that. "Good luck. I'm seeing Desi today. We have a lunch date."

"Glenda's invited me to have lunch at her house."

Raven sighed. "She's pregnant and that has to be a hellish blow, your husband's murder, especially since he was one of the best."

Blaine nodded. "Like I said, I've got a lot of fish to fry, so I'll be moving it. I'll talk with you this afternoon. Swap notes."

A tall, lanky, light brown-skinned young man came in. Dressed in faded blue jeans and a white T-shirt, he had an athletic build. His puckish face was framed with close-cut, crisp, black hair. At twenty-one, his demeanor said he was checking out the world and would find his place in it. He was Will Ryalls and he was smart and only at the TV station for a year or so, then onward and upward.

"Morning, Will," Raven greeted him.

"Raven," he teased her. "I'm here on a mission. The big enchilada asked me to tell you that he's tied up on that conference call and needs to delay your appointment until midafternoon."

"He's the boss. How're you this morning?"

"I can't complain. It wouldn't help. From the looks of those roses, I'd say you're in clover." Will smiled. "I like sending women roses, but with my gaggle of girlfriends, it'd break me."

She could never determine if he was joking or serious.

Again, Blaine rubbed his hand over his hair. He had a wife and two small children. "I saw the roses, of course, but I wasn't going to be nosy. I just admired. We're spending so much time on the Carr case, I'd better get my wife some roses or something else nice. She's beginning to hint that I'm neglecting her."

Raven laughed. "Roses will do it every time."

Blaine smiled now. "I am going to be nosy enough to say you look happy, Raven, and I'm glad. You've moped around enough. Today you've got that old joie de vivre back. Keep it up."

Will pursed his mouth. "That's French, but what's it mean?"

"Didn't you have French in school, junior?" Blaine teased him.

"Yes and damned near failed it. I like English better. That's why I'm majoring in communications."

"Hm-m-m, I can hear it now." She deepened her voice. "'This is Will Ryalls signing off for WMRY. The eleven o'clock news.' Then you'd squire not one but two beautiful women to dinner, *after* you'd closed everything up."

"Ah, you know me well, but WMRY is not where I plan to finally land. Something big like CBS or ABC."

"CNN would be more your speed," Blaine intoned. "They're edgy enough for you."

"Hey, you know me well. It's nice talking to you guys, but the boss has me saddled with a lot of sometime chores. I don't let on how easily bored I can get."

Raven wrinkled her nose at him. "At your age you should never be bored."

"Sez who? Take care of the roses. They're gorgeous. If they're missing, you'll know I took them to give to one of my sweeties. Bye for now."

He went out and Blaine turned to her. "Wish me luck talking to Glenda. She's trying to be brave, but she's still hurting bad. They had a great thing going, I understand."

"Yes, they seemed a perfect match. Cree was so settled, so sober…"

"Yeah, a really good guy. I still miss him a lot. "You're taping your time with Desi?"

"Yes, of course. I learned a long time ago that small things can crack a case wide open. Nuances, timbre of voice can all mean so much."

"Yeah. You're looking really well today. I have to say it again. You know you're one of my favorite people, so keep me posted. Roses, and you're glowing. Is this the start of something good, or what?"

"I'll keep you posted and you do the same."

As she began to get into her car in the parking garage under their office building, Raven's cell phone rang. It seemed she knew before he spoke that it was Adam.

She couldn't help grinning.

"Hi, totally lovable woman."

"Hi yourself. You're the lovable one."

"Keep that up and you can have all my year's paychecks. How are you? Sleepy?"

"Just a minute. I'm getting into my car and going to meet a friend for lunch." She got in, closed the door and sat holding the phone and beaming. "It's funny. I'm not a bit sleepy. I feel like I've had a good supply of sleep."

"That goes for me, too. Would you like me to take you to dinner tonight?"

She hesitated for a moment before she remembered. "I have to take Merla to a friend's house; they're having a doll party and she wants me, rather than Viveca, to take her. I think my child's getting a bit spoiled."

"How long exactly have you been working on this case?"

"I started about a month after Cree was killed. Ken didn't think you guys were going fast enough and he wanted Blaine and me to dig up special dirt, if we could find it. He felt you'd discourage us if you knew about it. Now Blaine's got another hot case. I haven't found the smoking gun either, but I keep trying. I'll never give up. And Adam, I do thank you for all the effort you've put into this. Why do you ask how long I've been on this case?"

"I'm thinking about Merla. You've almost certainly been preoccupied and a child senses that, and maybe she thinks she's losing you. Raven, be careful, too, that Kevin doesn't use this against you to get Merla. He works for himself and can be off whenever he wishes...."

"You don't know Kevin," she told him. "He's a workaholic."

"He might get a judge who's the same and so, sympathetic."

"Don't remind me. How do you feel?"

"Like I've found the pot of gold at the end of the rainbow—if a certain someone doesn't take it away."

She smiled thinking that if things were different, she'd have found that same pot of gold, but fate made her unable to claim it.

"You say all the right things, push all the right buttons and I'm grateful for the rush you give me, but take what I've said about the age difference seriously."

"I *am* taking it seriously and I know how little it matters, unless you let it. Raven, let's get the boat into the water and see that it *can* sail. Okay?"

"I can't help feeling fragile about love."

He sounded exasperated then. "I'm only asking that you give us a chance."

"You know," she finally said, "I really am going to give us a chance—but just to be friends."

"I'll take that if it's all I can get. Listen, we think we caught the guy who mugged you. He's an old offender and we've been looking for him for three sexual offenses along with his robberies. He'd staked out that area. A lot of women are going to be happy he's off the streets."

"I'm glad. Maybe my poor knees will stop shaking now. I guess from dealing with Kevin, I really get rattled at the thought of a sexual offense—and battering. I never used to think about that."

"The world's changed. We've all got to be more careful. Dinner tomorrow night?"

"Oh, yes, I'd love that."

"Great. You'll hear from me again. Do you mind frequent phone calls?"

She felt tender toward him. He had saved her from an almost certain worse attack. And he had kissed her with fervor that went to her bone marrow. "I love frequent phone calls when they're from certain people."

"That had better mean me," he growled.

"Back off, just a little," she said laughing merrily, thinking this felt too good to give up just now. She would go along for a short joy ride. And her heart responded, a *thrilling* short joy ride.

Chapter 4

Adam sat at his desk in his office with his feet propped on the desk, leaning back in his chair with his hands behind his head. A smile kept tugging at the corners of his mouth when he thought about Raven. Last night's kiss lingered in his mind and he held on to it. He felt his whole body tense with wanting her.

But other things kept crowding him too. He wasn't given to daydreams, but he was daydreaming now and he had to snatch the time to do it. The Carr case infuriated him every time he thought about it. Cree Hawkins had been a friend of his, at Howard at the same time Adam attended the University of Maryland. His fingers beat a tattoo on the desktop. "I'm coming for you, Carr," he muttered. "I know you're sharp and you've got the best lawyers imaginable, but I think you killed Cree or had him killed. It's a gut hunch, but my gut hunches have usually been right."

A rookie cop knocked and came in. "Detective, I've had the DNA tests run that you wanted. Here are the reports." The rookie shook his head. "I don't think this is what we're looking for."

Adam took the slender sheaf of papers. "Thanks for working this to the bone," he told the officer. "I hope it helps." He looked at the summary and swore. Negative. They had picked up a suspect in another murder and Adam had been fairly certain they had the culprit. Now the name leapt mockingly from the page. The guy was clean, at least of this murder.

Sighing, angry, he thought about the creep who'd tried to attack Raven as he picked up his mug shot. Albert Jones was his name, and they had picked him up in the early morning hours with Raven's credit cards in his wallet. He'd assaulted and robbed two more women by the time they nabbed him. They'd run his name through the computer. Three cases of murder and rape. Adam was usually a forgiving man, but there was nothing he hated more. He breathed a little harder when he thought about it, clenched and unclenched his fist. He was going to see that they threw the book at this bastard. Albert Jones. He could still see him in his mind's eye. Big and stupid and threatening. Preying on women.

Adam Steele was a passionate man. His mother often teased him about it and his father had looked at his son, musing on that passion. He had a temper held in tight check from childhood, aided by his childhood training. "If you're gonna love," his father had often told him, "you've got to exercise *restraint*. Feelings run powerful when you care and they can easily get out of control. Go where your heart tells you to go, but *think* about it first. Now, I'm not saying not to be spontaneous, but use that old left brain too."

From the beginning he had had it all, so nothing he had experienced had prepared him for Kitty's death. The heavens had poured their tears onto him and God had seemed to turn his back. For five years he had been sad and lonely. Ricky and his family had meant everything in the way of solace and comfort, but not until he'd met Raven at that CCG Ball had his life taken an upward path. Met her and lost her in one fell swoop. Now he had found her again and he didn't intend to let her go.

Thank God for work he loved. In the beginning, he had seen himself as the Black knight charging to the rescue. There were the good guys and there were the bad guys and he was mostly a good guy. His father had warned him about this. "You're gonna find your fellow citizens are a mix of everything," his father had said ruefully and often. "Don't waste time hating. Oh, I know people have got to be punished for the crimes they do, but at least *try* to understand. There, but for the grace of God, go you and I."

And he had held on to this until last night when facing the cretin who he was sure had intended to attack Raven, he had felt no mercy, only the raging need to protect his woman. He smiled grimly. She wasn't his woman, not yet, but she would be if he had anything to say about it.

Raven waited for Desi Howe at a restaurant in the Adams Morgan area of D.C. They specialized in Caribbean food.

When Desi came in with her fine ginger-skinned figure swinging, Raven got up and hugged her. Desi was cute, vivacious with natural blond hair. She seemed to Raven to live on the edge of danger. Desi dated shadowy figures, but they always had plenty of money to lavish on her. She went on cruises, to Vegas and lived in the fast lane.

"Hey, don't you look special," Desi exclaimed. "What you been up to while mama's been away?"

"Not much."

Desi laughed. "Your face says your mouth lies."

"It's not like I've had three months in Puerto Rico."

"Ah yes, girlfriend, envy me. I envy myself." Then added, "I'm going to have the jerk chicken and some fine cooked mustards and turnip greens. I understand nobody does the greens like this place does, and some macaroni, heavy on the cheese. I haven't been here lately, but Cree and I used to come. Lord, I miss that guy."

She looked down for a moment and Raven placed her hand over hers. "We *all* miss him. Cree was such a great guy. Think about what Glenda's going through."

"I know. I've had lunch with her a couple of times and she's being brave, waiting for the baby. Do you see her often?"

"Often enough. She's going through hell, but she's really cooperating with us."

Desi nodded. "I'm praying that with just a little luck…" She took a small playing card-sized object from her purse. "Look at this. It went with me everywhere when I worked at CCG and was wearing a lot of jumpers and skirts with big pockets those days." Her mouth set in a straight line. "I recorded every conversation I had with Tom while I was at CCG. I played tapes last night, a couple of tapes. I gave Cree a third tape that's dynamite. The day before he was killed, you were in New York for a couple of days following another story. You see, I had this gut feeling Tom was going to fire me. He began to criticize everything I did. I should have quit. I had fair leave and a little money stashed away. You and I talked about how I wanted to stay to see if there was any more info I could dig up to find who killed Cree."

"Ken has hinted that he'll give me and Blaine the high

sign to work more closely with the police. At first he didn't trust them, griped about their blunders and really fretted about the time it was taking them."

"They can be stupid, but sometimes they're brilliant. I know I've heard that this Detective Steele is brilliant. The case is his."

Raven felt a shiver of delight course along her body at the mention of Adam's name. "I met him again last night."

She recounted her meeting and Desi grinned. "Sounds like there might be something going on."

"No, I just find him good company. I've never been a bit attracted to younger men."

"You want to give him to me? I'll handle his care and feeding."

"He's not mine to give. I just met him. Young men these days get tired of their conquests pretty quick, and by the way, I don't intend to be one of his conquests."

Desi put her head to one side. "From the dreamy look on your face, kiddo, I'd say you already are. How old is this wunderkind?"

"Ripe old thirty-three, and let's be fair to him. He seems sober enough to be forty or better."

Their food came and both exclaimed at the fare. Raven grinned at the waiter. "That looks good enough to eat."

The waiter laughed heartily. "I'm new and haven't seen you ladies here before, but come again and again. You add that touch of class we need."

"I think we're going to be hooked if this is as good as it looks." Desi hunched her shoulders a bit as the waiter left and Raven said grace.

"You look a little down," Raven offered. "What's up, girlfriend?"

"Love problems, or just plain old lack of love."

"That's a bit cryptic. You haven't mentioned any new men in your life."

"I've got enough trouble with the *old* men in my life. Forget new ones."

"Oh well, I'm not privy lately to the old men in your life either."

"I mentioned that I have a couple of men who date and dine me. Nothing serious with any of them... Nothing hot and heavy going on."

"Until now. Your face says this is serious."

Desi nodded. "You bet your sweet bippy it's serious."

"Is he married?"

"I wish. I've dealt with that before. No, he's just un-available—to *me*, that is." She stopped eating and seemed on the verge of tears.

"Do you want to talk about it?"

Desi shook her head. "Not now, but when I do, I promise you're gonna get the shock of your life."

"Oh, this sounds great. You're not hanging out with Tom Carr, are you?"

"Funny girl. The more I saw of Tom, the more I wished I didn't know him. I hadn't been at CCG too long when Cree was murdered, but we were really close, closer with him being your cousin and all."

Raven nodded sympathetically.

Desi sighed deeply before she continued. "The little machine here is yours. It's a tape recorder. I have a couple more. Right now there's just this one tape, but there *will* be one more when I can find the other one. And there's the one I gave Cree. Raven, the more I talk about Tom, the more I dislike him and his assistant, Allen Mills. They're as slimy as cooked okra. When I think of the mandate they're entrusted with—to raise money for the needy—and the way they're rumored to be siphoning it off into *their* pockets, well, I really get mad."

"I feel the same way. But I do want you to be careful." Raven reached out and scooped up the recorder, put it in her purse. "Should I listen to this as soon as possible?"

Desi shook her head. "No need to. I want you to be where you can concentrate. Listen and tell me what you think. Tom had a conversation with someone when I was in the room. I pretended to be absorbed in reading something he asked me to read. He spoke of the possible indictment several times and I wondered. I couldn't put two and two together, but you know more about the case than I do. Do you think Detective Steele might be interested, that is if Ken gives you the okay sign?"

"Could be. If he does, I'll call Adam, run it by him. I'm expecting Ken to bring this up when I get back. If he doesn't, I will."

"Great, girlfriend."

"Now, about this new man in your life…"

"He's really not so new, just getting more painful every day."

"Oh, you poor baby."

Desi looked really stressed. "I think I'm in love, Raven, for only about the second time in my life. You know I was married once and it didn't work. No children, thank God, and the clown I married moved to South Carolina. I don't talk about it to anybody, but he was a real loser and the relationship left scars. Now comes this—what shall I call him? He's certainly not a man in my book. He's a sadist. I know that much."

Desi's eye filled with tears she blinked back. "Boy, I can really pick 'em, can't I? You'd think a twelve-year-old would do better. Here I am the ripe old age of thirty-one and I'm getting taken like bets at a race track."

"Don't beat on yourself, sweetie. We all make mistakes. Maybe you should talk with a mental health worker, or your minister. You're suffering, Desi. Maybe you don't have to."

"Thanks. I'm not much on shrinks, that kind of thing…"

"Doesn't have to be a shrink. Social worker. Psychologist…"

"Well, I'm pretty close to my minister and his wife. I think I'll try that route. I've got to get away from this monster. He's messing with my mind, pulling all my emotional strings so I'm choking. Thanks for the sympathy, love."

"Let me know how you come out."

"Believe me I will. A woman I still talk to at CCG told me Tom Carr is out of town today, back day after tomorrow. He and Allen traveled together this time. From what she tells me, they seem to be getting tighter." She glanced at her watch. "I've got to be going because I'm meeting someone."

Raven glanced at her sharply because Desi suddenly looked sad.

"One other thing," Desi said. "We've talked about it. Tom's arrogant. I think he feels he's got something all sewed up. He'd figure he's way ahead of you because you're a woman and thus stupid, or largely so."

"That's the impression I get of him. I hope he's in for a rude shock, but I think he likes Blaine."

"Everybody likes Blaine. He's Cree's counterpart. A real doll. Hey, this has been great. Let's do it again and soon."

"For sure."

It was two-thirty P.M. when Raven sat in a padded chair across from Ken in his office.

"We could have had the appointment we're having over Peking duck, my dear, but you had a prior engagement," Ken teased her, then grew more somber. "How's Desi?"

"Ah, she's seen better days."

"Is Carr still giving her trouble? He fired her. Or is she having my gender trouble."

"Well, since he fired her, so far Tom isn't hassling or hustling her, but she is having man trouble. Why do you think you men are so hard to get along with?"

Ken smiled and looked at Raven, running his tongue over his bottom lip. In her pale yellow sheath and tan leather pumps, she was something he'd like to take home. "Don't look at me. You could have me body and soul and I'd give you *no* trouble. I'd be puppy-dog-eager to please."

"You all say that before we get you."

"I'll bet Dr. McCloud never said it."

"Touché. He was reserved and cool from the beginning. I thought he was being respectful, tamping down ardor. I was naïve and way too old to be. I should have seen it coming."

"Talk to me," Ken said. "Even I get hot under the collar when we talk about McCloud. What did Desi have to say?"

Raven told him about the conversation and he listened intently.

"I wonder what the voices on the tape will say; I don't have time to listen now," he pondered.

"With Tom talking, it could be anything."

"Well, I know you'll be on top of it. Be careful, Raven. I don't mind telling you I'm worried about you. I think you're working too hard and I'm worried about those telephone calls. Tomorrow morning, I want to listen to that tape with you. What did Steele have to say?"

"Okay. There's not much he *can* say. He'll have my phone monitored. I called the phone company and they're on it."

"We all have a special interest in the CCG thing, but we've got lives too. And that damned mugging last night… That's close enough for me. It's bastard-city out here these days. You don't think he had anything else in mind? Rapes are becoming more common in the past month or so, but I don't want to frighten you any more than you are. Was Steele around when you got the telephone call later at home?"

"Yes. His being there soothed me at least some."

Ken looked at her sharply. "I remember that stud from the CCG Ball. He didn't want to let you go after you danced with him. Thank God he got a call and had to leave. I was prepared to be a real boor and monopolize you the rest of the night."

"That's not very sporting of you, Ken. It's not like we're lovers."

"Your choice, not mine."

Her face got warm and her eyes narrowed. "Fight fair. You know I'm off men for a long time. After Kevin…" She sighed heavily.

He leaned forward. "I ran into Kevin yesterday. He was cordial, looked happy."

"Then he's up to no good. That's the only time Kevin's happy."

"He really did a number on you, didn't he?"

"Yes." She didn't feel like taking this conversation further. She had never talked very much to anyone about Kevin and her marriage, not even to Papa Mac.

He respected her reticence and didn't say more about that particular topic. "Word's out that Special Investigations has a good case against Carr. If our grapevine is right, he'll be indicted within a couple of weeks."

"Forgive me if I'm cynical. Even if he gets caught holding the moneybags, he's got lawyers who can get him off. An indictment's one thing and a conviction is something else. We need smoking-gun evidence."

Ken shook his head. "No, I don't think so this time. We've got plenty. Glen Thompson's a firebrand; he intends to be a judge one day, so he's pumping hard. I wouldn't want to be in Carr's shoes this time."

"If he killed Cree or had him killed I hope he gets the maximum."

"So do I." He was silent a moment. "I wonder how Laverne Carr's taking this."

"Yeah, sometimes I wonder too. I was at Howard with Tom and Laverne. She's a charming woman, but a rather cold one. I run into her from time to time and she's restrained, friendly. He provides the means to keep her supported the way she's used to being supported. Her late father was a real estate mogul. Owned a lot of land in the old Foggy Bottom. She still owns some of it, I understand."

"You know, Raven, if Tom does go to prison, it's going to do him in. He's a very proud man. A dirt-poor boy who made good. Selfish as hell, but I guess that's understandable."

"Well, he should have considered his pride when he began to raid the cookie jar. And he's hurting people, Ken. Families need the money he's taking. Kids need it for treatment. There could be enough to go around, but not if the selfish top-level people are going to steal it all for their own selves."

"You're right, of course. Dinner tomorrow night?"

She blushed. "I have a date."

"We haven't had dinner in quite a while." He sounded wistful. "Have dinner with me soon."

"Sure."

He sat up straight. "Well, I guess it's back to the grind. I've got two more conference calls to complete before five. But what I'd like to do is put you on a pedestal in here and just look at you for the rest of the afternoon."

She held up a protesting hand.

"Okay, I'll cease and desist. At least give me credit for being well-behaved most of the time."

High up in a hotel in Manhattan, Tom Carr and his right-hand man, Allen Mills, sat at a big table in the living room of their luxurious suite.

"We're taking off, kid," Tom chortled. "Everything's coming up roses. Never underestimate handpicking your board of directors. Only Paul Turner is a holdout and he's outvoted. Our bonuses add up to a million and a half; a million for me, a half mil for you. You're satisfied with that? There's more later."

"Chief, you know I am. I'd work for you for a quarter of that. Hell, for nothing. With you as a mentor, the sky's my limit."

Tom smiled. He liked being a big man, physically, and in his job. He'd known in school that he was going to be a big man, known it since he was a small boy hustling newspapers and later handling a large distribution route and another job as assistant manager at an exclusive men's clothing chain.

His single mother used to tell him, "Son, take some

time for yourself. Life ain't all about work. Play's something you need too."

But play had never interested Tom. He had to be somewhere near the top of any heap he landed on and he intended to go higher, much higher. His job as CEO at Citizens Charity Group was made to order for him, but a few more years there and a few million dollars more and he was on his way to opening one of the largest consulting firms for financial planners.

He rubbed his jaw thoughtfully. He'd done all right for himself. If Cree Hawkins had had an ounce of common sense, Tom could have made him a rich man. But he had threatened to blow the whistle on the whole game. His eyes narrowed to a slit. He, Tom, had never been a man to mess with.

He relaxed a little. Funny thing how he could ponder things with Allen right there. They were that close.

Tom didn't think anybody suspected him of having anything to do with Cree's death. Cree must have talked plenty with Special Investigations because the investigators had come prowling around. Trouble was one of his board members now hated his guts and would do anything to bring him down, and that member had managed to get another board member in his corner. Tom rubbed his chin with his forefinger. Where had he gone wrong? Still, he couldn't shake the feeling that he could have handled it all to his advantage if the McCloud woman and her boss, Ken Courtland, hadn't started their damned investigation. He narrowed his eyes. He had plans and they were both going to pay for this. But he hated the woman more than the man. Women who rebuffed him or whose interest he wanted and couldn't arouse angered him.

In the beginning when she'd come around questioning him, he'd asked her out several times and she hadn't even bothered to be charming when she'd turned him down. She'd let him know quickly and in no uncertain terms that she didn't care for him and that had rankled him, hurt his ego. Getting even was going to be a pleasure.

Ken Courtland's TV station had begun asking questions, too, and were ready to begin a series on various CEO's, big and small, the power they exercised, the risks they took, the perquisites, the fat salaries.

Well, he wasn't really one of the big guys, but this was better. He operated with little oversight and he'd always taken advantage of that. He and his late partner had cobbled CCG together and he'd done well.

Allen worked with a sheaf of papers. Tom peered over his shoulder.

"You work too hard, lad," he said. "This is a pleasure trip as well as business."

Allen smiled. "Thank you. I'll be finished here in a sec."

Tom went back to thinking. Then, there was Laverne, his wife. Thank God for his other women. He tried not to overdo it, but he liked to collect beautiful women and the money helped. He hadn't married for love. Laverne knew he hadn't and he suspected she didn't love him either. Laverne was plain, but was a snappy dresser and a great hostess. He gave her really expensive presents to show his gratitude for the way she stood behind him.

In the beginning it was her father's money that gave him a stake and he liked his widower father-in-law, had been close to him and missed him after he died. Neither he nor Laverne wanted children and if she ever minded the other women, she didn't say. He felt she was happy that he didn't bother her for sexual favors. They had separate bedrooms and separate lives. He was satisfied and hoped she was.

Tom got up and went to the wet bar. He'd had it stocked with the best Scotch. He asked, "What're you having, Allen?"

"Same as you, chief."

Tom poured two on the rocks and brought them back to the table. Allen looked at his boss narrowly for a few minutes as Tom gulped down his drink. Allen got up and got a bowl of cashews from the sideboard and brought it back. Tom immediately grabbed a handful.

"Cashews are my favorite nut," Tom said. "Did you know eighty percent of them come from Aruba? The raw ones are far superior to the toasted ones."

"No, I didn't know that. Yes, sir, I prefer the raw ones." But Allen *didn't* prefer raw cashews; he liked the toasted ones better. But Tom liked you to agree with him and that was easy for Allen. He intended to pick Tom's brains to the limit, so it didn't hurt to follow his lead even in small things.

Tom cleared his throat. "I don't mind telling you again I'm worried about Raven McCloud." He rolled his eyes. "I'd like to have a go at that one. She's something else. Classy. Smart enough, but not too smart."

"She's sniffing around all right, but we can handle her."

"What d'you think about her friendship with Desi?"

"What I think about it is that we're so far ahead, so covered, there's not a damned thing they can do to us. We're drum tight, Boss. I've seen to that."

"You've seen to a lot of things, Allen, and I'm grateful. I want you to know that. But what do we do if Raven and her boss at that crummy TV channel she works for come too close?"

Allen hesitated a long while. "I'd be in favor of taking her out."

Tom looked up. "I've been thinking about that. This would be a last resort. Killing's a dirty business. I don't like it, but I know I'm never going back to the life I grew up in. I couldn't take it. I'm going up, not down. And you're going with me, all the way. We're gonna be kings of the hill. I just feel it in my bones."

That night Raven and Adam listened to the tape Desi had given her. The conversation was between Tom Carr and Allen, his right-hand man. Raven breathed shallowly, not sure what to expect, although Desi had said it sure wasn't a smoking gun. Then she relaxed as the two men talked about CCG and the direction in which Tom was taking it.

"It was a two-bit operation when I took over," Tom snorted. "They weren't raising nearly enough money, weren't paying the top brass nearly what top brass deserves. They weren't advertising widely, didn't have first-rate connections."

Raven could imagine Tom pounding his desk lightly the way she had seen him do on interviews. Adam listened steadily, his eyes narrowed. He had been taught to read voices to a far greater degree than Raven had learned. He shook his head lightly. Tom certainly didn't come off as a very nice guy; all his warts were showing, but you can't send a man up for being unlikable, Raven thought.

For a moment Adam and Raven tensed when halfway through the tape Tom asked, "What are we going to do about the McCloud woman, Allen? She's gotten to be a pain in the ass. We have to be careful, but it may be a good idea to put a good, old-fashioned scare into her. That may make her back off. She's too damned uppity."

"Yeah, but she's pretty feisty. She won't scare easily."

"I've got some underworld connections that'll pay off now."

Raven and Adam looked at each other, anticipating what would be said next. Then Allen said, "Look, Boss, I don't want to interrupt, but you told me to brief you on your meeting with the mayor in the morning and I've got a lot of things I think you need to know. You said you had to leave earlier than usual…now I've got all the time in the world."

Tom laughed. "Sure thing. It always riles me to talk about Raven McCloud. Sends my blood pressure way too high. One day…okay, let's get started because I intend to make a great impression on the mayor tomorrow. A buddy told he he's solidly in my corner."

The two men began to talk about Tom's appointment with the mayor and both Raven and Adam were disappointed as the tape whirred on with details that were useless to them. She let the tape play out and tried the other side to find it empty. She shut the recorder off and could have wept with frustration.

Adam hugged her. "Did Desi say there was something important on this tape?"

"No, not really. I guess she wanted me to hear what Tom had to say about me, but he only hints at what he'd like to do. He makes no mention of Cree. Of course, she gave the tape to Cree where he *does* threaten Cree. She referred to that one as dynamite."

"And that's the missing tape? Of course, you've talked with Glenda about it?"

"Not just talked, I went to her house after I left work and we looked the place over. Glenda's very well organized, the way Cree was. It wasn't there. Adam, we may never find that tape. Glenda's been looking for it since Desi told her about it. And Glenda says Cree didn't go up to the cottage on Green Mountain between the time Desi gave him the tape and he was killed. Glenda'll keep looking, of course, but she's sure it's not there."

Adam pressed his hand to his head. "So near and yet so far," he said, "but I get the feeling that Carr's arrogance is going to be what takes him down after all."

Raven called Desi then. She was surprised at how drunk Desi sounded. Raven sighed. "Girlfriend, that tape doesn't tell me much."

Desi hesitated a long moment. "Yeah, well the second tape'll tell you more. I've got to think where I put it. I've gotta go now. Got late company coming."

With the open line humming in her ear, Raven wondered who Desi's company was.

Chapter 5

Adam's wolf whistle was long and low as Raven answered her door chimes. He leaned against the doorjamb, admiring her. "You *do* light up the scenery," he told her.

Raven blushed furiously, her lovely amber skin suffused with pleasure. "Hey, you're the one. You look like you stepped off the pages of an *Esquire* special." She looked at his tall body draped in a greenish blue Harris tweed jacket and his dark brown gabardine trousers. His shirt was pale blue and his tie was color coordinated. But it wasn't the clothes. It was the man.

Adam laughed. "Thank you. And you look like you stepped down from heaven." He was a man who appreciated the finer things of life, he thought now, and she was surely the finest. Dressed in cream silk pants and a leopard-print sash, her only jewelry was a wide gold bracelet. He inhaled deeply, the better to enjoy the jasmine fragrance that surrounded her.

"Thank you. And double thanks for coming here for dinner instead of going out. I hope you like the fare. You said you like oysters and we're having them fried."

"I love oysters and I never met a fried one I didn't like. I don't eat much fried food these days, but I'll make an exception for oysters anytime."

"And I have oven-fried white potatoes and a humongous garden salad. Simple, but I think it'll be good. I don't eat much fried food either. D'you like green peas and baby pearl onions?"

Adam grinned. "You've put it all together and I don't mind telling you I'm pleased."

"Are you laughing because you're pleased?"

"That—and the fact that my sibs and I used to mark certain foods as aphrodisiacs. Oysters and green peas were high on the list."

"Oh? Well, I didn't have that in mind, but if they are, they are."

"Not that I need certain foods around you." At a mock disapproving glance from her, he laughed again. "Okay, I'll knock it off. Raven, I just can't help feeling I've known you a long time."

She hesitated. "I feel the same way and I feel it in my bones that we're going to be really good friends." But she realized she was nervous around him, skittish. He aroused feelings in her she hadn't felt for a long time and she didn't want to deal with these feelings just now.

"How's little Miss Merla?"

Raven glanced at the big grandfather clock as it struck eight P.M. "She really wanted to talk with you, but she had a long day and she simply fell asleep on her feet. By the way, you can play your harmonica for me anytime. My grandfather plays a harmonica."

He nodded. "Later, I'll be glad to oblige, and Cree told me about his grandfather's harmonica. That's why I brought it."

She smiled and shook her head. "You remind me of my grandfather."

"I'm grateful for any crumb."

Then he glanced around him. "I see you brought the roses home. I'm glad you liked them enough to do that."

"I love them. They're the most beautiful roses I've ever seen. Where on earth did you find them?"

"Over in Georgetown. I've got a friend who owns a floral shop over there and he sets out to make his place the best. He says they'll last at least a week if you use the life extender in the package."

"I did that. And I cut the stems on a slant. I'm going to press a few of them. I can't thank you enough."

"None needed. Beauty calls for beauty."

"I'm—" she began and stopped.

"You were going to say…"

"Again that I'm not beautiful, but I'm glad someone thinks so."

"Just someone? Not me especially? I'm wounded."

Raven chuckled. "You're something of a wag, Detective Steele."

"Adam to my friends and I'm hoping we'll be friends." He added under his breath, "And more."

"How does it grab you to come back to the kitchen with me and handle the oven fries while I finish the salad?"

"I'd like that." His heart was thrumming as he thought, *Just keep me near you, close to you and I'm happy.* But he wasn't happy enough; he wanted to be closer than close. In a word, he wanted it all.

As she stood at the counter tearing romaine lettuce into small pieces, she told him, "I've got something special to talk with you about. Something serious."

His face reflected tender concern. "Not something bad, I hope."

"No, something that could prove very useful. I won't talk about it until after dinner. Do you like Ben and Jerry's Chocolate Chip ice cream? I have several other flavors. Pick your poison."

"Chocolate's fine."

"And coconut rum pound cake?"

"That I haven't eaten before, but it sounds great."

"I made it."

Adam finished checking out the fries and stood up, walked over to the counter to stand beside her. "Hard to believe you can be the goddess you are and cook too."

She smiled. "You're laying it on with a trowel."

"It comes from the heart. I'm not one to bridle my tongue."

"You've got a honey tongue. But never mind, I've been through a dry spell and I need a bit of flattery. Just don't take it too far."

"Why? You admit you need some of it and I'm sincere. I think you know that. Tell you what. Let yourself relax a little. I'll be on my best behavior. I won't kidnap you and run away with you and I won't kiss you again until you want me to. You call the shots and I'll let you. Try it. You *may* find you like it."

Raven shuddered a little. His nearness made her tense. He left no doubt where he stood, but she had her life all lined up. She knew she *wanted* him; she didn't lie to herself about that. But she didn't *need* him. She didn't think she'd ever need a man again. She had needed Kevin, and what had it gotten her?

But she surprised herself by saying, "Okay, I'll try to relax a little. You do make me laugh and you're something of a rascal, I think, but I find myself enjoying being with you and I haven't enjoyed myself for a long time. Not since Kevin and I were first married and that spell didn't last long."

He looked at her long and hard and she thought he had a way of kissing her with his eyes and it flustered her. He did it now.

"I'm sorry," he said, as simply as she had told him she was sorry about his wife's dying.

It was time to take the potatoes out and the salad was together. "I've got an idea," she said. "Do you like oyster loaves? I've got soft French bread."

"Yeah. I do. I make myself one now and then. I discovered them in New Orleans."

"Then I'll make us a couple of big ones. Did you like New Orleans?"

"Loved it. I only went once for Mardi Gras."

"I lived there for a few years. Loved it."

Everything was all finished a bit later and they sat at the rose-damask-covered table set with her best silverware and china. She had put together an arrangement of maidenhair fern and gladioli.

"All this for me? It's really something."

"Who else?"

The food was superb. They laughed merrily as they ate with napkin bibs and napkins covering their laps to catch occasional drippings from the delicious feta cheese and sun-dried tomato dressing on the oysters and the salad.

"You've got a birthday coming up."

She felt suddenly somber. "Don't remind me. I've left the land of youth and entered unknown waters."

"Stop it. That's how I felt when I left my twenties. You're

lovely, talented, successful, and—put this first—you've got a great kid. Those things are going to last you until forever."

She nodded. "Merla's going to grow up. I'm almost sorry to subject her to an adult's heartache."

"You survived it. I did. And if we're good to ourselves…"

She looked up, but he didn't finish the sentence.

"Like I said, you've got a birthday coming up and I want to take you to a place called Enchanted Farm to celebrate it. You and Merla, Ricky and me. Down in the Tidewater area. All the scary rides, cotton candy, prizes to win. My niece, Ashley, and her husband own it. How does it grab you?"

Her face lit up. "Oh, I'm loving it and Merla will be in heaven. I've been to concerts by the gorgeous Ashley. This will be one of the best birthday, or any other day, presents I've ever gotten."

Raven leaned forward and put her elbows on the table. "I remember the fabulous Singing Steeles with your half-brother Frank and his wife Caroline and two of their children: Ashley and Whit. Ashley's a great gospel diva now and Whit is one of the best gospel singers around. I have so many of their records and CDs. And yes, I remember the original Singing Steeles with your father, Mel, and Frank and others. You come from a very proud lineage, Adam, and you do them proud."

Adam leaned back, tickled that she was pleased.

Then she blew him a light kiss in gratitude and it went through him as if her body were pressed hard against his. He felt sad that she was without someone to share all that love she so obviously possessed. They were meant to be a pair and he intended to prove it.

He helped clear the table and dish up the dessert. She

scraped the dishes and put them in the dishwasher, turned it on.

"Why don't we take this up to the family room and listen to music? I told you there's something I want to talk with you about."

"Sounds good to me. By the way, how's the fridge coming along?"

"I think it knows it's on its way out because there hasn't been a peep out of it."

"Good luck. I've had mine for ages. It'll probably blow any time. That's another thing. You've got to see my castle. The only thing it lacks is a woman's touch."

"You're so handy. Maybe you don't need a woman."

"Heresy! I don't just *need* a woman like you, I'm desperate."

"I'm sure you could have your choice."

"I'm picky. Hard to please."

"You say you like me. That means you're *easy* to please."

"Don't knock yourself. I know a Kohinoor diamond when I see one."

She thought then that that's what *he* was. A diamond and a fully polished one. And he didn't seem to know it.

At the foot of the stairs she was suddenly overwhelmed with visions of him kissing her two nights ago. Tonight he had said he wouldn't kiss her again until *she* wanted him to. Well... She didn't realize she had paused.

"What is it?" he asked.

She shook her head as if to clear away the cobwebs.

"Nothing. Just a thought."

He looked at her. The ice cream and cake were sweet, but she was sweeter. And he thought he plainly understood that she wanted something and he was willing to move heaven and earth to give her what she wanted.

In the family room, she set her tray down and switched on the new Bose entertainment center, asking, "What's your preference in music?"

"Depends on what I'm up to. At times like this when I'm trying to keep myself under control, I like classical. Or when I'm trying to think, working on a case."

"Would you like some Dvorak?"

"Yeah."

"What would you like to hear?"

"His Eighth Symphony is a favorite."

"Third movement?"

"Yes. I'd really enjoy that."

She selected a CD that featured excerpts from certain symphonies with the Dvorak Eighth Symphony's third movement first. They sat on the sofa, eating dessert from small trays and he felt better than he'd felt since Kitty died. He was grateful to Raven for bringing him back to life as he'd once known it.

She drew a deep breath. "When you rescued me yesterday, I was coming from an interview."

"An interview with?"

"A woman whose grandson died from Carr's thievery." Raven also told him what Desi had said about overhearing Tom and Cree quarreling before Cree was killed. "It seems Tom told Cree he'd see him dead and in hell before he'd let him rat him out. Cree laughed and said, 'Speaking of hell, the devil himself couldn't stop me.' Then Tom told him, 'Don't make me do something I don't want to do.' She said they were both furious."

When she had finished, Adam was silent a few minutes. "And she never came to the police with this info?"

"No. She was afraid. Her boyfriend is an ex-junkie and he didn't want her to."

"That's good info. You didn't give me her name."

"I'm protecting my source. You know every once in a while some journalist goes to jail to keep from divulging a source."

"Yeah, I'm well aware of that. Could you lean on her to talk with us? I'd offer her protection."

"What you can. You guys are so budget-strapped these days."

"I think I can swing it. Talk with her, please. We'll just take her statement."

"Adam, I'm not sure. I don't want to get her into trouble. She's a helpless soul."

"How did she happen to overhear this conversation?"

"She worked at CCG for a little while. She was fired."

"So Tom has no idea she overheard him and Cree arguing?"

"That's just it. She thinks he might be suspicious, thinks it might even be the reason he fired her, but she just doesn't know. She says the two men were in a semi-closed-off part of an office being renovated. It was after five and most people had left. She wanted a quick smoke and didn't want to go outside."

"So she's afraid she might follow Cree in Tom's plans?"

"Yes and why wouldn't she be?"

"Raven, this is all the more reason she should talk with us. You can believe Tom hasn't forgotten that she may have overheard. He's covered his tracks very well and he isn't about to let someone like this woman trip him up. Don't help her get herself killed."

Raven sat, thinking that she agreed with him, but she'd have to talk with Desi. Now she said, "She told me there was bad blood between Tom and her; he'd hit on her often and seemed annoyed that she always turned him down.... Okay, I will talk with her again."

"Thanks. I don't think you'll be sorry. You may very well save her life. Please do it soon. She's probably going to require a lot of leaning on." He sat forward as she nodded her assent.

"That was a wonderful meal and I thoroughly enjoyed myself, but put me out. I've got a rough day ahead."

"I enjoyed your company. You're nice to be around."

"Not exciting?"

She smiled. "I think you know the answer to that."

She was tense, but she felt a certain ease she'd never felt with Kevin. She trusted Adam. She was pulling him to her and she couldn't stop herself. Her heart tripped the light fantastic, but her mind said, "Go slow."

"I said it when I came in. I'll say it leaving. You look beautiful. No, that begs what I'm thinking. You *are* beautiful, all the way through. Being with you, I'm glad I'm passion's fool. I can't think of a saner, more sensible way to live."

He saw a shadow of fear cross her face and wanted badly to know what the hell McCloud had done to her. He wanted to scoop her up and run to some summer wooded spot and make love to that exquisite, full body until he calmed her fears and brought out all the ardor he knew she possessed.

"I mean it," he said. "You're going to have to throw me out."

Since the time she'd met him again the day before, she'd constantly surprised herself by wanting to gently tease him, play with him and she didn't consider herself a playful woman. But she reminded herself that as a girl and younger woman she *had* been playful, lively, even though she had been caught up in pain over her parents. She had been that way with Kevin at first, but that hadn't lasted past him trying to take Merla over. Now she murmured, "I told you. You're much too nice to throw out."

He leaned forward and kissed the corner of her mouth as she sat still. Her heart was thundering under her full breasts. The sensation of wanting him to stay, of *wanting* him, period, raced along her veins like wildfire.

"All right," she said, "we both need to get some sleep."

He grinned when she said that, thinking loving thoughts of holding her in one of their big beds. But then he wanted the *whole* woman, wanted her badly.

They both stood at once and this time he touched his lips to her cheek as she thought he'd kiss her lips the way she craved, but he didn't.

"Raven?"

"Yes."

He drew a deep breath. "I said I wouldn't crowd you, but how about lunch as often as we can make it? We're really working on the Carr case and a couple of others, but I have to eat. Dinner's an option, too, if you're willing. Movies and plays are out right now—not enough time—but keep October fifteenth in mind, will you?"

"Uppermost in my mind. I haven't been to a farm since I was a child and that was a very long time ago."

"Hush. It wasn't that long. You're eight years ahead of me. Don't make it twenty-five."

He wasn't just eye candy, she thought to herself, but more *soul* candy—the exquisite Belgian chocolate kind.

She showed him the tape Desi had given her and played it for him. There wasn't much of interest.

"There're two more," she said. "The second one is

more damaging to Tom and she thinks the third one will nail Tom. He threatens to kill Cree on that one."

"Where are the tapes?"

"She's got them stashed somewhere in her apartment. She promised to look for them. Desi's not exactly one to keep her word."

Before he left he asked if he could look in on Merla, and it moved her as she led him to Merla's bedroom and opened the door. "She's a precious kid," he told her softly. "Ricky's wanted a little sister for a long time."

As they closed Merla's door she couldn't stop smiling. "How long have we known each other? A day? Two days?"

"A lifetime," he said huskily. "I count the time back at the CCG Ball. I started falling then and I haven't stopped. I don't think I will be stopping. Maybe a day after forever."

"You're a romantic, Adam."

"Yeah. Doubly so where you're concerned."

At the door, she found she didn't want him to leave her, but he pulled the door open to find a short-stemmed, dark red rose lightly taped to it with a piece of notepaper taped to the stem.

Frowning, he asked her, "Admirers?"

With a lurch of her heart, she replied, "I hardly think so."

She was breathing too fast and her heart turned over with fear and a premonition that this was not good.

Adam said quietly, "Let me," as he pulled the rose off the door and opened the note. He swore under his breath as he showed the message to her. It read:

Short stem for a short time to live. Red is the color of blood, your blood that I will soon spill.

Raven stood rigid with shock and fear and Adam caught her close as he shut the door and held her, listening to her heart pound even as his own thudded. He had just found her, he swore, and nobody was going to take her away.

Adam put the note and the rose on a table and turned to her. "I'm going outside to see if there's anybody out there who may have seen who put this here."

"I'm going with you."

"Raven I—okay. I'm not doing a thorough canvas tonight."

Outside there was only one woman to be seen sitting on her front stoop. This was a new neighbor Raven didn't know and she introduced herself.

Adam was pleasant, gentle.

"Ma'am, we're wondering if you saw anyone go up to this lady's front door within the past couple of hours."

The woman nodded. "I certainly did and I got envious because I thought, aha, a romantic man pinning a note to his beloved's door, then slipping away. I wondered afterward, because I've been out here a couple of hours and other than neighbors, I haven't seen anybody else. The neighbors are mostly over at Ft. McNair at a party."

"Did the man speak to you?"

"No, he kept his head down and he was walking really fast." She described the man as being tall, but beyond that, she didn't remember any outstanding characteristic. She did describe what he wore: a slouch hat pulled down and dark clothes. "My husband's in the hospital and this was the first opportunity I've had to get some time for myself. I've got a hectic job as counselor as a juvenile center. Let me tell you I've got my hands full. What about this man?"

"I can't say just now," Adam told her, "but it's the opposite of romance."

The woman's eyes opened wider. "If there is anything I can do, like answer questions formally…"

"Thank you," Adam said. "It may come to that."

Other houses in that part of the complex were dark. When they got back to Raven's house, Adam stepped inside and took her hands in his. "You're trembling. Should I stay again?"

She shook her head. "Just check to make sure my security is still tight. I told you this has been going on for a few months. You never get used to it." There were tears in her voice as she told him, "I'm mad as hell about this. I'd like to punch the living daylights out of whoever is doing this."

"Understandable. I'd like to punch him out before you have to. You're getting extra patrolling around here since that first night. The only problem is this is an isolated section. I'll take the note and the rose to see if we can pick up fingerprints. I'm going to call you often, Raven, and I'm going to tell you whether you want to hear it or not. You're precious to me already. In my mind you're my Amber Love and I'm going to hold on tight."

She looked at his earnest, handsome face and felt her heart expand. "I wish with all my heart that what lies between us could be different. I just don't think I'd want to survive again what I went through with Kevin. And yes, I will tell you about it sometime, but right now it hurts too much."

"Do you think he could be doing this?"

"Kevin would hire someone to do it. It's the type of thing he would do."

"And of course there's Carr."

"Yes." She laughed then, again with an edge of hysteria. "Wouldn't it be funny if the two of them got together."

"Nothing about this is funny, love."

She noted how quickly he called her love and she smiled. Maybe one day she'd find a man like him who made her feel safe. He stayed another hour soothing and comforting her and when he left she missed him and wondered at the intensity of that missing. She had been alone the other times when the culprit followed her or she thought he did, called at odd hours and hung up, or breathed hard into her ear on the telephone, and she had withstood it. Why did she feel like clinging to Adam Steele as if she were drowning and only he could save her?

She didn't expect to sleep and she didn't. She couldn't stop thinking about it all and one word fastened itself to her mind: *soon.*

Chapter 6

Raven gazed out on the beautiful farm owned and run by Ashley and her husband, Derrick. The view was breath-taking with its hills and valleys and the Chesapeake Bay rolling a short distance away. She thought that October 15th had come around so fast. Her birthday, and Adam had been good for his promise. They had come down to the Tidewater area out from Norfolk in a van. Raven, Adam, Merla, Ricky, Viveca and Carey Sloan and last, but far from least, Papa Mac.

The group was gathered a short distance from her, talking to Derrick and it gave her time to think. They hadn't heard from the cretin who was stalking her since he'd left that rose and the note taped to her door. But he didn't need to do anything else. Her nerves were more frazzled each day as she waited for some new onslaught. Who? and Why? swarmed her mind. And, more important, when was *soon*?

Both Tom Carr and Kevin were certainly capable of having someone do these deeds. Kevin wanted custody of Merla and Kevin was a cold, cold man who felt he deserved whatever he wanted. And Tom? Well, Tom was a man who never intended to be poor again, and more than that, she suspected that he intended to be richer still. His greed knew no bounds, she thought now, and woe be unto anyone who stood in his way. And Raven certainly stood in his way.

Her boss, Ken Courtland, was the one who ran the show, but it was Raven's baby. As it had been Cree's baby. Now Cree was dead and Raven was pursued by a stalker whose last note had delivered a chilling promise. *Soon.* In the brilliant, warm October sunlight, her arms peppered with goosebumps as she shivered. Adam came up behind her and gripped her shoulders from behind.

"Why so pensive? It's your birthday."

He gently turned her to face him. "I know and thank you. This view is gorgeous. I wish I could stay here forever. After all, I've got the people who mean most to me right here."

He looked at her gravely. "Do you know what you're saying? You're including me in that group. Did you mean to?"

She drew a deep breath, laughed a little shakily. "I didn't think about it before I said it, but yes, I think I did. Adam, we can be the best of friends. I do think the world of you and I never thought I *could* feel so close to you. But I've had my lumps with love and I rule with my mind now, not my heart. If things were different, I'd let myself go and love you with all my heart and accept your love, but I..."

"You're living with fear of what's happening inside and outside of you. I'm going to get to the bottom of the fiend who's stalking you, or the fiends. But you have to understand, feel, what my love means and can mean to you." He tipped her chin up and kissed her mouth lightly. "I give good love, the best. Try it, at least for a while. You'll never be sorry."

But she leaned slightly into him and thought, if I let

myself go, I could love you *more* than you say you love me. My heart and my soul would be yours. And what if you change? You're not so young that you don't know your mind. You've had a deep love. I know now I feel I couldn't stand losing you. A part of me would die of heartache without you then. I remember how I felt when my parents went away, when my grandmother died. And when Kevin turned out to be nothing like he had pretended to be. Lying, and womanizing, and physically pushing me around. I got smart fast and fought back, but not fast enough. The scars have never healed.

As if he had read her mind, Adam told her, "I'm not Kevin, Raven. I'd never hurt you, and I'm going to see that no one else hurts you."

Very gently she told him, "We don't always mean the hurt we deal each other, but we deal it all the same. My parents and my grandma didn't die to hurt me, but the pain is still there."

"You need new, fresh love to replace the love you've lost."

She didn't get a chance to answer.

"Hey, you two, you're in a world of your own." Viveca and Carey came up behind them. Raven thought Viveca looked a little haunted and Carey looked bothered. Ricky came up with his little pal, Merla, in tow.

"Hey Dad," Ricky said. "You oughta see the Shetland ponies. And the goats." He proceeded to make goat sounds as Merla laughed and tried to do the same.

"And there's a huggy bear stand on the other side of the hill," Merla gleefully told them. "Hey Mom, Adam, they're great." She turned to Adam. "Will you win me one?"

Before Raven could answer, Adam said, "You bet, or I'll break my arm trying."

"You should've asked me," Ricky said. "I've got a pitching arm that's almost as good as Dad's."

Raven laughed. "It may take both of you, plus Papa Mac and Carey."

"Okay. *Soon*?" Merla piped up.

At the sound of the hated word that threatened her so, Raven shivered again, but she kept it down. Her child knew about none of this. "Yes, darling," she replied, but she didn't say the word.

Ashley and Derrick were the best of hosts. This was a weekday and Enchanted Farm wasn't crowded, so they had the chance to briefly visit each part of it which was also an entertainment center that drew people from hundreds of miles around. Various animals, games like those of county fairs, horseback riding, really good food, and a small yacht anchored in the bay where rides were given on the sparkling water twice daily.

Adam's glance constantly strayed to Raven in her aquamarine wool pullover and stonewashed beige jeans. She was so precious to him it pulled at his heartstrings just to look at her.

Ashley and Derrick's fifteen-year-old son, Corby, and their eight-year-old daughter, Eleni, were out of school for that day. The four children hit it off and cavorted like fairy elves.

"If we can leave the twerps behind, I'll show you how to pitch horseshoes," Corby told Ricky.

Ricky laughed loudly. "Twerps," he said. "I like that word." He smiled indulgently at Merla. "Hello, twerp."

Merla looked at him saucily, not sure whether to be pleased or offended. "You're a twerp. A *big* twerp."

"Ahh-h-h-h, girls," Ricky moaned. "How come they're necessary?"

"How come *you're* necessary?" Merla shot back. "You're *not* necessary."

"I sure am. What would you do without me?"

Before she could answer, Papa Mac, Adam and Raven, Derrick and Ashley came up.

Merla immediately ran to Papa Mac who could be depended on to champion her.

"How're you kids doing?" he asked. "Enjoying yourselves, are you?"

All four chortled their delight.

"They're fighting, but I'm behaving myself," Eleni said in her best grownup manner. "Why don't we play some pitching games?"

A visiting small family came up. "We're the Moores. Are you singing today?" the mother asked Ashley who smiled and shook her head.

"Not today I'm afraid. Sore throat, but I should be all healed in a few days. Are you from around here?"

"Just from around Newport News. We come here several times a year."

"Then please go up to the house and leave your name and write down the title of your favorite spiritual and drop me a line to tell me when you're coming back. I'll be sure to sing your song and dedicate it to you."

The woman hugged Ashley and said to her family, "You hear that? I told you she was a love."

The family got as enthusiastic as the mother and Ashley introduced them to the others.

As if in payment for the teasing of the boys earlier, Eleni told Merla, "See that Shetland pony over there, the brown and white one, he's mine. Want to ride him? The boys are too big."

"Oh, could I?" Merla breathed, pleased at a chance to get back at Ricky.

Adam helped seat her on the horse that trotted off to be met a short distance away by Derrick.

"Well, right this minute we're going to walk over and play the pitching games," Adam said. "I have my orders to win you a—well, whatever I *can* win."

"Dad, if you can't, I can, I think maybe," Ricky cut in.

Adam smiled. "I'll even let you go first."

At the huggy bear pitching stand, there were stuffed bears of several sizes and colors. As a broadly smiling middle-aged man gave Ricky several very large golden rings to throw around the small crown that was fastened atop the bear of his choice, Merla held her breath until it occurred to her, "Couldn't I throw for myself? You and Mom always say to do things for myself."

"Of course you can, sweetie." Adam patted the little girl's shoulder.

Merla drew a deep breath, took a round hoop and threw it at the bear of choice—and missed. Her little face showed disappointment.

Adam patted her shoulder again. "Rome wasn't built in a day. Here, try again."

But after four tries in which she missed each time, Merla turned to Adam. "Maybe you had better do it."

"No. My turn's next," Ricky intoned.

"Okay hotshot," Adam said, grinning.

But Ricky's aim was no better.

"We can do more of this this afternoon," Ashley told them. "It's your birthday complete with fabulous Devil's Food cake. You've got a really good farm dinner coming up, so let's let Adam throw and he'd better win you something, hadn't he?"

Merla nodded and looked at Adam who took the hoops and began pitching. He, too, missed on the first throw and redoubled his efforts. On the second throw the hoop went around the top crown on the bear's head and it was a win.

"Voila!" Adam exulted. "So, the old man's still got it."

Raven reached up and kissed Adam's cheek. "Thank you. I was getting anxious."

Ricky cocked his head to one side, admiring Adam and Raven. "I think it'd be great if you two got married." He looked at Merla. "The twerp and I would like that. Wouldn't you?"

He smoothed Merla's hair and all was forgiven.

"Oh yes," Merla breathed.

Papa Mac smiled from ear to ear. "Hear ye! Here ye! I like the sound of that." He looked at Adam gravely, then at Raven. "Honeygirl, I haven't had a chance to see much of Adam, but I sure like what I see. And I'd like to see you and Merla settle with a good man."

Raven flushed. "I notice you never got married after Grandma died."

"Touché. I never fell in love again." His eyes twinkled. "Seems to me your case is different."

Raven's tongue went lightly over her bottom lip. She told herself she wished Adam didn't look at her so lovingly before all these people. They were friends, not lovers.

Merla's little face lit up with joy as she hugged her bear, then she kissed and hugged Adam who beamed.

"Now after dinner, we'll win Mommy a bear," Adam said.

"Or maybe I'll win her one," Ricky promised.

"That would be nice." Raven ruffled the boy's hair and he blushed.

A little later at the big, white clapboard house that

could have been pulled from the pages of a *House and Garden* magazine, Raven and Viveca found themselves on the semi-wraparound front porch with the warm fall sun shining.

"Honey, something's bothering you," Raven said as they stood by a trellis. "Can I help?"

Viveca blinked back a few tears. "Can *anybody* help? I'm afraid my marriage is running into trouble."

"How so?" A quick look of deep concern crossed Raven's face.

"How do you tell if a man's cheating?" Viveca asked bitterly.

After a moment, Raven offered, "There are said to be ways. The advice columns frequently run letters to help you tell if your mate is running around. Kevin never cared if I knew after I tried to keep him on the straight and narrow for the sake of our marriage. But why do you feel Carey's cheating?"

Raven thought she knew what Viveca would say and she did. "He's away so much working so late. We used to go places together, just sit and hold hands and cuddle. Carey's got the makings of a great husband.... Raven, did I make a mistake? Carey and I are from different races. We've played that down, or rather we haven't had to. His father and his mother taught long years at Howard University and at Hampton. They had absolutely no objection to our marriage; they like me a lot and they're so supportive. My mother was pleased that Carey's such a nice guy. Only my pop was a little bothered. He adores me and he doesn't think anybody is good enough for me, but he finally came around. Now he's downright enthusiastic about Carey and us as a couple."

Viveca paused, thinking, and her face was sad. "You like

Carey a lot; he talks to you. He used to talk to me. Now he's always rushed."

Raven hugged her friend. "Baby," she said simply. "It's going to be all right."

"Do you know something I don't know?" Viveca looked at Raven hopefully, but Raven shook her head slowly.

"You're always so good to talk to and you've got such great common sense," Viveca told her. "Now how about it if you use that great common sense to seal you in with Adam Steele. He adores you, Raven, and you need a good man, even if you don't *want* one. Your daughter needs a father and Ricky needs a mother. You're the only one who's out of step. I'll listen to you if you'll listen to me."

Raven hugged her again. "You drive a hard bargain, love. Dry those tears and we'll find the group and get ready for dinner. I've told you how deeply I've come to feel about Adam. But I'm scared, Viveca, *so* scared."

Viveca hugged her tightly as she murmured, "Sometimes we have to go ahead and *do* what we're scared of."

Derrick presided over the groaning dinner table with great pleasure. His blessing was long and spirited and each person added a short Bible verse. The group from D.C., Derrick and Ashley, Corby and Eleni were all there. A two-year old baby, Abby, was brought in to meet the group from D.C.

Ashley introduced the cook as Mrs. Funchess and added, "She's a culinary genius. If anyone ever tries to steal her away, they'll have me to answer to."

The woman beamed. "I don't plan to go nowhere."

Ashley smiled her thanks and patted her baby. "I'd let her have her high chair and be with us," Ashley said, "but she's been fretful and I want her to get plenty of rest. She's such an active child."

When the older woman brought the baby to her, Raven felt her heart squeeze nearly dry. What a beautiful, loving child. She thought about Merla's birth and it seemed light years ago. She felt this child in her womb and in her heart. Oh yes, she *wanted* a baby. With a ragged breath she looked up to find Adam gazing steadily at her and she wanted to run away with him, to hold him tightly to her, make love, make a baby.... Heat suffused her body when Adam smiled crookedly as if he knew exactly what she was thinking.

And Adam felt his heart lurch with hope when Raven looked at him the way she did. He dreamed a quick kaleidoscope of wildly sensual, loving scenes that ended in them holding their baby close. Ah, Lord.

Papa Mac saw it too and smiled. He and his Aurelia had known the joy of love and kids and he wanted the same for Raven. She had known the joy of one child, but never the love she should have had from a man. He had come to despise Kevin, but he altogether approved of Adam Steele. Any fool could see he was head over heels with Raven. And he wondered sadly when she would get over the hurt Kevin had dealt her.

Music poured from the sound system. They had requested Ashley's gospel recordings and that music filled their ears, soulful and perfect.

"This is *dinner*?" Merla piped up. "At home I have dinner at four-thirty and Mom eats around seven. You said this is dinner?" She spoke to Derrick.

"It *is*," he replied gravely. "You see, in the country we have breakfast, dinner and supper where you have breakfast, lunch and dinner. Different strokes for different folks."

Merla frowned. "What d'you have for supper?" The word felt funny to her.

"All kinds of good things," Eleni told her.

Merla sat forward with deep interest. "Sometimes I help Mrs. Reuben cook, but not often."

"You never showed all that much interest," Raven told her.

"I'm interested now. Tomorrow could we have supper and I could help Mrs. Reuben make it?"

The grownups laughed and Raven demurred. "Sweetheart, our lifestyle doesn't fit that scene. We're not home at noon, but you certainly can help Mrs. Reuben cook anytime you wish."

"Goody!" Merla was all smiles.

The table was simply but beautifully set with cream damask, good silver, crystal, and a centerpiece of varicolored mums broadleaf fern. Raven thought the food was the best she'd tasted lately. The sideboard held beautiful cuts of roast beef, rare and well done, baked turkey, spiral honey-cooked ham, beef stew in a crock pot. There were salads—vegetable and potato. Flaky rolls were in napkin-covered baskets. Candied yams, asparagus, baby corn, collard greens with bits of ham lending color. It was a feast and they settled down to enjoy it. As they talked, a middle-aged woman brought in a cart of desserts and began to serve dinner.

Ashley smiled at her uncle. "Adam, you're looking prosperous—and happier than I've seen you in ages. Is something going on you haven't told me about?"

Ashley gazed from Adam to Raven, then back to Adam.

And Adam looked at Raven. "There's a lot going on, but I'm not sure I'm at liberty to talk about it. If I ever get a breakthrough, you'll be the first to know."

Papa Mac smiled with half-closed eyes as he looked at Raven. "And you'd better let me be the first to know—and soon."

Soon. Raven jumped a bit, startled again at the word. Was she going to have to remove that word from her vocabulary? Was the man who stalked her bluffing to scare her out of her wits? Or was she simply slated to die—*soon?* Her breath nearly stopped just thinking about it and she began to cough.

Adam got up and came around to her. "Let's go out on the porch and stop that cough," he said urgently. "Go on with dinner," he said to the others. "She's a little upset. It'll be all right."

"If you're sure," Ashley said.

"I'm sure," Raven said between coughs.

Out on the porch Adam had Raven draw deep breaths. "You were thinking about the evil bastard who's stalking you, weren't you?"

Raven nodded. She couldn't speak and there seemed to be something lodged in her throat which felt bone dry.

"Your grandfather said the word 'soon' and I watched you. In response to your grandfather, I know you're undecided about whether you want me or not, but this had to do with that word, as your stalker uses it. Sweetheart, I would do anything to spare you this, but you can't let it get you down. That's what he wants."

"I know," she said evenly, "and you're right. I won't let it get me down. Adam, I care about you. In a little over a month, I've come to care for you the way I've never cared for any man." Her voice sounded tremulous and it lifted him until she said, "If anything happens to me, I want you to know that."

Adam gripped her shoulders. "Nothing's going to happen to you. We're going to grow old together...." He stopped then. He hadn't meant to say that. Easy, easy, he told himself, he wasn't going to crowd her. Not now, because her words, the look on her face, even with the fear reflected there, gave him hope far beyond anything she'd given him before.

He hugged her then, held her trembling body against his and knew fully that she was his woman, the woman he had to have.

"I'm better now," she suddenly said. "Thank you. Adam, how did you get to be so sweet?"

"Your sugar's rubbed off on me."

They both smiled then and he kissed the corner of her mouth, his tongue darting a bit in which made her shiver, this time with deep pleasure.

Back inside, the others looked up anxiously when the two came back. Adam seated her, then himself.

"Is everything okay?" Ashley and Derrick asked at once. Ricky and Merla seemed to hold their breath.

"I'm fine now," Raven said heartily. "Let this delicious meal proceed."

"Look, you've got to come back to a catfish fry late one afternoon or at night; we have both." Derrick sought to add a soothing touch.

"Hey Dad, sounds neat," Ricky said. "How about it? I've sure liked the others I've been to down here. Raven, you'd love that."

"I expect I would and I'll look forward to it."

Merla looked beside herself with joy. "Hey Mom, you'll bring me?"

Raven laughed. "How could I go anywhere without you?"

Ashley chuckled as she reached over and ruffled Ricky's short dreadlocks. "Both you boys are growing like weeds."

Adam laughed. "The way they eat, they'll be grown and married before we know it."

Ricky looked suddenly somber. "I'm not ever getting married."

The group looked startled. Adam asked, "Why, son? I've never heard you say that before."

"But I've thought it. Wives love you and die and it hurts too much."

Adam and Raven both got up and went by Ricky's side, hugging him. The boy didn't cry, but you could see tears lingering.

"Would you like to go outside and talk about this? You, Raven and I?"

Ricky shook his head. "Not now, but I'd like that later." He turned to Raven, asked fiercely, "*You* won't leave me, will you?"

And Raven, as well as Papa Mac, noticed that there was no hesitation in her voice. "I won't leave you," she said softly. "I won't *ever* leave you."

Adam thought then about whoever pursued Raven and bitter anger caught and held him like giant pincers. He took Raven's hand and held it to his lips for a few moments. She *was* growing to love him and he wondered if she knew.

The desserts were all scrumptious—blackberry and peach cobblers with flaky melting crusts, small kegs of vanilla, chocolate and strawberry ice cream. Butter-rum poundcake.

They all stood up when the gorgeous three-layer Devil's Food cake was wheeled in. Set on Ashley's best heavy Steuben crystal, it blazed with forty-one chocolate-colored candles.

"Step over please and blow them out." Ashley was so pleased at the way Mrs. Funchess' cake had turned out.

Drawing a deep breath, Raven walked over and blew until the candles were all out. Then Adam held his ginger ale glass to hers, and as the crystal tinkled he made a toast, "May your future be bright and may you know and accept love that lasts forever."

"Yay!" the kids all cheered her.

She congratulated Mrs. Funchess on the cake and the woman blushed and thanked her.

The older woman laughed as she chatted while serving. Eleni got up and explained, "I always help Mrs. Funchess serve."

"Oh Mom, could I help too?" Merla was restless with joy.

"You bet you can," Ashley told her. "All your wishes are our command today."

The food was so delicious and Raven felt the old torment slipping away from her. There was only the matter of Adam and her to be resolved. Her trained mind said he was too young for her, but her heart pled its case; he felt altogether *right* for her and that was all that mattered.

That afternoon, Ricky won a very large huggy bear for Raven after strutting his stuff with his pitching arm. Carey won a smaller bear for Viveca. Then they all met and mingled with the small crowd of other visitors and petted the animals that were available to pet. Merla was simply enamored of the Shetland pony and kept looking wistfully at him.

Then it was time to go on the yacht and all four children were wildly enthused. "I've been on it before," Ricky bragged. "Many times."

The two girls looked at him adoringly.

"Nothing, dude. I'm on her most every day," Corby bragged back.

But the boys had long ago forged a bond and always looked forward to seeing each other.

The yacht was sleek, white and carried a friendly crew of four. The captain, a big, hearty man, made his visitors feel at home. Today on deck there was a huge crystal bowl of strawberry punch and a variety of delicious cookies. All that walking had made the children and the grownups a bit hungry again and they sampled the refreshments, some smacking their lips.

"Hm-m-m, these are great," Raven told Ashley. "Your wonderful cook again?"

Ashley laughed as she nodded. "Don't call her *my* cook. She's her own woman and she's the freest woman I know."

Raven's laughter matched Ashley's as she said, "Sorry. The world has changed and I keep forgetting."

The visitors toured the yacht and some danced to pop music and rhythm and blues. Then gospel music took over and they were reverent and mostly silent, listening intently.

A young woman came up to Ashley as she stood with the D.C. visitors. "Miss Ashley," the woman said, "you've been a favorite with me for quite a few years now. Long may you reign."

Ashley thanked her, then signed the autograph book the woman held out.

The Chesapeake Bay winds rippled and sunlight sparkled on the bluish green waters. As Adam gripped Raven's hand, she found herself wishing she could stay in this place and this time with the ones she loved. She was far away from the stalker and his evil. She felt safe here. But was she? Gradually he was insinuating himself into her life, his evil coming between her and the sense of safety. She said nothing to Adam, wanting him to have some moments free of worry.

Then for a little while, Adam mingled with the others and Raven stood at the railing watching the ship plow the waters as Carey came to her.

"I don't want to be nosy, but you and my wife were talking. Viveca's unhappy and I'm the cause, I'm pretty sure. I want to share a secret with you, Raven. May I?"

"Of course you may."

He put a hand on the rail as if to steady himself. "I'm putting in a killing amount of time at work because I'm angling for a promotion that I've been told I have a very good chance of getting."

"That's wonderful."

"Yeah. Viveca is kind of restless. She really wants to quit her job at WMRY when she gets pregnant and I want her to. She's been fretting about what we'll do to make ends meet when she's not working for a year or two. Of course there's no baby yet, but we're trying and keeping our fingers crossed. With this new job, she could stop for a long while, maybe for good. So I see it as a challenge and a necessity."

"Why can't you just tell her this?"

Carey shook his head. "I want to surprise her. Viveca loves surprises."

Raven shook her head. "In the meantime, she's thinking the worst."

"Which is?"

"That you're cheating."

Carey threw back his head and roared with laughter. "Me? God, that woman fills my every waking thought. And my dreams. I wouldn't cheat on Viveca with the Queen of Sheba. She ought to know that." The laughter subsided and he sighed. "Look, I know I'm a stubborn cuss, but when I get my mind set…" He went cold sober then. "We have to *trust* each other. Maybe this is a test. In the end my parents split up because she didn't trust him. I can't let that happen to me."

Raven placed a hand on Carey's as it lay on the rail. "You know Viveca has been my best friend for a very long time and I've come to feel almost as close to you. When will you tell her your secret?"

"Things should be clear in a month or so. In the meantime, I'll bring her candy and flowers and small gifts."

Raven chuckled sadly. "All time-honored actions for a man who's cheating. Hadn't you thought about that?"

He laughed ruefully. "I guess I hadn't, but I'm *not* cheating, so I expect her, as I said, to trust me."

"Carey, you're reliving your parents' life and you're headed in the same direction."

"Hey, don't *say* that. What Viveca and I have is for keeps."

"I certainly hope it is. You might reconsider."

"No. The more I think about it, this is a test. She's got to trust me."

Suddenly Adam's voice spoke behind them. "May I join you?"

"Please do," Raven said.

Carey smiled at Adam. "Any idea where my wife is?"

"Yeah, in the cabin admiring the yacht, along with a gaggle of others."

"Then I'll go and admire too. This is a great yacht. Finer than many I've been on that were larger. Not that I've been on that many."

Carey left them and Adam put his arm around Raven's shoulders, hugged her. "Penny for your thoughts."

"They're so jumbled. Adam, I almost hate to go back. It's so peaceful here."

Her words tore at his heart. He would have given anything to be certain he could keep her safe.

Merla and Ricky came strolling up, looking somber. "Well," Adam intoned. "How's it coming? Enjoying yourselves?"

"Yeah," Ricky said, "only we've got something on our minds. Want to hear it?"

"Always," Adam assured him.

"And you, Mom?" Merla asked.

"Of course, darling. You know that. My, but you two look serious."

"Yeah," Ricky began, stopped, then blurted out, "We want you two to get married. We'd make a great family. Another little sister or brother and we'd all have it made."

Raven's heart expanded, beat too fast. Out of the mouths of babes. The children's faces were so earnest, so innocent. She and Adam looked at each other and he said to her with his heart in his eyes, "Well, honey?"

She placed one hand on Merla's head and the other on Ricky's arm. "Darlings, marriage is more than a notion."

"Dad *wants* to marry you. Why don't *you* want to marry him?"

Raven surprised herself by saying, "What makes you think I don't?"

Ricky whooped. "Then you *do*! And it's all settled. Merla and I'll help you set up everything. Oh boy!"

Raven's body went hot with the thought of Adam holding her, stroking her to fevered desire, shielding her body and her soul. And Adam felt a surge of power in his brains down to his loins until he was nearly undone with wanting this woman with a hunger so sharp it was almost frightening.

Merla was right in there pitching, dancing up and

down until Raven sobered and told them, "Now wait a minute, you two. I didn't say I would. I said I *wanted* to. You both know the difference."

Two faces fell flat until Raven soothed them. "Let's all just keep *thinking* about it, mulling it over. I'm not a great believer in fate, but maybe it *is* in the stars."

Then Ricky spoke in a voice gleaned from suffering the loss of his mother at such a tender age and he sounded bitter. "My dad loves you, Raven. Don't you love him?"

How to answer this? Raven thought, and honesty seemed best. She looked at Adam as she said, "I love him, all right, more than I ever thought I'd love a potential mate again. I love him, but I never want or intend to hurt him or either of you. That's why I've got to have time to think about this."

Adam's smile was wide then, pleased, and the children whooped again. "You love him and in a little while you two will get married," Ricky prophesied. He wasn't going to accept any other answer.

"Why don't you kids wander about some more?" Adam told the kids. "Make hay while the sun shines."

"You say that all the time," Ricky said, grinning again. "The sun's shining, but there's no hay around."

"There really is, you know," Adam said, "in that big red barn. Hay and oats for the horses. Now scoot."

The children left and Adam turned to Raven. She looked so lovely standing there and her eyes were warm and starry. "Did you mean it when you said you love me?" he asked her.

"I wouldn't lie to the children. I'm sure you know I love you, but marriage is such a big step. I've hinted at why I'm so reluctant. I want to talk about it, and I will as soon as I can bring myself to do it." Then she added, "I'll

never hurt you in any way I can help." There were tears
in her voice when she said, "Sweetheart, I *want* to marry
you, but I…."

She had not used terms of endearment with him often,
although he constantly used them with her. Lord, everything, she thought, was on *him. He* did all the reaching,
all the waiting, but she also knew she lured him on with
silent promises of good things to come. And she decided
the change would begin now. He brought joy and passion
into her life with a depth she'd never felt before. She was
going to let it happen and damn the fear that stifled and
shackled her. She was going to be free to love him with a
passion that matched or transcended his.

"Adam," she said softly.

He wasn't smiling anymore. "Yeah, baby."

Did he guess she was going to say it? He seemed to
know so much else.

"I love you. I know today that now I really love you.
There's something about being here with you. It's so
peaceful and quiet and we all fit together."

She drew a deep breath. "And the trouble I've been
having makes me know it too. The possibility of my death
has made me clutch at life."

He pulled her to him, his powerful hard frame outlin-
ing her lush, soft body. He could have wept with frustration at the blight that lay on their happiness. He had
wanted her for a long time; now she finally wanted him.
But there was still the shadow of the pain Kevin had dealt
her. And there was this new evil, this sorry bastard who
pursued her now with sworn death on his mind.

She felt herself throwing caution to the winds. "I want
you so much, *need* you so much."

He gripped her shoulders tightly. "I said I wouldn't

press you, but I'm so hungry for you. I'm going to ask you again...."

"Darling, yes, I'll marry you. We'll talk about when."

Adam let out a whoop of joy and caught her in a hug that threatened to break her ribs. "Baby, baby," he whispered, "this is forever."

For a little while then, Raven felt peace again, in his arms, in his heart. And she kissed him fervently, moaning slightly and pulling him closer to her. They were completely alone in the midst of others.

"Probably newlyweds," one nearby woman commented.

"No," her husband responded, "I saw kids with them. Maybe they weren't theirs, though."

The man pulled the woman close. "Let's share some of that romance." He kissed her and held her as she beamed. "What a wonderful day we picked for an outing. Let's come here often."

Chapter 7

"There's gonna be a killing!"

Raven clutched the telephone tightly as her blood chilled. Dear God, she hadn't even had time to wake up and think about Adam and their newly found joy. She had groggily picked up on the second ring, expecting Adam's voice. The creep had never called in the morning before, only in the early evening and at night.

"Who *is* this?" she demanded.

But he had hung up and the hum of the empty line mocked her. At least he hadn't said "Soon."

She lay tense for a few minutes, then picked up the phone and dialed.

"Adam?"

"Yeah, babe. How's my wife to be?"

For a moment she lost her voice.

"Raven, what's happened?" But he thought he knew what had happened before she spoke.

"He called again, just a minute ago."

"Oh hell! What did he say?"

She forced herself to steadiness. "That there's going to

be a killing—but he didn't say soon. Adam, I'm clutching at straws."

"Okay, I'm coming over. Just hang on."

"No. I'm taking up so much of your time and you've got a job to do."

"And you don't? Listen, sweetheart, I'm with you all the way, and I'll be there for you always. You've got me now. We've got each other. Just hang on."

She hung up, drew up her knees and hugged them as Merla came bouncing in. "Mom, I heard the phone. Who is it? Adam?"

"Yes, honey. Adam."

"Mom, you look upset." Merla hopped onto the bed beside her mother. "And I want a kiss and need a hug."

"And you'll get plenty of both." Raven hugged her child, kissed the soft, tender cheeks and held the delicate, thin body close. "Do you know how precious you are to me?" She swore fiercely that she would always keep her safe. But her own resolve mocked her. She couldn't keep herself from being threatened.

"Adam loves me too. He told me so."

"How could anyone not love you? You're such a lamb."

"Mom, are you gonna marry Adam?"

Raven looked at her for a long time. Why not tell her now? "Yes, sweetheart, I'm going to marry Adam."

Merla rocked back and forth with laughter, flung her arms around her mother's neck. "I want to tell Ricky. Can I call him now?"

Raven smiled at her daughter's happiness, forcing herself to concentrate on this and forget about the hated call. "Honey, I think we'll wait until later. Besides, Adam will tell him. What's your rush?"

"I'm happy. I get a new daddy." She hesitated a moment. "Will my old daddy be mad with us?"

Raven was taken aback. "I'm not sure. Why do you ask?"

"Well, he always asks me if you say anything about getting married again, and he asks me who you're taking up with."

"You never told me that before."

Merla shrugged. "He said it was a secret between us, but I don't like keeping secrets from you. I love you, Mom."

Raven hugged her again, held her. "And I love you more than you'll ever know."

She showered in one bathroom while Merla showered in another. Alone, she had time to reflect on the call. The voice was disguised, but nothing could hide the evil it held. It was meant to intimidate and it found its mark. She let the warm water wash over her and tried to attach a human to that voice. Tall? Short? Probably a hired man, and she shuddered as it came to mind. *A hit man.* She realized then that each time he called, she saw herself lying in a crumpled heap on the ground. Merla would be devastated. Now there were Adam and Ricky who would grieve.

She shook herself and turned the icy cold tap on. Might as well let the outside of her feel like the inside. As the sharp needles of water stung her, she told herself sharply not to be morbid. For the sake of others, she had to keep it in.

Mrs. Reuben was early. She let herself in with her key and called out her usual greeting, "Good morning, you two."

Raven was in the kitchen by then. In deference to Adam's coming over, she had begun to prepare a breakfast of oatmeal, sliced bananas, sausage and eggs scrambled with very sharp cheese. She slid the bowl of beaten eggs onto a counter to wait until he got there.

Mrs. Reuben took off her coat and came back. "Let me handle the rest. Did you all have a good time in the country?"

"Wonderful. Mrs. Reuben, Adam and I are getting married."

The older woman's joy was nearly as profound as Merla's had been. She closed her eyes and seemed to breathe a sigh of relief. "Oh thank God you'll have someone. I've been worried about that monster who's bothering you. I feel better with Mr. Steele being a detective and all. Here, give me a hug."

The two women hugged as the phone rang.

"Want me to get that, Mom?"

"No, baby, I'll get it." What happened if Merla picked up and he said what he said about a killing? A man like that wouldn't care about a child answering. He had a message to deliver.

Viveca was relentlessly cheerful. "I just want to apologize for being such a wet blanket yesterday."

"You weren't a wet blanket. You had reasonable things on your mind, so don't give it a thought. I just hope you two clear everything up in a hurry. Listen, Viv, I've got some news that will please you and Carey. I'm going to marry Adam."

Viveca laughed delightedly. "You wise woman. I'll bet he nearly passed out with surprise."

"Oh, I think he felt it coming. You know, Viveca, I've loved Adam from the start, just as he says he's loved me."

"He never had to say it. It's there for any fool to see. Talk about besotted. Oh, love, I'm so happy. Carey, pick up!"

Then Carey was part of the conversation and his pleased comments only added to the joy she felt.

Raven didn't mention the early morning call. She

hadn't forgotten it for a second, but it seemed too bizarre to talk of threats of death in the midst of life the way she'd never felt it before.

The door chimes sounded and Merla danced with glee as she opened the door. "Adam!"

"That's not what I'm looking for," Adam teased her. "I'll settle for no less than a big hug and a bigger kiss."

Merla hugged and kissed him fervently. "You gonna marry Mom? You told Ricky?"

"So many questions from such a little girl. I told Ricky and he's as happy as you are."

Merla looked at her mother with a worried frown. "Have you told Papa Mac?"

"I told him before we left the Enchanted Farm. I couldn't keep it from him."

"Oh, that's neat, Mom. When?"

"When do we get married?"

"In a very little while," Adam told her. "Just be patient."

Merla settled down. "You're gonna have breakfast with us. We've got some great raspberry Danish. I'll help Mrs. Reuben put it all together."

Only then did Adam look at Raven and the worry in her eyes tore at him. "Baby, I am so sorry." For a moment he felt gut-wrenchingly hopeless, then resolve flooded him as he took her in his arms, held her, smoothed her hair.

She forced herself to relax a bit.

"I'm so grateful for your love and so happy that I can let myself know I love you, take the chance on us and accept whatever happens."

They sat on the sofa and he drew her close again. "I think we ought to get married as soon as possible. What about Elkins?" He spoke of a town in Maryland that had a three-day waiting period.

"Listen, I know that's a short time, but I want you with me all the time."

Raven nodded. "Okay. I find I want that too. But am I being fair to you? I sprang this on you so quickly...."

"You could never spring it quickly enough. I can really protect you now. I love you, love you, *love* you. You've given me back my life."

Chapter 8

In her office that same morning, Raven felt a little more relaxed. She and Adam had spent most of the weekend together, with a delirious Merla and Ricky in tow. The four of them had made wedding plans. The ceremony would be at Adam's house because it was larger and she had gone to visit that house for the first time and found it lovely.

Adam's parents were away but they were wildly enthusiastic about the coming wedding when they spoke with Adam on the phone.

Earlier, Adam and Raven and the two children had gone shopping for a ring. In the small, exquisite jewelry store, Adam had said to Raven, "I want you to pick the most beautiful ring you see."

"Sweetheart," she had protested, "price has to be an object."

He had shaken his head. "No. Remember I told you shortly after I met you that I had inherited a nice sum of money from a wonderful old man who felt I'd saved his son's life. He said he had a lot of money and he wanted to spend it wisely. So you don't have to bother about the cost."

Now she looked down at the big, round white diamond that flashed its perfect fire in the office lights. She wasn't aware of Ken's coming in until he whistled long and low. "So DeBeers has moved to D.C.," he said, laughing. "That's some rock." Then his face shadowed. "What's going on?"

She looked at him happily. "Adam and I are getting married."

"Which is usually the reason for engagement rings. I would have gotten you a bigger ring," he teased. "That's a rock. I'd have gotten you a boulder."

She smiled and half closed her eyes. "I like rocks."

He came in and sat down at the side of her desk, asked wistfully, "Are you happy, Raven? Is he really the one you want? You've known Adam Steele such a short while."

She looked at him sharply. He did seem sad. "I'm happier than I thought I could ever be. Actually I've known him since that ball in April."

"Hell, you danced with him once or twice, talked with him a while. That doesn't count," he scoffed.

"It counts," she said, "for both of us. We couldn't forget each other."

"Okay, then I guess I'll have to congratulate you because I want you to be happy. I love you that much."

Raven blushed, then smiled at her boss. "Thank you, Ken. You've been such a good friend."

"And I've wanted to be much more. How's the fight with the beast coming along? Have you heard from him lately?"

She hesitated. "I hadn't heard from him in a little while since I told you about the rose and the note...."

"And nothing's happened about that?"

"No. Leads like that are almost impossible to track

down. I told you a woman saw him leave it, described him as being tall and could go no further."

"There's something else. You've gotten tense as hell."

"This morning he called again."

"Yes, and he breathed hard or said what?"

She hesitated a long time and didn't want to repeat the hated words.

Ken finished for her. "He said 'There's gonna be a killing.' I can see that from the expression on your face."

She nodded. "It could be some crazy teenager playing games."

"You don't believe that. Tom Carr plays games all right—hardball. Cree is dead and I surely believe it has everything to do with the Carr case. We've got a witness who swears she overheard Tom and Cree arguing vehemently, heard him threaten Cree."

"A witness who won't testify because her boyfriend won't let her."

"Witnesses change their minds sometimes."

"This one's in love and controlled by her man."

"Then there's the missing tape that Cree held."

"And we've been unable to find."

"In time maybe. Have you heard from Glenda?"

"She's grieving Cree's death so hard I almost hate to bother her. Glenda's a basket case. After nearly five months, she's still on the verge of a breakdown."

"She'll grieve less if we can find out who killed him. You're grieving too."

"God, yes."

Viveca, Blaine and Will came in together. Viveca handled advertising for the station and was almost as good as Carey, who worked for an outside advertising firm.

"Let's take a vote," Viveca proposed. "Let's just have

our morning meeting in here instead of in Ken's office. I like looking at big diamonds."

Blaine and Viveca and Raven all voted *yea* and Will growled. "Don't look at me. I'm just the gofer, and not so glorified either."

Viveca patted his back. "You poor baby. Your title is investigative assistant."

"I keep reminding myself," Will growled again.

Ken grinned broadly. "It's at moments like this I enjoy being boss. The meeting is in my office because I've ordered a variety of hot doughnuts and my secretary promised me the best coffee we've ever had here."

"Oh, oh," Raven said. "I'm defecting. I don't need the doughnuts. I brought along a bran muffin."

"Throw it out the window," Ken told her.

"I've got to shape up before my wedding."

Ken rolled his eyes. "If you shape up any more, I can't stand it."

Raven chuckled as she looked at Blaine and Will. "I haven't told you I'm getting married."

"Viveca could never keep anything like that to herself," Blaine said.

"Congratulations," Will said, holding out his hand which Raven shook. "So the roses *meant* something. If I ever settle down to just one woman, I'll remember that. And maybe it'll work for two or three."

"Hey buster, polygamy's not legal in D.C.," Viveca said, laughing.

Will leaned back where he stood and grinned. "It's gonna be for me."

As Raven got up to go to Ken's office with the others, her cell phone rang and Adam's warm voice came on the line.

"How's my baby?"

"I just left you a couple of hours ago. I think I'm okay now. How're you?"

"Well, you were upset and I worried. Other than that, I couldn't be better. How's the rock holding up?"

"So beautiful it scares me. Adam, I'm going to have a copy made and keep it in my safe-deposit box."

"It's insured."

"It's too precious to have snatched." She thought about the man on New Jersey Avenue who had tried to rob her and she flinched. Bastard that he was, he had given her a head start with Adam.

"Sweetheart, I need you to come by here to meet Allyson and answer a few questions about the guy who mugged you. Others have come forward and we're building a good case against him. I'd offer to pick you up, but I'm hog-tied here. Can you get a taxi?"

"I can and I will. What time?"

"Make it as soon as you can. Allyson's got to be in on a couple of depositions later, so she's in a hurry."

"Raven, I want to introduce you to my right hand and for that matter, my left one too, my sergeant Allyson Welles."

No doubt about it, Raven thought a bit sourly, Adam was beaming beyond his usual good humor.

Raven extended her hand and noticed that the other woman's smile didn't quite reach her eyes. "I've heard so much about you and I'm glad to finally meet you."

"Well, I'm hearing a lot about you too," Allyson said.

Each woman covertly looked the other over. Good Lord, that sylph-thin body, Raven thought. I'd kill to be in that body for my wedding.

And Allyson thought, *How lush she is. Talk about your Coca-Cola bottles.* But she felt smug because big women were out of style these days. Thinness was *in.* And she, Allyson, was thin, model-like. Adam had been attracted to her, she was sure. If she had her way, he would be again.

"I don't want to rush you," Allyson began in her actress's husky voice, "but I have a dozen things to do this afternoon, so could we get started?"

Adam took Raven's hand. "Sure. When you get through with her, bring her back to me, and don't keep her too long." He kissed her cheek as Allyson looked away.

Raven glanced around her as they traversed the long dark green and cream-colored hallway. Their budget crunch was obvious, but the building was clean and bright. Allyson led her into a small cubicle and once they were seated, she frankly looked Raven over with her masked cop's glance. She didn't seem friendly at all now.

"The night when the perp—that's perpetrator…"

"I know," Raven said.

"Well, when he accosted you as you walked along. . . Are you in the habit of going into that neighborhood often?"

"I'm an investigative reporter and I…"

It was Allyson's turn now. "I know. Mrs. McCloud…"

"*Ms.* McCloud. I'm divorced."

Allyson smiled tightly. "I know. Excuse me. So you had a special reason to be there.…"

"I did. As Detective Steele's right arm, I'm sorry, his *sergeant*, you'd know about the Carr investigation. I was there to interview a witness whose grandson had died largely as a result of money they didn't get from CCG."

Allyson's face went cold sober. "Yes, I'm afraid I know all about that. Ms. McCloud—"

"Please, call me Raven."

"I'm sorry, but I always keep the distance of last names with people I question. I'm sure you understand."

Oh yes, I understand, Raven thought, *that calling me Ms. McCloud keeps you from facing the fact that I will soon be Mrs. Raven Steele.* She became aware then that the other woman had said something and she missed it. Allyson looked a bit miffed, then repeated her question. "Mr. Hawkins was your first cousin."

"Yes."

Allyson offered no sympathy and her face mirrored none.

Raven was there less than a half hour and she was happy to leave the cubicle and start back to Adam.

At his closed door, Allyson turned to her. "I'm afraid Detective Steele is busy just now and he may be for quite a while. You might not wish to wait for him."

Raven smiled then, as narrowly as the other woman smiled. "I think I'll wait anyway. My boss told me not to hurry back, so my time is my own."

A merry smile lit Allyson's face then as she said, "Sounds like you have a good boss. Lord knows, I've got the best."

Raven decided not to wait. On the sidewalk outside the police station there was no taxi in sight so she decided to pick up a supply of toothpaste on sale from the corner drugstore. As she began to pass the first counter, Glenda, her cousin's widow, came to her, hugged her tightly.

"Raven, I'm so glad to see you. How are you?"

Raven held Glenda away from her and looked at her closely. The hazelnut skin was still smooth, but Glenda looked gaunt and peaked. "The question is how are *you*?

I'm about as well as can be expected. I called and told you I'm getting married in early December."

"Couldn't wait 'til Christmas," Glenda teased as Raven blushed. "Girl, that is the wildest diamond I've ever seen."

"Thank you. That's about the face of it. Couldn't wait." And she asked again, "How are *you* coming along?"

Glenda was silent a moment, looking down. "It's *hard*, Raven. I miss him so, but I have to be strong for my—our baby. I've been looking all over for that tape, but I've had no luck. Before Cree was killed, he talked to me a lot, but I was in ecstasy over the baby and I didn't always listen. Nothing else seemed to matter. Now I know it mattered. I don't think they'll find my husband's killer. Sometimes evil *is* stronger than good."

Raven patted her back. "I'll keep trying as long as I have breath. I miss him too, and just keep doing the best you can."

"I told you I went up to our cabin on Green Mountain and looked there with no luck. The tape has to be somewhere. You've said it's very important. I've tried so hard to help and I'm getting nowhere." There were tears in her voice.

Raven hugged her again. "Just take care of yourself. I have faith that we'll find it, and that we'll find the killer."

Glenda glanced at her watch. "I always enjoy talking with you and I want to hear more about your wedding, but I'm kind of rushing to get to my doctor's. Will you bring your fiancé around so I can meet him?"

"You bet I will. His name is Adam Steele."

"*Detective* Adam Steele?"

"Yes. You would have met him when Cree was killed. It's his case." Her eyes misted. "He was shot to death three blocks from Detective Steele's stationhouse."

Glenda nodded. "Very nice guy. You both are lucky to have each other. I'll bet Merla likes him." She didn't comment on Raven's remark about Cree.

Raven laughed. "She's about to take him away from me."

Glenda laughed then and her face lit up. "I miss you and Merla. You've been kind in letting me have time alone to grieve." Her voice got wistful then. "I wonder if the pain will ever go away."

Raven shook her head. "Remembering my parents' death, it takes a very long time. Remember the glory of the days we had him. Those memories are ours forever. No one can ever take them away."

This time Glenda's smile was sad. "You're sweet and like I said I miss seeing you the way we used to see each other so often. How're Viveca and Carey?"

"They're both fine."

"They're so in love. Give them and Merla my best. I'll call you."

Raven took her hand. "Please do, but only when you feel like it."

"And I'll keep looking for the tape."

"Again, only when you feel like it. You're way out there now and you need all the peace and calm you can get."

For a few moments Glenda was very quiet, then she said in a ragged voice, "My very soul seems to tear up all the time. Cree was a man straight from heaven. Maybe what we had was too good to last."

"Don't say that. You had every right to have your love last, but some devil cut it short. We'll find that somebody, Glenda," she said fiercely.

"It's been nearly five months. Cree wanted this baby so bad."

"I know he did."

"I have to go now." She kissed Raven again and walked slowly away as Raven's cell phone rang. Adam's voice was warm, teasing.

"Hello, heart of my heart."

"And soul of my soul," she responded.

"Why didn't you wait around for me?"

"Why? Well, your—*sergeant* said you'd be tied up for a while and she was pretty adamant about my not taking up more of your time." Had she sounded testy? she wondered. If so, well, hew it to the line and let the chips fall where they may. She wasn't too fond of Allyson Welles and it hadn't taken long to know that.

Adam laughed heartily. "Allyson carries the world on her shoulders when we're into a case and we're getting more cases than we can handle well. She works like a galley slave and she's really dedicated."

Raven waited for him to say he didn't know what he'd do without Allyson, but he didn't.

"I'm asking a little ahead of time, but I want to give you a prolonged tour of my palace. You've only been by there on infrequent rush visits. When's your best time?"

She thought a moment. "The weekend would be perfect. Saturday. Because all this week the group and I are working on plans for our December dinner-dance. Too bad we can't go back to the days when CCG pulled with us, but money still has to be raised."

"Yeah. Some things can't be helped. Glen Thompson, of Special Investigations, is trying to get Tom Carr indicted as soon as possible."

"And he usually succeeds at what he undertakes."

"Is there anything you'd like to do tonight?"

"If you'll come by after work for a quick kiss, I'll hurry home then let you go."

"I may not be able to go. It gets harder every minute."

"You're not playing in that field by yourself. Eight o'clock?"

"With bells on."

Chapter 9

Raven had loved Adam's house each of the few times she'd seen it. Of course, while she was trying not to love him, she had demurred when he'd wanted her to spend time there. As Adam pulled into the driveway the following Saturday morning, she thought now that because she let herself love him, welcome him all the way into her heart, she wanted to love the house the way she loved him.

As they sat in the driveway, she told him, "You and Ricky did a magnificent job. How long did it take you?"

"Well, when we began with a vacant lot, Ricky was ten, not four years ago. We had the help of a lot of friends and I've got a construction foreman friend, Mike Barnes, who'd want to be a member of the wedding, but he's with the Peace Corps and overseas. My brother, Marty, is my best friend, but I guess Mike's next. I'd guess it took about three years. A labor of love."

"You're way up near the Maryland line. The houses on upper Seventeenth Street are some of the most beautiful in the city. I love it up here."

"Are you keeping your townhouse in southwest?"

"Yes, I'm renting it to a friend who's delirious to get it."

They sat in Adam's burgundy Lincoln Town car admiring the outside of the two-story cream brick house with its beautifully landscaped exterior surrounded by a black wrought-iron fence. Gold, yellow, bronze and white chrysanthemum bushes in full bloom were massed in borders and big stone pots of frost-scorched broadleaf fern adorned the stoop on each side of the front porch.

Adam leaned over and hugged Raven, touched his lips to hers. "You never had time to see the garden house."

She laughed a little. "I lied. I had time, but I was fighting my attraction to you and I didn't want to be alone with you too much."

"I could tell. You'd be surprised to know how much I could tell. That's why I could play a waiting game so well."

"Braggart."

"No. You're just not too good at hiding what you feel, for which I'm grateful."

Inside the house, they stood in the living room with its arches and décor of plum and cream. There were four bedrooms and four baths upstairs and a guest room and powder room downstairs. Big modern and antique furniture was artfully arranged and potted plants were everywhere.

"Who takes care of all these plants?" Raven asked.

"Well, I do my part, but a plant caretaker comes in once a week."

"They're beautiful. Mrs. Reuben, Merla and I take care of ours."

"And they're just as beautiful."

The dining room held a spectacular large china closet of glass and mahogany.

"I love that piece," Raven told him.

"Mom gave it to me when Kitty and I got married and

when she died, Dad said if I got another woman they didn't like, they'd take it back. They were only half kidding."

"I loved meeting your parents last year. I hope they come to like me half as well as Papa Mac likes you."

"He's a grand guy. I'm looking forward to being closer to him. He'll fit in nicely on Dad's and my brothers' fishing trips. I got a chance to really talk with him down at Enchanted Farm."

"I'm glad." She reached over and kissed his cheek. For a moment she was frightened of the outpouring of love she felt for him as he took her in his arms and pressed her soft, warm body close to his.

"If this is as close to heaven as I get," he told her, "I won't complain. Honey, I saw something like fear cross your face. What else are you afraid of?"

She wasn't going to deny it. "I'll tell you very soon. Maybe that will help."

"You don't want to tell me now?"

"I'm putting it together. It hurts, Adam. That's why I don't like to talk about it."

He caught her closer. "Take your time, sweetheart. I'm not going anywhere."

Adam's kitchen was magnificent pale yellow with dark red floor tiles. There was a lovely dining alcove that looked out on the huge backyard and garden house which was made of the same cream brick as the house.

"All it needs is a swimming pool and you'll be in luxury's lap."

"*We'll* be. All it really needs is you."

She held up her hand with the glittering ring. "This says you have me."

He looked at her somberly. "And does your heart agree?"

"Oh, it got to be yours long before my frightened mind did."

"I'm glad."

Adam put on gospel songs sung in duet by Ashley and Whit. "Strange to see how my niece and nephew could have those glorious voices and I can barely carry a tune in a bag."

"I think you've got a great speaking voice anyway. It surely moves me."

"Thank you, ma'am. Your voice is musical and I love it."

"Listen, my stomach is saying, 'Feed me or I'll bite you.'"

"A few chips and a glass of orange juice should stay it until I get your dinner. Now, you said you wanted homemade pizza with pepperoni, onions, double cheese, green and red peppers—oh hell, the whole works."

"You've got it. I'll help you."

"No, this is my treat. You get to rest."

"You work harder than I do."

"I'm bigger. More stamina. Haven't you heard about us men?"

She grinned and patted his shoulder. "There are some who contend that you're the weaker sex. Get the pizza going, Steele, or I'm going to go under with hunger."

He got out the pizza stone and began to slice and chop the ingredients of a pizza he was frequently complimented for. But after a few minutes he relented and let her do the salad of romaine, vine-ripened tomatoes, cucumbers, peppers and radishes.

She moved about humming merrily as she finished the salad and set the table.

He came to her. "Taking over, are you?" he whispered as he held her. He took a dish cloth from her hand and threw it on the table. "I want nothing to come between me and a long, long kiss."

She was full of surprises at herself today when she answered, "I want nothing to come between us in any way."

As Adam held her, he could hear the thunder of his heart. Lord, it had been so long since he'd felt passion like this hot in his veins, racing and tumbling, mad for release. He pressed the small of her back to his body and held her prisoner.

"Bad idea," she said shakily. "Both of us are volatile now."

"Isn't that the best time?" he asked huskily.

"Oh you," she whispered, smiling. "Dinner first."

"What if I refuse to let you go?" he murmured as he rained kisses onto her face and her throat, opened the front buttons of her scarlet wool jersey blouse she wore atop a short black wool skirt. "You look so damned good in red," he told her. "I could eat you alive and not leave one morsel."

She couldn't say it, but the heat in her loins was her undoing. She felt languid, melting with desire and her breasts were swollen against him, aching to be stroked before his hands found and cupped them, squeezed gently, then did the craved stroking. His tongue had a life of its own and it probed the sweet, sweet inner sanctum of her precious mouth.

He stroked her body through her clothes and felt himself about to explode sky high.

"The pizza, honey," she whispered. "Can we eat first?"

And his question was a challenge. "Do you *really* want to wait?"

Her sigh was telling. "No. I want you now."

Then her tongue was fevered in his mouth. He kissed her all the way across the room to the stove and let her go for just a minute or so until he opened the oven door and removed the pizza stone, setting it on the stove top. She was languid, melting against him. He turned the oven off, scooped her up in his arms and took her up the stairs.

At his bedroom, he paused and she opened the door. "Watch out for your back," she told him as they went into the room. "I don't want to hurt you ever."

"I'm a very big man," he told her. "You're going to find that out."

He put her on the bed and they hurriedly undressed each other, driven by love and aching desire. The lacy red underwear she wore heated his blood to steaming and when they were both naked he fell to her big, firm breasts and suckled them hungrily. *A feast fit for a god*, he thought. Would he ever get enough?

She moved beneath him, moaning softly as he began to kiss her ardently, his mouth hot on her flesh that craved him so. He roved her face, her throat, patterning wet kisses that thrilled her to the bone. Her breasts were feverishly reaching for him, swollen and pebbling. And when he finally reached her midsection and made circular kisses around her navel, his tongue going into the indentation, she felt herself coming apart in a glorious melding.

With bold sweeps, he traversed her belly with its tender, silken amber skin. Then he stopped and murmured, "My Amber Love." But she could barely hear him because he was going to her center, slowly with small kisses that were driving her crazy with desire.

On his knees, he pulled her to the edge of the bed and laved the tender bud of her center as she cried out.

Something in her wanted to hold back, needed to hold back, but what he did to her was too exciting, too enthralling, so her right brain that gave such pleasure took over almost completely and her left brain that signaled control was overruled. His mouth traveled down her thighs to her calves and he kissed her well-tended feet with more wet kisses, then again. "Dear God," she cried out. "How much more of this can I stand?"

He stopped long enough to say, "There's so much more I want to give you. Do you want me to stop?"

"No, Adam, no! What you're doing is wonderful. Please don't stop."

After a few minutes, he paused and looked at her for a long while, stroking her body, then alternately kissing and stroking.

He got a condom from the night table and slipped it on. She stroked his shaft that was greatly swollen with love and lust and desire beyond the telling. He parted her legs with slow gentle movements and entered her body that ached for him.

"I want all of you," she whispered. "*All* of you."

He smiled and raised her legs across his shoulders and slid all the way in, his body bursting with the urge to know her in every way a man can know a woman. And looking at her face, he thought she was more beautiful than anything he had ever seen. There were mountains and oceans and starry skies, but nothing in his life had affected him the way she affected him now. He had loved a woman with all his heart and lost her, and he had not hoped to love that way ever again. But he *was* loving this woman with all his heart and soul. He was coming home.

He rolled over then to place her on top of him. She called his name, and no music had ever sounded sweeter. Pulling her hard onto him, he penetrated to the bottom and she moaned, "Adam. Oh, sweetheart, I love you!"

He fought against orgasm then, but she was already wildly bucking above him, her hands in his hair, pulling his mouth hard onto hers. She greedily suckled his tongue as if she could never stop.

He had thought it was all over and he knew what he was capable of, but they both felt the rapture of the first orgasms and two rapturous others, then lay spent. She thought nothing short of heaven could be like this. Oh Lord, if it could only last. Yet even in the midst of paradise, she knew there must be torment, something to take it all away.

Adam rolled over, drunk with happiness and hugged Raven to him. "This makes you my woman," he said, smiling. "As if you weren't before."

"I *feel* like your woman," she whispered.

"And God knows I'm your man."

The shadow crossed her face that he had seen from time to time since he'd know her, even on the night of the CCG Ball.

"Honey, what is it?" he asked. "All of a sudden you look sad."

"Adam, we have to talk."

"Anytime. Why don't we do it now?"

"It felt so wonderful to have you inside me. I can still feel you there."

"I still feel it too. This is what lovemaking is supposed to feel like."

"I know, but I never thought I'd experience it this way."

"All the years with Kevin, didn't you enjoy making love at least sometimes?"

She hesitated a long moment, not wanting to make it worse than it had been. "In the beginning, it was okay, fairly pleasant, but I told myself I dreamed too much, expected too much. I married at thirty—and I hadn't had much experience. I just never seemed to fall in love, and I know now the kind of lovemaking I wanted comes only with love."

"Amen to that."

"Kevin pressed me hard for sex before we were married and he didn't believe I had only had two lovers. I preferred *dreaming* of what I wanted to what I found I could have. He was rough from the beginning and I told myself it was because he was in love and wanted me so badly. That's what he said. It was all so wrong, Adam, right from the beginning, but I admired what Kevin had accomplished. He was *Dr.* McCloud, attractive, a big man, and I was fool enough to think this could be a substitute for love.

"I think Kevin despises sex. I know he does. After we were married he used to chide me for my feelings. 'Don't carry on like that,' he used to say. 'You sound like an animal. There is sex for humans and sex for animals. I like the carefully controlled, human kind. Never let your feelings run away with you. Control is the key to successful living.'"

"You must have been in hell."

"That doesn't tell you the half of it. I fell in love with you the night you stayed because I was frightened when I'd been mugged. We talked and you said your father had lovingly called you 'passion's fool' and told you to be glad you were."

There were tears in her eyes then and he kissed them away. "Go on," he said. "I want to hear all of this."

"Day after day and night after night, Kevin and I went on like this. You see, love, I knew when you said it that I, too, am passion's fool. I would give anything I'll ever have—except my daughter and the child I hope to bear for you—for what we just knew. My body feels alive, *has* felt alive since I've known you, and I was only half alive before."

"Couldn't you have gotten a divorce earlier?"

"Merla came a few years later and there was her welfare to consider. I said Kevin is a cold man, but he loves having a child to look up to him, to control in a way he could never control a woman. But when Merla was five he changed toward me. I think now he was *trying* to drive me away. There was nothing about me he didn't criticize. He wanted me to quit the job I love. He accused me of having an affair with Ken, even picked a fight with him and publicly accused me of running around with him.

"In the end I was emotionally battered. We quarreled over raising Merla, everything. Then one night when I refused to go to bed with him, he struck me, bruising my breasts and blackening my eye. I wasn't about to bring up my child in an atmosphere like that, so I filed for divorce. There was the other incident of disciplining Merla. He counter-filed and charged me with adultery."

"A really nice guy." Adam shook his head.

"He's a genuine bastard and I'm sorry he's my baby's father." She touched his face. "So you want to know why I'm sad. I can still feel Kevin's spirit like a blight on my own spirit. Day after day telling me how licentious, how wanton I am. Accusing me of having every man who paid me a bit of attention, complimented me. I moved out after I filed for the divorce and one night when I wouldn't let him see Merla, he accused me of sleeping with Ken again and called me a whore. I held my temper with a lot of effort but I wanted to slap him and I knew for the first time I could kill. That frightened me, Adam."

He took her in his arms, saying, "Baby, baby, I understand that feeling all too well. You didn't even strike him. You have nothing to be afraid of. You're home free."

"There has always been gossip about Ken and me. He tells me he's in love with me."

"I'm afraid that's his hard luck. You're mine now."

Sharp thrills coursed along her spine. "I love hearing you say that. Now tell me you're mine."

"I'm yours, sweetheart, have been since the moment I saw you and always will be."

"Be patient with me if I seem to go away from you sometimes. A man like Kevin isn't easy to get over."

He hugged her close. "You bet I'll be patient. Just promise me when you *do* feel like responding to me you'll let yourself go—the way you just did."

"And a part of me feels ashamed—like an ani—"

He placed the edge of his hand over her mouth. "Don't you dare say it. You're an angel, a goddess, and they have deep feelings. Passion is our trademark and that's never going to stop being true of us."

Her stomach rumbled then and she grinned. "It's back!"

He began to get up and she stopped him. "Where're you going?"

"To get you a snack. Be right back."

Her hand stayed him as she stroked his shaft, loving it because it was a part of him and her tender hands stroked his rippling biceps, pectorals, the washboard abs and flat stomach. "You're a beautiful man, Adam Steele. I hope you know it."

"I'm not even in the ballpark with your beauty. You go beyond beauty, Raven," he said gravely. "There's something so tender, so precious about you. I keep wanting to lock you up to make sure you're mine forever. *Will* you promise to be mine forever?"

"You have my word, if you'll do the same for me."

He fell back on the bed, took her in his arms and kissed her with fervor that shocked her, even after what they'd just known. "D'you know something?" he said, "I want you all over again."

"And I want you more. Hurry back, my love."

"I'll do that. I'll get a robe for you."

"Yours? You haven't got a woman's robe here, or have you?"

He nodded. "I've kept some of Kitty's clothes, but my Mom and my sister spend the night here sometimes when Dad goes fishing. You have nothing to be jealous of."

"If you owned the Hope Diamond, wouldn't you be jealous of it?"

"You flatter me so. I'm surely not the Hope Diamond."

"You are to me."

He grinned. "There you go, binding me to you so tightly I couldn't break away if my life depended on it."

He got up and got robes from the closet, brought one back and helped her into it. Then he put on his pajama bottoms as she stood up and stretched, smiling all the while. When he paused at the doorway she blew him a kiss and told him, "Hurry back!"

After he left she padded barefoot to the window. Lord, it was beautiful out here. Adam had a quadruple-lot backyard. Oak and linden and sycamore trees grew in abundance, tall and stately, fast shedding the red and gold leaves left on longer than usual by an off-and-on-again warm fall. The garden house intrigued her; they could make love there. And she smiled to herself. They could make love anywhere. What she had just known with him was a miracle. All these years of tormented wanting, suppressed passion and frustrated God-given sexuality/sensuality. Her body felt weightless now, fast freeing itself from its hated shackles of despising the glory she felt, was meant to feel.

And down in the kitchen Adam thought about Raven as he prepared a good-sized tray of mini-pizzas, sharp cheese, wheat crackers and crunchy peanut butter on salt wafers. He felt so good he couldn't believe it. What if she hadn't come to him? He'd been prepared to wait. But she had come and all his life he'd thank the heavens for what he already knew with her, secure in the knowledge that what they had would grow stronger all the days of their lives.

He prepared more fresh orange juice, this time mixed with cranberry juice and went back up the stairs, tapped on the door and went in. She sat on the edge of the bed, her eyes sparkling. "Thank you," she said as he came in and set the tray on the night table. "If anyone had told me I could shuck Kevin's evil this fast in bed I wouldn't have believed it. Thank you for that."

He bent and blew a stream of air onto her face. "The way I plan it, you're going to have a lot more to thank me for. I've got one more thing I've got to bring up."

"Hurry back."

"You bet." He kissed her again, blew another stream of air onto her face.

"You can't cool me down that way," she teased him.

"Then how?" he teased back.

"I'll give you one good guess."

He grinned. "When I get back—hold that thought right there."

And he was very shortly back with an ice bucket and a tray holding a bottle of champagne, two flutes and a bowl of maraschino cherries. Setting the articles down, he popped the cork on the champagne and poured two flutes almost full.

"A toast, then it's time for the robe to come off," he said.

"You're so anxious, *you* take it off." Her voice was sultry, caressing.

"In a minute, I'll oblige you." He touched his glass to hers and the crystal rang. "Life doesn't get any better," he said solemnly. "May we last always."

With a slow smile he bent and took off her robe, threw it aside, then removed his own robe and pajama bottom. He sat on the side of the bed and looked at her, his heart in his eyes and she knew she would come to him completely now.

He took three cherries and placed them between her full breasts, then poured a little champagne in his hand and into the valley of her beautiful globes. He closed his eyes against the powerful surge of love and desire he felt for her. His shaft was mighty then, wild to claim what welcomed him.

And he thought then that they were building a new world for themselves and their children. In each other's arms they created love and life.

She looked at his beloved face and murmured, "Cherries and champagne—and you."

"And *you*," he told her. "If I were to die this minute, I would have known wonder the way I suspect most people never know it. Thank you, God, for sending me this woman for my own."

She turned her face to heaven saying, "And thank you no less for sending me this man."

He bent then to the cherries in the crevice of her breasts, ate one, then the other two and licked the champagne from the tender flesh. Then with maddening slowness, he poured little amounts of champagne down her belly and into her valley of desire, following the pattern he had first taken. The bud of her desire ached with wanting him inside her as she held his head in to her body and cried out his name. All the ancient words that drove him on, started a fire in his loins and in his brain that made him want to possess her forever, *own* her for himself. Raising up, he slipped on a condom and entered her tremulous body and was held like a hot magnetic glove that could not let him go.

He worked her slowly, expertly with all the passion he knew and her response was all he could have wanted as he darted little kisses onto her face and ran his tongue along the edges of her sugar-sweet lips and into the corners. Then his big thumb outlined her lips with feathery strokes. Both gestures made her shudder with delight.

He had said that she would know how big he was and this time he filled her with his shaft and his love. But he could have been any size and she would have nearly fainted with the intense joy of her love for him and his for her. He lifted her legs over his shoulders and with a harder but still smooth and tender stroke, went past her womb and buried his face in her breasts.

"Am I making it good for you?" he asked her.

"Sweetheart, it couldn't *be* any better. I feel so relaxed, so open to you. It's as if I've known you always."

He squeezed her tightly. "I feel the same way. Now do you truly know our age difference doesn't matter?"

"I knew it when you began to protect me, take care of me. Knew it by the way you treated my daughter and the way you held back until I was ready. You're very much a man, Adam, a man after my own heart."

"And Lord knows, you're a woman after mine."

They were slow then, relaxed and easy as wonderful time passed before he withdrew to the edge then slipped in harder again and again until she felt the rush of fever invade her brain and body and the glory began to shake her mercilessly with a tender violence she could hardly believe.

"Adam?" she whispered.

"Yes, my darling."

"Thank you so much, love, for giving me yourself like this."

He planted a wet kiss in the hollows of her throat. "Thank *you* for responding the way you do. Like the song, I may never get to heaven, but this is close enough for me."

Later, they showered in the big cream and peach bathroom. She burst two bath gel capsules of some woodsy scent and spread the liquid on both of them, then turned on the triple headed shower and felt the sharp needles of warm water sluice over her. "I think I'll get triple heads. I love the feel of this."

"See what you've been missing, and I had to beg you to come to me."

"I just felt you'd despise me too."

He took her wet, slippery body in his arms and hugged her tightly, kissed her wet face. "Raven, you're the best there is. I want you climbing to the skies with me, crying out my name the way you did a little while ago. I want you to let yourself go with me completely. We're going to know each other the way biblical men and women knew each other, with love and jubilation. We're going to be happy, my darling, the way we were meant to be."

There were hot air jets in the corner where they dried off and rubbed lotion onto each other.

"I love your house," she told him. "It must have cost a bundle."

"Not really. I told you about the money I inherited. I hardly had to touch it. The guy I mentioned to you, Mike Barnes, was able to get everything at a discount. And his friends pitched in for beer and great meals. They would take very little money. I'm glad you love it, because it's yours." He smiled then and her heart got full just watching him. "The way *I'm* yours."

There were tears behind her eyelids when she told him, "The way I'm yours. Please don't ever leave me."

"I won't and you'd better not ever leave me. I couldn't take it if you did."

There was a pot of blossoming white mums on a table. He reached into the drawer and got a pair of scissors, snipped off a long-stemmed blossom and put it behind her ear, kissing the side of her throat.

Sheathed, he steadied himself against an onslaught of passion. Holding her warm, naked body very close to his, he stroked her silken back and buttocks, thrilling as her soft flesh melded with his hardness. On the cream plush rug, he placed her on her knees and entered her scorching body that gripped him again and held his shaft prisoner. Looking at the outlines of her voluptuous amber-skinned body, he half closed his eyes and smiled. Bending, he kissed the flesh that intrigued him so, groaning deep in his throat.

He had her lower her chest to the floor and his shaft lingered in the steaming home she made for him. With deepening rapture he heard her soft moans and it spurred him on. This woman, this place, this time was all he knew or cared about and everywhere he ever wanted to be.

"We are so good together," he told her. "We are the very earth itself when we're together."

And she lay in blazing torpor, claiming him as her own as her body felt the intense heat of his and she moved evenly, slowly, achingly under him for a very long time. Then heat flashed between them and she went into a rhythmic siege of holding and letting go and holding and letting go that sent her into heavenly orbit. And she felt utterly content for the first time she could remember.

Completely enthralled by the woman beneath him, Adam's heart and being climbed to an emotional mountaintop and stood there, his woman beside him, and knew the glory he would know again and again as long as they were together.

Chapter 10

An hour later Raven and Adam were on bicycles on their way to a restaurant in Maryland that specialized in pizzas. "I'd swear they're better than mine," Adam told her as they rode along, "and that's saying something."

"Don't make me hungry. The mini-pizzas certainly took the edge off." They smiled at each other companionably, while trying to keep their eyes on the road.

"I'll call Merla a little later," Raven said. "She likes to keep in touch."

"And Ricky will call *me* a little later. He *means* to keep in touch."

"We're fortunate to have children who like each other so much. Big boys and little girls don't always get along. The boys consider little girls pests."

Adam laughed. "I think Ricky has been so hell-bent on getting himself a mother, he'd settle for any little sister. Pinch me, sweetheart. Are we really getting married? We'd better be."

"We're getting married."

The restaurant wasn't crowded; they picked up their

food, sat and shared a jumbo diet 7-Up and went to their bicycles. As they rode along, they were mostly silent, both remembering the lovemaking they'd just known. Then Adam said, "Six months ago, if anyone had ever told me I'd be holding you, that you'd be my wife-to-be, I would have doubted it. First off, I thought you were involved with Courtland...."

"No, as I told you, I was pretending. I didn't *want* to fall for you, not after you told me how old you are."

"Now you see it doesn't matter. *Love* is what matters. Do you agree?"

"All the way. I can't imagine my life without you now. I can't wait for our wedding. Your family will all be back by then. Whit's tour is over. We've got a warm winter forecast, so if we're lucky..."

"Baby, I can't wait either. Tomorrow or even today would have been fine with me. You've given up the idea of going to Elkins and doing it quickly?"

"Yes, Papa Mac is hungry for a wedding. He said this one should obliterate the one to Kevin, and I agree. I don't want a big wedding because it would remind me of that one. Viveca and I are pulling this one together in a hurry. Early December! Oh, happy day! I love you, honey. Did I ever tell you that?"

He grinned. "Not often enough."

"Adam?"

"Yes, love."

"Nothing. I just like to call your name."

Her cell phone rang and she reached into her skirt pocket and got it, answered. Mrs. Reuben's frantic voice came onto the wire. Her voice was so choked, Raven could barely understand her. "Ms. McCloud. Someone has taken Merla away from me."

"Taken her away? What do you mean, kidnapped?"

"Yes." Mrs. Reuben was crying then, but she tried to control herself. "I've called the police."

"We'll stop on the shoulder," Adam told her as he caught the gist of the conversation.

They stopped their bikes and Raven continued talking. "Go on. You called the police."

"Yes and they're coming out. There was a crazy call…"

"What did he say?" There was no doubt in her mind that it was a he, the same man who'd bedeviled their lives for so long.

Mrs. Reuben could barely talk, she was crying so hysterically.

"Please calm down, Mrs. Reuben. I'll be right there, but can you tell me what the man said?"

"That—that there's going—to be a killing. Oh, my God in heaven!"

Raven's blood ran ice cold and her shaking fingers could barely hold the phone. She looked at Adam with haunted eyes. "Just hold on," she said. "We'll be there in a very short while."

She relayed the conversation to Adam and he scowled. "We'll hurry. Are you going to be able to ride home to my house?"

"I think so. I'm forcing myself to be calm. This is no time for me to go to pieces. Thank God, you're with me."

They didn't talk on the short trip and in a very little time they were in Adam's car and on their way to Raven's house.

They found Mrs. Reuben calmed a little, pacing the living room, wringing her hands. "Why haven't the other policemen arrived? Detective Steele, you don't know how glad I am to see you both. My Lord, the man on the

phone sounded like the devil himself. How could anybody do this to such a sweet little girl?"

Adam questioned Mrs. Reuben further. She talked as
best she could. Merla had asked if she could visit the little girl around the corner. Mrs. Reuben had called the
girl's mother and she'd said send her along. A very little
while later, the woman had called to ask when Merla
would be coming because they all wanted to go to a
nearby ice cream parlor. Alarm bells had gone off in Mrs.
Reuben's head. Merla should have been there. She had
known right away that something was wrong.

Mrs. Reuben wrung her hands. "I should have been
more careful. I should have watched her more closely. I
can't forgive myself."

Raven took the still hysterical woman in her arms as she
tried to keep her own hysteria from overwhelming her.
"Please don't blame yourself. You've always been as good
as gold. You couldn't have known. Merla's eight; we don't
watch her the way we would a younger child. You've got
to calm down. You'll be sick."

"I'll try," Mrs. Reuben said, still sobbing.

In the meantime, Adam was on the phone with people
in the police department who would handle the abduction. It helped that the kidnapped girl had ties to someone in the department; they were only human.

Adam paced the floor relentlessly, stopped to soothe
Mrs. Reuben along with Raven who was quiet and half
frozen with fear. She fought to keep her brain from fogging over. Merla was a brave child, she thought, who felt
the world was on her side. But the child had known Kevin's temper, had often been cowed by it and Raven wondered if she would handle herself poorly, be reminded
and overcome by memories of Kevin's out-of-control

anger. Her heart tore up for her little girl and hot tears burned her eyes.

It was Adam who said, "While we wait, let's kneel in brief prayer." And the three of them prayed to a God they worshipped who had seen them through other misfortune.

In a few minutes a squad car pulled up in front of the house. A male and a female officer got out and shortly they were inside talking. Adam fielded most of the questions at first, but Mrs. Reuben and Raven had to be questioned too.

"And you say there was a phone call and a man, or what seemed to be a man, said 'There's gonna be a killing'?" The male officer was tense, already deeply involved.

Mrs. Reuben looked at them with frightened eyes. "Yes, that's what he said."

"And nothing else."

Mrs. Reuben shook her head. "No. Nothing about ransom or why or anything, just—that. Would he hurt her?"

The police sergeant sighed. "I sure wish I knew the answer to that."

Adam put his arms around Raven and wished he could protect her from this nightmare. Of course, in retrospect they should have guarded Merla more closely, but the creep had been after Raven, had focused his attention, his evil on *her*. Still, he thought bitterly now, they should have considered this possibility.

And Raven alternately stood up and sat down, thinking along the same lines. Why didn't you keep on after *me*? she asked the monster. Who would hurt a little girl because of anger at her mother? Well, *this* one would anyway.

Adam went out and came back with two aspirin and a glass of water.

"Do you have any tranquilizers?" Adam asked Raven.

"In the medicine cabinet. But I don't want to be tranquilized. I have to know what's going on."

"You will, believe me. They'll just take the edge off. I've taken them before. We've all got to keep clear heads."

"Ms. McCloud," the female officer said. "Is your little girl the calm sort, or does she get rattled easily?" The policewoman's voice was soft, kind, compassionate.

"Oh, she's very calm. We've talked with her about strangers and I think she's well grounded there. But she's a child and children just can't *know*." She couldn't help it, fantasies of Merla lying in a heap somewhere, badly injured or worse, rose in her head and she fought them down. Stricken, she looked at Adam and muttered to the absent perpetrator, "*Don't hurt her. Please don't hurt her. Whatever you want, I'll get it for you. Please…*"

The phone rang then and Adam signaled to Raven to answer it. He went into the kitchen to pick up the extension, leaving the door open between the rooms.

They hadn't expected another call so early. The voice was sly, evil, muffled. It might well have been a fake voice coming from a machine. It could be an expert at mimicry. "Hello," Raven said, her own voice sounding remarkably calm.

"So I win again," the hateful voice said. "I've got your kid. You may never see her again. Think about it." Then the voice went lower. "I mean to *hurt* you, Raven, the way you have hurt me."

"Who *are* you?" she pleaded. "How can I do something about this, if I don't know who you are? I've never hurt anyone intentionally."

He said nothing.

"Wait," she cried then. "Is she all right? Please let me

talk with her. Promise me you won't hurt her." The words spilled from her.

But the dial tone was all she got, and she stood clutching the phone with cold, numb fingers as if that response could bring the fiend back onto the line.

Adam came back in slowly, his face set in granite. He could not remember a time when he'd been this angry or felt this frustrated.

"A voice from hell," she said tremulously.

"A voice from hell," Adam echoed.

"I'm wracking my brains to think of who would hate me so much," she said slowly. "I've got to hold together for Merla's sake."

Adam came to her, took her in his arms. "Cry if you want to cry. We're all under a world of stress."

But Raven didn't want to cry. She wanted to confront this monster and tear him to pieces.

An announcer at WMRY had given the news of Merla's abduction, pleaded for her safe return. Station reporters would be around in a few minutes to interview Raven and Mrs. Reuben. Now Raven heard the door chimes and in a moment heard raised voices.

"I'll see if she can see you," she heard Mrs. Reuben say.

"By God, she'll see me all right," Kevin's harsh voice came through and in the same instant he pushed in. "What the hell's going on here?" he demanded.

"You heard the news," Adam said.

"And what're you bums doing about it? You damned policemen who coddle criminals even when they kill people and give tickets to upstanding citizens for the least infraction."

Kevin glared at Raven. "I told you you didn't have the

means to take care of my daughter. If she'd been with me..."

Adam faced Kevin, shielding Raven from his ire. "It could happen to anybody, McCloud," Adam said.

"You keep out of this." Kevin turned to Raven, sneering. "If a two-bit cop is all you can do for yourself, I pity you. I promise you this will go against you in a custody hearing."

Raven laughed a little hysterically. "Stop it, Kevin! How can you think of a custody battle at a time like this?"

But Kevin was beside himself with rage. "I'd like to throttle you."

He made a step toward Raven and Adam was in his face. "Don't touch her," he said quietly, but his voice was deadly.

Kevin drew back. "You can't guard her forever."

"But I can get a restraining order for you," Adam threatened, "if you give her trouble."

Kevin's face turned red as he looked at Raven hard and mocked, "Well, well, what have we here? A ring. Are you really going to marry this jerk?"

"Kevin," Raven told him, "I won't have you coming here to harass me. We need all of us pulling together. Merla's been kidnapped!"

Kevin looked a bit ashamed then, but still very angry as he muttered, "I'd like to shake you until your teeth rattle, break your neck."

"All right, McCloud, let's cut it out," Adam seemed to grow in stature.

"Why?" Kevin seethed. "She's surely got it coming, and as for you, I've learned my rights from the criminals you cops coddle. I only said what I'd *like* to do. Don't play me for a fool."

Adam's face was a mask of controlled anger. "Then stop acting like one."

"Have I hurt you, Kevin? Are you behind this?" Raven asked.

Kevin looked crafty then; his eyes were slits. "Am I *what*?" He roared with harsh laughter. "I could kill you for asking me a question like that. I've got time for Merla, time to properly protect her. You better be careful…."

"Or you'll do what?" she retorted, but Kevin didn't answer, just scowled.

The door chimes rang again and in a minute the living room was full of Raven's coworkers. Blaine sometimes did the weekend noon news and he interviewed her, his face sympathetic and warm. They got all the particulars and interviewed Adam the longest. This was top-rate human events news with a police detective involved with a woman whose daughter had been abducted.

"My daughter may have been unhappy." Kevin cut in.

"And who are you, sir?"

"I'm *Dr.* Kevin McCloud, the child's father, and I don't mind saying that if I had been given full custody this wouldn't have happened."

"Kevin, for God's sake," Raven cut in.

But Blaine spent a few minutes getting Kevin's side of the story. They all moved to the living room and Raven stood near the door when the bells chimed and she opened the door to Viveca and Carey who hugged her, tears in their eyes.

"We heard and we came right over," Carey said. "Lord, this is a body blow."

No sooner had they spoken when Glenda and Desi arrived. Both women hugged Raven, but Raven was surprised to see that Desi spoke coolly to Kevin who also seemed cool in return. Desi had never liked Kevin that much, Raven thought now, but this seemed beyond that.

"What have you two heard?" Viveca asked.

"Just the bare outlines."

"I know it's early," came from Glenda, "but do you have any leads?" She walked over to where Adam stood fielding questions. "What happens next?"

Adam began to explain that most of the radio and TV stations would soon have the news on the air. Adam had seen to it that wire services had photos of Merla. Already flyers were being printed, giving Merla's name and showing her photo.

Suddenly Kevin blurted out, "What if they kill my daughter?"

Raven's head jerked up. Her voice was scathing. "It's a little early, isn't it, to come to that conclusion? Kevin, why don't you go home? You're not helping here."

"Good idea," Adam said firmly.

"Oh no, I'm not going anywhere until I get some more news and Steele here tells me exactly what our inept police department plans to do. I don't wonder that Merla's been abducted. Criminals rule the city these days and we pay men like Steele to sit on their asses and do nothing about it."

Adam looked at him levelly. "I won't dignify that with a remark. It might be best if you went home and stayed by the TV or your radio. The media is on top of this and you'll soon know whatever we know."

Kevin drew himself up to his full five ten, but Adam was the bigger man in every way. "You were unwise enough to get tied up with my crazy ex-wife who probably does your bidding, but you're not tied up with *me*."

Adam told him evenly. "For which I'm grateful."

Mrs. Reuben prepared and served dozens of miniature pizzas, soft drinks, milk and Danish pastries. Raven had baked two coconut-pineapple cakes the day before and they went quickly.

Another TV station had sent its people out and the questioning began all over again.

One fresh-faced female reporter from another station asked Raven, "How are you holding up, ma'am?" And it was all Raven could do not to cry. Adam saw the distress on her face and was quickly at her side, his arm around her shoulders.

"Please go easy on her," he told them. "This is news from hell. She needs all the help she can get." And he squeezed her shoulders. "Maybe you should lie down; it might help."

"How long have you two been engaged?" a reporter asked. "I noticed the ring."

"Not very long," Raven answered.

"Today. Yesterday. A month. A year?" The reporter was after his story and this was a good one.

"That's the best answer we can give," Adam said.

The same reporter asked, "D'you think your kid is sharp enough to outsmart the kidnapper? Some kids save themselves. Is she a plucky kid?"

"My God," Kevin raged, "that's an ignorant question if ever I heard one. My kid's eight years old. Hardly a match for a criminal."

The reporter looked levelly at Kevin and shot back. "Do you have enemies you know of who might have perpetrated this?"

"I've got lots of enemies," Kevin said, as if he were proud of the fact. "Any man worth his salt has enemies. You might ask her mother. God knows she's got a choice few. She's always hounding somebody about something or other."

Another reporter asked, "You a medical doctor, McCloud?"

"I'm a Ph.D. Doctor all the same."

Kevin was willing to talk all day and the reporters took full advantage of it. One asked, "Would you say little Merla is a happy child? Was anything bothering her?"

"Pardon me," Raven cut in. "She's eight. Things *do* bother children. Certainly I hadn't noticed any unhappiness. Merla is an even-tempered child who makes friends easily and is usually happy."

Kevin looked at her slyly. "Last time she was with me, she gave indications that she'd like to stay with me."

It was more than Raven could take. "I don't believe that."

"You're so damned busy, you don't know *what* to believe." Kevin narrowed his eyes and moved in for the kill. "My kid didn't care much about her new daddy-to-be. When she doesn't talk much, it means she doesn't like what's going on."

Raven clenched her hands at her sides. "I don't want to talk about something like this with what's going on, but Merla *adores* Adam. She likes him far better than she likes her father."

Adam smiled grimly. "And I adore her."

"In a pig's eye she likes him better. My daughter loves *me*."

"Kevin, *please*!"

Raven looked up then to Desi's face and found her staring at Kevin with what could only be described as vivid hostility. Kevin didn't seem to notice. The two TV crews were leaving and one reporter said to another reporter, "This is gonna make a helluva story if there's not some simple explanation."

And Raven prayed the silent prayer she had prayed from the beginning. "Dear God, please bring her safely home."

The house seemed so deserted after the TV crews left, but Viveca, Carey, Desi and Glenda stayed.

Raven turned to Glenda. "You're standing too much, I think. Why don't you go up and lie down? We've got all kinds of food and drink here too. You look a little peaked."

"Yes, Glenda, you do," Desi said. She patted her own flat stomach. "What I wouldn't give to be in your condition." Her voice was soft, wistful.

Glenda blushed. "You're such an attractive woman, Desi. Get started."

"How I wish." She smoothed her blond hair.

Raven didn't have time to focus on anybody but Merla, but she couldn't help noticing the extreme bitterness on Desi's face that had begun when she was looking at Kevin a little while back.

Glenda went up the stairs as Kevin sat down, then abruptly changed his mind. "I'll be going," he said, "but I'll be back." Then he waggled a finger at Raven. "I want you to keep me apprised of everything that's going on. You've got my cell phone number."

He left then as Raven reflected that he was getting meaner by the day, stranger, and she wondered as she had wondered before if he had anything to do with making her life a hell on earth. He was the only one she knew other than Tom Carr who disliked her so intensely. No, she rethought, *hated* her.

Adam took her hand. "I think it would be a good idea if you went somewhere else for some peace. Unfortunately, it doesn't help to leave because your stalker could call again at any time. Honey, you're going to have to brace yourself. The devil you're dealing with may be someone who has access to heavy cash and he may disguise himself and Merla and go God knows where. He may even have a private plane."

"Oh, Adam, *no*." Her hand went to her throat. She hadn't let herself think of that.

Everything was being set up swiftly. Adam's office had set up listening posts on phone lines. He told Raven that some of his best men were working on this. And the FBI would get involved if the abductor crossed state lines.

Raven watched three other police—two men and a woman—move through the group and talk to Adam. All three smiled sympathetically at her.

Raven massaged her temples as a bulletin came over a TV station telling of Merla's abduction, but one question crowded Raven's mind as she turned to Adam. "What did the hellhound mean, Adam, that he wanted to hurt me the way I'd hurt him? Two men are twisted enough to feel I've done them wrong: Tom Carr and Kevin. They can't see the beam in their eye for looking at the mote in mine."

"They're both pieces of work all right," Viveca said tiredly.

Three TV sets were on in the house and two radios. Raven got up and paced. Hot tears choked her chest and the pain was terrible. Adam got up and went into the kitchen; Viveca followed and they soon came back with a cup of hot hyssop tea.

"Drink this and you'll feel better," Adam said. Viveca asked if anybody else would like tea or coffee. No one did.

At a first hurried sip Raven burned her mouth, but said nothing. This small pain took something away from the larger pain. The telephone rang and they all jumped. Raven got up and answered.

"Things ought to be getting interesting." The voice was the devil's own, but he sounded smoother, as if he gloated. He breathed heavily the way he had been breathing, but had not lately. Then his silence frightened and enraged her.

"How is my daughter?"

Nothing save heavy breathing. Then like a shot from hell, it came. "There's gonna be a killing."

"*Damn you!*" she raged. "You want *me*, not her. Let her go and tell me where to pick her up. I'll come to you, anywhere you want me to come."

His voice clearly carried the gloating this time. "Well, maybe I've got what I needed all the time. Yeah, I'm sure this will serve as payback...."

Her voice pitched to a near scream and she was losing it. She needed to keep control, but she was losing it. "You'd better not hurt her." And she thought she was doing everything she shouldn't do.

"Good-bye, Mrs. McCloud, and pleasant dreams."

Afterward, she couldn't remember hanging up. Looking at her stricken face as he quickly hung up the extension and came from the kitchen into the living room, Adam came to her, took her in his arms and held her trembling body as she struggled to calm herself.

"Would he hurt her?" she asked.

"Baby, we can only hope for the best."

Desi, Viveca and Carey all came to her, wanting to know what had been said.

Carey spoke first. "You once told us he often told you that there's going to be a killing. Has he said that lately?"

Raven nodded. "He said it this time too. Oh God, why isn't there something we can *do*?"

They decided then that it was best to pray in a group again and Raven led the prayers this time and her heart seemed a little less burdened. They had hardly finished praying when the phone rang again. This time Adam got it. He didn't feel Raven could take anymore just now.

The voice was melodious, smooth, asking for Mrs. McCloud. When Adam asked who was calling, the man identified himself. Tom Carr. Adam covered the mouthpiece with his hand and asked Raven if she wanted to take the call. She did.

"Yes, Mr. Carr."

"Ms. McCloud, I just want you to know how sorry I am about your little daughter. I'll be brief. In spite of the bad blood between us, if there is anything I can do, you have only to call me. Will you?"

"I'll remember," Raven said numbly, then added almost as an afterthought, "Thank you."

She relayed his message to the others as they scoffed. "I wouldn't trust Tom Carr as far as I could throw him," Viveca said as Carey and Desi nodded.

Desi looked thoughtful. "Tom is a slick one and he won't change anytime soon. He hates you. I *do* know that."

Mrs. Reuben nodded, then said she was going to prepare soup and sandwiches, that they had to keep their strength up.

"I can't eat anything. I can hardly swallow. Perhaps later." Raven's eyes burned and her stomach felt as if it were weighted with lead.

"You could swallow a milk shake, or some of one." Adam took her hand and kissed it. "Try for me."

She nodded. "Okay."

Mrs. Reuben went out to prepare the food and the five of them were left alone. When the phone rang again Adam answered and it was Kevin. "Any more news? Did the creep call again?"

Adam thought a minute before he answered. "He called again with pretty much the same line."

"Tell me everything he said."

"It wouldn't help, McCloud. You've heard it on the news. The words haven't changed." He had no intention of telling Kevin anymore than he could help. What if *he* were behind this? A man like Kevin would kidnap his own daughter for his purposes. And he wished this were true because Kevin wouldn't hurt her. This way she'd be safe.

He reflected, too, that he and others had asked the media not to quote the message that there was going to be a killing. So far, no one had broken ranks. They didn't want to stir up some psychotic soul's urge to copycat violence.

When Adam went back to the group Raven looked at him with haunted eyes. "Do you think Kevin could do something like this?"

"Anything's possible, love. It might be better if he *is* behind it."

And Raven thought, better for Merla but more dangerous for her, Raven, because she was convinced now that Kevin would kill her to have full custody of Merla. More and more she wondered about Kevin's sanity.

"You should lie down for a brief while anyway," Viveca said.

Raven shook her head. "I couldn't rest."

"Did the tranquilizer help at all?" Adam asked.

"A little, but the only help I really want is Merla back."

Chapter 11

The afternoon passed with no further word from the perpetrator. Raven's nerves were screaming. Carey said they had to go home for a while, but would be back.

"At least *I'll* be back," Viveca said crisply. "I can never count on where Carey will be. Can I, love?"

"Viv, zip it. This is neither the time nor the place."

"Speaking of times and places, we're getting so far from where we started."

"Viv." His words were a warning as he turned to Raven. "We'll be back. Keep us posted on any new developments."

A still sleepy Glenda came down the stairs. "You'd have awakened me if anything new happened, wouldn't you?"

"Of course. Did you get a good nap?" Raven asked.

"I guess you'd call much of the afternoon a good nap."

"Somebody should be with you now all the time," Raven said. "You're only three months or less away from giving birth."

"My mom's coming to be with me. She had surgery and couldn't make it sooner. You always did worry about me. I'm a big girl. Truly I am, and a healthy one. And I'm

going to go now because I need to get home. Please call
if anything new happens."

Adam and Raven assured her that they would and
walked her to her car in Raven's driveway. Glenda's big
belly reminded Raven of the time she carried Merla so
close to her heart. Now she wished it had been Adam
whose child she carried.

They watched as Glenda drove off and Adam drew her
close again, whispered, "I wish I could bear this whole
thing for you."

"You don't know how much you help me. Just having
you here."

His lips grazed her face and he pressed her so close he
could hear her heart beating swiftly as if it were tired of
waiting as patiently as it could.

Carey and Viveca lived in southwest D.C., too, about
fifteen blocks from Raven. As they parked and Carey
helped her out of the car, Viveca said saltily, "You'll need
to keep the motor running, won't you? You'll be off to
God knows where."

"I've asked you to stop saying things like that. Where
I'm off to is my office and more work than I've ever seen
in my life."

"I'll bet. We don't even have much of a love life anymore. You're tired all the time. When do your headaches
start as in 'Not tonight, honey. I've got a headache.'"

"I never saw this side of you before."

"That's because you never deserved it before."

Carey frowned. "I hadn't planned to handle it this way,
but Merla's kidnapping has made me think. We're not
only not promised a rose garden, but we're not promised
life itself. I still can't tell you what I'm up to these days,

but I can tell you a little more. I really haven't been fair to you and I'm sorry."

"Is there someone else?"

Carey gave a harsh laugh. "Hell no. It's you, baby, all the way and all the time. Come on, we've all had a rough day. I promise we'll talk later."

By nightfall, the late evening news still carried the abduction bulletin and flyers were posted all over the city. Adam would stay, of course, and Mrs. Reuben decided to spend the night. Desi seemed subdued, deep in thought. Finally she rose and stretched.

"I don't want to leave you, but I have to. I've got to see someone."

"I really appreciate your coming over," Raven told her. "You're not in any trouble of any kind, are you?"

Desi looked at her thoughtfully. "This is no time to dump my burdens on you. There's something I have to work out with someone, then I'll tell you all about it. Raven, we've been friends since I worked at WMRY, which I wish I still did. But enough of that. Know that I'll be praying all the way for Merla and if there's anything at all I can do, just call me and I'll come running."

Raven stood up and as the women hugged, it seemed to Raven that Desi was suffering and she wondered why. But she had little time to wonder. Merla filled her whole being. Where was she? And *how* was she? She couldn't stop the horrific visions filling her mind.

"We'll walk you to your car," Adam said. "You had to park down the street."

"Okay. I'll take you up on that."

The three of them walked slowly under a starlit sky and it broke Raven's heart because Merla was a star-gazer. She loved studying the heavens. God, she loved the world she lived in, most of all her mommy whom she had already begun to call "Mom" sometimes. Merla. The cry was strangled in her throat and she stopped with tears scalding her eyes and Adam held her.

On the sidewalk nearly to her car, Desi touched her friend's back. "Hang in there, love," Desi said. "Call me if you need to talk and I'll check from time to time. Raven, please take care. I love you so very much." She kissed Raven's cheek and got into her car.

Back in the house, Mrs. Reuben said she thought she'd turn in early, so Raven and Adam were alone. Raven was surprised to hear her door chimes.

"Let me get it," Adam told her. And in a minute, she heard him exclaim, "Allyson! Come in."

Allyson came to Raven. "I hope I did the right thing in coming by, but I wanted to offer any help I can give. We've gone over all the fine points of this case, and we've set everything in motion to find Merla. All that's left are prayers." She blinked back a few tears. "My heart really goes out to you."

"Thank you. Please have a seat," Raven said. "It was good of you to come."

"Oh, I'd have come earlier, but we've worked really hard and I'll be going back when I leave here, so I'll only stay a few minutes."

Adam shook his head and looked at his sergeant like a proud daddy, or a proud husband, Raven thought.

He put his arm around Raven's shoulders. "It's at times like this when I know I have the best in someone to work by my side."

Allyson blushed furiously. "You're always kind."

* * *

In his office, Tom Carr sat with Allen, who looked at Tom with admiration. "That call you made to Raven was a great move."

Tom smiled tightly. "Well, it was an *expedient* move. Raven McCloud is a smart woman and she isn't going to be too easily thrown off. But, as I said, it was an expedient move. Now, where do we go from here?"

Allen grinned. "You call the shots. Where do you *want* us to go from here?"

"I'm thinking," Tom said. "I'm thinking. I don't dirty my hands with unnecessary evil, but in this world some evil is necessary. I'm on top now, Allen, and I intend to stay on top and I won't let Raven McCloud stand in my way. She's choosing her own poison. So be it. Her death will be on her own hands. She had her chance to back off."

"Do you think Paul Turner is going to turn on us? I had my doubts about putting him on the board."

"Well, he's just our latest pick as a board member. We've been fortunate with the others; they're hand-picked and they're in my pocket. Paul was a mistake."

"Yeah. Have you heard anything else about the kid?"

"Merla?" He looked crafty then. "A little. I'm sure it'll turn out in our favor whether the news is good or bad."

Allen looked thoughtful. "Some people's kids mean more to them than they mean to themselves. I'm glad I don't have kids. They can get in your way. Aren't you glad you don't have any?"

"Hm-m," Tom said, "once I was glad not to have any. Now…" he cleared his throat. "Let's change the subject. It's spooking me."

Tom frowned. The kid's abduction would sure put a scare in Raven, but he was far from certain what the kid's death would do. Raven McCloud was a fighter. She didn't back down.

Allen smiled. "I've got to say it, boss man, you're a winner, all the way." He lifted his hand in an imaginary toast. "The absolute king! Long may you reign!"

Raven tossed fitfully on her bed. Adam had insisted she lie down to try to get at least a little sleep. Several times he had come in to check on her. The second time he placed a hand on her forehead, then got a thermometer and took her temperature.

"You've got a little fever," he told her.

He left and came back a moment later with two aspirin that she took. She drank the water slowly and found she could hardly swallow.

"Don't worry," she told him. "I get fevers when I'm under stress." She jumped when the phone rang. Adam ran to get the extension in the kitchen as she reached over and picked up the phone.

"Ms. McCloud?"

"Yes, this is Raven McCloud."

"I want you to listen closely."

Raven could have danced for joy when Merla's sleepy voice came on. "Mommy, come and get me."

So choked she could barely get the words out, Raven told her, "Oh, I *will*, honey. Where are you? Are you all right?"

Merla cried a little then. "I don't know. I was blindfolded." The little girl stopped and asked the man, "Where am I?"

"Never mind where you are. Get back under the covers."

"Mom," Merla cried. "Come and get me." Then frantically, "Will you come and get me?"

The man shouted. "I *told* you to get back under the covers." Then he turned his attention to Raven. "I'm still trying to make up my mind what to *do* with her. I can think of lots of interesting things that would make your blood run cold."

"Please don't hurt her."

He laughed nastily and it occurred to her that he had never laughed while talking with her and it frightened her.

"Your theme song is 'Don't hurt her.' And it gives me ideas. If I hurt her, then maybe you'll know how it feels to be hurt, to be destroyed. Yeah, it certainly gives me ideas."

"I've never hurt you. If you think I have, tell me and I'll try to do something about it."

"You're hurting me all the time, but payback is due and coming soon." And he laughed the nasty laugh again and told her, "*Gonna be a killing.*"

Panic took over in her completely as she begged him, "Wait! Please tell me at least a little more. We can work this out."

But she talked to a humming line. He had hung up when he got to the last word of his statement and it hung in the air like poison fumes.

Adam came back in, sat on the edge of the bed and took her rigid body in his arms, held her close. She was sobbing then, unable to stop. He stroked her back, kneaded her shoulders.

"Oh God," she cried. "He's going to kill her. I just feel it in my bones."

"Baby, don't *say* that. He wants to stretch you to the breaking point."

She was tied up in knots, every nerve screaming when the phone rang again. Adam ran to the kitchen again to get the extension. This time she was numb when she picked it up to hear Papa Mac's welcome voice.

"I'm on my cell phone. We went fishing and I just heard the news. I tried to get you, but your line was busy, so I just set out. I'm coming in to D.C. right now and I'll be with you in a minute. Listen, Raven," he said fiercely, "you hang in there. Everything's going to be all right. I've been praying since I heard."

"Thank you." Tears were choking her now. "We'll wait for you."

Raven's hand stayed on the receiver, willing the abductor to call again, tell her something about her baby. And she prayed endlessly, trying to conjure up Merla's image and when she did, holding her close. *Dear God.*

Adam came back into the bedroom and, standing by the side of the bed, told her, "You said yourself you have to be strong for Merla's sake."

"I can't take it if he kills her, Adam. I'll track him down like a dog and kill him. I swear I will."

"No, because *I'll* do it first. Sweetheart, you've just got to pull yourself together."

"I'm going to get up now and get some coffee. I got a little sleep, but I don't need anymore. Papa Mac will be here in a little while."

But the minutes began to drag, and it seemed to Raven an unusually long time before Papa Mac rang the door chimes and Adam let him in. Papa Mac came immediately to Raven as she sat at a table in the kitchen, wringing her hands.

"Baby girl." He called her the old, old name. "Be strong

for your child's sake." He asked Adam to tell him what had happened and Adam did, looking grim and infuriated.

"So we're just waiting," Papa Mac said.

Adam shook his head. "No, there's a lot more going on than that. We've got a battle plan and neighboring police jurisdictions are cooperating with us. Trouble is, this fiend could have taken Merla far away by now. We've got our work cut out. We suspect who's probably behind it, but we can't even be sure of that. I've got a gut feeling about this and I think everything's going to be okay. It's a feeling I just got since the last call."

"Son, I couldn't be happier that my granddaughter chose you for a husband. You're everything she needs, and you'll make a perfect father for Merla."

At the mention of Merla's name, fresh tears began to course down Raven's cheeks. "Go ahead and cry," Adam told her. "Tears will wash away some of the rage."

Mrs. Reuben came in, greeted Papa Mac, saying, "I thought I heard voices. I was coming out to make fresh coffee, but you've already done it."

This time the phone seemed to jangle. It was Kevin calling.

"I've been riding around and I see lights in your kitchen. I've left you alone for a little while. What is the news about my daughter?"

"Nothing new," Raven told him. "Everything's the same."

"You sure you're telling me the truth?"

"Are you sure *you're* telling the truth? Kevin, for God's sake, do you have anything to do with this?"

"You keep saying that. You want Steele and the other cops on my tail. Well, it's not going to work. Hassle me and I'll put a suit on the police department that'll make their heads spin. You've got no proof of any kind...."

Raven said dryly, "Methinks thou doest protest too much. You can be cruel. I know that much. Very cruel. If you kidnapped her to get to me—"

"Let me come by and we'll talk."

"We have nothing to talk about and I don't want you here."

"If she'd been with me—"

Raven hung up the phone. She could take no more of Kevin. He didn't call back.

Each person held a mug of coffee. Raven liked cream in hers, but this very early morning she took it black and appreciated the faintly bitter taste.

"You think Kevin's playing games with you?" Papa Mac asked.

"It's possible," Raven answered. "With Kevin, anything is possible."

"He sure brought a lot of hell into your life, baby girl." He turned to Adam. "You'll make it up to her, I'm sure."

"I'll sure try," Adam reassured him and Raven.

They sat around the kitchen table sipping second mugs of coffee, saying little, taking some degree of comfort and warmth in each other. And Raven thought that not even her parents' death had engendered this kind of despair. Folks said the death of a child brought deeper pain to parents than anything else and she found herself repeating constantly, "Please God, don't let him hurt her."

Raven didn't know how long they sat there when she felt a measure of peace and looked at the wall clock that reflected four A.M. This time when the phone rang, a sense of dread threatened to overwhelm her.

"Raven," the hellhound commanded, "listen well because I won't repeat this. I've changed my mind and I'm coming after you directly. You can get over the kid one day, but your own death—you won't be getting over that. Now listen carefully. Come to Bailey Road and Peterson Place at the edge of Alexandria, Virginia. Turn right and three stoplights beyond that, turn right again. You'll find Merla where I put her out. Now you hurry because I researched this area and a crazy woman keeps pit bulls that she's not too careful about. They break out sometimes. Are you listening, Raven?"

"Yes." She tried to keep her voice from trembling. Her body was hot with both hope and fear. "I'm listening."

"Well good. I'm sure you've found out by now from your cop lover that they can't trace my calls and—"

"Please let me go. I've got to get there to get her."

"Shut up! You go when I *tell* you to go. Is that clear?"

"Yes."

"That's more like it. You're not so high and mighty now, are you? Maybe I'll demand that you stop being an investigative reporter. I can make it bad for your health. You hurt people and they hurt you back. Law of life. Okay, Raven, you know where to find your kid. One, two, three, I'll hang up now." Then he paused. "The killing will come a little later. Go!"

Adam made the quick, necessary calls to Allyson who would relay his messages to others in the police department. Then time crawled as they drove out onto the highway, rushing to get to the spot where the abductor had said they'd find Merla. Adam tried to force himself not to speed; a wreck wasn't going to help, but his speedometer crept up and in a few minutes they heard a police siren. A state trooper pulled them over.

Chapter 12

"What's the rush? You were doing seventy-five by my clock," the trooper said.

Adam explained what was going on and the trooper swore. "I'm going to follow you and help in any way I can."

On the highway again with the trooper trailing, they could go faster and with a sigh of relief they neared the space where the abductor had said they'd find Merla. To Raven it seemed to take forever. There was no one in sight. The three got out of their cars and looked around anxiously in the still-dark morning.

"Where is she? Is she hiding in the bushes?" Raven asked and she called to Merla. No answer. She thought about what the abductor had said about pit bulls and her chest squeezed tight.

Raven's stomach plummeted with disappointment. The beast was playing games with them. Her heart was thudding now and she shook with fury. Where *was* her child?

The trooper removed his hat, scratched his head. "You remember exactly what he said?"

Adam put his arms around her. "I was listening and I'm sure we got it right."

"Dear God," Raven prayed. "Please keep her safe."

Adam prayed with her when suddenly her cell phone rang. "Is this Mrs. Raven McCloud?" a woman's pleasant but hurried voice asked.

"Yes it is."

"I've got your little girl. You must be going crazy with fear, but she's safe and right here with me."

"Mommy!" Merla's glad cry brought tears to Raven's eyes.

"Here. Speak to her, ma'am. Talk to your little girl."

"Honey, I love you so much. Where are you? Please ask the lady where you are."

Raven heard the question Merla asked the woman and in a minute the woman was on the phone giving directions. "I was out watching the moonlight with my dog and I heard Merla crying and went to get her, brought her back here. What kind of creep would put a kid out at this time of the morning?"

The woman gave Raven an exact location very near where they stood and she told the woman their location.

"You're right near me," the woman said excitedly. "I'll leave my porch light on. We'll wait for you."

Raven's heart filled to bursting and she silently gave thanks as they drove the short distance and parked in front of the woman's house with the porch lights on. As they got out of the car, the door opened and the woman and Merla came running down the steps and sidewalk and Merla went into Raven's arms.

Merla laughed happily. "You're squeezing me too tight. I was so scared."

Merla hugged Adam tightly then. "You came and got me." And she said again, "I was so scared."

"Did he hurt you in any way?" Raven demanded.

Merla shook her head. "No. He was nice. He read me nursery rhymes and stories. He said he wouldn't hurt me, but I was scared anyway."

Raven looked at Adam. "It's the kind of thing Kevin would have had done, and he would go out of his way not to hurt her." She patted Merla's head, squeezed her fragile shoulders.

"Well, come in," the woman said. "I made coffee for myself after she came. You got yourself a state trooper to help." She broke off and stared at the trooper. "I've seen you somewhere before. Ohmigosh, *Lonnie Williams!* Weren't we in high school together?"

The trooper laughed heartily. "Lorraine Craddock. I never forget a charming face. It's been a long time. You got married early."

"And divorced not too long after."

Merla looked from one to the other. "Can I have a little sip of coffee too?"

Raven couldn't stop hugging her daughter. "You can have a whole cup of hot milk with a little coffee in it. You can have anything you want, baby."

Raven and Adam talked about the abductor to Lorraine and the trooper who nodded sympathetically.

"Well, you were lucky. There's so many creeps out here nowadays. They'll stop at nothing."

"You're right about that," Lorraine said.

With the coffee ready, the woman sliced coffee cake and served it on pretty, small china plates. "I don't have much company and I don't mind telling you it's nice to have such pleasant people here." She grinned. "Y'all come again, any time."

The trooper looked over at her. "Well, *I'll* be back anyway. My wife walked away years ago. Never looked or came back. She divorced me."

"Kids?" the woman asked and the man shook his head.

"Me neither," the woman said.

They were both in their thirties and the looks in their eyes said there was hope, lots of hope, and they both smiled.

Adam and Raven looked at each other, happy to be in on the birth of this new relationship.

The woman talked about rescuing Merla. "Oh, she was scared all right. But she must have known she could trust me. She came to my arms like a homing pigeon. She's so sweet and so pretty. You must be really proud of her." Then her voice got wistful. "I'd give anything to have a little girl like her. Or a boy. I'd be satisfied with either one."

"I've got a fourteen-year-old son," Adam offered. "You'd enjoy meeting him."

"Oh yes," the woman said and there were stars in her eyes.

"I don't want this to be the end of this relationship," Raven said. "We're so grateful to you for bringing her with you and calling me. It means so much. Can we see each other again?"

"You bet we can. I'm happy to have done what I could. I love kids." She looked at the trooper obliquely. "One good turn deserves another."

"Yeah," the trooper said, "you brought us back into each other's lives."

"I've got an idea," the woman said. "A friend gave me some great pan sausage. It's low fat and scrumptious. Why don't I fix us some sausage and eggs, some quick biscuits and plum jam? Grab you? I don't mind admitting I'm holding on to all your company."

"Sounds good to me," Adam told her as Raven nodded, delighted at the invitation.

Raven got up. "I'm going to call Papa Mac and he can tell the others. I'll be right back."

When she returned, she found a wide-eyed Merla watching the woman take fat sausages from a package. The child looked a bit nervous, but she was alert and focused on the food.

"Oh boy, I love sausages," Merla cried.

Raven looked at her little girl closely; she seemed almost hyperactive and she kept darting glances at Raven who patted her hand. "I'm sure you must be hungry. Did the man give you anything to eat?"

Merla wrinkled her nose. "Cheese crackers and Vienna sausage. A lot of junk food…"

"You're sleepy, aren't you? Did you get any sleep last night?" Raven asked.

"That man made me go to bed early and he got me up too early. He wasn't mean, Mommy, he was nice to me."

"And I'm glad for that. But he wasn't a nice man, honey." She hadn't wanted to question Merla about the abduction, wanted to let her get over the shock a bit, but it seemed an opportune time to ask the question. "Honey, how did you happen to go with that man? Did he threaten you?"

"He did. He came up from behind me and told me to get into the car or he'd hurt me. I was scared, Mom. Would he have hurt me? It happened so fast. We rode off really fast. I guess he wasn't so nice."

Raven was thoughtful and still very angry in the midst of her happiness over having Merla with her. "He could have hurt you," she said. "Thank God he didn't."

Adam made the last of his calls to Allyson who would have the news put on the wire and they sat down to a big, country breakfast.

Merla squealed with delight. "Mom, can I stuff myself? I'm a growing girl."

"You bet," Raven told her. "Eat all you want."

"There's more where that came from," Lorraine told the child. Then she looked at Raven's hand with its blazing diamond ring. "I don't want to be nosy," she said, "but that's a beautiful ring, so you and the detective are engaged, but not married yet?"

"We soon will be," Adam answered.

"You're in love and it shows," the woman said as Adam's eyes met Raven's and blazed like the diamond. Aware of his legs under the table, she thought about the time when they'd first had dinner and his leg had kept bumping hers. That had been the beginning when she'd known how much she wanted him, no matter how hard she'd fought the feeling.

Finally the trooper said, "I've got to report in again and I'll have to be leaving. It's been nice meeting you folks and I'm happy everything turned out okay. Lorraine, give me your number and I *will* call soon."

He left then and Lorraine looked after him fondly. "He always was one of the best," she told them.

They stayed only a short while after and they were on their way. Merla sat between them on the front seat. And they heard it on the radio on the way home, that Merla had been found safe. The police had still to catch the abductor.

"Hey, I'm a celebrity!" Merla said. "That's *me* they're talking about. Just wait'll Ricky hears this."

"He's kept up with it all," Adam told her. "Your soon-to-be big brother loves you very much."

As Adam, Raven and Merla rounded the corner, they were surprised to see several cars and the WMRY news van on the street in front of Raven's house. As they pulled into the driveway, Ken met them, grinning. "I just couldn't resist making a show of the wonderful news," he said. "Allyson put me on track for this one." He hugged Raven, then Merla.

"I hadn't expected this," Raven said.

"I know, but it's such a heart-tugging story," Ken pleaded.

Then the other WMRY employees drew around them. "You've just gotta let this go through," Will Ryalls begged her. "This is news with a capital N." Will screwed up his face the way he often did, making Raven laugh.

"All right, okay," Raven told them and the process began.

In the midst of the taping, Kevin drove up, got out, walked swiftly to where they stood and hugged Merla. "Baby. Daddy is *so* sorry about what happened to you. Are you okay?"

The child nodded and tried to console him. "I was scared, but the man was nice to me, Daddy." Then added, "Most of the time."

He hugged her again. "I'm so happy to see you because I was so worried. I wish you lived with me. It would never have happened."

Merla looked uncomfortable and Raven started to protest, but thought better of it. Adam's eyes met hers with sympathy before the cameras turned to Kevin as he held Merla in his arms.

"I don't mind telling you there's going to be a custody fight after this," Kevin said. "I can best protect my child, and I have so many resources at my command that my ex-wife doesn't have."

"Kevin, please," Raven finally said. "This is neither the time nor the place."

Blaine was interviewing and she stayed away from Kevin as much as she could, focusing on Raven and Adam. Viveca and Carey, who had recently arrived, stood in the background giving them the A-okay sign.

At last it was nearly over and Ken came to her. There were tears in his eyes when he bent and picked Merla up. "Baby, you just don't know how glad I am to see you."

He hugged Merla as she smiled. "I'm glad to see everybody. I was scared."

Putting the child down, Ken turned to Raven. "We're all here for you if you need anything. I know you have Adam, but other people are necessary too." He glanced at the ring on her finger and regret ran raggedly through him. He had loved this woman for a long, long time, now he had lost her.

In their southwest town house, Viveca and Carey began to settle down. She changed to blue short-shorts and he whistled at her legs.

"Are you giving me a Mrs. America show?" Carey grinned as he watched his wife, ardor rising in him.

Her irritated glance swept over him. "Would it keep you home if I were?"

He looked uncomfortable. "I'm not going anywhere."

"Not now maybe, but you won't stay long and you'll be off again."

Carey was exasperated and he looked like a hurt little boy. "You've *got* to trust me, honey. A good marriage is based on trust."

Viveca sighed. "Trust isn't easy to come by, love. You were on campus, so you know my well-to-do parents had all the basics. Teachers didn't make a lot of money, but he bought her candy and flowers at every opportunity, gave her negligees and other expensive presents. My father was an affectionate man and he was handsome."

She paused as a few tears gathered in her eyes and she angrily brushed them away. "But he was a womanizer for all that. He was careful, discreet, but word got around and he was gossiped about. My mom held her head high, but she suffered and I suffered.

"And I found the man of my dreams and we were going to be married, but he decided to become a priest...."

"Why are you rehashing all this?"

"Because I think you're cheating."

He went to her, held her tense body in his arms and cuddled her, kissed the hot tears on her face.

"You're the love of my life," he said, "and I don't want anybody but you. You've just got to trust me. You know my parents broke up because she *thought* he was cheating. He wasn't. I think my mother came to know that when it was too late."

"I just don't know," she said miserably. "God knows I *want* to trust you."

His long, lean fingers stroked her back. "In a little while I can tell you what this is all about. You'll be pleased. Just trust me, please."

Desire began to flood her then as the scent of his beloved body began to get to her. She nestled her head against his throat and gave herself over to wanting him, needing him.

He groaned at the pleasure that began to sweep through his body as he held her, kissed her with a lust and love that matched her own. Slowly he began to undress her and she was relaxed, compliant in his hands.

When she was naked, he simply held her away from him and studied her wonderful body with love-blinded eyes.

Silently she undressed him, feeling the warmth of his muscular body, gasping for breath at the depth of her feeling. Oh Lord, she wanted him, but she had to protect her heart. She wasn't going through life a broken woman like her mother.

And Carey knew he had spoken the absolute truth when he said he loved her. She was the love of his life and he didn't intend to let her go. But he was stubborn in his resolve that she *had* to trust him. There could be no marriage without that.

Both held uncertainty at bay as their bodies yearned and met and he entered her, standing, his eyes half closed, desire galloping in his bloodstream like unleashed horses. A gorgeous yielding wonder began in her body then, but she fretted. This was *so* good, but what if she got pregnant while she wasn't sure she could trust him? She only knew she had to take the chance on him, had to gamble on their love.

Chapter 13

"This morning an indictment was handed down for Thomas Tillman Carr for forgery, embezzlement and fraud. Mr. Carr is CEO of the Citizens' Charity Group of Greater Washington and has been one of the luminaries of this community for a number of years. Most of his board members are solidly behind him as he protests his innocence, but one has sworn he will testify against him.

"This TV station has led the fight to oust Mr. Carr, feeling that he has lost his effectiveness as a leader for this group and that many people are being badly hurt. We will keep you posted.

"This is Raven McCloud, investigative reporter for WMRY-TV, filling in for Marian Sims."

Raven leaned back in her chair and drew a deep breath. It was Monday and she had slept most of the day Sunday. Merla had begged her to let her stay home from school, saying she wanted to go to work with her and Raven had agreed. Now Merla sat across the room from her in a small chair kept on hand for small-fry visitors. Raven beckoned for her to come over.

"Know what, Mom?"

"No. What?"

"When I'm a big lady like you, I'm gonna be a TV reporter. Will you let me?"

Raven tweaked Merla's nose. "When you get to be a big lady, you can be whatever you decide to be. It'll all be in your hands."

Raven had to shake her head. Merla seemed unharmed by her ordeal that had just passed. She had taken a couple of naps the day before, had played with her paper doll city and seemed happy. But once in the night she had cried out and Raven had come to her, taken her into her own bed and cradled her. She had immediately gone back to sleep and had slept well from that point on.

Raven, Adam and Merla had discussed the abduction in depth and Raven had wondered whether she should take her to a child psychologist. "My niece, Annice, is one, as you know," Adam had said, "but why don't we wait a bit, see how she pulls through this?" So they had decided to wait.

The staff members were always charmed by Merla when she visited. She was sweet, delightful and took an interest in what they were doing.

Marnie, a station secretary, came to Raven and Merla. "Li'l bit," she said to Merla. "Have I got something for you? When you visited last time, you said you liked paper dolls. I found some in my closet. And I've got honey popcorn with peanuts. Come wiz' me, my girl and we will explore."

Merla laughed at the accent Marnie affected and started away. But after a few steps she turned and came back to Raven and threw her arms around her neck, hugged her tightly, then left with Marnie.

Raven thought she knew what that was all about, a delayed reaction to the kidnapping.

Fifteen minutes later, Marnie was back. "Mr. Carr is here to see Ken and you, Raven. He says he doesn't have an appointment, but hopes you'll see him. He's quite a charmer, isn't he? And such a handsome man."

Raven frowned. "Well, I've got my work cut out for me today. What does Ken say?"

"He told me to check with you. He can sandwich him in if you can."

Raven swallowed a lump in her throat. Did Tom Carr have anything to do with what had happened to Merla? Was he behind the trouble she was going through—the calls, the hounding? "*There's gonna be a killing*" reverberated in her mind, and she shuddered. Someone had said these words while he held Merla prisoner, but nothing else had happened. Was that person playing games at the behest of Tom? Or Kevin? Were the two men working in tandem to wear her down?

"I'll see him," Raven finally said, "but only for a brief while."

They met in Ken's beautifully appointed, large office. Marnie was right. Tom Carr was a handsome man with a leonine shock of black hair and chiseled features. He was tall, trim, fit and gloried in his masculinity. But Raven thought he looked a bit haggard. Tom wanted nothing in the way of refreshments and he greeted them both with a brilliant smile. "I don't mind telling you I appreciate both of you seeing me. I think we need to get a few things worked through."

He turned to Raven. "Ah, beautiful as usual, Ms. McCloud." She smiled tightly.

They were seated in plush chairs in a semicircle. "What can we do for you?" Ken was at his best facing an adversary.

The big man clasped his hands in an earnest gesture.

"First, I want to say again how sorry I am about your little girl's abduction. Abduction of a child is always heartless."

Raven and Ken nodded as Tom drew a deep breath. "I'll try not to take up much of your time and I'll be blunt. I'm asking you to back off on your editorials and on your reporting, Ms. McCloud. We're running extra time for fund raising because of slimy gossip and what's being openly said about me is affecting the money we had hoped to raise.

"This year, the Office of Personnel Management had promised to put us on their roster of fundraising organizations for the first time. This would have been quite a feather in our cap. I think you can see where reining these attacks in would be necessary."

Ken put his hands behind his head, leaned back. "And because of the indictment, they're changing their minds?"

"They haven't said yet, but if you could be kind enough to soft-pedal the indictment. We still live in a land where people are presumed innocent until proved guilty. Grant me that. WMRY is closest to the African-American community."

Ken shook his head. "An indictment has been handed down. That's news and I'm sure you know we owe it to our listeners—"

"Yes, yes, I know, man, but I think even you would say you've overdone it. You've given far more coverage to this than it's deserved. I'm not the only CEO who has been accused of wrongdoing. Our butts are always exposed. There's envy abroad here. Wannabes are moving in on our tracks."

"You've got a board member who has said he'll testify against you."

"Ah yes, a man who hates even himself, but my other board members are solidly behind me."

Ken looked at him levelly. "It's said you have a packed board. That the group of you have all but gutted CCG. I think even you'll admit there's a need for an investigation."

Tom shrugged. "Investigate away, but don't crucify me until my story has been told. I took a small, struggling organization and I've put it on top. You know how much our community needs CCG. We've raised a lot of money, helped a lot of people…"

"And you've *hurt* a lot of people," Raven said.

"I don't think you can prove that," Tom said a bit huffily.

Raven laced her fingers together and began. "There's a small community center—Keats—that you were sworn to help. Their administrator told me they'd gotten less than half the money you promised them. Three children with infectious diseases died because the money to treat them wasn't available. Do you know how painful it is to have a child die unnecessarily? The administrator said you had promised him that money and there wasn't time to raise it from somewhere else. He was heartbroken, and we're heartbroken too."

Tom Carr was silent for a long moment. "I'm truly sorry about that, but all organizations like ours run into problems. I think we've done wonders."

"I've gotten other complaints from the field," Raven said. "At another small outfit you had promised to fund an afterschool club that would have helped an entire community of children have some place to go instead of roaming the streets. There was to be a playground, after-school study groups…"

Tom Carr scoffed. "They didn't turn in a well-defined plan. They had their chance and they blew it."

"Or did you and your board blow it?" Ken ran a finger around the inside of his collar. "The money your annual report said you'd raised was enough to cover everything it was supposed to cover."

Tom sat up straighter. "There are rules, Mr. Courtland, regulations that must be followed. Just back off a bit, give me the benefit of the doubt. You know how much this station means to this community. The citizens love it, swear by it. And by attacking me, you're hurting us all. We've raised a quarter less money than last year. Can't you see what this is doing to us? This community needs us."

"And especially you," Ken said smoothly.

"Then you're focused too much on me and you're not going to stop," Tom said flatly.

"I'm afraid not. Special Investigations handed down the indictment, not me. I can assure you the other stations will be on top of it."

"But not the way your group is. Editorials, almost daily now. Ms. McCloud's probing personal indictments against us. I can well understand your personal anger, Ms. McCloud. Cree Hawkins was your first cousin and I'd heard him say that you were closer than most brothers and sisters. When Cree was murdered it couldn't have hurt me more. He was one of the finest young men I've ever known and he did a stellar job for CCG. I miss him and we can never replace him, but you shouldn't do personal vendettas in your line of work."

Very coolly Raven told him, "Cree told me a lot about you. He admired you so much in the beginning, but he began to find out things that were less than flattering. How you were one thing in your public life and another in your personal life. You liked Cree in the beginning and you wanted to groom him, but he didn't like you very much in the end. So you groomed Allen Mills and he fit your plans precisely.

"Mr. Carr, we have sworn statements against you from people who are, or in Cree's case, *were* in a position to know what you're about. Willing women and a high style of living aren't what I would think people want in a leader of an organization like CCG."

"Harsh statements, ma'am, and I don't think they're provable."

"More provable than you know," Raven retorted. "And I keep thinking of the three children who died of infectious diseases who might have been saved if the money to treat them had been there."

Ken nodded again, in support of Raven.

Finally, Tom Carr tapped his knee with his fist. "Then you won't back off for at least a little bit?"

"We can't," Ken declared. "We're watchdogs for the community we both serve and we'd be letting them down if we backed off. If half of what we think is wrong with CCG really *is* wrong, you more than deserve everything we're slamming you with. You had a choice. You needed to be and you could have been like Caesar's wife: beyond reproach. Instead, you've chosen to play it fast and loose with other people's money.

"You're going to find that we have information you don't dream we have and in the end we're going to win. We're certain of that."

Tom Carr smiled then. He didn't think they were going to win. He had high-powered, brilliant lawyers, the best the East Coast had to offer and he had covered his tracks well. Cree Hawkins was a mistake he didn't know how to rectify, but what he didn't know, his lawyers did.

Tom began to get up. "I'm sorrier than you know," he

told them, "but I am blameless and in the end I'll prove that. I thank you for your time and I can only hope that you'll change your mind and be fairer about this. As street people say, 'Cut me some slack.' I wish you a pleasant day and thank you again for seeing me without an appointment."

Back in her office with Merla at her side, Raven thought about the days just passed. She glanced down at her beautiful ring and sighed. So much had happened. Merla sat at a small table in the corner that had been put there for her when she visited. She turned around, smiling. "Look at the new dolls Marnie gave me. Aren't they pretty?"

Raven examined the paper dolls carefully. There were a man and a woman and two children. "Very nice," Raven told her. "You're getting a lot of dolls."

"Well, it's a paper city. I need a lot of people."

"Right. And you're getting them."

"Marnie wants me to come back out and keep her company. She's going to order me some more dolls and I'm going to help her go online. She says I'm smarter than she is at computers. Am I, Mom?"

Raven laughed. "You're a kid and kids are smarter on computers than grownups are these days. I expect you're smarter than Marnie *and* me."

"Oh goody. Daddy doesn't always think I'm so smart. He says I can be pretty dumb."

"Don't pay any attention to that. You're smart, baby, and don't you forget it."

"Adam says I'm smart." Merla hugged herself. "I'm so glad Adam's gonna be my new daddy. Will he stay for always?"

"I hope so, baby. I surely hope so."

Viveca came in carrying a florist's vase of flowers. "I just wanted you to see these," she told Raven and Merla. "From my ever-loving husband. The man is keeping me spinning. Just when I think he's away so much he doesn't care anymore, he does something nice like this. Lilies are my favorite flower. And look at this note."

"They're beautiful," Raven and Merla said at once. Then Raven read the note. "Lilies are your favorite flower and you're my favorite woman, my *only* woman."

"The man loves you very much," Raven assured her.

"Ah, I keep telling myself."

Merla showed Viveca her paper dolls and she admired them. Then looking happier, with no strain from the past day and two nights, the child turned to Raven. "Mom, can I call Papa Mac?"

"May I, sweetheart. And yes, but don't keep him on the phone too long."

"Why? He loves to talk to me. He said he did."

Raven smiled. "And so he does, but please don't talk too long."

"Okay, I won't." She happily took Raven's cell phone, went back to her table and began to dial.

Viveca put her flowers on Raven's desk and sat down. "So what did the lord and master, Tom Carr, have to talk about?"

Raven began to discuss Tom's visit when her phone rang and Marnie announced Allyson on the line. The sergeant's voice was warm now, no more Miss Efficiency. How long would it last? This woman adored Adam and she didn't always hide it well.

"Ms. McCloud, I would appreciate it if you could come in sometime today to talk with me a bit about your daughter's kidnapping. There're some loose ends still hanging and I find that personal interviews are always more satisfactory. Detective Steele said he thought it would be wise."

Raven drummed her fingers on her desk. No doubt about it, Allyson's voice went all soft and fuzzy when she called Adam's name.

"I was going to come to you because Detective Steele has told me how hectic your schedule is, but something very pressing has come up here. Could you possibly find time to come over?"

The thought of seeing Adam again pleased Raven as she said slowly, "I think I can make a little time. How long would this take?"

"No more than twenty minutes. A squad car could take you back, pick you up, if necessary."

"No. A taxi is usually very easy to get outside. Would two this afternoon be satisfactory?"

"It would be perfect. I'll see you then."

Raven hung up and stared at the telephone for a moment.

"You look a little flustered," Viveca said. "Who was it?"

"Adam's right-hand woman that he absolutely could not do without." She spaced each word.

"And you'd like to do away with her altogether."

"Fat chance of that."

"Oh love, take your own advice that you constantly give me about Carey. At least he's with you all the time."

"When he isn't with Allyson."

They went back to discussing Tom Carr when the phone rang again. This time it was Desi who sounded frantic. "I've got to see you before the day is over," she said. "Tonight's fine if you can't make it earlier. I wish you'd come here to my apartment. I can talk better here."

For a moment, Raven pondered her schedule. "Merla's with me. I could let her go home with Viveca and pick her up. You sound bad. Whassup?"

"Plenty, but it can wait until you get here. My phone may be tapped."

"Desi?"

"That's who I am for the next few minutes. After that, who knows?"

"Desi, you sound awful."

Then Desi was crying and Raven asked, "Do you want me to come over now? You sound as if you need someone."

Desi coughed then and laughed shakily. "You know me. Miss Hysteria of the Century. I don't really want you to come now because I have a lot of things to pull together to tell you about. Come after work. That should be perfect and I won't hold you long."

"You don't have to worry about that. You can spend the night with Merla and me. I'll bundle you into my car and pick her up and we'll have an old-fashioned chicken dinner. How does that grab you?"

Desi seemed more relaxed then. "Baby, you're the best," she said. "Adam's getting a jewel and I hope he knows that. Men don't always appreciate what they have."

She sounded sad again and Raven thought she'd talk with her a while longer, but Desi said she had to hang up. There was someone at her door.

Getting a taxi to the police station was a little harder than Raven had anticipated and she thought she'd probably let a squad car bring her back to work. Adam didn't seem to be anywhere around and Allyson was crisp and efficient. She seated Raven in her small office and asked a battery of questions about the abduction and what had transpired, taping and writing it all down. And something came to Raven's mind. The alliteration of names: Adam and Allyson. Why hadn't she thought of that before? Then, she thought grumpily, enough had gone through her mind about those two. She was marrying the man and Allyson wasn't. Why wasn't that enough?

"You're something of a celebrity in this town," Allyson said, "so we'll need plenty of info on hand. The more personal the better. I get the feel of the whole case from talking with you here for just this short time. Sure, I had most of it before but you answered my questions beautifully and that always helps."

Someone tapped and quickly burst through the door. "Allyson, about this…"

Allyson's pale face reddened and she looked up as Adam came in, stopped short and grinned. He gave a long "Hell-o-o-o," came to where she sat, bent over and kissed her on the mouth as quick fire flamed inside her.

"Hello yourself," she told him as their glances held.

Adam felt the same fire and it blotted out everything else. Allyson got up and said, "Well, we're all through here, so I'll be running along. See you later, Detective."

"Yeah," he said absentmindedly, his attention focused on Raven.

As soon as Allyson closed the door, he pulled Raven up and hugged her, then said, "Maybe we can make love in my office. Baby, you look so good."

"Don't talk," she whispered. "I want you to hold me, just hold me."

A few minutes later in his office with the door locked she went into his arms and her heart thundered desire.

"I want to strip you, put that big, luscious body on the desk and make love to you until you faint with ecstasy. I can feel your legs around me, feel myself inside you deep and loving every second of it. My Amber Love."

"You've got me turned on so high I'll never be able to walk out of here," she told him. "You're gonna have to carry me out if you don't do something about my passion for you."

He laughed. "And to think I thought you were so up-tight when I first met you, but I knew in that restaurant when you teased me about hitting on you that you had fire in your veins, wildfire, and I knew I had to stoke that fire. Stoke it and put it out in my own. Listen, I'm talking to try to calm down. If I don't, I'll eat you alive right here, right now."

"But we can't here."

"Let's go to a hotel," he teased her. "Spend the afternoon."

Her mind came back to itself. "I left Merla at the office. She's going home with Viveca. And I have to see Desi after work, something important. My mind needs to be clear."

"Making love will clear both our minds."

"I'll want to stay in your arms a long, long time and let you stroke me and make love to me again."

She sagged against him, weak again with wanting him so badly she could hardly stand it. He showered her face with wet kisses, then her throat, his lusting tongue licking and kissing the tender flesh until she whimpered. Then he undid her bra under her front-buttoned blouse and suckled the heavy breasts gently at first, then harder.

"How do I love thee?" he asked, his gold-flecked eyes fogging over with passion. His hand moved down to raise her skirt and slip under her panties. His index finger slid into the syrupy wetness of her body and she moaned against his neck.

"Don't make me faint," she told him. "I keep warning you."

He was intent on what he did to her and his shaft swelled, a nature-driven creature in pursuit of pleasure, heaven bound to utter glory. He placed his shaft on the edge of her secret place and she leaned back to let him inside to joy beyond the telling. She knew nothing beyond this moment and sweetness flooded her very veins.

The phone rang harshly three times. "This is a special call," he told her groggily, trying to snap to attention. "I have to get this."

He picked up the phone and answered, "Yeah?" Then "Okay. How much time have I got? Okay, thanks a lot."

His eyes on her were still very tender, but something had interfered with the passion.

"Damn!" he said. "The chief is on his way over. I thought we still might have time, but I don't want to risk it for your sake. Baby, talk about your poor timing."

"The three rings let you know there was something special?"

"Yeah, that was Allyson. The three rings means the call is special."

"I see," she said slowly.

He took her shoulders and shook her gently. "Stop it, Amber Love. Nobody on earth comes between you and me as far as I'm concerned. Let me take you and Merla out for an early dinner."

She shook her head. "I have to see Desi tonight. Adam, she sounded bad, frightened. I wanted to go over after I left here, but she wants me to wait until later. Something's up and I wonder what it is."

"Poor kid. She's seemed unhappy since I met her. I just

wonder what her story is. She'd be better off cooperating with us."

"Maybe she's decided to."

He grinned. "Maybe. Should I come by later? We need to finish this."

Raven's face got hot. "After Merla's asleep. Call me and we'll set something up. I'm with you. We need to finish this; we had a great thing going there."

"Hell, mine's still hanging fire."

"Like I said, I'm with you. Now let's get this act together. You don't want your chief to catch us *en fla- grante.*"

Adam laughed and kissed her throat again as they straightened their clothes. Raven longed for the wedding to be over when they had time to know each other again and again.

Chapter 14

A weary-looking Desi greeted Raven very late that afternoon. "You don't know how glad I am you could come."

The two women hugged and Desi told her, "Your baby's
back home safe, you're engaged, you've got Tom Carr on
the run. Your world's on top of it. Girl, how I envy you."

Desi had a big, beautifully furnished apartment in a co-
op in southwest D.C. She wasn't working and she hadn't
lived there long.

"Desi, what's going on? You were okay Saturday. That's
just two days back. What on earth has happened?"

"First things first. I was housecleaning to calm my nerves
and I found the second tape I recorded of Tom Carr and
Allen. There were three main ones in all as I told you. I
gave the third one to Cree and Glenda can't find it."

"That's great. This should go a long way."

"I'll play it in just a moment, but the third tape is the
killer. Tom says flat out he's going to have Cree whacked
if he keeps on threatening to go to Special Investigations
with what he thinks he knows. Of course Tom knows that
Cree is a friend of Adam's. And Cree was killed before he

could take that tape to Special Investigations. Oh, that tape, if we only knew where Cree put it."

"Glenda's still searching and having no luck. She's even driven up to their cottage in the mountains and found nothing. Cree had come to be hell on Tom. He intended to see him go to prison because he was furious about those three kids who died."

At the mention of Cree's name, Raven felt her heart begin to hurt. She missed him; she'd always miss him, but it would help if they could find his killer. Tom Carr was a brilliant man and his lawyers were even more so. Raven and Ken were trying to move mountains and they were having only minimal luck.

"Could I get you a drink?" Desi asked.

Raven shook her head. "No. Nothing. I need a clear head."

Desi looked glum. "No, you need a cloudy head for all this. It's going to shock you, but I ask your forgiveness in advance." She got up and poured herself a drink from her wet bar.

"Are you talking about the tape?" Raven asked.

"And something else. A confession I need your forgiveness for, but let's get to the tape."

Desi inserted the tiny tape into the recorder and began to play it. Tom's and Allen Mills' voices were clear as they talked about the weather, CCG, then Cree.

"Cree Hawkins has become much more of a nuisance now," Tom said bitterly. "He's trying to wipe out what I've spent a lifetime building. I don't intend to let him do that."

Allen's distinctive voice was sympathetic. "I'm with you, boss, but just how do you intend to stop him?"

"Ever heard of hit men?"

"How would you find a hit man?"

"I've got a couple in my pocket and I'll tell you how when the time comes. Soon."

Raven was reminded of her stalker's use of the word *soon* so often. She was reminded, too, again of Cree when Desi stopped the tape.

"Just for a moment," Desi explained. "Tom had come to hate Cree. I hid my tiny machine deep in his file drawer full of old papers where he never looked. For all his brilliance, Tom apparently never seemed to think of checking to see if his office was bugged. He's so arrogant. Ah, but that proved to be my advantage. Shall we continue?"

The tape played on with the two men talking about CCG. "There's plenty of money for us *and* the community, but our share comes first. I built this organization and I'm due my cut of the spoils—*our* cut."

Allen murmured, "Right on, boss. I bless the day you hired me."

"I'm the one who blesses that day. You're like a son to me."

"Thank you. My father was never like you. He just didn't give a damn. You're a man after my deepest heart."

"I'll get going on this hit man thing. We've got to head this hombre off at the pass before he does us some real damage. Paul Turner's an ass. I knew the minute he got on the board that he wasn't going to work out, but I didn't expect him to be a total ninny. Going to Special Investigations, siccing them on our tails…"

"Maybe we ought to have *him* whacked. He's rich, influential. Don't you think he can do us far more damage than Hawkins?"

"No, not as much. I made the mistake of trying to take Hawkins under my wing. I told him a bit too much about what was going on because I was interested in him. Well, it didn't work, but I got you. Special Investigation's full of questions, thanks to Turner and Cree. You know my story, that Cree Hawkins was the one who was siphoning off money. Hell, he was an accountant. Listen, boy, I've got great lawyers who think of everything."

The two men talked then of how they would set it to look like Cree had been on the take, had been allied with mobsters who had ultimately killed him. They set it all out.

Then near the end of the tape, Raven's name came up.

"What about Raven McCloud?" Allen asked.

"Leave her to me," Tom said, laughing. "I hate an uppity woman and Raven is uppity with a capital U. Her fate is sealed, but we'll talk about it later."

"Lord, but you're a smart man. You deserve everything you could ever get from this outfit."

"Yeah. CCG's my baby. I built her from scratch and like you said, I deserve my cut. A huge cut if you ask me."

The men talked desultorily then about the weather, about the CCG Board of Directors and Tom's wife.

"You figure prominently in my will," Tom said. "I don't mind telling you that. My life with Laverne hasn't been a happy one. She had all the money when we married. Rich daddy and she never let me forget it. She's gotten a whole lot sweeter since I got rich, but I'm not leaving her what she thinks I'm leaving."

"Thank you, sir. You know how much I respect and admire you and it may embarrass you for me to say it, but I love you too."

Tom coughed. "Then it's full speed ahead with taking care of Cree and the McCloud woman. She's a beautiful creature; I've got to give her that. With that Rubenesque figure and those beautiful eyes. I'd like to roll her in the hay just once before I have her taken out."

Allen laughed. "Boss, you're a card."

Desi let the tape run a minute, then cut it off. Raven wet her lips and anger swept her. "You had this on tape and you didn't go to the police or Special Investigations with it? Desi, you're supposed to be my friend."

Desi hung her head. "I've got to have another drink."

"No, you've had enough to drink before I got here. I think I deserve an answer to my question."

Desi hunched her shoulders. "The last tape, the one we can't find, talks about me too. They planned to kill me. I told myself they wouldn't harm either one of us. That's what I wanted to believe."

"But you *know* you should have told me. You owe me that much."

"He wouldn't let me go to the police or tell you about it. Oh God, Raven, you're going to hate me the way I hate myself for this."

"Who're you talking about who wouldn't let you tell what you know?"

Desi looked absolutely miserable and it was a long while before she spoke. "Kevin. It's—or it *was*—Kevin."

Astonishment lay on Raven's face. "Kevin McCloud, my ex-husband?"

Desi nodded. "No more, no less. Kevin and I were lovers before you two separated."

Raven sat numbly at first. Then she became even more furious. "How *could* you? You know how he hurt me, know what kind of person he is."

"I know and I'm sorry, but he told me he loved me, that he'd loved me a long time and he wanted to marry me.…"

"You're a good-looking woman. You've had other boy-friends before.…"

"Oh hell, let me be honest. From the beginning I fell

in love with who Kevin is, the all-powerful *Doctor* Kevin McCloud. He gave me money like you wouldn't believe and he told me I was just what he wanted in bed. I realize now he controlled me completely.

"He's what I wanted in a husband, and I didn't let myself think about what he'd done to you. I told myself I was different; he'd never hurt me. He said he loved me, that he'd loved me a long time, that he wanted to marry me. I'm repeating myself. I'm thirty-one and nobody's asked me to marry him for a very long time. I'm sorry, Raven. I'm really sorry. Can you forgive me?"

Desi looked at Raven's ring that she was toying with. "It always seemed to me that you had everything and I had so little. I was only getting what you didn't want and that was enough for me."

"I gather you've broken up with him. That now you know the score."

Desi nodded. "I know the score, all right. When Kevin told me he had another woman he was going to marry to give himself a better chance to win custody of Merla, I lost it.

"I told him I was going to you and to whatever judge would handle his coming case for half-time custody. It could well be a woman judge. He went ballistic and he struck me. I had a friend make pictures of the bruises, so I have all that. I'm sorry I've been such a fool."

Raven didn't comment and Desi went on. "He offered me a quarter of a million not to go to you or write a judge or have him arrested for assault and battery. It was the second time. The first time, I backed down."

Raven said slowly, "So you were willing to let me go through hell for the sake of a man who hates me and said he loved you?"

"What the hell are you talking about? You're talking about something else other than how he mistreated you when you were married."

Raven thought then about the fact that she hadn't told Desi about the stalking, the savage phone calls. She'd always wondered why. Had some sixth sense warned her? Very heatedly Raven said, "Well, for starters the last thing that happened, Merla's kidnapping."

"Kevin wouldn't do that. Tom Carr's probably behind that."

"Do you know if Tom and Kevin know each other? Are they more than passing acquaintances?"

Desi nodded. "They know each other very well. But you know something that doesn't show up on the tapes? Very rough-looking men, mob types, three of them, went to Tom's office when I was there late. Most of the time they came when Allen wasn't there." She shuddered. "They didn't look human. I think *they* killed Cree."

Raven looked at Desi levelly. "I'm so disappointed in you, that you'd possibly sacrifice my life and your own."

And she went on to tell her of the telephone calls, someone following her around the city, the threatening words.

"Oh Lord, I'm *so* sorry." Tears slid down Desi's cheeks. "And I've lost the best friend I ever had for nothing. Kevin laughed in my face when he said he'd never marry me, that he'd never loved me, and that he was just getting back at you."

Desi looked so miserable that Raven wanted to take her in her arms and comfort her, but she was angry at her betrayal.

"I know you're mad and I don't blame you, but I asked you over to hear the tape and tell you about Kevin and me. You'll be happy to know I'm going to Special Investigations and I'm going to talk with Adam Steele. Lord, you're so lucky to have a man like him."

"Don't I know that."

Desi looked at her with haunted eyes and finally she said, "Raven, like I said, I'm going to talk with Adam and with Special Investigations. Maybe Kevin *is* in cahoots with Tom Carr. Something's going on. Why would he be so adamant that I not go to the police with what I know?"

"I think you're right and I'm glad you finally changed your mind. Do you think Carr has any idea of what you overheard?"

"No, I don't and I was a fool to tell Kevin. I was in love," she said sadly, "and I thought he wanted to marry me. I'm so sorry." She clenched a balled piece of Kleenex in her hands.

"There's something else I didn't tell you."

"What is it?"

"You've heard the first two and I gave Cree the third. It concerns you even more than the others. I told myself it was all bluff. Kevin wanted the tapes. I didn't tell him about the third.

"I refused to give them to him. I told him I'd destroyed them, but I don't think he believed me. It was the only time I stood up to him."

"Have you *any* idea what Tom's link would be to Kevin?"

"Yes, you know Tom was trying to get him on his board. Tom knew about the bad blood between you and Kevin and he and Kevin both have it in for you. *You're* their common bond."

"I see. And you say this tape has more on it about me?" She took the second tape from Desi and slipped it into her purse.

Desi put her hands to her face. "Just go listen to the tape

again. It's not a smoking gun, but I'm ashamed to listen with you. I should have told you, but Kevin strung me along until day before yesterday. There's more, Raven. I was leaning toward giving him the tapes I had. I never told him about the one I gave Cree."

She paused then a long time before she continued. "If I had given him the tapes and he betrayed me, I think I would have killed him. Do you, *can* you understand?"

"It's all right. We all make mistakes. Just talk to Adam and Special Investigations. At least we can bring Cree's killer to justice."

"I won't even ask you again to forgive me. How could you?"

"You're going to have to forgive yourself. That's what matters."

"I don't know if I can. Oh Raven, if we could only find the third tape. That's when I was hiding in that room and overheard and taped Tom threatening Cree. That's by far the ugliest one of all and the most damaging."

"Glenda's still looking and wracking her brain to think where he could have put it that's secure. It wasn't in his safe. She says he didn't go to their mountain cabin."

Raven's cell phone rang. She reached down to the bag by her side and answered. It was Adam.

"You said you were going to Desi's by taxi. I'd like to pick you up, take you home when you're ready."

"Fine. I'll be leaving in fifteen minutes or so." She gave him directions.

Desi's eyes were wet. "Kevin always treated me badly, but he always said he loved me, wanted to marry me. He was using me; I know that now."

Raven reached across and hugged Desi's shoulders as they sat on the sofa. "I'm angry with you, yes, because I loved

Cree so much and because you've jeopardized my life and yours by holding on to this information, but I do forgive you. Will you go talk to Adam tomorrow?"

"Yes, I'll talk to Adam first. I believe he'll be easy to talk to."

"I think so too. Desi, promise me you won't get cold feet."

Desi shook her head. "No. You'll stand by me? I need my hand held, I'm ashamed to say. Let me call you in the morning before you go to work, or you call me early, around six or so. Help me pull myself together."

"Of course I will. I wake up early, so I'll try first probably."

"You're the best friend I've ever had."

Raven patted her back. "You're well on the way to helping to right this situation. I'm going to go downstairs to wait for Adam."

Later, with Raven beside him, Adam drove past the turn for Raven's house, then drove on and parked on a section of the Tidal Basin. He turned to her. "I've got a few things I want to say before we go in. I'll only be a minute. First, I love you for all time to come."

"And I love you the same way. Adam, Desi is coming to see you tomorrow morning. She gave me the second tape tonight. I have it and I want to listen, with you listening too."

"Hey, that's great! We're still missing the last tape but we now have the second. Her testimony and the other tape will mean a lot."

She told him then about Kevin's actions with Desi and he swore. "The more I hear about Kevin McCloud, the less I like him. I loathe men who mistreat women, savage them." She was sick of talking about Kevin.

"What did you want to talk about, love?" she asked.

"Our wedding. Can we push it up? My folks are com-

ing back a little earlier than they planned and Whit will
be finished with his tour, so he can get here. I don't mind
telling you I'm on my head to have you for my own,
reaching over at night to touch you and hold you. I'm
having wild dreams of going into your luscious body and
filling you with my seed. We need to move fast."

She thought a long moment, then leaned over and
kissed him on the mouth. "What about November fifth?
That's enough time. Damn the preparations. We'll wing
it. The important thing is that you'll be my husband."

"And you'll be my wife. My cup runneth over, not to
mention my private sperm bank."

Raven giggled as they looked out on the wind-rippled
waters with the city lights sparkling on them and she
knew both joy and sadness. Joy over Adam and her coming marriage and sadness over Cree.

Merla flew into Raven's arms as soon as they got into
the door. "Mommy, I helped Mrs. Reuben cook dinner.
We have lamb chops, wild rice and I'm fixing the asparagus on toast. We thought Adam might come and we
fixed enough for him."

"That's very kind of you ladies," Adam told her.

"Hey, I'm not a lady, but I want to be," Merla said,
grinning.

"And in due time, before you know it, you *will* be."

Raven rolled her eyes. "Oh, she and we and everybody
will know it. My little one is chafing at the bit."

Mrs. Reuben had dinner with them and Merla chattered happily. It was as if she had not just gone through
a frightening ordeal.

"When do we get married?" Merla asked in the middle of dinner.

"Do you want to answer that?" Adam asked Raven.

Raven looked at her daughter and smiled. "How about the fifth of November?"

"Wonderful!" Merla exclaimed. "Then I'll have Adam for a daddy. I'll be so glad."

Adam reached out and ruffled her hair. "Not half as glad as I'll be to have you for a daughter. I look forward to much more of your scrumptious asparagus on toast."

Merla giggled. "One day I'll cook as good as Mommy and Mrs. Reuben."

The child and Adam smiled at each other. "You're sure headed that way."

With dinner finished, Raven insisted that they would scrape the dishes and put them in the dishwasher so Mrs. Reuben could leave. She drove her own car.

Afterward, Merla soon grew sleepy, but she fought sleep because she enjoyed Adam's company. So she yawned and asked, "Have you got your harmonica with you?"

Adam made a wry face. "As a matter of fact, I haven't. Sorry."

Merla's face fell. "You make such pretty music."

"Thank you." He put his hands to his mouth and simulated an old nursery rhyme tune and the child was entranced. She put her hands to her mouth and nothing like what he was playing happened.

"How do you do that?"

"It takes some practice, but I'll teach you."

"Promise?"

"Promise."

Merla happily trotted off to bed then, every once in a while putting her hands to her mouth.

They both came to tuck her in and Raven asked, "Do you need a bedtime story?"

"No, I'm real sleepy. Adam, give me a kiss."

"What?" Raven asked in mock consternation. "Are you deserting me already?"

"Uh-uh. I need a kiss from you too."

They both kissed and hugged Merla and Adam laughed. "I can see that this just gets better all the time."

With Merla asleep, they sat and listened quietly to the "Adagietto" from Mahler's Fifth Symphony. Raven sat with Adam's head in her lap.

"It's said he wrote that for his new bride." Raven's voice was dreamy.

"I'd love to be able to do something like that for you."

"You don't have to. You do everything for me just by being with me, loving me."

She bent forward and kissed his face.

"We have unfinished business from this afternoon." He winked slowly, provocatively at her.

Her face got hot and her body hotter. "You have only to talk to me and my body burns," she murmured. "Adam, how long will this wonder last, do you think?"

He laughed. "It's lasted for my ma and pa for lo these many years. Somehow I think we'll be the same."

"You're so sweet."

"No, you're the one who's sweet. Men are snakes and snails and puppy dog tails...."

"Hush. I know what you are to me. As much as I hate to, we've got to listen to the tape."

Raven got a recorder and slipped the minicassette in. They listened carefully as Tom's and Allen's voices talked about CCG and their plans to siphon off even more money. She heard for the second time parts she wanted him to hear.

"I think we've got our tracks well covered," Tom said. "I set this outfit up, so I know how to handle everything."

"I hope you don't take this the wrong way, but do you even *think* of getting caught? You know I'd go to hell and back for you."

Tom laughed easily. "Now that we've taken care of Cree Hawkins, the only fly in our ointment is Raven McCloud. Of course Ken Courtland runs the show, but she does the digging."

"What do you plan for her?"

Tom didn't answer for a moment, then, "More than she'll ever dream. She's got a kid. People love their kids. I just want to hassle her at first. Now I've decided she has to go."

"You mean…?"

"Yeah, the ultimate. She knows too damned much. McCloud is interested in getting total custody of his kid. He'd cooperate."

"Not with harming his kid, he wouldn't."

"That was a thought, not a plan."

Tom and Allen talked of desultory things again and finally stopped.

Raven switched off the recorder.

"So he intends to kill me," she said and a deep chill went to her bones. "He's said it before, but this time it sounds final."

Adam's face was set, grim as he took her in his arms and held her fiercely. "Not as long as I have breath in my body."

It was late when they came together in the guest bedroom downstairs. As they undressed each other, her body felt groggy with desire that filled her mind. She was badly frightened too, but the fear made her cling to him more desperately. At least she had him and this moment. He was everything she had ever wanted and he entered her heart and her soul no less than her body and she was happier than she had ever dreamed of being.

Much later he said, "I thought maybe it's best that Merla not wake up and find me here. And there are things I need to pick up at home for work tomorrow. I want to get in early to prepare to meet with Desi. But I'm not going to leave you, not now. I'll sleep down here and you go to your room before Merla wakes."

"Thank you." She kissed his hand.

"Desi," she said slowly. "Hearing about her and Kevin was quite a surprise."

"Do you care?"

"I care that she betrayed me. She's the one who was torn up, and I am angry that she didn't tell me the full story about hearing Tom threaten Cree. It'll make all the difference."

"Yeah. We can prove it's Tom's voice, but his lawyers can say it was all a bluff."

"I know. Poor Cree. He had his whole life planned around giving his family the good life. He and Glenda were really in love."

After Adam slept, Raven went upstairs to her own bedroom. In passing, she looked in on Merla and found her sleeping on her side with her fist tucked under her cheek. She went to the bed, bent and kissed her forehead, smoothed the soft hair, then went to bed.

She missed Adam's hard, warm, no *hot*, body and his sometimes soft, sometimes wild kisses. In less than three weeks, they would always be together and she could reach out and touch him. She felt the hard surface of her ring. Mrs. Adam Steele. Raven Steele. The clock downstairs sounded one o'clock as she fell asleep.

It seemed she had slept only an hour or so when she came awake. It was six-thirty and she was still dead for sleep. Six-thirty! Desi hadn't called; she'd probably overslept too. She reached the bedside phone and dialed Desi's number. No answer. Had she gotten cold feet after all? Had she decided to run?

Mrs. Reuben would be there at seven. She decided she would go by Desi's apartment before going to work because her friend probably needed more reassurance. Her sleep had been profound and she had dreamed only of Adam, but now her stomach held a queasy feeling and a sense of dread filled her. She went downstairs, woke Adam and told him of her worries.

"Why don't we drive over if she doesn't call in another half hour? She may have kept on drinking and passed out."

"That *has* happened before. I'll take a quick shower."

That was a perfect idea, she thought. She was probably overreacting and everything was going to be all right.

Chapter 15

At Desi's apartment building a little later, a resident let them in as he was going out, and at Desi's third-floor apartment door Adam knocked softly, then more sharply, frowning. Raven put her ear to the door. Silence. He tried the door and it was firmly locked. Both called Desi's name softly.

After a few minutes Adam said they'd need the help of the resident manager who they had noticed lived on the first floor near the entrance. Downstairs, Adam knocked and in a few moments, a middle-aged woman with a puffy face and tousled gray hair opened the door.

"Ma'am, I'm Detective Adam Steele and we're here to see Ms. Howe in three-fifteen. We've knocked and there's no answer. We have reason to believe she might still be ill as she was when we left last night. Could you please let us in?"

As he talked he showed the woman his detective badge and she was instantly friendly and helpful.

"Oh, Ms. Howe," she said. "I thought she's looked a bit peaked lately. You wait here just a minute and I'll take you up. She's fortunate to have friends like you to look after her. I've got two hundred and twenty-two people in here and Lord knows I can't see after all of them."

It didn't take her long and they were at Desi's door. Raven felt her nerves would snap with tension. As the door opened, the woman called out, "Ms. Howe" several times in the little vestibule. Then they saw that the apartment had been ransacked. It was plain a search had taken place. There were overturned tables as if someone had been in a rage and papers were strewn everywhere.

Adam glanced around and went to the bedroom first. He came back out and beckoned to the two women who started in as a small scream escaped Raven's throat. Desi lay face up on the floor beside the bed in a pool of blood that came from her chest. Her arms were over her face as if to protect herself. She wore a thin blue shortie gown that was twisted up to her crotch.

"Oh my God," Raven moaned.

Adam got thin plastic gloves from his overcoat pocket, bent and felt Desi's pulse and heart. Her eyes had rolled back in her head and she stared blindly. His gloves were full of blood when he stripped that pair off and got another pair.

"I'm pretty sure she's dead," he said.

For a moment they all simply stared at the body, then Adam went into action. He made several calls. "To the forensic team," he explained to the women with him.

"If you haven't had coffee, we'll all need it now," the resident manager said. "I had just finished making some downstairs. Will you join me? It may seem cold of me to ask, but I've seen this scene before."

Adam shook his head. "Thank you, but I need to be busy up here. Raven, why don't you go and have a cup?"

"I want to stay with you and help as best I can."

"It may sound callous," the manager said, "but if you're like me, you simply don't function if you aren't stoked with caffeine. What I'm gonna do is get you some coffee on a tray, bring it back. Lord, it wasn't long ago that I had a similar shock like this. I've been here fifteen years and we've had two murders. One, two years ago. Do you want cream and sugar?"

Raven wanted cream and sugar and Adam wanted black. The woman all but backed out the door. Adam paced then feverishly, thinking, planning. In a very short while the forensic technicians would be here and the spadework on this particular murder could begin. He was in his element. There was nothing he hated like the wanton taking of a life, especially a woman's life. He was so successful at solving murder cases because he put his heart and soul into it. He felt deeply that he owed that much to the ones whose lives had been so ruthlessly snuffed.

"Sit down," he said to Raven. Then he went to her, took her in his arms and simply held her.

There were tears in her eyes as she told him, "Don't take time to coddle me. You've got your work to do. I've seen dead bodies before, murdered bodies. There was Cree. I can take it. I want to help you all I can. Tell me what to do."

"Honey, there's nothing you *can* do. I've got my battle plan mostly laid out now and when my team gets here, the work will begin. What're you going to do about work?"

"I'll call Ken later and I'll be going in late."

"This has to be a major blow. I'd advise you to at least take the morning off."

She shook her had. "I'm an investigative reporter, remember, and this is almost certainly a part of my case. I think Desi was the woman who knew too much. And again, both Tom Carr and Kevin had cause to kill her."

"Yes."

The resident manager was back with the coffee in big mugs and they drank it standing.

The forensic team came then, letting themselves into the building with their special police keys. Allyson was with them. Adam answered the knock and Allyson swept in, drew Adam aside and he explained the case to her. Raven couldn't help reflecting that there was that closeness between them again, a closeness that almost shut out the rest of the world. People didn't always realize who they loved. They reached for others they *thought* they needed. Stop it, she told herself sharply. This was no time for childish jealousy.

There was a photographer, an aide, a fingerprint man. They all gathered around Adam who explained what he knew about the case. This done, they fanned out and began their jobs. It came as no surprise to Raven that they joked as they worked. She had worked with and around the police before, so she knew they joked to relieve the sheer horror of their task.

Allyson made the deduction Raven and Adam had already made. "You're right, whoever did it was looking for something and was apparently enraged at not finding it. Adam, I'm going to leave this to the rest of you. Now that I've got a little background, I want to begin running checks on the lady." She turned to Raven. "Ms. McCloud, you knew this woman. Was she a close friend of yours?"

"I thought so."

Allyson glanced at Adam obliquely, then back at Raven. "Had you quarreled?"

"Lord no. Let's just say I found out I didn't know her as well as I thought I did."

Adam cleared his throat. "I'll fill you in on the details, Sergeant. I think she's still a bit too shaken to be questioned."

"Of course." Allyson's fair skin blushed bright red.

The team got very busy then. It seemed to really come home to Raven when the photographer drew the chalk outline around the body.

"We'll get DNA and hopefully that will give us lots of clues," the aide told Adam.

"Let's hope," Adam said grimly. The pounding of his heart reminded him sharply that threats had been made to his beloved and the same people who had hated Desi also hated her.

It filled Raven's mind that one of the things the killer sought could be the tape she held. Had the killer watched her and known she'd come here? Then, too, Kevin would surely have told Tom about the tapes. There were no tapes in the apartment. She felt icy walls closing in on her.

It was nearly eight-thirty A.M. when Raven stepped out into the hall to call Ken at home.

"Raven! I was already up and around, going in early."

"Ken." Her voice sounded strangled to her.

"What the hell is it, baby?"

"I told you about Desi, just how she was involved in Tom Carr's case."

"Sure you did. What about Desi?"

"She's dead, Ken. Murdered. I'm at her apartment now with Adam and his team."

"Good Lord! When did it happen?"

"I saw her last night. I spent a while talking with her.

There're a lot of things I need to tell you. She gave me another tape she hadn't given me earlier. And of course the third one's still missing, the one she gave Cree."

"Lordy Lord. I talked with Glen Thompson a few minutes ago. He thinks they've got a pretty good case, but it would be so much tighter with that second and that third tape and Desi testifying. At least we've got the second one."

"That's the hell of it. She told me last night she *would* testify and why she had refused up to then."

"That's interesting, I'll be eager to hear about it. But why don't you take the morning off to pull yourself together and come in this afternoon?"

"No, it would be best if I were at work. I want to go on the air at noon because I want to personally announce this murder. I'm going to say there's more evidence than we've told so far."

"I'll wait for you then."

She went back into the apartment and told Adam she was going to go home, get dressed and go in to WMRY. He looked at her gravely.

"Are you sure you feel up to it? You had known Desi a long while, and you were once very close."

"Adam, I wouldn't miss this. If you think it's all right, I'm going to say you have a lot of evidence and invite the public to provide more. Then, I'm going to lean on Ken to provide a twenty-five-thousand-dollar reward. Tom and Kevin have got to wonder what we have."

Adam nodded. "Sounds like a good show to me.

As soon as Raven stepped into her office, Ken came in. "I know this is short notice, but I want you to anchor the noon news. You were a friend of Desi's. You can put a meaning to it that the regular anchor could never do. Can you do it?"

"I can handle it," she told him. "It certainly has meaning to me."

"How about lunch if you feel up to eating?"

"Thanks for the invitation, but I have to meet Adam at his office. Allyson needs a statement from me and he wants to take me somewhere."

"I wish I were Adam these days."

Raven looked at him carefully. "You're a handsome man, Ken, a charismatic man, so you'll find someone. I'm sure of it. We're still great friends, I hope."

He shook his head slowly. "A female diplomat; there are no better. I have found someone, only she's left me and moved on to another love. You bet your sweet bippy we're still friends. If I have anything to say about it, we always will be."

She was on her way to check with the woman who handled makeup for the show when she met Viveca in the hall. Her friend took her in her arms. "You must be shocked beyond the telling," she said.

"I am," Raven said. "My stomach just won't stop churning. Why, Viveca? Who would do it?"

Viveca's look was speculative. "You don't like gossip, but Desi led a pretty swift life, I gather. I have known a couple of her girlfriends when she worked here and they chattered quite a bit about her. She couldn't seem to find herself. I'm not criticizing her."

"There but for the grace of God go I," Raven murmured.

"What can I do to help soothe you?"

"I think time is going to be the only answer, but I really appreciate your wanting to help me. I'm just torn up. I have a couple of things to tell you."

Will came up, his caramel face sad. "I heard about Desi. Ken told everybody. I didn't know her well because she had gone to CCG when I came. Desi was one of the nicest women who came around here. From what I hear, I guess she just got lost." He pressed Raven's shoulder and moved on, then turned back. "I talked with her a couple of times. She really admired you. Listen, if there's anything I can do, anything at all, just let me know."

Raven nodded. "That's kind of you, Will. You've got to be one of the most helpful ones on our staff. I wish you weren't going back to school this summer."

"Thanks. I may wait until fall, or even later. I'm enjoying this place and the people."

Raven surprised herself with the smoothness with which she broadcast the news of her friend's death. It was a newscast, so she wasn't free to give her feelings, but her words were warm and effective and they mourned a life taken. She ended with a note that Adam had asked her to end with. "Police have two men under surveillance who will be questioned closely." Adam had said grimly that he wanted to put Tom and Kevin on the hot seat, throw them off guard, whichever way they chose to respond.

The Grand Jury that had indicted Tom Carr would probably meet in a month or so, she reflected as she finished. Such a long time of bilking the public, raking it in from the top, lying, stealing, betraying. Broadcasting this news didn't make her happy, but it did give a sense of satisfaction that this particular public perfidy was coming to an end.

Ken and Will waited for her as she came out of the broadcast room. Ken took her in his arms and hugged her tightly. "You're just the best," he said. "No question about it."

Will's face was somber. "I'll second that opinion."

As she walked slowly toward her office, Viveca came to her. "This is hardly the time for any other kind of news, but you'll probably want to hear it. You're so fond of Carey."

Raven smiled wanly. "I love you both. You know that."

"Carey called me a few minutes ago. He wants to talk with me tonight. It sounds grim. You think he's leaving me?"

Raven said with an edge of teasing, "I'd leave if you gave me a hard time like you've given him lately."

Viveca shook her head. "Don't tease. I'm scared. I love the big rascal. What'll I do if he leaves me? I *had* to give him hell. The one thing I won't take is a man playing around. I'll tolerate most anything else."

"You need more proof that he is before you take off on him."

Viveca's response was prompt. "Never at home, preoccupied when he is, doesn't really listen, falls asleep on me when I want to make love. What other proof do I need?"

Raven looked at her watch. "It's twelve-thirty, you'll be home about five-thirty, so you've got five and a half hours to sweat it out. I'd say surprise him, let the past bury the past. Go in and give him the hottest kiss he's ever had. If he's leaving, you can make him change his mind. I know for a fact you had him going when you two were courting and for the first few years of marriage. This trouble hasn't been happening too long."

Viveca bit her bottom lip. "The women out here these days are so lush and so bold."

"You're lush. Can't you be bold?"

"You're teasing me again. I guess Adam has his work cut out with this murder."

"I'm meeting him for lunch. He has a surprise for me and I wonder what it is."

"Since it's Adam we're talking about, I'm sure it's nice. Now you talk about a guy who's drooling. I get hot when I see him looking at you. Oh, you two make a great couple. I'm so happy for you."

"Hm-m-m, all I can say is if you and Carey break up, you're my used-to-be friend. I'm on Carey's side."

"And in a minute I'm going upside your head, girlfriend."

Chapter 16

Raven found a harried Adam when she got to his office a few minutes later. She drove there because she had to get some money from the bank later at Waterside Mall and she didn't feel like walking. In his office he kissed her long and hard, running his hands up and down her back, his tongue going into the corner of her mouth. She thought then that he had only to look her way, touch her and her very soul warmed. He held her away from him.

"My baby's torn up over Desi," he said softly. "I got a lot of info from you when we both were there this morning, but Allyson needs a more formal statement. Please give it to her, then I want to take you somewhere."

"The surprise you mentioned. Adam, I'm ragged. I don't think I need another surprise. Tell me what it is."

He brought her hand with his ring on it to his lips and kissed her soft hand. "Okay. My parents came back early and I'm taking you all to lunch. Granted I can't take a lot of time because of this case, but you've got to see them. They wanted to see you again before the wedding. The sibs will be at the wedding, but you may not meet them again much before then."

She smiled and pursed her mouth. "Oh Adam, I'm probably a mess. It's been such a day."

He looked at her in her navy woolen reefer coat with a silk flowered scarf around her throat. She looked sad and caring and beautiful and he wanted her again.

His look was somber. "The Steeles can see right through you. They'll know you're solid gold."

Adam walked Raven down the hall to meet with Allyson. She was her usual, cold, crisp self as she wrote down what Raven said as another cop sat a bit away from them. The recorder was old and whined a bit.

Allyson sighed and her voice was softer. "Ms. McCloud, just tell me what you saw, what you felt and I'll ask you a few questions. This won't take long."

And it didn't take long, but just once Raven thought Allyson flushed. That was when she mentioned going to Desi's apartment with Adam so early in the morning. And she thought, *Get used to it, lady. He's mine now.*

But Allyson was twenty-eight to Adam's thirty-three, at the top of her game and a looker. Why did it have to hit her now, she thought fretfully. Desi's death burdened her, Desi's declaration of love for Kevin made her feel betrayed. Would Adam one day feel he'd made a mistake in marrying a woman eight years older than he was?

From the beginning, Raven had felt she had known Mel and Rispa Steele all her life. The molasses-colored Rispa and the very fair-skinned Mel were the soul of cordiality as they hugged and kissed her. Adam's face was like the sun.

"Oh, my dear, you look lovely! Welcome to our family."

"And so are you a wonderful group," Raven responded.

"My boys sure know how to pick 'em," Mel chortled.

The restaurant Adam had chosen had come to be one of her favorites and her favorite waiter was on duty today. He bowed and smiled from ear to ear. "You're in luck. We have fabulous braised ribs, asparagus and wild rice. And I asked the chef to make peach cobbler because I know how much you and Detective Steele love it." He bowed then to Mel and Rispa. "I think you, too, will find this dessert delicious, but I can tell you about others you might like as well."

Rispa nodded at her husband. "I think we'll like the peach cobbler."

"Good. You will be served shortly." They ate bread sticks and sipped sparkling water and Rispa reached into her tote and brought out a narrow, navy satin package with a beautiful, intricately fashioned blue bow. She handed it to Raven. "For you, with our love. It's a simple present from the heart. You have wondrous amber skin and this will reflect that beauty."

"Why, thank you," Raven responded. "Oh, I'm so happy to see you both."

"Open your package, love," Rispa encouraged.

Raven carefully opened it. "I want to keep the wrappings."

Inside, on a white satin bed, was a strand of round amber beads, each bead separated by a small, gleaming gold bead.

"This is beautiful," Raven told them as her eyes misted.

"We got it in Puerto de la Cruz after Adam told us about you. My daughter helped pick it out. It comes from one of their fabulous shops and we're glad you like it. Adam will surely be taking you there soon."

"He surely will," Mel agreed. Mel closed his eyes and

tapped his foot to the piped-in guitar music that played in the background.

Rispa kept smiling and finally she said, "I'm slender, it's true, but my husband also likes full-figured women."

"And I'm partial to charming women who's presence reaches out to me," Mel said. "My dear, Adam couldn't have pleased me more if I'd chosen you myself."

For a moment Raven looked down, her eyes misting again because she felt so completely accepted and her voice was a little husky as she said, "Thank you both so much."

"His sibs are going to love you too." Rispa's eyes were warm and tender on her future daughter-in-law. "Even Damien is taking time off from his beloved recording business down in Nashville. When we find him someone, we'll have ten children instead of five."

Raven saw then the depths and the wonder of the family she was marrying into and her heart expanded with gratitude.

The meal was superb and the aroma made it perfect. The snow-white tablecloths reminded Rispa of the restaurants in Puerto de la Cruz and she reached across and silently took her husband's hand, smiled at him. And Raven thought, Adam and I will be like this in the years to come. Now the painful time with Kevin seemed light years away. Even Desi's death, the stalking and the danger was held at bay.

Rispa's eyes sparkled again. "I began dreaming of your wedding the day Adam mentioned it. Mel and I were married at sunrise. I've never forgotten it. In my grab bag that I call my tote, I've got an old blue garter that my mother gave me when I married Mel. I want you to have it." She reached into her tote and handed Raven a yellowed envelope. Raven looked inside and found a wide blue ruffled satin band with the elastic still firm.

"They don't make elastic like this anymore," Rispa said.

Mel grinned and squeezed his wife's hand. "They don't make women like this anymore either. Ninety-nine and forty-four one-hundredths as good, but not quite."

Adam laughed. "You always had a silver tongue, Dad. That ninety-nine and forty-four one-hundredths percent is good enough for me. I'll supply the rest for Raven. You're looking at a man who's in a hurry for November fifth to come."

Rispa teased her son. "The old country song, 'I'm in a hurry and I don't know why.' Except you completely know why."

"Yeah." Adam grinned.

By the time the peach cobbler was served with a touch of brandy and whipped cream, the four people were secure in the company of each other and they hated to see this time ending.

"I could stay here all afternoon with this group," Adam said, "but I'm working on a new case and I've got a lot of fish to fry." He didn't mention that the case involved a friend of Raven's. He would do that when he called them later. He turned to Raven, "What's on your agenda, babe?"

"I'm driving over to the bank to pick up some cash and deposit a check. Then back to the station." She thought then that she'd stay at the station for a while. She welcomed the thought of going home to Merla because Adam would be working late. She didn't want to have time on her hands to think and brood.

Outside the restaurant, the group hugged each other and took their leave. "It's been wonderful seeing you again and we look forward to the wedding and a lifetime of knowing you." Rispa laughed suddenly. "We raised our three boys to be good husbands, so yours is well trained and we'll help keep him in line."

Adam hugged Raven and laughed heartily. "Just having her for my own is all I need to keep me in line—forever."

Back in her car a couple of blocks away, Raven sat thinking, satisfaction flooding her like a blessing. They were the nicest people and she was the most fortunate woman. The feel of Adam's big body washed over her and it was as if he were by her side. No, pressed against her, the outlines of his hardness thrilling her the way he always did.

She had locked her doors and was still in a state of warmth and love when she became aware of someone tapping on the passenger side car window. It was Kevin! He started walking around to the driver's side from the front and she had the desire to start up and run right over him.

He tapped on the window. "I need to talk to you. Please let me in." He could have stayed on the passenger side and she wondered why he didn't and the thought came, the closer he got, the better he felt he could control her. Should she let him in? Flush from successfully meeting her future in-laws, she nodded. "Okay."

He walked back to the other side and got in, sitting too far over on her side and she involuntarily moved closer to the door.

"Don't move away," he said. "I'm not poison and I don't bite."

"Except sometimes you do."

"I watched your noon news," he said slowly. "Am I one of the men Steele wants to talk with?"

"You'll have to ask him that question."

"I'm asking *you*. You're pretty good at getting under a man's skin, getting his secrets. And is the other man Tom Carr?"

"Again, I can't help you."

"So Desi's dead. I saw you go into her apartment building yesterday afternoon. I happened to be driving along that way."

"Driving? Or following me?"

"Why were you going there?"

"Did you kill her?"

"I didn't. I wouldn't. What did you two talk about?"

"Among other things, you. You like savaging women, don't you, Kevin? That's the way you get your thrills."

"You came out pretty good. Fat alimony. You're marrying within a few years of dumping me. I'd say I left you intact."

"I seem to remember your battering me a couple of times."

"Everybody loses it sometimes. I just lost it."

"You threatened to kill her, she told me that."

"I threatened to kill you a few times, and didn't. I'm hot tempered."

"I didn't tell you I was going to press charges against you for battering me the way Desi did. That kind of thing would make it far more difficult, if not impossible, for you to get fuller custody of Merla."

He didn't respond to that, saying instead, "I gave Desi a lot of money. That should have counted for something. I didn't love her, wasn't going to marry her. No way. She had no class. And maybe I've never gotten over you."

"Don't give me that."

"I loved you, Raven, whatever else. But I'm sure you

know if that love hasn't turned to hate, it's something like it. But I didn't kill Desi."

"Did you kidnap Merla?"

"Hell no. You asked that question when the abduction took place."

"Are you behind what's happening to me?"

He looked at her sharply. "What *is* happening to you, Raven? You're beginning to sound like the jerk you're marrying. Questions. So many questions. What's happening to you?"

"You probably know, and if you don't, you won't hear it from me."

"I guess you're proud of yourself. Turning suspicion onto me and old Tom. Working with your cop boyfriend to get us hung. Tom's got a bad heart, so watch it. My heart is in top-notch condition and I've got lawyers who'd make your head spin, but I'm sure you know that. Your station may face a big lawsuit if you keep it up. Tom and I both have reputations to maintain and I, for one, intend to maintain mine.

"He's a public figure and he has to be a helluva lot more careful about his reputation than I have to be. I want my daughter to be proud of me when she's old enough. She told me she'd like staying with me."

"I don't believe that, but if it's true, you spoil her dreadfully. And Kevin, a man doesn't make a child proud by battering women, savaging them."

"You've used that word twice now in a short while. You were cold, Raven, oh, not at first, but later. No man likes a cold woman."

Raven thought about Adam and desire filled her heart, and her body grew very warm. One thing she knew, she wasn't cold.

"What did you want to talk with me about?"

"I just want to warn you to lay off. You and Steele may be a team, but my lawyers and I are a team too. You and Steele don't have the money to fight the kind of lawsuit we'd file."

Raven raised her eyebrows and thought about the inheritance Adam had. Not that she'd ever ask him to use it, but he was the kind of man who'd do it anyway. She wasn't about to tell Kevin about the evidence Desi had against Tom and him. He'd never heard the tapes.

"What else did she tell you about me, other than the ridiculous allegation that I threatened to kill her?"

She hesitated a long moment. "I can't talk about this, Kevin, not anymore. I've said all I'm going to say. I'm not afraid of you or your lawyers and this conversation is over. I have things to do."

"Yeah, well, I have more things to do in a week than you have in five years. I'm ahead of you, Raven. I was *born* ahead of you and I'm always going to be. My lawyers can make any judge believe that Desi was at fault. Gold digging, that was her game. She wanted money, not me."

Raven shook her head. "She wanted you, badly. She loved you."

He snorted then. "I'll never believe that. Gold digging was her game," he said again.

She looked at him sharply, beginning to be angrier, but a bit afraid too. She had run into Kevin's sudden and violent temper before and it always shook her. The will to murder always lay just behind his eyelids. But she hid her fear well and her own voice was as cold as his. "You'll have to get out, Kevin."

"Okay, but take my warning seriously. I'm not playing."

"Neither am I," she said as he got out and slammed the door hard.

* * *

That night, Viveca looked up from her ad sheets. "You're staying in. What a surprise."

Carey looked exasperated. "I said I wanted to talk with you. Did you forget?"

He looked so miserable, she relented. Shaking her head, sick with anxiety, she murmured, "I didn't forget." If he wanted to leave her, she was going to make it easy for him to say so. "Sit here," she said, patting the sofa cushion next to her.

He sat down and to her surprise took her hand in his, squeezing it.

Clearing his throat, he told her, "I'm going to be blunt about this. I've been wrong…"

She was going to be blunt too. "Is there another woman, or worse yet, another man?"

He laughed then and his face lit up. "Hell no, babe, you're *it* for me. I said I'd be blunt. I've been working, Viveca, all kinds of screwed up hours because my boss has told me he wants me for a top manager in a couple of months. You could quit then and have the babies we want so bad."

Hot tears filled her eyes. "And I thought…"

"Yeah, and I don't blame you. You knew how my parents split up…. Mom accusing him of other women when there weren't any. He told me later he decided he might as well be killed for being a lion as being a lamb and he did find one other woman and he and mom were divorced. She filed when it wasn't true. She died without finding anyone else."

He took her in his arms and kissed her thoroughly, licking her satiny face, his breath coming fast. She melted into him as her heart thundered. He looked at her and closed his eyes. "I decided you had to trust me implicitly. Our relationship was empty without that trust. I can be miserably stubborn and I know that now. Then Desi was murdered and I realized completely that we're not given tomorrow.

"You needed to know what was going on with me. Trust is based on good communication between two people and I wasn't being fair to you." He stroked her back and kissed the hollows of her throat.

A wild sense of joy filled her as he asked, "Can you forgive me?"

Snuggling close, she whispered, "Can you forgive *me*?"

He grinned. "You bet I can. Come on, tiger, let's go start on our first ankle biter." He squeezed her breasts gently, then more vigorously, arousing her to fever pitch.

"Better yet, we can start right here."

Chapter 17

Nature cooperated fully that morning and sunrise proved to be gorgeous coral, lavender and yellow rays on the horizon. The wedding day at Adam's house had finally arrived and Raven felt she had never been so happy in her life.

The stalker had not struck since the abduction and her nerves were a little steadier. He still lay in wait in the back of her mind and she was more certain than ever that Tom Carr and/or Kevin was behind this. More and more she and Adam favored the scenario of the two of them acting in tandem.

Her wedding gown was lovely. It was off-the-shoulder heavy cream silk lace over silk satin with long sleeves that ended in a V over her hands. She wore a band of baby gardenias in her hair and Adam thought the scent was entrancing. Her bouquet was of gardenias. He had visions of what was going to happen to those baby gardenias when they were alone.

Raven felt her mouth water when she looked at him in his tuxedo, his big body at its best. No way could she stop the desire that flooded her.

Viveca, in pale blue silk crepe, was her matron of honor, Ricky was the ring bearer, and Adam had teased him earlier. "You're a trifle big to be a ring bearer." But Ricky had been adamant. "You got a smaller son? I really want this, Dad." And Adam had relented.

Adam's oldest brother, the tall, ruddy-skinned Marty, was his best man, clad in a smart tuxedo. But it was Merla who stole the show. Bright-eyed, with her mop of curly black hair, she was her effervescent self and she simply glowed. Before the ceremony began, Raven took her in her arms. "You're stealing my thunder," she teased her. "I'm supposed to be the beauty today, not you. But sweetheart I can see now what kind of bride *you'll* be."

And Merla hugged her tightly, seeming to understand. "You look so happy today, Mom. And you're so beautiful. One day I'm gonna marry and I'll be as happy as you are."

"You will. I promise you."

The outsized living and dining rooms were packed with wedding guests sitting on rented, padded chairs. The air was bright with anticipation as Nick Redmond's combo softly began "Promise Me." The minister from the church Adam and Raven attended began the words that heralded a lifetime of truth and beauty. But it was only when he reached a certain part that Adam felt his heart turn over with thrills.

"Do you, Adam Steele, take this woman to be your lawful wedded wife, to love her and cherish her for all your life until death do you part?"

"I do."

Adam's voice was choked with emotion as he responded to their minister's question in the wedding ceremony he and Raven had written. He looked at her now and felt the love in his heart nearly consume him. Then

Raven answered that same question about him in a tremulous voice that told of a love so deep it was painful. The minister's mellifluous voice droned on as each of them read their parts of the rest of the ceremony until the words were said, "I now pronounce you man and wife."

The minister smiled broadly then, observing the couple's deep joy before he intoned, "You may now kiss the bride."

Adam swept Raven into his arms and held her and they could have been alone as he kissed her ardently, his tongue briefly teasing her mouth. It was done! Lord, it was done and Raven was his for all time!

Raven relaxed in his arms, glorying in the meaning of this moment. But she also became aware of the sweet ripples of laughter around them at the long kiss. Adam drew away a bit, but it was plain he didn't want to let her go.

The minister shook hands with Adam and kissed Raven's cheek. "What a beautiful bride you make, my dear. I think you two will be very happy."

And in the midst of all that joy, Raven thought about Cree and how much he would have enjoyed knowing she was happy at last.

Adam saw and asked her, "You're suddenly sad. What is it?"

When she told him she was thinking of Cree, he said gravely, "We'll find his killer, love. This will never be a truly cold case as long as I have breath. The same goes for Desi."

Raven's happiness came back as they cut the wedding cake. Ordered by Rispa from a fabulous, world-famous Baltimore bakery, it was from an old New Orleans recipe. Nutmeats, plump golden raisins, sweetmeats, cherries and other delicacies, Raven found it one of the best cakes she had ever eaten. Smiling, she fed Adam.

"If you're not careful, I'll eat your fingers along with the cake." And he whispered, "I'm hungry for you, baby. How long can I wait?"

She felt thrills of desire flood her body and her blood ran hot as she grimaced. "I'll get you for that turn-on remark."

"You can't get me soon enough."

The wedding celebrants crowded in on them with hugs and kisses and heartfelt congratulations.

Papa Mac was first. He had spent the night with Adam and Ricky because he didn't want to miss a minute of this wedding. Now with tears in his eyes, he embraced his granddaughter and hugged Adam again. "I always wanted me a grandson," he said. "Now I've got you and Ricky, a great grandson. Be happy, son, the way I know you two will be. If I had picked you myself, you'd be the man for Raven."

Viveca and Carey were in the forefront, happy for their friends and happy for themselves. With tears in her eyes, Viveca hugged Raven. "You are gorgeous," she said, "and you're going to be ecstatic with Adam. I feel it in my bones."

Adam introduced her to family members she hadn't met, having long ago explained that although one had a different mother, they and he considered themselves whole brothers and sisters.

There was Frank, his half brother, with his wife Caroline. Both were noted gospel singers who like Mel had once headed a famous group, "The Singing Steeles." They were the parents of Ashley and Whit, whom Raven had already met, and Annice. Then there was Marty, who had served as best man, and the twins Damien and Dosha, teasing, tan and ebullient.

Raven couldn't help exclaiming, "Now I know where Adam comes from. You're all such a magnificent bunch!"

Adam's sibling twins came to where the wedding couple stood. Dosha's eyes were sparkling. "You'll be at my wedding next summer and I hope it will be as lovely. I think you'll be the sister I've always wanted."

"You owe me a dance," Damien said to Raven, "and if I'd seen you first, old Adam wouldn't have you now."

And Raven understood then why he was considered the playboy charmer of the family.

Whit came to the couple and his sibs, his handsome face merry. After clapping his Adam on the back, he kissed Raven's cheek. "You make a beautiful bride, lady." He had liked Raven from the first time they met.

Ashley and Annice came to them with their handsome husbands in tow. They all gave effusive congratulations and the women kissed Raven's cheek.

"It's plain you're going to fit right in," Ashley offered.

"Thank you."

Annice grinned. "If bro here ever gives you any trouble, just send him to me."

Raven threw back her head, laughing. "I'll be sure to do that."

Luke, Annice's husband, laughed too. "She sure keeps me in line," he teased.

There were hugs and kisses all around, cries of joy and satisfaction. And Merla was again the hit of the wedding as she sparkled happily.

Raven's coworkers from WMRY had invitations and almost to a man they came, bringing joy and lovely gifts. And there were others in her line of work who came and honored her. Ken headed the group, with Blaine and Will bringing up the rear.

"Let me monopolize her for a few minutes," Ken said to Adam.

Adam glanced at his watch. "For a few minutes only.

Ken said to Raven, "You're so beautiful. Be happy."

"Thank you. I am happy."

With the ceremony over, Raven went midway up the stairs and flung the gardenia bouquet down to waiting female arms. She smiled widely as Mrs. Reuben caught it with a gasp of delight.

Raven went upstairs and into the master bedroom and changed into a snug, ruby wool jersey dress and black suede pumps. She stood in the room for a few minutes remembering the first time she and Adam had made incredible love on this bed when they couldn't wait for the pizza to finish baking. She didn't want to remember that that had also been the day Merla had been abducted. Shuddering, she tried to dismiss that thought. Her daughter was doing fine. *Look how happy she is today,* Raven thought.

Rispa and Viveca knocked and came in. "We wanted to help you and we got tied up in the hullabaloo," Viveca said. She held up the wedding dress that lay on the bed.

"Save it for Merla," Rispa said, laughing. "I've fallen in love with your daughter."

At the thought of Adam waiting downstairs, ready to whisk her away to Pennsylvania's Green Mountain for a short honeymoon, Raven's emotional cup overflowed. She felt ageless, of an age with Adam as he was of an age with her. She swore she was never going to let the age difference matter again.

Back downstairs, caterers were serving a wondrous selection of food. Damien had insisted on fried wild rabbit, his whimsical touch, and there was Peking duck, baked turkey, ham and roast beef. German and American potato salad lay on a bed of crisp iceberg lettuce, surrounded by bright red tomato wedges and slices. Baked macaroni and cheese and macaroni salad. Plump fried oysters, done immediately before eating. New England clam chowder. An array of raw and cooked vegetables.

Raven explained to the guests. "This is really brunch, but it's a little too early. We decided to just be informal. You won't need to cook all day. There's plenty to take doggie bags, and we're planning on keeping you for a while."

As Nick's combo played soft, romantic music, the door-bell rang and Nick got up, smiling. "That'll be my lady, Janet, I'll bet." He answered the door and hugged the lovely woman who stood there, brought her back and introduced her around.

Adam put his head to one side as Nick rejoined his group. "She's ten years his senior and theirs is quite a love story that I believe, like ours, it's going to last forever."

The dancing began and Mel came forward. "I think I'll steal you for one dance. My son can be a possessive man."

Mel proved to be a formidable dancer, light as a feather and an excellent guide. "Now me, I like these new young-people dances. They give me a chance to shake a leg." He grinned then. "But there's nothing like soft romantic tunes to build a mood. You look really happy, daughter-in-law, and I think my son can keep you that way."

"I just hope I can keep *him* happy."

His face grew somber then. "The boy was so broken for so long and at times we despaired for him, but he knew he had to go on for Ricky." He paused. "Then you came and the world changed for him. We love you for that, and we thank you."

Raven shook her head. "He's given me more than I could ever give him."

Adam cut in on them and swept her away. "I'm gonna give you a treat when I get you alone."

She wrinkled her nose at him. "You're a rascal, Adam, but along with that you're one sweet man."

"You keep saying…"

Adam's sib, Marty, cut in then. "Don't monopolize the bride; we love her too."

They stood for a moment. "Yeah, so I see. Damien keeps looking over here. He'll be next to horn in. Can't a man keep his bride all for himself on his wedding day?"

"Nope," Marty answered. "It doesn't go that way. You've got a lifetime to dance with her. She's really lovely. I like your taste."

Marty's wife, Caitlin, swept by in someone's arms and they winked at each other as Marty told his brother in a heartfelt voice, "I'm so happy for you, bro. You'll never know how happy."

"Just paint us a wedding portrait free of charge. That's all I ask."

"And you'll get it. It will be an honor. Now surrender the lady."

The repartee between the two men was so full of affection and love, Raven couldn't stop smiling as she went into Marty's arms. Nick's combo played an old, old tune made popular by the African-American singer, Billy Daniels, "Old Black Magic," and like his father and his brother, Marty proved to be an excellent dancer.

The dance was over too soon and Marty told her, "You're a smooth dancer and I intend to claim you later for another round. Make old Adam jealous. He can't keep his eyes off you."

Before she could answer, Adam cut in, grinning. "Don't you two enjoy this too much." And as Marty moved away, smiling broadly, Adam's voice was husky as he asked her, "How's my bride, my love, my wife, my baby? My woman."

Raven teasingly fluttered her eyelids at him. "How could I be less than elated with you calling me all those pretty names? Look, honey, Glenda looks a bit down. Let's go and cheer her up."

Glenda sat near a window in a pretty navy wool maternity frock with a wide, lacy collar. "Bride and groom," she said as they came to her.

"How *are* you, love?" Raven thought she looked down at heart.

Glenda sighed. "I've been better. I guess this reminds me of my wedding." She patted her big abdomen. "And junior's chosen today to act up. I think he wants to come out in a hurry."

Adam and Raven took hassocks at Glenda's feet as she told Raven, "I've given you the keys to the mountain cabin. I know a honeymoon leaves little time for anything else, but you'll want to continue searching for that tape. I've wracked my brain to think where Cree might have hidden it. He felt it really is a smoking gun and, Adam, you can use it. I told you Cree said Tom threatened to kill him if he testified against him. He felt that Tom had simply gotten overwhelmingly arrogant with his army of lawyers and thought he was beyond the law. Cree said Tom was acting crazy."

"Believe me, we'll take the time to look," Raven said. "You have my cell phone number. Now, call me anytime."

"You know I wish you the most wonderful of honeymoons. Cree and I certainly enjoyed ours. Mr. Curtis is our caretaker up there. He called and said his wife had stocked plenty of delicious food and the cabin is snug and cozy. You'll love it."

"I'm sure we will." Adam's glance on Glenda was warm, sympathetic. "You've got to dance at least once and I want that one."

Glenda smiled. "It seems I'm always slightly tired these days, but I think I'll risk one dance with you. I may need to go home early."

"Lie down here," Adam said. "And if you need someone to take you home, Raven and I will do it before we leave."

"Oh, you're kind and I thank you, but I think I'll be all right. I've gotten used to feeling like this. I think it's just junior's way of keeping me all to himself."

Looking at Glenda, Raven felt a few tears gather in her eyes at the thought of Cree's and Glenda's beautiful love-filled life. And Cree's horrendous death.

Adam's captain and the police chief were both there in natty civilian dress and she danced with both men. She had met his captain and immediately liked him, but she had not met the chief until today. Allyson was out of town helping the aunt who raised her who now had a sprained ankle.

The chief danced with her first. He was a husky, ebullient pecan-brown man and he told her, "You make a lovely bride and you dance superbly. Detective Steele is a lucky man. I don't mind telling you your husband is going up. He's a magnificent officer and we're all very proud of him."

Adam's ruddy, brown-haired captain claimed her for the next dance and he grinned, "After dancing with those smooth dudes, the chief and Adam, I sure hope I don't leave your feet crushed."

Raven laughed. "I'm sure you'll do fine, Captain. You look like a man who's got rhythm to me." She grinned at him impishly, and the captain flushed, got somber.

"Adam's like a younger brother to me and I suffered with him when he was alone so long. Now you two have found each other and I know you'll be happy. I have only to look at you together."

Nick Redmond clapped then for attention. "We have a great happening coming up. I'm going to play you a song I composed for the happy couple. It has a special meaning to them and it's called "Passion's Fool."

Raven's breath caught as she looked at Adam who grinned. "You didn't tell me about this," she chided.

"You'll find I'm good at keeping secrets, except I won't keep any more from you." He kissed her lightly on the lips.

Damien was passing and he teased, "The honeymoon is later, not now."

Nick's splendid maple-front guitar began to moan as he flashed a smile at his wife and his group joined in. Nick sang solo:

> *Night after night we loved each other.*
> *For you I've broken every rule.*
> *Got no regrets, no shame, no teardrops.*
> *JUST CALL ME PASSION'S FOOL!*

> *We came together in the winter*
> *Every cell of us on fire.*
> *Winter winds made us draw closer.*
> *Hot with love, weak with desire.*

> *You left without a word of warning*
> *Broke my heart and crushed my soul.*
> *Now you're back and say you love me,*
> *And my fool heart has lost control.*

> *You said you never meant to hurt me.*
> *With you I just can't play it cool.*
> *I'll take the chance because I love you.*
> *JUST CALL ME PASSION'S FOOL!*

A saxophone crooned softly like a lover's kiss as Raven and Adam looked at each other. Nick finished with another chorus and the celebrants clapped heartily. Raven walked up to Nick and kissed him on the cheek. "Beautiful!" she said.

At that moment Raven's eyes met Adam's and held, fire flashing between them. "You don't know the half of it," Nick murmured. "I've made a recording and Adam has the cassette. A honeymoon cassette. My gift to a couple I idolize."

"You're sweet," Raven told him. "We idolize you too."

"Hey!" Adam said. "That's what you always tell me— that I'm sweet. I'll share nothing about you with any man." His eyes were hotly teasing.

"Okay. Okay," she said, laughing. "You're the sweetest of them all."

Adam put his arms around her shoulders and whispered, "You're beautiful. That song is turning me on and I can't wait."

And she murmured back. "You're wicked, love, and I wouldn't have you any other way."

It was a little after noon when the festivities began to wind down a bit and Adam and Raven were ready to leave.

Dosha, Adam's sister, came up to them with her twin, Damien, who grinned and said mischievously, "It's about time you two shoved off for the mountain. It's a two hour drive and you've got work to do once you get there."

"Damien, behave yourself." Dosha smiled at the couple. "You look so happy, you two. Just a minute." She stopped one of the waiters and handed each of the three a glass of champagne and kept one for herself. Then she raised her glass and they raised theirs as she toasted: "May life be all that it *can* be for you, and may you be happy and in love always."

Dosha's eyes filled with tears as she remembered Adam's loss and his suffering and her heart filled with hope at the love he knew now.

"What a wonderful family I'm marrying into," Raven told them.

Adam smiled and looked at Raven. "All this love feast is turning me on. Baby, we've gotta go. I like to look at the mountainside as we drive."

"Yeah. Likely story," Damien teased.

"Okay, Turk," Adam shot back. "Dosha's turn is next summer. That just leaves you. Isn't it about time you stopped chasing fillies and settled down?"

Damien raised his eyebrows. "All in due time. In every family there's one who chooses to be different. Find me a woman like Raven and I'll happily settle."

"You find your own woman. God knows you've courted enough."

"All the good ones are taken."

Mel and Rispa came up. "It's a wonderful gesture to have Nick write that song," Mel told Adam. "I didn't know you remembered what I said about being passion's fool."

Adam hugged his father. "Dad, I've remembered just about *everything* you ever told me. It was wrapped in too much love not to remember."

Papa Mac came to them, asked Raven, "Are you happy now?"

"You know I am."

"Look, you two had better be hitting the road. I remember your grandma's and my honeymoon." Mrs. Reuben was nearby and Papa Mac kept glancing her way.

Within a half hour Adam and Raven had taken their leave. Merla was happy to be staying with Mrs. Reuben and Raven had promised her a big teddy bear.

As they got in the car, they were peppered with rice Adam couldn't shield her from. They waved and waved, got into the car and before he started the engine, Adam turned and grinned at her, pressed her thigh. "You're gonna have to help me drive. I'm in a bad way."

And Raven teased him. "A good man in a bad way. What a combination."

Chapter 18

The trip to Green Mountain in Pennsylvania was uneventful with Adam driving the first half of the way and Raven the second half. As they pulled into the carport, Raven groaned. "We've got this food to unload and I'd like a nap."

Adam grinned. "You'll have time for a nap later—maybe. This afternoon and tonight, love, you belong to me. Your time is mine and I have plans for you."

"Like I don't have plans for you. The nap was a joke." They looked at each other and both caught fire as Raven said, "Let's begin unloading." She dug into her bag and handed him the ring of keys.

"First things first," he threw back over his shoulder as he went to open the door, then came back to where she stood beside the car. "Walk with me a few steps," he said.

"To where?"

"Don't get contentious on your wedding day. I'd hate to have to give you a light spanking first thing."

"Okay, I'm walking. I know when I've met my match."

At the doorway he paused and put his arms around

her, then picked her up and pushed the door open as she kissed his face. "Oh sweetheart. I'm too heavy for this. We have to protect your back for better things."

"What's better than carrying my bride across the threshold—leading up to more passionate activities?"

He held her up for a full minute before settling her on her feet. She quickly drew away and peeled off her coat as he did the same. As they came together in a heated kiss, he stroked her back covered with the soft garnet wool jersey and his hands moved down to her buttocks and gently massaged.

"We've got to unload the car," she whispered.

"Uh-uh," he whispered. "The food is packed in thermal containers. It'll keep. I've been hurting through a whole wedding. When the preacher said 'Kiss the bride,' and you kissed me, it was all I could do to keep from taking you in my arms and racing upstairs. With you, I'm not a patient man."

She smiled impishly at him. "And I'm going to lead you on." Her kiss was wild then as she licked his lips, then his face before he growled and caught her close, forcing his tongue deep into her mouth as she clung to him as if she could never let go.

He stood holding her, squeezing her soft, silken body gently, and shook his head. "I can see where this is going for me. I'm hooked on you forever and I'm satisfied to be."

"Me too." She drew out of his arms, turned. "Unzip me, honey."

"I'll do better than that," he said as he slid the long zipper down. She stepped out of the dress and the slip that pooled around her ankles. He undid her black lace bra, leaving the full, beautiful brown breasts exposed. Then he went to his knees and slid the elasticized-top panty hose, then the black lace panties down and off her legs and she shivered as he kissed her crotch and thighs.

"Lord, but you're beautiful," he groaned. "I'm going to spend myself on you."

Raven murmured, "Now you." And he stood in torpor as she began to undress him, beginning with his belt which she unbuckled and slipped off hurriedly. She unbuttoned his shirt, then unzipped his pants, doing it slowly while he held his breath. His shaft was big and swollen with love and lust and she stroked it tenderly. Oh Lord, she thought, he was one gorgeous man, with his well-developed pecs and biceps and washboard abs. A thin line of black hair ran down his front then ended covering his crotch.

When he was completely naked, she stood against him and he stroked her ardently, kissing and kissing her mouth, her face, the full breasts, her shoulders and bending to kiss her belly until she thought she would faint.

"Let's go to the bedroom," she whispered.

There was a glint in his eye. "See that table," he said, pointing to a sturdy mahogany table in the corner, "I can barely make it to the table. The bedroom will have to wait."

He danced her to the table with imaginary music thrumming in both their ears. She sat up on the table, her feet a few inches from the floor, legs spread to welcome him and he entered the syrupy wetness of her, aching with passion and love and desire. He lightly nipped her bottom lip, then traced her lips with his tongue. Glove-close she gripped him and he groaned as he touched her womb and held fast there.

Her breasts were sweet, ripe melons against him and he bent and suckled her slowly, maddeningly, licking the flesh around the big pale tan aureoles and the darker brown circles. Soft, then harder.

"Do you know how much I love you?" Raven was feverish now, moving in concentric circles beneath him. She caught his buttocks and pressed him deeper into her body, stroked him fervently and moaned deep in her throat.

"Baby," he told her, "I will never, never get enough of you."

"That's the way I feel about you. Thank you for helping me free my mind. I was so emotionally numb when I came to you. I was afraid no man wanted a libidinous woman who craved him. Thank you, sweetheart."

She knew she talked to slow herself. She didn't want this to be over.

"You're very welcome. I'm glad we've been able to add to each other's lives because we're together for good, and I'll gladly take all you care to give me all the time."

And his saying it made her dizzy with joy as she drew him closer again. His tongue devoured her mouth then and she went spinning, spinning to the edge of the world with him deep inside her, a blessing she would know forever.

She felt the first tremors of multiple orgasms and let herself go in an orgiastic fever.

"I wanted to last a long time for you," she told him, "but…"

He laughed softly, "But it just got too good for you. I want it to always be that way. We've got plenty of time and plenty more where that came from, baby."

He worked her gently, then a little more roughly until he hoarsely called her name. And with a hard gasp, he felt his loins quake and his own multiple orgasms began, flooding her body with his naked seed, glorying in every drop. He wanted a child from this ecstasy, a baby to hold close to their hearts, to love, to nurture.

And Raven thought no less than Adam did of the child she hoped would come from her womb and his seed. Now they were deep into the meaning of life itself.

With the orgasms slowly diminishing, he still held her close, but she became more aware of what lay around her. Soft snowflakes had begun to fall heavily outside as they made love. "Look," she cried. He turned and saw the big, dry flakes.

"I want to go outside, let it fall on us." He saw with joy that his mate's eyes were shining and her face glowed. She smelled of the Shalimar bath oil she favored and her own pheromones, and it was getting to him yet again. He smiled at himself. Would he ever get enough of this woman?

"Adam? You've gone away from me."

"No. I'm still inside you. So you're tired of me already. You want to go outside."

"Please, trust me. When we come back in, I'll give you love you haven't even thought about."

"There's not much I haven't thought about where you're concerned, but I'll take your word for it. Okay, honey, let's get dressed and go out, romp in the snow."

They lazily donned the same clothes with their heavy coats, scarves and gloves and went out into the side yard. Outside Raven really noticed the lovely mountain cabin for the first time. Coming in, she had been too full of passion for her mate. The cabin was fieldstone and snug, but roomy enough. Cree and Glenda had owned it for only a year when he was killed.

Once they were outside, the snow began to fall much more heavily and Raven wrapped her scarf around her head. Adam was bareheaded.

"I don't want you to catch cold," she said. "Shouldn't we go back and get you a cap? I put one in my suitcase for you."

Adam shook his head. "I'm hardy. I seldom have colds. I try to stay really fit."

She chuckled. "Judging by how we just made love, I'd say you're super fit." She shook her head. "I'll never find the words to tell you."

"You don't have to. Your body and the way you give yourself to me says it all."

She touched him, crying merrily, "Tag," and went racing to the other side, with him in hot pursuit. In a minute he had caught her fast from behind and held her tightly against him. When he slacked his hold, she dropped to her knees and rolled over on the snow-covered ground. On his knees he caught her and rubbed a few flakes of the sticking snow on her face.

"That's one way of cooling me down," she said, laughing.

"But I've got far better ways. Ways that will thrill your very soul. Come to Papa, baby."

And she snuggled in his arms as if they were in a warm bed as the thick snowflakes fell faster and faster. The heavy outer gear shielded them from the cold, but each wanted to feel the flesh of the other. They were part of the earth out here and mother nature did what she does best, increase mankind.

"We may get snowed in here and spend the rest of the winter," he said.

"I love being absolutely alone with you."

"Same here. Sweetheart, we'd better get the things in. Speaking of colds, I don't want *you* catching one."

"Um-m-m. I'm fit too, but you're right."

Struggling up, they unpacked the car and got the suitcases and the food inside and stored it. Then their eyes were on each other again, heated and intense.

"Well, so much for snow cooling us off," he said. "This

really is a great-looking place, and you're a great-looking woman. And to me you *feel* even better."

"Um-m-m," she said, "you don't feel so bad yourself." They fixed and ate small bowls of New England clam chowder with oyster crackers and had slices of ultra-sweet honeydew melons imported from Chile.

"Let's not eat too much. I want no interference with my plans," he told her.

She looked at him from under her thick eyelashes. "And those plans are?"

"To drive you crazy, completely out of your mind."

"If I don't drive you first."

Sitting across from him, she put her foot on his chair between his legs and his breath came quick. "You're asking for trouble, woman, and I'm the man to give it to you." He stroked her foot as it pressed against his shaft.

"Promises," she teased him. "Lots of promises. When do I get some action?"

"I'll have you moaning 'Uncle' before I'm half through."

She teased him more. "Oh, this food is so good. I think I'll fix something else. I'm hungry."

"You're not fixing anything else to eat right now. I'm hungry all right, but for *you*." He smiled deep inside thinking how she had come out from under a sexual-sensual complex cloud of numbness and fear into a splendid star-and-moonlit space that made him and her burst with happiness. And he thanked God for this gift.

He looked at her and told her, "You've come a long way, baby. Yeah, a long, long way, but I'm going to take you even further."

Chapter 19

Early Tuesday morning, Raven and Adam were still in their robes, getting ready to leave for D.C. She walked around the house, again remembering when Cree had been here. All at once, his presence seemed palpable and she felt a lump in her throat.

They had gotten up very early and begun a thorough search of the two-bedroom cottage. After the first rooms had turned up nothing under Adam's trained hands, they had gone to a pantry stocked with canned food. They were nearly finished and were sick with disappointment when Adam climbed on a stepladder to reach a corner top shelf. There he found a small metal box and handed it to Raven, who opened it.

Inside were five tapes and a note that read:

My darling Glenda,

Pray that I am able to destroy this note and you never read it. I didn't tell you, but I came up here to hide these tapes. They all concern my beliefs about Tom Carr and CCG, but one is more important than the rest. That is the one Desi gave me and I have listened to and heard Tom Carr threaten my life. The other four are Desi's and my conversations and my thoughts about CCG.

If you read this, know that I love you more than you would ever dream. You've been my life and you are my soul. I leave you many things to remember me by because I want you and our son or daughter never to forget. Sweetheart, I love you, love you, love you—forever.

Your love and lover,
Cree

Tears ran down Raven's face as she handed the note to Adam who read it closely.

"We don't have a playback machine here," he said. "We'll listen to the tapes as soon as we get back."

As she stood in the doorway between the living and the dining room she turned to Adam, saying, "Pray that the one tape has what we need. Why else would he hide them where he did?"

Adam looked thoughtful. "I hope you're right, love. That would take us a long way toward making his killer pay."

"And the same person almost surely killed Desi."

"Yeah. The wheels are in motion now. All we can do is pray. At least, thank God, no one has struck at you since Merla's kidnapping. My guess is that he realized he had overtipped his hand and is aware that more policemen are watching you since then."

She hugged herself and shuddered with a sudden chill. "I don't know, love, it's almost as bad waiting until he strikes again and I'm sure he will. I haven't felt followed.

No calls, no nothing. In spite of myself I've gotten a rest and it surely is a welcome wedding present."

"You'd better believe it. Enjoy your mini-honeymoon?"

She hugged him hard. "Thanks to you and your expertise, it was fabulous."

His lips roved her face with small, wet kisses. "Thanks to your response. You're the fabulous one. Honey, you *are* wonderful."

"Um-m, *you* are. Okay, we both are with each other. May it never end!"

"I don't expect it to. We'll tend our love carefully and thank God for it every day of our lives."

She patted his face that was so dear to her. "I'm glad we packed and loaded the car last night while we still had the energy. Now for breakfast. What would you like?"

He glanced at his watch. "Six-thirty. We have plenty of time. Oh, pancakes and eggs scrambled with sharp cheese, bacon."

Raven heard the music of her cell phone then announcing Merla's call. Smiling she picked it up. "Hey baby, how're you?"

The child's voice reflected happiness. "Mommy, Mrs. Reuben said I should thank you for calling me every day, so thank you. When are you coming back?"

"How does today grab you?"

Merla laughed merrily. "Super. Mom, there've been a lot of policemen around here since you and Adam went on your honeymoon. Well, maybe not a lot—Mrs. Reuben says I exaggerate—but two or three."

"I'm glad, love. They're supposed to come around."

"One had coffee with Mrs. Reuben and me yesterday."

"Oh?"

"And Papa Mac spent nights with us. Did you tell him to?"

"Sweetie, it's just another way of keeping you safe."

"I'm glad. I know I keep saying I was scared, but I was."

"I would have been too. You were so brave. Listen, we've got to rustle up some breakfast and I'll see you in a few hours."

"What did you get me?"

"Well, we haven't stopped anywhere to get anything. This is a country setting. No stores. What do you say you and I go shopping Saturday and you can take your pick— that is if you don't break me."

"Break you?"

"Break my bank account."

"I won't. Mom, I love you—a whole lot."

"And I love you even more."

"Let me speak to Adam, please."

"Sure thing." Raven handed the phone to Adam.

"How's my princess?"

"Great. I just want to say it's super having you for a dad. You're the best."

"Then that makes us a mutual admiration society of two. I love you, baby. I couldn't love you more."

"Me too. Hurry back."

Adam hung up then and handed the phone back to Raven. "Lord," he said, "I'm making out like a bandit. A woman I worship and another kid I couldn't love more." He chuckled. "You notice Ricky's called every day. He really loves you, honey, and he's as happy as a clam at high tide."

She went to the blinds in the living room and opened them, looked outside at the car and frowned.

"What is it?" Adam came closer and looked out too.

"On top of the car, there's a big white envelope. See it?"

"I sure do. Let me get into my pants and I'll go see what it is."

"I'm going with you. I'll just put on my coat. We won't be out but a minute."

Adam felt a finger of dread trace along his spine and Raven felt her heartbeat accelerate. All at once she thought of dangers. Letter bomb? Another threat?

"Maybe someone is passing out flyers."

"Best thing is just to check."

Clothes on, they went out into the icy air where Adam eyed the envelope at first, then patted it gingerly thinking it was too flat to be a letter bomb. Written on the front were the words RAVEN and ADAM.

"What the hell?" Adam exploded. The envelope was perfectly flat, so it was almost certainly another threat and his stomach cramped with fury. It was not sealed and there was no clasp, so he opened it and slipped out a couple of eight-by-ten color photographs.

And both gasped with shock because the photographs were of them romping in the front yard the first day they were at the cabin.

"My God," Raven whispered, her throat dry with fear.

Adam swore then, ugly words he never used, because for the moment he felt helpless before a flood of strength rose in him along with the savage anger. "Let's get inside," he said. "We'll fix something to eat and we'll head back. I want to have this checked by a lab that can do it quickly."

And they both thought this meant that the killer had watched them, maybe followed them up from D.C. He had watched as they had taken their suitcases out and put them in the house. And Raven felt violated deep inside herself. Their passion belonged to them and was private, but some monster had declared war and said no, everything about them belonged to him and they *had* no privacy.

They went inside and he took her in his arms, said grimly, "Baby, you're trembling. Listen, you're my woman. I love you. I'll protect you or die trying." He kissed her face, soothed her.

She felt sick then that she had brought this horror and heartache into his life. He was a peaceful man who had known only one terrible trauma with the death of his first wife. But how long would *this* last? Bitterly she felt it could go on forever.

Chapter 20

Adam and Raven were quiet as they began the trek home. Suddenly she shivered and hugged herself in the warm air of the car.

Adam glanced at her. "What's wrong, honey?"

"Goose going over my grave, I guess. What in the hell could be the meaning of these photographs?"

"It's possibly a prank of some teenagers who live in that neck of the woods."

"I don't think so. I think it's the hellhound's work."

Adam was silent for a long while. That's what he thought too, but he hated to see her so upset. And he was just as upset. He began to say it was their honeymoon and they weren't going to think about bad things, but that wasn't possible. They both lived largely in reality, the good and the bad, and this was close to the worst.

She glanced down at the floor at the metal box holding the tapes. "At least I'm glad we found these. Even if the missing tape isn't there, there's probably other evidence we can use. And I'm a willing witness to what Desi told me."

Adam sighed deeply and thought, *A witness and it puts*

your life in danger. More and more he felt that Tom Carr and Kevin were twin culprits, each with his own ax to grind. And he, Adam, was going after them both with no holds barred. Poor Desi.

Raven glanced over at him and put her hand on his thigh. "I keep thinking how much Cree and Desi would have loved the wedding and teasing me about our honeymoon. Both were romantics to the core. I wish you'd known Desi better. She didn't always run her life to her advantage, but she meant well, had a wonderful heart."

"She surely didn't deserve what she got."

They were halfway home when Raven switched on the radio, saying "Let's have a taste of broadcast reality."

And they had almost missed it. The classical music station was giving a brief spot of hourly news. "Tom Carr, CEO of Citizens' Charity Group, commonly referred to as CCG, suffered a massive heart attack this morning and is in intensive care in a local hospital. A spokesperson for the hospital said Carr is doing as well as can be expected."

The announcer moved on to the weather then and Raven's fingers on Adam's thigh tensed. "Good Lord," she murmured and sat up straighter.

Adam grunted. "This sure changes things. We'll listen to the tapes and I'll call Glen Thompson. He'll need to know what's on the tapes, even if it doesn't sound like much. And if we're lucky enough to hit pay dirt…"

It was eleven when they pulled into the driveway and Adam looked at his beautiful house. "The old girl never looked so good," he said.

Adam parked near the front door saying he would park in the garage later. As they got out of the car, Adam said, "Wait."

"Okay. Why?"

He caught her hand and walked a short distance to the door in the cold December air that was no colder than the fear that permeated her body.

At the door, he unlocked it and smiled softly as he picked her up and carried her over the threshold. As he put her down, his voice was very gentle. "I'm gonna love you for the rest of my life. Remember that."

"I will," she promised, "but you could never love me more than I love you."

He got their bags from the car, the metal box tucked under his arm.

They decided to listen to the five tapes before they called Ricky and Merla and the others. They were both tense with anxiety, but both felt a closeness they hoped would last forever.

The five tapes were neatly lined up in the box. The first tape was simply conversations between Cree and Desi about CCG and where it was headed. Cree said he was beginning to despise Tom's leadership and was working with the board member who intended to go public with his dissatisfaction and with formal charges. "We've both got to be careful," Desi said. "Fortunately for us, Tom's arrogant. We're his hirelings and he'd never think of us going against him."

"Yeah," Cree said grimly, "but Allen might think about it. He's a different fish in that kettle."

The second tape recorded conversations again about CCG leadership and where it was going, but there were snippets about Tom's life. "Laverne's got him over the barrel about his womanizing, I hear," Desi said. "He's riding high, but Laverne's holding his feet to the fire. I know a second cousin and he tells me a lot. You know she had all the money in the beginning. She's sort of cold to his heartless heat. Now he's made plenty of money, but she still has the long-time social standing and as a man who began life poor, he seems to dote on that. They manage to stay together, but the cousin says she's the wife from hell. I'd say they deserve each other."

Raven sighed. "Interesting, Cree and Desi, but where is the tape Desi gave you, the one we're looking for? The one we *need*?"

And about a quarter of the way through the third tape, the recorder went silent with only the whirring of an un-recorded tape as Raven and Adam held their breath. Then they heard it. Cree's taut voice accused Tom. "It's a damned shame what you're doing to CCG and I'm tell-ing you I've found evidence, solid evidence about what's going on."

And Tom's unctuous voice. "What evidence have you found that'll stand up? I'm a big man in a pretty big city here and who are you?"

Cree laughed harshly. "I'm one of the concerned citi-zens that make up this group as well as an accountant in a position to know what you're siphoning off. I know you've got your own special man in to doctor the books— cook the books—but I've been able to see where you're taking this outfit and you have a choice. Stop it or I'll blow the whistle on you."

Raven cringed as she listened. Cree, no, she told him silently. You don't threaten a rattlesnake, you move on it. But then Cree being Cree would have wanted to simply stop what was going on, make Tom realize the error of his ways. He never wanted to hurt anybody and he paid for that benevolence with his life.

She was so deep into seeing Cree as Adam sat with half closed eyes that only Tom's angry voice on the cassette brought her back. "Watch your step, Hawkins. If you know what you say you know, then you know too damned much. I can have you taken care of so you won't be shooting off your mouth to anyone."

"Are you threatening me?"

"You're damned right I'm threatening you. You've got a pregnant wife. You've got a good job with me and I once considered taking you under my wing, but you were always a little too goody-two-shoes for me. A churchgoing old boy. You need to grow up, Hawkins."

"And you're an example?"

"I've got the life you'd like to have and you're going to lose the one you have if you keep going down the road you're going."

"You *are* threatening me. Don't make the mistake of becoming a killer in addition to everything else."

"Oh, *I* wouldn't do it, Hawkins. There are other ways. But I like you, so I'm going to make this emphatically clear. You go to the cops with this and you're dead meat. I'll see you dead and in hell first. No, *I* won't do it, but I'm sure going to set it up."

There was silence again, then Cree said with a heavy sigh, "I'm sorry, Tom, really sorry. I thought you were made of better stuff than this."

"And I sure thought you were made of *smarter* stuff, boy. Here I'm offering you the world. Name your price, man. Name it and it's yours. I'm not looking for trouble. I just damned sure intend to keep what I have." His voice held a desperate edge. "I don't mind telling you I'd kill to keep what I have, only I don't have to. I can pay to have it done. That's all I've got to say. Now if you're as smart as I think you are…"

The machine played only the whirring sound after that and the harsh words hung in the air between Adam and Raven.

Adam bent forward, let the tape run on with nothing else recorded. "Well, I can smell the acrid smoke of *that* gun," Adam said as the tape ran out. "Any voice-proofing machine will verify Tom's and Cree's voices. And of course it's only a threat, but it gives us reason to go after Carr. Only he's lying in intensive care in a hospital. Make a copy, honey. I want to get this to Special Investigations this afternoon, see what Glen thinks of it. It's the best thing we have."

"Yes, and if Desi told Kevin about the tapes and Kevin told Tom—and we're pretty sure he did—then that would be a reason to kill her, or have her killed."

Adam moved over on the sofa and took Raven in his arms. "This is such a damned, snarled mess."

She looked so tense, so bothered that Adam hurt for her. He kissed her face and throat and simply held her for a very long time.

Then Raven called Merla and Adam called Ricky and it wasn't long before both were there, Merla first with Mrs. Reuben and Papa Mac.

By then, Raven had brightened. "Oh," she said to Papa Mac, "you're still around, are you?"

"You bet I am." He smiled at Mrs. Reuben. "I like the silver fox's company."

Raven laughed. "The silver fox, huh."

Merla went into her mother's arms for hugs and kisses. "I had a real good time, Mom. Papa Mac said those are glorious times you had on your honeymoon. Am I going to have a glorious time on *my* honeymoon, Mom?"

Raven gave the child another squeeze. "You bet you are, honey," and Merla moved over for more hugs and kisses from Adam.

Ricky came a few minutes later. He had stayed with his Uncle Marty and his Aunt Caitlin.

As Ricky came in for a bear hug, Adam teased him. "Ah, I see you managed to do without me for a few days. You look good to me."

"Hey! Uncle Marty and Aunt Caitlin are fun! Their twins are more fun than a barrel of monkeys. Talk about lively! Oh boy! They sure kept me hopping. Pop, any chance of us having twins?"

"Ask your Mom."

Teasingly, Ricky went to Raven. "Hey, Mom. Can you have Merla and me some twin brothers or sisters? Please."

Laughing, Raven ruffled his hair. "I'm not sure, but one thing we do know is if you marry a woman with twins in her background, you're likely to have your own set. You've just got eight or nine more years to wait."

Ricky groaned. "I'm impatient. Gramma says it's in my genes. I get it from you, Dad. That's too long to wait. Oh well, I'll keep asking—and wishing."

"And who knows," Adam said with half closed eyes, "but what wishes sometimes come true."

Adam's cell phone rang. He picked it up, walked back to the bay windows to talk, then came back.

"Honey, that was Allyson," he said. "Some early DNA evidence has come back on Desi and she needs my help to decide on the next steps. I'll be back in a couple of hours, and I'm going to drop that tape by Glen's."

Raven nodded and he squeezed her hand.

Before she could blot it out, she had a crystal-clear vision of Allyson in Adam's arms as she, Raven, had been. Allyson was twenty-eight, younger than Raven had been when she married Kevin, young enough to be sure to give Adam healthy babies without worry. Would Adam regret marrying her, Raven, one day? Maybe even now? A tender note he probably wasn't aware of always crept into his tone when he spoke of Allyson.

Adam was gone by the time she finished thinking and Papa Mac came and sat beside her. "Hey, you're in a dream world. Tell us as much as you can about your honeymoon on Green Mountain."

And Raven thought, dream world? Both a precious dream *and* nightmare.

"Yeah Mom, tell us," Merla chortled.

And going along with their program, Raven told them, "I'll make it into the fairy tale it was and I'll begin with once upon a time."

But she couldn't tell them about the photographs on top of the car the morning they left Green Mountain, and she couldn't tell them about the after-knowledge that someone, likely the hellhound, had malevolently watched them, plotting and planning his evil deeds.

Chapter 21

At her office the next morning, as Raven walked about the newsroom, she listened to the buzz about Tom Carr's heart attack. He had once been a frequent visitor to WMRY and the station had been very much a part of CCG's annual ball. Now, Raven reflected, the station's annual dinner-dance was going to be a very different affair this year.

Viveca came into the newsroom from her cubicle and hugged Raven. "Carey's coming over a bit later," she began as Carey walked in the door, came to Raven and hugged her.

"We're racing, you know," he said, "and right now we're ahead."

Raven understood that they were talking about the baby race and she smiled. "So you're ahead. Twins run in Adam's family you know." Then it dawned on her. "Oh, you're pregnant! Honey, you're *pregnant*! Congratulations! Maybe *I* am already, too."

Viveca's face lit up with all the warm thoughts that went with a baby's birth. "Oh, that'll be fun. Have you picked a godmother?"

"Adam wants us to ask Dosha and I think she's a very good choice."

Viveca and Carey both nodded their agreement. Carey frowned, saying, "Too bad about Carr's heart attack."

"Yes," Raven said. "This throws a monkey wrench into our investigation. I hope he pulls through; he's a fighter."

Ken's secretary, Hilary, came to them. "Ken would like to see you as soon as possible."

"Bye babes," Raven told them. "I'll see you both later."

Ken looked rumpled, as if he hadn't slept well as he got up from his desk and walked over to two chairs. "Sit down, love. You look a bit hassled as I'm sure I do. How was the honeymoon?"

She didn't want to talk about the hellhound's photographs this morning, but Ken had asked her to always tell him what was going on. She thought she'd begin with the good stuff. "The honeymoon was wonderful and thank you for asking." She was silent then for a very long moment and he studied her.

"But there's something else. The hellhound?"

"Ken, I'm beginning to wonder if this is ever going to stop. I'm frazzled and getting used up."

His face clouded with anger as he leaned forward and patted her knee. "I'm sorry and I wish I knew when it'll be over. If they can only get a break in Desi's case. That missing last tape…"

"I have it for you to listen to. You were with a couple of people when I came in. We found it and it's in my tote bag. I brought a recorder."

"Hey, that's great. I'll listen in a little while. Is it all we thought it was?"

"It is and more. We hear Tom directly threaten to have Cree killed if he intends to be a witness against him." She shook her head. "I didn't call and leave a message because I wanted to tell you this face to face and you were out."

"Yeah, I was."

"I'm wondering about my mind, Ken. I'm beginning to forget things. Maybe I just want, or need, to forget."

Ken's eyes narrowed and he spoke slowly, watching her face as he asked the question. "Did anything untoward happen on your honeymoon? God, I hope not."

Her breath shallowed with anxious memory. "Something happened all right."

She told him about the photographs as he frowned. "Good Lord."

He got up then and began to pace from his desk and back to her then, to the door and back. "What is Adam saying about all this?"

"What can he say? You know they're doing all they can to catch the killer and we're assuming this is the same man who killed Desi."

"I think it's a good assumption."

"I'm having lunch with Adam. Now that Tom's in the hospital and unlikely to get well soon from all the info we can gather, maybe things will slow down. But of course there's always Kevin. If nothing slows down, perhaps that will be our answer."

Ken sat with clasped hands. "I get mad as hell when I think about what Kevin put you through. Both he and Tom had reason to kill Desi. She had something on them both and they are malevolent men."

"Ken, could we not talk any more about Tom or Kevin or the hellhound? Just for the minute?"

"You've got it. This is hell on you." He grinned crookedly. "Viveca's talked with me about taking time off when she gets pregnant. You're so efficient, you probably got pregnant on your honeymoon. What am I gonna do around here without either of you? You're my favorite people and you're my special favorite." He sat forward then, his hands clasped. "I'm gonna miss you, love."

Raven laughed a bit. "I'll be around quite a while, even pregnant, but you're kind to say you'll miss me." She started to tell him about Viveca's pregnancy, but decided she'd let Viveca do the honors.

"Quite a while isn't long enough. I suppose you've got a godfather."

She nodded. "As a matter of fact, Adam's brother, Marty, wants to be godfather." She broke off with a little laugh. "All this deep conversation and I don't know that I'm pregnant. All this trouble with the hellhound makes it more difficult to conceive, I'd think."

He leaned over and took her hands in his. "I'm with you all the way, all the time, babe. I just wish I were in Adam's shoes. Now don't get embarrassed. You've heard this song before."

"You're a dear friend, Ken," she said slowly, "and you've always been there for me."

"And I always will be."

Raven got the recorder with the tape in it. Ken stopped all calls, locked his door and they listened. Several times he rewound and listened more intently. When it had ended, a deep frown creased his forehead and he breathed harder.

"Glen is gonna love this. Get it to him right away."

"This is a copy. Adam took the original to Glen."

In the hallway Raven's cell phone announced Adam. She dug into her jacket pocket and answered.

"Hello, honey," his baritone voice caressed her.

"You're the honey," she responded. "You're just the sweetest man on earth."

"With the sweetest woman at my side. I want to run something by you."

"What and when?"

"You're a feisty broad and you're not gonna like this one damned bit, but I think it's necessary. There's a little Italian restaurant almost halfway between us. Great food. Do you know where I'm talking about?"

"Gino's. Yes."

"Can you meet me there at one?"

"I'm free. Not much is going on. I'm going to go farther on downtown after I meet you. I promised Ricky I'd pick him up one of those video games he wants, so we can't take long."

"I can order the food and they'll have it ready."

"Just pasta and a salad for me and oh yes, tell them to make sure it's with their meat sauce I hear is scrumptious."

"You want it. You got it."

She smiled when she hung up the phone. She'd just left him a few hours ago and already she hungered to see him again. Like a schoolgirl she sat mooning and thought: *My love, my one and only romantic love.*

At the tiny restaurant, they sat in a booth in the crowded room. Gino's was warm and friendly and Gino brought their food almost as soon as they sat down. The short, roly-poly owner stood over them. "Detective and Mrs. Steele," he greeted them. "You don't come often enough with your beautiful wife, Detective."

"Keep up the good work and it's for sure I'll be bringing her more often." Adam and Gino had a wonderful camaraderie and Raven fit right in.

They ate quickly in silence, drinking merlot wine. And not until they were finished did she ask what he wanted to talk about.

His eyes roved her beloved face and he looked very somber. "I'm going to get you a bodyguard."

"Oh Adam, they're prohibitive, and I *hate* the idea."

"I've got that inheritance in the bank and I can't think of a better way to spend it. Hell, for that matter I'd spend the last nickel of my pay. We both make good salaries. I've been calling around, checking out guys who've gone into the very best security agencies. They don't come cheap, the really good guys, but they're worth it."

To take the edge off the gravity of what they talked about, she teased, "Whitney Houston and her bodyguard fell in love in that movie."

Adam laughed. "You fall in love with yours and I'll fall on you hard." His eyes twinkled as he amended, "I'll fall on you with a love that will sweep any bodyguard away."

It was her turn to get sober and she was surprised to find tears in her eyes. "I don't *want* a bodyguard," she blurted out. "I don't run scared, Adam, ever. Or I like to think I don't."

Adam looked at her levelly. "Everybody runs scared at some point, love. It's the better part of common sense. You were shaking with fear the night you came back into my life. I've felt your heart thud after one of the hellhound's calls. You were ashen with fear when Merla was abducted. We're both scared, sweetheart, and we've reason to be. Too much has already happened…"

"Tom's heart attack may make a difference."

"Don't grasp at straws, honey. There's always his man, Allen, to carry on. And there's always Kevin."

"I don't want to live my life in a cage."

"Better to live in a cage until we can get to the bottom of this than to lose your life. I'm sure not going to stand still for that."

"I'll think about it."

His face got set then. "You think fast because I'm convinced this is best. I want you to begin interviews day after tomorrow."

"I'll think about it," was all she could manage to say as her stomach churned.

"I need to move on," she said, "and pick up that video game."

"Ricky loves you, you know. You've been wonderful for him."

"And you've been wonderful for Merla."

"We've got it in spades, sweetheart. Make up your mind you'll go along with me. It's best, I know."

It felt good walking the six blocks to pick up the video game. The air was crisply cold and she drew her belted navy melton cloth coat around her. She couldn't stop thinking about Tom Carr in the hospital lying helpless. Would this change things? Not if Kevin were involved with him.

In the store, she also selected a junior video game for Merla. The fact that Merla loved Ricky didn't make the little girl any less competitive. He called her "My Merla" sometimes and it tickled the child.

Raven was walking briskly down the street when she became aware of a man looking at her, following too closely behind her. She looked in every shop window for two blocks and he was always there. A tall, slender man with pecan-colored skin and curly black hair. He certainly didn't look threatening. And she couldn't help wondering if the hellhound looked threatening. Some of the world's worst murderers looked like perfectly ordinary citizens.

Her heart began to thump painfully and she wished Adam were beside her. Maybe she did need a bodyguard. It couldn't hurt. It was just that she wanted an ordinary life for herself and her family. She would argue for a week to decide.

She stopped suddenly, throwing the man who was just behind her off balance.

"Why are you following me?" she demanded in a bold, harsh voice that she hoped hid her fear.

For a moment he stammered, then he said, "I'm sorry. I didn't mean to scare you. I won't hurt you."

"I'm not scared of you. What do you *want*?" Was she being a fool to talk with him?

The man shook his head. He was actually a very decent-looking man, but he looked sad beyond belief, and shaken. Had *she* scared *him*? Was he drunk? On drugs? Crazy?

"What do you *want*?" she demanded again when he was silent.

"The woman I love walked out on me. I was fooling around and she left me. I saw you as you walked to the store and I stood at the window and watched you shopping. God, the two of you look so much alike. I thought you might be like me now, alone. It happens."

Angrily Raven felt pity along with fear and it made her angrier still. Why was she sorry for him? He could be the hellhound.

"I won't bother you again," he said. "You probably already have someone who loves you the way I'd love you."

"Get a grip on yourself," she told him. "Don't you have friends you can talk with?"

He shook his head as she saw the glint of tears in his eyes. "No. We were always enough for each other until I got scared of being in love, afraid she'd leave me, so I began to leave first. You think I'm crazy, don't you? Well maybe I am. I don't suppose you'd talk with me."

Her first impulse was to say yes and she felt on the edge of hysteria.

"No! Stop following me!" Why did she want to help him?

"Okay, but thanks for talking with me even this little bit. It's helped me. You're so beautiful. I could love you the way I love her."

She had to say it. "Ask her to forgive you, take you back."

"She's with another man now and they love each other. I *did* ask her. She laughed at me. Thank you more than you know."

He turned then and she watched him slowly walk away and was embarrassed when he turned to get a last look at her and found her looking at him.

That night when she told Adam about the encounter he was angry. "Why would you stop to talk with a man who could be your tormentor? I'm insisting that we get a bodyguard for you. The interviews with me have already begun. Fear takes his toll on our minds, baby. It clouds our judgment. I don't think you should have talked with this man at all."

"Are you mad at me?"

"No," he said sadly. "I love you. I just mean to keep you safe."

In spite of everything, she slept soundly in Adam's arms. Before drifting off, she asked him to make love to her which he did with fervor.

Then at one in the morning she came awake, got up,

went down to the kitchen to get a glass of water because her mouth was dry with continuing fear she kept trying to master. She stood with her back to the sink sipping a bottle of water when the cell phone she carried in her robe pocket rang.

She flipped on the talk button and said "Hello," her voice hoarse with anxiety.

There was a chuckle on the line this time, low and malevolent.

"This is your executioner," the hateful voice said. "Your time will be very soon."

Chapter 22

Next morning, Raven still felt the torment in her bones. They all got up early because they were driving to Mel and Rispa's. Adam held her close and stroked her. "Maybe you'd better give up the cell phone. We can cut down on the bastard's calls if Mrs. Reuben answers the phone when she's here and I answer it too."

Raven shook her head. "I don't let the children answer the phone anymore and Mrs. Reuben works here; she shouldn't be exposed. Besides, he calls on my cell phone most times. Honey, I'm an investigative reporter; that's my *job*. I have informants calling me at all hours with truly good information. No, that won't work. I just have to tough it out."

They sat on the side of the bed and Adam continued to rub her back. "A day in the country will do us both good. Informants and tips or not, leave the cell phone here."

"I can't. Ken needs to get in touch with me from time to time. He doesn't take advantage of that, but there are times…"

"Okay, but today, let me answer all the time."

"We've tried that and the hellhound just gets nastier when I do answer. He's commanded me to answer my own phone."

"And you're afraid to cross him? Honey, we both know that won't work."

Sick with frustration, she felt hot tears in her eyes. "Then what *will* work? You don't know the half of it, love. Yesterday, I was ready to tear into that strange man, I was so scared. I was nearly over the edge."

He hugged her again. "I can certainly see why."

"Then I remembered you, that I have you on my side and by my side and I calmed down. I have to get a grip."

Ricky and Merla knocked and came in, fully dressed.

"Have you two had time to shower?" she asked.

"Hey, we were up at the crack of dawn. We've even had cereal and I made coffee. Country, here we come!"

The kids came to them for their morning hugs and kisses. And Raven sat beside Adam thinking her life would be one prolonged blessing if she didn't have the hellhound lurking with his evil intent in the background.

Adam had called his family intermittently on the way to say where they were. As they drove up, Raven thrilled at the beauty of the Steele estate with its big stone house, painted a glistening white with dark blue shutters and massive shrubbery. A black wrought-iron fence surrounded it and acres of woodland lay on the sides and in back. Oh, it was a wonderful place and the newly fallen snows simply enhanced its beauty. Several cars were parked in the driveway.

As they pulled over the cattle guard and into the driveway, the front door burst opened and people spilled out.

Dosha reached them first with fervent hugs and kisses, then Mel and Rispa and Marty and Caitlin.

Marty clapped Ricky on the back. "I swear boy, it won't be long before you've outgrown me."

Ricky grinned, looking up at his tall uncle. "That'll be the day."

Mel and Rispa hugged Raven and Adam and Rispa's eyes on Raven were a bit sad, remembering what she was going through.

"Where're the twins?" Adam asked.

"Inside where it's warm, chafing at the bit. Ah, those two," Caitlin shook her head. "I've found my first gray hair, but I'm happy."

Dosha had moved back from D.C. into an apartment in Minden. Adam asked her how she liked it. "I love it. I'm composing now along with my teaching. I hired a woman to cook, clean up."

At the doorway they were greeted by the big major-domo of the house, Roy, and his lively wife, Sarah. More hugs. And the twins stood before them, still for once with fingers in their mouths. Adam scooped up Caleb Myles with a bear hug and Raven held Malinda and kissed the fat, peach-fuzz cheeks.

"How in the world do you put them down long enough to do your work?" Raven asked Caitlin.

"Believe me, it isn't easy. They've long been spoiled. We have someone now to stay with them during the day, but they're ours come nightfall. I don't mind telling you they're a handful."

Raven looked around her, struck by the simple home-yness of the place. Spacious living room and parlor, a dining room all done in pale plum and a country kitchen and breakfast nook to die for, all done in yellow enamel and stainless steel. The furniture was mixed modern and traditional, the floors carpeted in deep plum with oriental throw rugs. And there was a huge fieldstone fireplace, very much like the one in Adam and Raven's house.

Raven felt a calmness then at the center of her being. Her doctor had said she thought they could tell if Raven were pregnant at around a month or before. That was one blood test she longed to take.

Rispa's lovely face glowed with happiness because she was surrounded by her beloved family, except for Damien, and her heart hurt for her young twin son who could never seem to get it together the way the rest of his siblings did. Oh, he was successful enough with his recording company in Nashville and his songwriting, but he flitted from woman to woman, with the chief woman in his life one Rispa didn't really like.

At a small scream from Caitlin, Rispa turned. Caleb Myles was gleefully pulling Malinda's hair and she was punching him with tiny fists and crying.

"Here, here!" Caitlin cried. "How many times do I have to tell you?" She firmly pulled the two apart and they reached for each other, hugging and kissing.

"No!" Caleb Myles declared. "No, no!" Then said it a couple more times for emphasis.

Caitlin sighed. "I don't have to tell you they're beginning the "No" stage early. They're not two yet, but they're into the "terrible two's" already. Lord, doesn't that give us something to look forward to."

"No," Caleb Myles said again and this time his twin took it up as Marty lifted his son who now clutched a yellow plastic duck.

"Let's put this aside for the moment," Marty said. "You'll have it in your mouth in a hot minute."

"No!" the baby shouted again, laughing. And said it twice more.

"Okay," Marty said, "we'll see about your 'no's.' How about half a raisin oatmeal cookie?" He walked over to the buffet with the child in his arms, picked up a cookie and cut it with a case knife. "Now, let's see," he teased his son, "Want a cookie? What d'you say?"

But Caleb Myles was set in his path and yelled "No," again as he took the cookie and began to stuff it in his mouth.

Marty's face was wreathed in smiles as he shook his head. "Lord, let noon come quickly. That's their nap time—when they let it be. You talk about your barrel of monkeys, they're it." He put Caleb Myles down and picked up Malinda who had her chubby little arms stretched toward him. "You wanna be daddy's girl, do you? Kid, where *is* your mother?"

Caitlin laughed. "Right here, resting for my turn. We're gonna have to settle for these two. I'd be terrified of getting pregnant again, afraid of another pair of livewires like these. We'd have to hire a battery of nannies."

Dosha watched the scene, dreaming. Her body quickened every time she saw her niece and nephew. She couldn't wait to have her own kids to love with the kind of love she'd always known.

Suddenly Malinda got fretful and began to cry, rearing back hard in her father's arms. "Baby, what is it? Does something hurt you?" Marty looked at her carefully.

He tried to hold her close, but she wasn't having it. Her little brown face was reddened with wails nobody could stop. "Oh yeah," Marty told her, "I think I remember another time like this. Let's have some music, y'all. That'll soothe this savage beast." He patted his baby's back.

Adam came forward, grinning. "I think I can help here." He reached into his shirt pocket, brought out a harmonica and blew a long, lonesome riff. Malinda quieted, looked at the silver instrument and held out her hand to it.

"Like it, do you?" Marty smiled and kissed Malinda's face. "I see you're planning to be like your Uncle Damien, musically inclined."

And Malinda lisped, "Moosic," pursing her lips.

"What would you like to hear, kid?" Adam asked Malinda.

And the baby repeated, "Moosic."

"Pretty good for not quite two," Marty said. "Boy, these two are really something."

"Hell," Adam said as he stopped playing a moment. "They come from Dad here and Frank's Singing Steeles, how could they miss?"

Adam played "Londonderry Air" and Caleb Myles came to him and hugged his leg as Adam reached down and picked him up. The baby lay against his chest, soothed by the tune before he began to giggle.

Marty moved close to them. "Like that tune, do you?"

Caleb Myles was predictable. "No."

Roy came in. "Sarah wants you to know we're eating dinner early on account of the kids."

"Fine," Rispa said.

By then Mel was on his hands and knees giving Malinda a horsey ride and she was loving every minute as she pounded his back and yelled, "Giddyup horsey!"

"They're precocious," Raven said.

"Thank you. We love them so much and they're doing so well," Caitlin told her. She knocked on a wooden table nearby, saying "Please God, let it always be so."

Mel set the CD player up to play gospel music then

and they sat around listening to the Singing Steeles as the music soothed them all.

> *Go down Moses, way down in Egypt land*
> *Tell ol' Pharoah to let my people go!*

In the midst of that gorgeous music, Raven's cell phone rang and she tensed. Coolly, Adam took the phone from her and answered. It was Ken. "Just checking to see if Raven's doing okay."

"So far, so good," Adam answered. "Hold on to speak with her."

She sat where she was and chatted with Ken a few minutes before he said, "I wouldn't have horned in on your family gathering, but I was bothered about you and I wanted reassurance that you're okay."

"Thanks, and yes, I'm doing okay," she answered hollowly. "Let me talk with you tomorrow or Monday, but we may spend the night here."

"Sure thing. Take care, Raven. You're precious to me."

Raven hung up. The call had brought the whole terror back to her. She licked dry lips. What was it the fiend had said, "*This is your executioner*"? And the words went ricocheting down the corridors of her mind. "*Who are you?*" she whimpered inside and no answers came at all.

Merla sat by Dosha, silently adoring her. She would be flower girl the next July when Dosha got married. "Listen," Dosha said, "we're all going to put on our snow clothes and play in the snow a while. We don't have a snowman yet and we've got to have one."

The stretch of snowed-under lawn they finally chose was on one side of the house. Raven took her camera to record the lovely old white house nestled in the wind-swept, pristine snow. Drifted piles of snow invited Merla and Ricky to dive in and come up laughing and sputtering with wet faces. Strong sunlight made the house windows sparkle and Ricky and Merla couldn't wait to throw snowballs.

The twins in their snowsuits looked like chubby angels as Raven picked Caleb Myles up. He reached out and patted her face and looking at that smooth, smooth silken skin her heart felt full to bursting. Then she felt the pressure of Malinda's little arms around her legs and began laughing as she said to Adam, "I need some help here."

Marty came over. "Here," he said, "let me."

But Adam was there first. "You have them all the time, so let *me*."

Adam stood close to Raven as each held a twin. They looked up to see Ricky and Merla standing nearby grinning. "All we want to know is when do we get a baby?" Merla asked.

And Raven teased them. "When you grow up and have your own."

"You promised," Ricky said.

Even bundled in a snowsuit, the sweet weight of the baby in her arms made Raven glow as she looked at her husband and his heart leapt at the sight of what he saw in her eyes. Hers leapt in turn at what she saw in his.

Finally Raven and Adam gave the babies to Marty and Caitlin who alternately let them sit on the snow a little while then held them.

Ricky and Merla were in heaven as they rolled in the snow, then started the snowman under Mel's direction.

"Now we want one big enough to last a while," Mel explained. They were on a hill and decided to build the snowman halfway up it. Mel had brought a carrot, an old pipe, charcoal for the eyes, nose and mouth. There was a long broomstick he had saved all winter in anticipation of this. He had remembered to bring an old black derby hat, a jacket and a colorful red, yellow and green plaid scarf.

"Merla will do the head, Ricky the upper body, and the big, bottom part needs a man to handle it. That will be me."

"Aw grampa, I could do it," Ricky protested.

"Sure you *could*," Mel came back, "but you need something to look forward to. Now, when you're my age and have grandchildren of your own, you'll just instinctively know how to build the world's best snowman."

Ricky stood looking at his grandfather with awe. He had trouble imagining himself as a man his father's age even though he longed for that day to come, but to be Mel's age was beyond anything he could imagine. He liked the part about kids though. As an only child he wanted a dozen kids of his own.

Adam came to Raven as she stood a little apart, looking at the growing snowman and at Mel rolling the snowball that got bigger and bigger until he was satisfied.

"Oh, let me put his clothes on please." Merla was beside herself with joy.

"What do you know about a man's clothes?" Ricky scoffed.

"Hey, I helped Mom pick out some jammies and underwear for Dad. I know plenty."

Ricky rolled his eyes. "Well maybe."

At last the snowman was finished and stood in his naked splendor, until Merla slowly and painstakingly slipped on his clothes, taking care with the broomstick arms. Raven snapped photo after photo as the child completed her task and whooped with delight.

"Mom, make sure you snap one picture just for me."

Raven made the A-okay sign. "You bet I will and when you're finished, you can snap your own pictures."

Raven shuddered then and her breath shallowed. "What is it, honey?" Adam asked.

She shook her head because she was thinking of the night Adam and she had romped in the snow on Green Mountain. They had had a ball thinking they were alone when all the time there had been an evil interloper watching them with hellish eyes. Did he watch them even now? Her throat felt bone dry and a small chill coursed the length of her body.

It took her a minute to answer as she tried to smile. "A whole lot of geese have been going over my grave lately, I guess."

His eyes got haunted then and he took her gloved hand, then hugged her. He knew very well what she was likely thinking and his gorge came up again. There had been only that one call since Tom Carr's heart attack, but Kevin was always out there. Raven wanted to think things were slowing down, but were they?

Caitlin went in early with the twins, but the others stayed outside the better part of an hour and they came in famished.

Roy and Sarah had had a great time preparing this particular dinner. They were always happy when the sibs came to visit.

"I've got two specials for you," Sarah told them. "A young pig got run over in the road outside and Roy got him immediately, scraped him down, gutted him and I roasted him. You never tasted anything like this. And there's the cherry pie I put together, with another two, one for each couple to take home. Oh, and cherry ice cream goes with that pie."

"Oh boy!" Ricky licked his lips and rolled his eyes as Merla put her head to one side, saying, "I love cherry pie. Mom makes them, but not often enough. Mrs. Reuben makes a pretty good cherry pie, but not as good as Mom's."

"Well I hope you don't tell her that." Raven patted Merla's head.

"Mom, you know I don't. I know how to hold my tongue."

Dinner was the roasted pig without the head, crispy fried and soft-fried chicken and roast beef. The couscous and the wild rice were fluffy and the green peas and tiny pearl onions were full of Sarah's special flavor. The perfect candied yams were done with Splenda sweetener. Asparagus spears under rich, creamy sauce and collards were cooked with bits of ham. Cornbread as light and delectable as cake, dripping with sweet butter gave Raven an appetite she had not expected to have.

"Anybody want great rolls, they got 'em," Roy announced.

Rispa looked up at Roy and smiled as they were all seated. "Now, once you put the other few dishes on, what d'you say you and Sarah sit down here and enjoy your dinner."

"Well-l-l," Roy began.

"No wells about it," Rispa said firmly. "You always say I'm the boss. Well, just follow my orders here."

A slow smile spread across Roy's face. The people he and Sarah worked for were the best. He often felt he and Sarah were the luckiest couple in the world to have each other and someone like the Steeles to work for.

Merla studied the centerpiece of broadleaf ferns, glad-ioli and mums. "Gramma, the flowers are gor-ge-ous. Did they come from a florist's?"

"Uh-huh. I'm glad you like them. They *are* pretty. Does anybody feel they need rolls? I'll be glad to get some hot ones."

"Now you don't have to do that," Sarah said as she sat down. "You enjoy your dinner."

But everybody was enjoying the cornbread too much to want rolls. Raven's taste buds lit up with a mouthful of the roasted pig. It was absolutely delectable, unlike anything she had ever tasted before. And she sampled the whole cranberries with the hint of lemon flavor. It felt so good to be here with the Steeles, Dosha, Marty, Cait-lin and the twins who sat in high chairs, one on each side of Marty and Caitlin. The babies were noisy, joyful eaters who got as much fun out of pushing their food around as they did eating it. They leaned toward each other con-stantly, and Raven wondered if they remembered their togetherness in the womb. Somehow she was certain they did.

"Hey," Ricky said, "we're forgetting something. Gramma and Grampa, we brought you something. Merla and I chipped in from our allowance and the parents picked up the rest. You're gonna love this."

Rispa smiled. "Well you didn't need to. You all are present enough."

But Ricky had gotten up from the table and gone into the bedroom where they had all piled their things.

Raven shook her head. "I'm getting more absent-minded every day. Ricky's right. I do think you'll like it. We found it at a great estate sale out in Maryland. Lord, the stuff they had."

Then Ricky was back with the large, tissue-wrapped package done in gold colored bows.

"I'm not going to wait to unwrap this," Rispa said. "It looks too lovely."

Wrappings off, Rispa gasped at the large and beautiful white jade fruit bowl with the beautifully carved fruit on the sides.

"Hey," Mel said, "that's really something. It must have set you back a bundle."

"No one could deserve it more," Raven told them.

Rispa got up, came to each chair and kissed Raven, Adam, Merla, then Ricky. "I love this and I love you all. Thank you so much. This goes to use right away. I always wanted one like this, but never saw one anywhere."

"Bless you all for thinking of us." Mel's eyes held a glint of tears.

"It's really pretty," Sarah said, "and it was nice of you to bring it."

"Yeah." Roy smiled. "Reminds me of when I was in the Merchant Marines and over in China. They say jade brings you good luck and this family don't have nothing but good luck."

Raven was silent then. The family's luck had dimmed when Adam's first wife died. Was it going to dim again when the hellhound got through with her?

Raven felt the presence of God and His heaven with the glorious voices of the gospel music that was playing.

"There's one recording Whit's done lately and I made a copy," Rispa said. "He's going to send all of us one. It's 'Wade in the Water,' and I want you and Adam to have it now. Words and music can help sometimes just the way God can." And she said it because she knew about what was wrong in Adam and Raven's life. She wasn't a swearing woman, but nothing was too bad to wish upon the beast of prey who stalked Raven and had kidnapped Merla.

"I love that song," Raven murmured.

Later, when they had finished the cherry pie topped with refrigerator-made cherry ice cream and listened through Beethoven's Sixth Symphony, Raven went upstairs to gather their things. Rispa followed her.

She came to Raven and took her in her arms. "My darling, something new is wrong, isn't it? Hasn't the monster stopped? You haven't said anything."

Raven felt like sobbing. Rispa was so like her own grandmother had been. "It hasn't stopped," she said, but she didn't want to go into the details. She and Adam were doing everything they could. She knew that Rispa and Mel would suffer at her torment and she didn't want that for them.

Then on the drive halfway home the sense of dread took over as Merla dozed off in the back seat and Ricky listened with his earphones to hip-hop music. She moved closer to Adam and he turned, blew her a kiss. "I love you," he said suddenly. "Know that there will never be a time when I don't love you."

"And I love *you*. Can I ever make you know how much I love you?"

Chapter 23

The following morning, Raven came awake slowly with a sense of something being not quite right. Adam lay a little away from her where they usually slept spoon fashion and he murmured in his sleep. At first she couldn't understand and he thrashed around a bit. Then she heard him say, "I don't want to do this to you."

She listened then to hear more, but he was silent, breathing hard. Should she wake him? He slowly roused himself and frowned deeply as she leaned forward and kissed him on his forehead. He caught her close.

"How long have you been awake and looking at me? I was talking in my sleep, wasn't I? I could hear myself, but I couldn't stop myself."

She stroked his face. "Why would you want to stop yourself? Are you keeping secrets?"

He drew a deep breath then and a somber shadow crossed his face. "Sometimes secrets are necessary to protect someone."

"Honey, I don't ever need protection from you. I'm with you whatever happens."

"I know that, but you've got more troubles than one person can stand. I'm not going to add to your burdens. *Our* burdens."

His saying it brought it all back, all of it regarding the hellhound. Right now she could still hear his voice the other night and she shuddered a bit. Her *executioner*. And *soon*. Cold seeped along the marrow of her bones and she drew closer to Adam for warmth. He hugged her for a long minute but seemed preoccupied.

"Adam," she said after a moment. "You'd tell me if you ever came to feel our marriage was a mistake."

He turned and looked at her sharply. "What in the hell would make you say a thing like that?"

She was adamant. "Would you?"

"Why do you ask? We've been married two weeks. Let me be in paradise, will you? What're you doing today at work?"

Such a swift change of subjects. She wouldn't continue to question him, she thought. Let it play out. But she had never known him to be evasive before. And she thought again, she hadn't known him long enough to really know him. Oh, but she did know him in so many ways. For the past day or so he had talked about Allyson more than usual and Allyson had called the house whereas she usually didn't. Let it go, she told herself sharply.

She would coast along with his program. "What're we doing today? Well, Viveca and I are going out to The Gardens to talk with Malcolm about final plans for the December dinner-dance. He's already helped us make some great plans so it should be really nice. I'm thinking that Tom was always at our dinner-dance from the beginning. It's going to seem strange without him."

"Have you heard how he's doing?"

"Yes, I asked for info and it's not good."

"Carr's hurt a lot of people. We know he indirectly caused at least two people's deaths. He may be responsible for killing Desi and he may be behind or *be* the fiend who's stalking you. So we have to rein in our sympathy."

Then she said in a low, haunted voice, "Cree was always at those dances, too. Adam, how long does it take grief to ease even a little?"

He thought for a very long moment before he said, "Even with Ricky, I couldn't seem to get away from my grief. I missed Kitty so much I wanted to die, too, to be with her. Then I met you at that CCG Ball and I began to heal on a deep level. Thank you."

She pressed him to her breast, held him for so long a time. "Thank *you*," she murmured.

They were silent then until she said, "Honey, how about if I plan a special day for us? I'm off early Friday afternoon. Caitlin and Marty have Merla for the weekend. Ricky's asked to go to the Enchanted Farm and we said yes, so we're alone all that weekend. It would be a great time for us to get it on."

She looked at him then as he frowned, saying, "It's not the best time, sweetheart, but we'll see. There's a lot going on at the station house and I'm beginning to be run ragged, but I'll try to rearrange my schedule...."

There was hesitation in his voice again.

"Listen," she said urgently. "I don't want this between us. If there ever comes a time when you think you've made a mistake, maybe that there really *is* too great a difference in our ages—"

"There's not. I'm sure of that."

Her voice was tense as she asked him. "Then is there something else you're *not* sure of? Have you maybe realized belatedly that you love Allyson?" There, she'd said it.

He looked really startled then and he swallowed hard. "I love *you*. I just can't talk about this right now. As soon as I can, I will. And sure, go ahead and plan for a date for us this Saturday all day. Is there somewhere you'd like to go, something you'd like to do?"

She kissed his mouth hard. "Yes, I'd like to stay here and make love to you so deep it will stay with you for the rest of your life."

He smiled at her then, really smiled. "I'm afraid you've already done that."

She drew back then, looked at him and saw the withdrawn look again. He was saying all the right things, but something else was on his mind. *Talk to me, love*, she silently pleaded. *Please really talk to me.*

Out at The Gardens, Raven and Viveca were greeted by a jovial Malcolm who owned and managed the very popular restaurant and nightclub. "Ladies, it's early and already I'm getting my eye candy for the week, maybe the month. How lovely you two look."

"And you," Raven answered, "are your usual spiffy self." Malcolm had begun his day with a camel hair jacket and brown gabardine trousers. A beige shirt flattered his brown face and he was famous for his beautiful ties. His face lit up at the compliment and he kissed each woman's hand.

This morning Raven wore navy wool with a big draped cream collar and Viveca strutted her stuff with a closely fitted dress of scarlet wool crepe.

"Let's go to my office, ladies. I can have anything you want sent in for your indulgence—food, liquor, you name it."

"You're a doll," Raven said, "but we're full up. Just before we left the office, someone went out and, craven wretch that he was, brought back dozens of Krispy Kremes."

"Yeah," Viveca said. "I may be on a diet for the next month. Why is everything that's good *to* you bad *for* you?" Then she threw back her head, laughing as she thought about her pregnancy. "Only not always. *Not always.*"

Malcolm had noticed a slight thickening around Viveca's waist, correctly gauged her meaning and smiled.

"Okay," Raven said, "we'll put our cards on the table. We're aiming for the best December dinner-dance ever. You've got most of what we've laid out and these are the last minute touches." Reaching into her tote bag she withdrew a manila envelope and extracted a sheaf of papers. "You made the arrangements for the thousands of tiny white lights and the soft rose lighting?"

"I did. Tell you something else. I've added lamb to the menu. I've come across a truly fabulous recipe for roast lamb and a special merlot wine to serve with it. Your liquor bill is going to make you cry, I'm afraid."

Raven laughed. "Pull out all the stops. This has to be absolutely fabulous, so cost is no object. Our advertisers are the best and they deserve the best and we're growing by leaps and bounds. Lay on, daddy-o."

Malcolm grinned. These ladies had plans and he had bigger plans and this year's dinner-dance was going to be spectacular.

Back in the office, Raven and Viveca checked in with Ken who was in a good mood.

"How're my favorite dolls?" he greeted them.

Viveca smiled. "Women aren't dolls anymore, you male chauvinist. But I must admit I like the sound of being a favorite."

"It's not a bad thing to be," Raven intoned.

They fell to discussing the December dance and Ken was very enthusiastic. "So we're ready to rock and roll," he said. "Our ad revenues are way up this year and I feel you two have everything to do with it, so I don't mind telling you you'll be getting fat bonuses."

Viveca blew him a kiss. "Now, that's a man after my own heart."

Will knocked and came in, whistled as he looked at the two women, but his whistle was mostly at Viveca and her scarlet dress. He said to Raven, "You look very nice today, sweetie, and just about every day." Then he turned to Viveca, saying, "But you, mama, are *something else* in that ball of flame on your back." He growled low in his throat.

"Down boy," Viveca said easily as Will smiled broadly.

"You wouldn't say that if you saw my new wheels," Will chortled. "I've got a blood red Sting Ray, just about a museum piece and I'll be hostage to the payments the rest of my life."

"Go boy!" Viveca said.

"Too bad you're married. You and my car would go well together. Both classy."

Ken spread his hands, indicating that Will should join them and Will sat down. As they began to discuss the dinner-dance again, his secretary knocked, came in and pulled the door shut behind her.

She nodded to Ken. "I didn't want to get on intercom to announce the lady, but Mrs. Carr is outside and demands that she see you. She's in quite a state and I tried to calm her down, but she isn't having any. Shall I bring her in?"

Ken thought a moment, wondering how best to handle this. He said to his employees, "I guess this does it for now, people. I have to see what this is all about."

The employees got up, but before they could get to the door, a disheveled Laverne Carr burst through. Glaring at Raven, she raged, "I'd spit on you if I weren't a lady."

Raven didn't answer, kept her cool as she continued out. Hilary stood, uncertain what to do when Ken got up and nodded to her. "It's all right. I'll take care of this. Mrs. Carr, what can I do for you?"

The woman laughed hollowly and put a hand to her head. "We were once on a first name basis and I was the best-groomed woman anybody ever saw, but now...." Her words forced him to look at her sagging, statuesque body and her smooth brown skin that was grayed with suffering.

"Please have a seat." Ken indicated a seat across from his. "How is Tom?"

She sat down heavily. "I'll tell you in a minute how he is. Please ask Raven McCloud to come back in."

Ken buzzed Raven and in a minute she sat with them. Laverne Carr was silent a long minute, breathing harshly. "My husband is dying," she said dramatically, "thanks to your lies and your hounding him. He's a proud man. He's come so far, only to have you two destroy everything he's built up."

"Mrs. Carr," Ken began. "Laverne. Don't blame us. We were just the messengers. Special Investigations has found plenty of evidence that your husband was siphoning off money that properly belonged to agencies for distribution to the poor and the needy. A man, Cree Hawkins, who was an accountant at CCG was killed, we think because he knew too much. A young woman, Desi Howe, was killed, we think because *she* knew too much."

"Lies!" Laverne shrieked. "All of them lies. My husband never did anything to hurt anyone. We're important people in this city, Mr. Courtland, important the way you two will never be. The *Post* has done stories on us many times. I grace the pages of their Style section. I won't take this lying down. I'll fight you to the death."

She paused and her eyes filled with tears. "And speaking of death, I should be by my husband's side. I left Allen Mills, to stay with him until I could get back."

Laverne Carr's body went rigid then with hatred and fury. "My husband would heartily approve of what I'm doing, because he wants his name cleared. He is a good man, a conscientious man who has done everything to help this community, and I will avenge his heartache and if God so wills it, his death.

"Just know this, you two. I will leave no stone unturned to even the score. I will be at your throat until the day you die and there is nothing, *nothing*, I will not do to hurt you. *Live with that!* I am a devoteé of the Old Testament. An eye for an eye and a tooth for a tooth."

As she struggled up, Ken got up to help her and she spat at him, "No, keep your seat. Stop pretending to be the gentleman you surely are not."

The woman went out on unsteady legs and Ken realized he had smelled liquor on her breath. He followed her to the door and thought it best to say no more.

Ken came back in after Laverne had left the offices and sat down heavily. "I can't help but feel sorry for her," he said. "Her position in life is everything to her. And make no mistake about it, she really will stop at nothing to strike back."

Raven nodded. "Who knows if that striking back began when we first started to unearth the dirt on Tom." Raven clenched her teeth. "I might have some sympathy if it weren't for Cree and Desi. Cree was my *heart*, Ken, as you know. The brother I never had." Her voice went ragged then. "I wake up crying sometimes and I don't know why. Then I *do* know why. Cree isn't here any longer. God, Adam has helped me so much, but Cree and I had a special relationship."

Ken sighed. "Special and wonderful to watch. I'm remembering how he used to come by to pick you up for lunch and he'd chat with me. We were Cowboys fans, diehard, and we both liked hip-hop and rhythm and blues, as well as opera. Cree was the best, Raven, the very best."

"What d'you think Laverne will set out to do?"

"God only knows. Talk about watching our backs. She's got the gold to do plenty of damage, same as Tom and—"

Will knocked and came in, handed Ken a sheet of paper. "Hilary sent this," he said. "Thought you'd want to see it immediately. It won't be on the news for a little while." The lone TV in the office was turned so low it was almost impossible to hear it. At the moment, Ken was more interested in the clarity of the picture.

Ken looked at the paper for a moment, then passed it on to Raven. Tom Carr had died of a massive heart attack that morning at about the time Laverne would have been on her way to the WMRY building.

At home that night, Raven moved about thinking of Tom and Laverne Carr, but mostly of Adam. What was going on in her new husband's world? They were so freshly married and already were there seeds of dissent? Adam wasn't a man who could hide his feelings, yet there was *something* he was trying to hide from her.

Mrs. Reuben had gone home, Ricky was spending the

weekend at Enchanted Farm, Adam hadn't come in and Merla snuggled closer to her. Mrs. Reuben had done a crockpot beef-and-wine stew and Raven's mouth watered at the thought of it. Already, she had willed away the photographs taken on Green Mountain and the hell-hound's call a few nights back. She stroked her arms with their cold goosebumps as the voice resurfaced, call-ing himself *her executioner* and saying again her time would be *soon.*

Her life seemed unreal to her now, but she meant to keep it on an even keel. If she died, so be it. Cree had died. Desi had died. She was a fighter, but they had been fight-ers too. Now there was a wedge between her and Adam and it hurt her, scared her. So quickly he had come to mean everything to her. Suddenly she wasn't hungry anymore.

"Hey, I did the salad," Merla piped up, "and Mrs. Reu-ben said I put everything in it but the kitchen sink. But you like everything in it, don't you, Mom?"

"You bet I do." Raven reflected then that more and more Merla called her "Mom," not "Mommy." Her little girl was growing up. What would her life be without her mother if the hellhound had his way?

She smiled then because Saturday was the day she had planned for Adam and her to be here alone. She had new Shalimar bath oil and she had a new periwinkle tricot nightgown and old, old desires. When they were wrapped up in each other, perhaps he'd *want* to tell her what was going on with him.

Merla had eaten earlier and she waited for her good-night hug and kiss from Adam who came in around sev-en-thirty. Raven noted that he looked livelier.

"Hey punkin'" he greeted Merla who ran to the door at the sound of his key in the lock.

"I thought you weren't going to get here until after I was asleep," the child told him.

"Oh, I rushed it. Gotta get home to my two angels."

With Merla in bed, choosing to read herself a bedtime story, Raven and Adam sat down to dinner.

Suddenly Adam shook his head. "That Allyson is a seven-day wonder," he said.

"The eighth wonder of the world?" Raven hadn't intended for her voice to sound edgy, but it did.

Adam reached over and squeezed her hand. "Honey, don't be like that. Allyson and I have worked together for quite some time. She's a difficult person to get to know, but she's pure gold."

She didn't want to say it, but it slipped out, "And I am?"

"Pure platinum, with diamonds, big, sparkling ones."

She smiled in spite of herself.

"I talk about Allyson to let you know where she's coming from. She's had a hard life, both parents died when she was very young and an aunt raised her. You remember she couldn't come to our wedding because that aunt had sprained her ankle."

"I remember." And she had been happy not to have Allyson's presence overshadowing her special, splendid day.

Adam seemed all right now, she thought, but was he? They had done everything to communicate superbly with each other from the time they'd come to know each other—until now.

He had some reports to go over. "You don't mind?" he asked her.

"No. I'll just contemplate my navel and change tote bags. I usually change them once a month, but it's been nearly three months this time. You take my mind off everything else."

She kissed the top of his head and he looked at her absentmindedly and there was that new sense of wide separation again, as if he'd retreated into some deep place in himself where she wasn't welcome. Well, didn't everybody have such a place? She remembered all too well that she and Kevin had *never* known the closeness she and Adam now knew.

In the bedroom, she pulled her tan leather Coach tote from the closet shelf and threw it on the bed. Then she dumped the things from the black leather tote onto the bed and began to sort them. She was nearly through when she saw it: a small, sealed vial of blood.

What on earth? Her knees felt a little weak and cold as she picked the vial up and sat down on the bed. A shudder ran the length of her body. She had a slight sense of smothering, as if a fist had hit her in her stomach. Licking dry lips and swallowing hard, she wanted to run to Adam, have him hold her. Where in hell had this come from? She tried to retrace her steps, but it had been nearly three months since she'd gone through the contents of that bag. Because of its small size and shape, it could have been put in yesterday or even today and slipped down near the bottom. Okay, she asked herself, where had she been lately?

And it hit her, she had been in the drugstore she and Kevin had long patronized and he had come up and begun to talk with her.

He had smiled. "Still seeing ghosts all around you?"

"That's not funny."

"Ah, come on. You always were too serious."

She had looked at him levelly. "I have no wish to explain myself to you, Kevin."

"Okay. Tell me about Merla. How she's doing? Everything."

"You see her every other weekend. You know how she's doing."

And she'd frowned because Kevin seemed eager to talk, to be with her and she wondered why. He mentioned a new girlfriend and said he might be getting engaged soon, or married. Merla hadn't mentioned anything about it, but then Kevin believed children were meant to be seen, not heard.

Now she remembered that there had been a commotion in the store when someone was caught shoplifting and her attention had been diverted. Kevin owned and ran a biological lab. He had access to vials of blood. And he had had plenty of time to slip such a vial into her tote. Had he followed her into the drugstore? *Was* he the stalker? Or had he hired someone to do his dirty work? The latter two were old questions and she reflected tiredly that they had no new answers.

She wanted to go in to Adam, but something held her back. When she'd left him, he'd seemed so preoccupied. She was an investigative reporter and she would always be in the middle of some hot seat. He had his own dangers to deal with; he didn't need hers. But she'd have to tell him about the vial of blood sometime. Just not right now.

Questions kept flooding her mind. Was it human blood? She realized she was clutching the vial and she put it in the night table drawer. Changing her mind, she took the vial into the bathroom, put it on the back of a top shelf of the medicine cabinet and began to run nearly hot water into the tub for her bath.

The water warmed her body some, but a bone-coldness lingered. She had to keep a lid on her emotions. There were Ricky and Merla to consider. But it was getting harder and harder. She made herself relax and focus on the next day when she and Adam would be alone.

Chapter 24

The next morning Adam sat up in bed savoring the smell of the Colombian Supreme coffee Raven had brewed after dropping Merla off at Marty and Caitlin's. There was also the unmistakable odor of thick country bacon on the grill and he knew what the rest of the breakfast would be because she had told him the night before.

"You get breakfast in bed in payment for past services rendered," she had teased him. He rubbed the stubble on his face. She had commanded that he get a complete rest this Saturday. No shaving; she found his stubble exciting. He closed his eyes, smiling, and fantasized her moving about in the kitchen. She was so special and she was going to be hurt when he told her and she'd hurt even more for him because she was that kind of person.

He switched on the radio to a classical music station and the sweetness of Massenet's "Meditation" from *Thais* floated on the air. For moments he lay back, listening, until the melody was finished. He got up, whistling softly. He wanted no negative thoughts today. She had planned everything and he was going to follow through. He looked down at the bulge in his pajama bottoms and smiled again. She was in for a treat. He had been afraid that his negative feelings about his secret would keep him from making love to her, but he had put mind over matter. He patted the bulge. He was ready for her. But at any time the anxiety might kick in and render him unable to function and she would wonder. Okay, he thought testily, right now that wasn't happening.

Raven opened the door softly and stuck her head in. "Are we awake?"

"Yeah. You missed 'Meditation.'"

"Oh, sorry. I'll just put a CD of it on."

"Got a kiss for your old man?"

"If you've got one for your old lady."

She came to the bed and looked down at him, smiling, but his look was somber. He thought she looked beautiful in her watermelon-pink, fitted robe that displayed her voluptuous figure and made her amber skin glow. The robe showed cleavage and it turned him on. As she stood close to the bed, he reached up and brought her down beside him, slightly rubbed his stubbly face against hers.

"Um-m-m. You feel good," she said, "and you smell like Altoid mints."

"And you smell like Shalimar and love."

She laughed. "How does love smell?"

"Like you."

She touched his face. "I wanted to see if you were awake before I bring you coffee."

He trailed his fingers down her back. "You're waking me up. Let's have the coffee together later."

"You're so sweet," she said, "and I love you so much."

He drew her closer. "I'm glad because I need your love right now more than ever."

She drew a little away from him. "Honey, something *is* bothering you."

He placed an index finger against her lips. "Hush. We aren't going to talk about negative things, only the positive ones. Making love and making more love until we can't make anymore."

There was something in his voice that moved her, but made her wonder. He sounded almost desperate. Oh, my love, she thought then, I know you and what you stand for and if our marriage is a mistake, you'd make sure you gave it every chance and you'd stay if I'm pregnant. You've talked more about Allyson lately and you've sung her praises even more than usual. I love you so much and I want your happiness so much I'd give you up so you could be with her. Then she thought fiercely that she *would* have this day, this night with him.

"I love you," she said softly again.

"And I love you. Want to pitch some woo?"

Raven smiled. "Not on your life. I'm saving you for tonight. There's a full moon and I'm opening those blinds and we'll watch it and make the man in the moon green with envy at what we do with each other."

"Lead me on, lady. Lead me on."

"In the meantime, get it together and I'll bring our breakfast in."

She got up, padded to the window in her satin mules that matched her robe and partially opened the blinds, letting bright sunlight stream in. At the bedside again, she paused, bent and kissed the top of his head and started back to the kitchen. Everything was done; she had only to bring the trays in, so she flopped onto the bed again.

In the bathroom, Adam got himself together, found he was out of Altoid mints and reached up on a top shelf where he always kept an extra roll. Feeling the vial of blood, his fingers sought to recognize what it was and, puzzled, brought it down. *What the hell*? He looked at the blood hard and holding the vial went out to the bedroom where Raven lay on the bed.

"Honey, got any idea what *this* is?" He held out the vial.

She sat up abruptly. "Adam, I wasn't going to tell you just now. You've seemed upset and I didn't want to bother you. I found it in my tote when I changed them last night…"

"And you just put it on the shelf and said nothing to me."

She was silent a moment. "You've seemed to have something deep on your mind this past day or so. I just couldn't. You've been so good about protecting me from all the trauma I've been through. Now that you've got something going on that's hurting you, I just didn't want…"

Adam closed his eyes for a moment. What was he doing to their love? How was his life messing up?

He questioned her then and she told him how she'd come to find the blood and about meeting Kevin in the drugstore and when she'd finished, he hugged her and said, "I'm sorry. I want to help you with this all the way through. When anything happens, Raven, *anything*, I want to know about it. Monday, I'll have the blood analyzed to see if it's human or animal. I'd like to think Kevin's behind this, but we don't know."

He put the vial on the night table. "I'll put it in my briefcase and give it to a lab Monday morning first thing."

"I wanted us to enjoy this day, this night," she said wistfully. "Sweetheart, I need you. I'm so afraid."

"I know you're scared and I'm sorry."

"I'd hoped that with Tom's death it may be over."

"That's tilting at windmills, honey. There's still Kevin."

Suddenly she burst out, "I hate ruining your life this way. You had a calm life before you met me."

He looked at her carefully. "Calm, yes, and empty."

"You had a friendship with Allyson. Wasn't that, isn't that full?"

He hugged her fiercely. "Don't even go there, Raven. You've brought something into my life I haven't had for a long, long time."

She had to say it. "But you've seemed unhappy lately, as if there's something deep on your mind and I just thought you might be having second thoughts about us. Differences in people, age, life station, a lot of differences make a big difference. Adam, I want you to know if you ever change your mind about us, I'll let you go. I want you to have whoever, whatever makes you happy."

He hugged her so tightly then, her ribs hurt. "I love you. I want you. Some guys chase whatever woman turns them on. What I want, what I've always wanted is fused love and passion and desire and I have it with you. I've always found I'm happiest operating with integrity. It's the only way I can live. I have that with you. I'm going to be only partially honest with you because I can't be honest all the way right now.

"Yes, I *have* got something going on and I'll tell you, but I have to wait it out. You've got too much on your shoulders and I'm always going to be there for you long after this is over."

"If it's ever over," she said bitterly. God, how did her life ever get to be so entangled?

"We've put new shadows on Kevin, along with the old ones. He's under surveillance. We're tightening the noose around Allen Mills and Laverne Carr, too."

"They've played it so smart," she said then. "Threats

and more threats. You can't arrest a man for threatening when you don't know who it is. We haven't been able to find the man who abducted Merla."

"But I've got a gut feeling now about what's going on. Kevin's made a few slipups that I can't discuss yet. But Lord, I wish things were clearer. We go down a tunnel and we think we're nearing the end and sunlight only to find yet another tunnel."

They lay in silence a few moments, then they kissed slowly and softly, holding each other against the fear and pain.

Suddenly she said, "We're going to enjoy this day and this night, no matter what."

They showered together and slowly the romantic aura that had begun the day came again.

Breakfast was orange and cranberry juice, sourdough pancakes, sausage and eggs scrambled with swiss cheese and scallions. There was Adam's favorite whole-blueberry syrup for the pancakes.

Lying in bed with his top bare, Adam grinned at Raven. "Sugar and spice and everything nice. That's you."

Raven sat up beside him and both had breakfast trays on their laps. "I'm having a hard time concentrating on my food with all the beefcake you're exhibiting." She half closed her eyes and took him in. The well-developed pecs and abs and biceps. Not too much. Just enough to start her heart pumping, her blood running hot.

"I'm thinking," he said, "the videotapes we rented were a waste of money. I'm looking at your lush body and if I get any higher, I'm going to fly. I think I'll just have *you* for dessert."

She giggled. "We don't have dessert with breakfast."

"To each his own. I know what I'm having."

And for the moment, she let herself be happy. Adam had spoken of integrity, which he had in spades. But she thought now that wasn't enough. She needed his complete and undivided love.

After breakfast, they spent the morning lazily listening to a mixture of jazz, the classics, country music, rhythm and blues. They snuggled on the plush carpeted floor with big colorful pillows behind them. She turned to him, nuzzled his face. "If Barry White had never been born, we would have had to invent him. Oh, how he turns me on."

"Yeah, he does it for me too, but when did I need Barry or anyone to build me up when I've got you? I have trouble simmering down." He lightly licked her silken amber skin and murmured, "My Amber Love."

"You haven't called me that in a while."

"But I think it all the time."

She looked at him then, felt his warmth. He wasn't distant in this moment and she was glad. She had him here with her and the hated, threatening calls didn't matter, the vial of blood didn't matter, the frightening photographs didn't matter. No, she couldn't just push them away, but she had him now and she intended to enjoy him to the limit.

Adam saw the joy on her face and gloried in it. At least he could give her this much. If what he was afraid of came to pass, she would have these moments to sustain her. He bent his head to the exposed cleavage the cream silk lounging pajamas displayed and ran his tongue over and into it, licking, planting small, wet kisses until she gasped for breath. She pressed his head hard to her breasts, stroking, her fingers massaging his scalp.

Suddenly she laughed. "We said we'd drive each other crazy with daylong foreplay, then tonight we'll make love under a full moon."

He smiled at her. "The question is can I wait? Thank God it's not Daylight Saving Time. Hey, Mr. Moon, you can't come out soon enough for me." He took her by her shoulders and shook her lightly. "Who says we can't take a few quick bites, then come up for the main course tonight?"

"Greedy."

His look was somber then. "I keep remembering our first lovemaking encounter when I had plans for feeding you my best pizza to turn you on and you couldn't wait...."

She laughed then. "*I* couldn't wait. Why you..." She took a pillow and swatted him. "You were all over me. All big hands loving me up. Okay, so we were all over each *other*." She squeezed one of his biceps. "I still can't look at you, hear your voice without creaming. One day I'll get used to your being mine, but not yet." Her lounging pajamas had a leopard-print sash and she wore leopard-print mules. He wore a cream silk sport shirt and brown Dockers. They sat back and looked at the rented videos and couldn't take all that passion, so they made brief, mad love, then fell back into the rhythm they had planned. They were like children in their free wildness, yet adults in the depths of their passion and bone marrow-deep desire.

It began to rain in a slow, soaking pattern, sealing them in from the world. She was glad it wasn't snowing. Somehow that would have been too much like Green Mountain. Green Mountain would bring memories of the photographs the way being at Mel and Rispa's had done.

Dinner had been prepared by a caterer and left in the

fridge. They warmed and served it by candlelight together and sat down to eat at six, with champagne which they drank with dinner instead of regular wine.

Chapter 25

"Um-m-m, this is heady stuff," Raven said.

Adam chuckled. "There's a lot of heady stuff going on around here." They sat across from each other, savoring the roast Peking duck and the sweet and sour jumbo shrimp with lemon-orange sauce. There was wild rice and rich macaroni and cheese, baby corn, green peas with tiny onions and broccoli dipped in rich Australian butter. She had prepared tossed green salad with Vidalia onions.

"Imagine us," she told him. "This is our first champagne in a while."

"It'll be the last for some time. I want to stay mostly sober. I've got you to make me drunk—with passion."

She looked at him then as it washed over her in waves. "Just call me passion's fool," she murmured in a low, throaty voice. "That's what we are and I, for one, am happy about it."

"Double that." His eyes caressed her, roved her body with all the love he felt.

She slipped off her mules and ran her bare foot up and down first one of his legs, then the other.

He grinned. "Woman, I thought I'd given you enough to last until later."

"Oh, you're not the only greedy one around here. I may get my fill of you when we're very, very old. I'm not sure."

"Well, I know where I'm coming from and I'll be ancient and still wanting you."

There was that shadow again that crossed his face and it alarmed her. "Honey, what *is* it?"

He drew a deep breath. Wanting her went so deep it threatened his emotional balance, but that was only one part of his life to deal with. He wanted to tell her now, but how could he? She had all the pain she could handle in her life. He reached across the table and squeezed her hand. "It's nothing, love. I'm just crying inside waiting for the main course to begin."

After dinner they cleared the table and set up the dishwasher. And a few minutes later he put her up on the food-warming table with a thick towel cover and she sat there laughing. "My fanny is going to get so very warm here."

"And that will match the inside of you." His tongue laved the corners of her mouth, then flicked over her face with wet kisses as she breathed shallowly, glorying in the sensation.

"Did we really make love a little earlier? I can't believe we did. I'm still on fire." Her voice was husky, slurred with passion.

"Merely a taste," he told her. "An appetizer." He wanted her then with a savagery that shocked him. Wanted to go into that gently pulsing place that held him like a hot wet glove.

"Um-m-m, please give me more." She closed her eyes and let him help her slide off and undress her, then himself. He looked at her, murmuring her name. Then he said, "My beautiful Amber Love. And I don't mean just your body, but your heart and soul."

He pressed her hips and stroked them as he lifted her slightly and slid inside, hot and throbbing, intent on being one with the object of his desire. He kissed her throat and groaned with the feelings sweeping through him. But after a moment, she placed a hand on his chest. "We don't finish, not now," she murmured. "I have plans for you and they don't include your planting your seed just now."

This time there were no barriers between them and it was as if there had never been. She placed her hand behind his head and pulled his face closer to hers and he kissed her with a fervor that touched her heart. "Okay buster, stop it now," she told him.

"You tell me one thing, but you're pressing for more right here and right now."

He held her against him.

"I'm going to model something for you. I bought a gown just for tonight and you're gonna love it."

"I love your smooth brown skin a whole lot more."

She pulled away from him then and went upstairs to the bedroom with him hot on her heels in pursuit. She took the garment from the foot of the bed and slipped it on, then stood before him pirouetting. The nightgown was periwinkle nylon tricot with a plunging front and back bodice fashioned of sheer lace. The slightly shirred skirt hugged all the curves and his mouth watered with desire.

With half narrowed eyes he watched her beautiful, lush body, then went to her and held her to him. "Okay, I see the nightgown and it's beautiful and you're beautiful in it, but I can't get more turned on. I'm going to take the pleasure of pulling it off. Do you mind?"

"And if I *did* mind?"

"I'd do it anyway. I've never tried the warmer table before and I like the sensation. What do you say we go back?"

She touched his face lightly, then stroked it. "You're something of a nut."

"The kind you love, I hope."

"The kind I adore. Come to Mama, you big, loving brute." She stroked his biceps, letting her fingers slide over them, then pushed him a little away and stroked his pecs and his washboard abs. She touched his rigid shaft, squeezed him gently. She could have gone off just looking at him. Why was he so damned gorgeous?

"Do you love me?" she asked him and waited for his answer with bated breath.

He caught her by her shoulders and held her. "I love every cell of you. I'd swallow you whole if I could, then I'd never lose you."

And his answer surprised her because it was she who was afraid of losing him. She felt salty tears behind her eyelids and nuzzled his throat. She was so dizzy with wanting him that she hardly realized that he had maneuvered her back onto the warmer table and put her on it. This time when he slipped inside her and clutched her buttocks, she locked her legs around his back and held him in as he worked her mercilessly and suckled her breasts gently at first, then much harder.

"I don't want to hurt you," he whispered, "but I'm hungry for you, hungrier than I've ever been and that's saying something. If we haven't made us a baby, we'll make one tonight."

Even in the haze of her desire she thought, he was talking future again as if he hadn't been distant. What was going on with him? But she fell into the intense mood with him and felt happiness flood her bloodstream along with pure lust and love so deep it had to be divine.

Afterward, they dozed on their bed, spoon fashion, and she dreamed of meadows covered with red clover and beautiful clumps of violets. She and Adam sat on a bed of moss with a baby between them. Their baby had brown peach skin like Caleb Myles' and Malinda's and her heart was so full, tears came to her eyes. And with delight she thought, What if they had twins?

She had prepared the glassed-in sunroom for them earlier. Now she pressed her naked full breasts to him. "There's another facet to this night," she said softly. "Let's get to it."

He laughed. "Oh, I don't know. I like what we were getting on that warming table. You ought to do an article called 'How We Made Out Like Paradise on Our Warmer Table.'"

She put her head to one side. "You think it was good there? Wait until we get on the air bed on the sunporch."

It was still raining, slow and steady, sleep-provoking, perfect for making love.

They got on the air mattress that was covered with rose satin sheets. The pillows were king-size and covered with rose satin cases. The satin felt heavenly beneath their flesh and he stroked her, kissed her with wet kisses, until she drew away, then came back and kissed his leathery flesh with her own wet kisses. She laved his nipples and he shuddered. "That feels so damned good. Don't stop."

"Oh, I have to stop. I have better things to do with you."

Then he laved *her* breasts, suckling them hungrily as she moaned in the back of her throat and stroked his back. Gina Campbell's signature song, "Love Be Good to Me Tonight," was on the CD player and the dulcet, wondrous tones of love and desire went deep into both of them as he worked her relentlessly, moving with slow, expert rhythm as she held him inside her body and nourished him fervently with her juices and her own maddening desire.

"Peach juice and more peach juice. Bring it on, Mama. I can use all you've got to give me." He felt her womb against his shaft and went sky high with glory, thinking it just didn't get any better than this.

She felt a little crazy then with love and desire. "Still greedy?" she asked him. She knew *she* was.

"You don't know the half of it. Only I wouldn't say greedy, just hungry, hungrier than I've ever been in my life. And I won't be getting full any time soon, so you've got your work cut out for you."

"I'm not complaining."

She never wanted him to leave her body, but as low thunder rolled, she clutched his tight, hard buttocks and held him in as ripples of passion and desire took her body and she knew the wonders of that desire's momentary climax. Her body gripped and released him, gripped and released him. Then she was shaken hard and long like a vibrating machine that didn't want to quit.

And arched above her, he felt his full power flood him, felt himself bestride a universe and fill her with his seed. He was a god on Mt. Olympus, an African god, and he carried his mate with him as seas crashed in his loins. He was coming home. Lord, he was coming home!

He held her close then and kissed her face. She was so precious to him. When could he tell her? And he pushed the thought away. He had this time. Take it and run, run with all the fear he felt. A fear that now was as great as her own with just as much danger.

They slept tightly entwined and woke to near silence. Only the ticking of the grandfather clock in the living room next to the sunporch could be heard. It had stopped raining. Raven got up and padded over to the blinds that were set in two tiers. The bottom tier was closed, but she opened the top tier and cold, bright moonlight filled the room.

She got back in the bed and looked again at the moon when Adam grabbed her. "I'll bet you're jealous of what we just had," she murmured to the man in the moon.

"Don't make him come down and try to take my place," he said, laughing. "Rested?"

"Very."

"Ready for the next round?"

"Can't it wait until morning?" She was teasing him as he looked at the luminous clock dial. "It's nine o'clock," he said. "I'm not sleepy. I could make it on that little sleep for the night. I've got something else in mind. We haven't had you on top of me. We haven't gotten in a position for me to really go all the way in. We've just nibbled around the edges."

She kissed his shoulder. "Then by all means, let's get it on."

The room smelled of Shalimar, heady and entrancing, and their own personal odors that were vibrant, earthy and compelling.

He placed her on her knees and entered from behind, bent and his lips brushed her waist, hips and buttocks as thrill after thrill of wonderment shot through her and his big shaft found her womb again as she lowered her upper body to the mattress with the lower half held up.

Inside her, he worked what she could only feel was magic and he was the master magician. "Honey?" she whispered.

"Yes, love."

"Make it last a long, long time. I can't stand it if it ends."

What they knew there lasted a very long time and filled them both with love and pleasure even greater than they had known. It was as if each sought to sustain and reassure the other that this had to last, *would* last forever.

Chapter 26

Adam stood by the windows in his office as Allyson tapped and came in.

"There's a lady outside who wants to see you. Our receptionist told her you weren't taking visitors and brought her to me, but I think you'll want to talk with her."

Adam looked at Allyson who had been so valuable to him in the past and her eyes on him were warm and sympathetic. "How're you doing?" he asked her.

She nodded. "Hanging in. I'm just worried about you."

"Thanks."

"Have you told Raven yet?"

He shook his head. "Not yet. I'm waiting to give it time, let it play out."

"Oh yes, and Adam, the blood in that vial *is* human. For what it matters, type O positive like most of the population."

"I thought it would be human. It seems to me the type of thing McCloud would do, but then I'd think he'd know he'd be a prime suspect."

"From what you tell me Raven's told you, he wouldn't care. He's a man who sees life as a game and means to play it on *his* terms. And speaking of terms and games, Adam, the woman outside has an important story to tell. You've got to see her."

"Why so secretive? Send her in."

In a few minutes Allyson brought in a small almond-skinned, well-coiffed woman who looked very nervous. "Why, Ms. Heflin," Adam said cordially as he shook her hand. They sat catty-cornered to each other as Allyson went out.

"Maybe I shouldn't have come," she said in a birdlike, shrill voice. "God knows I didn't *want* to, but a citizen has duties.... I don't hardly know where to start."

Adam smiled at her, trying to put her at ease. "Just start at the beginning, Ms. Heflin. Relax and take your time."

"Well, there's not much to tell really. It's just when the police came to question me... You see, you know I live across the hall from the lady who got killed. And when you police came to my apartment and questioned me, well, I lied. I said I'd seen nothing, knew nothing. But I'd seen a man go in and out of Miss Howe's apartment real often and...."

"Yes, go on," Adam said easily.

"Well, the night she died...now I'm not usually nosy, but something made me go to the door, just a feeling... I saw a man leaving sort of sneaky like. He closed the door behind him real soft and he looked all around him like he'd been up to some devilment and he went down the stairs.

"Lord, you could have knocked me over with a feather when I saw this article in the style section of the paper yesterday on this big doctor who owns a biological lab. And it was him, that same man. I'd swear it on a stack of Bibles. See, the paper had a lot of pictures of him in his business. You're gonna think I'm just a crazy old lady. That's all. I don't know anything else. I never saw him again until I saw his pictures in the paper. I just kept having a hunch I ought to come forward."

Adam reached across and took her trembling hand. "I think you're a very, very smart woman, Ms. Heflin, and I thank you more than I can say. I'll have a police car take you home if you're not driving. Are you available if I need to question you further?"

"Oh thank you, Detective," the woman breathed. "Yes, I'm available. You don't think he'll find out and come after me?" She clenched her hands. "I had to come. It's been eating my conscience up." Then she shook her head. "But I have to turn you down on that police car offer. My neighbors'll wonder and I don't want to set idle tongues to gossiping."

His smile was kind and reassuring. "I don't think you have anything to worry about. Tell people you talk with you had something stolen, so you have reason to come here. You've done us a really fine service. Let me pay your taxi fare home."

"Well," she said, "Lord knows I've been scared. You're a very nice man, Detective, and I thank you for listening to me. And yes, I'm a little poor, on pension and Social Security you know, so I could use the help with a taxi. Thank you for understanding."

"I'm the one who thanks you for coming in."

He walked outside with her and flagged a taxi and handed the driver some money. As she got in, he told her, "Now you come by if there's ever anything you need to talk about, anything at all."

She smiled at him with all the warmth and relief she felt. Men this nice didn't come into her life all that often and yes, she would help him in any way she could.

* * *

Around ten that morning Raven sat in her office waiting for Mrs. Reuben and Merla to come by. Mrs. Reuben had called to say the child was feeling a bit poorly and she was picking her up from school. Then Merla had said she wanted to see her mother, so they were on their way.

Remembering the weekend she had spent alone with Adam brought a soft, satisfied smile to Raven's face. Her body still felt warm, entranced by Adam's incredible lovemaking. But she was still so worried about him. She'd call him a bit later. Her cell phone rang and she picked it up to hear his voice.

"I just want to see you and tell you some interesting news about your ex," he said. "Will you be around?"

She made a kissing sound which he returned. "I'd *stay* around for you, but yes I will be. Merla and Mrs. Reuben are stopping by. Merla isn't feeling too well."

"Sorry to hear that. I'll see you both shortly."

Raven teased him. "It seems she's like her mother and can never see enough of you."

Raven pressed the cell phone cutoff button and sat still, reflecting on how happy she felt. The hellhound had done nothing since his last call. And she didn't know just when the vial of blood had been put into her tote. But there had been peace and quiet before and it had ended. It was worse this way because he kept her dangling on edge. But she could take it. She had a husband and two kids to take care of. *Dear God,* she prayed silently. *Please let it end safely for me and them soon.*

Adam, Merla and Mrs. Reuben all came in at once. Adam kissed her on the mouth gently, making Merla announce, "When I get grown, I'm gonna have a husband who's always kissing on me?"

"If you're lucky," Raven teased her.

"Papa Mac kisses Mrs. Reuben." She gazed at the older woman who blushed as Merla asked, "Doesn't he?"

"You're just too much," Mrs. Reuben told her. "Little pitchers also have big eyes and tell everything they see."

Merla giggled. "You're talking about me. I think it's cute when big men kiss big women."

"*You're* cute," Raven said and drew her child to her bosom. "You don't seem to be feeling all that bad."

"Well, maybe I just needed to see you."

"Didn't you have a good time at Marty and Caitlin's? You said you enjoyed playing with the twins. They took you to school this morning."

"Oh, I did. I did, but I didn't see enough of you and Adam and I missed you."

Raven's buzzer sounded and the receptionist announced Kevin. Bristling inside, remembering that Adam had something to tell her about him, Raven told her to send him in.

Kevin was natty in an expensive black-brown tweed suit and plain maroon tie. He looked rich. He *was* rich and he meant for the world to know it. He coolly greeted the others and got right down to business. "I won't take up much of your time," he said, "but I need Merla to stay over this Sunday night. There's a lady I want her to meet who won't be in town until then and will be leaving shortly after. I'll let her sleep Sunday afternoon and she can stay up late instead of coming back to you."

With a scowl, Merla spoke up. "I was going over to Mrs. Reuben's after you bring me back home. Papa Mac's gonna be there and we're making pecan fudge. We've been talking about this a long time."

"Well, you can do that another time, Merla. This is important. You can make fudge anytime."

But Merla could be stubborn and her little brown face began to redden with temper until Raven said, "She doesn't seem to want to stay longer with you, Kevin. I guess I'll have to insist that you bring her back at the usual time, four o'clock."

Now it was Kevin's turn to show temper. His voice crackled with anger he didn't try to hide. "She's the kid and you let her run the show. One day you're going to be sorry for that, Raven. The further we go, the more I know she'd be better off if I got broader custody. The roles really ought to be reversed with my getting chief custody. I'm seriously thinking of getting married again, so I would be best for her. The woman I'm seeing is what I would have liked you to be."

Adam looked at him coolly, said nothing. Kevin took this time to walk over to Raven's side and pat his child on her head as Merla drew away.

"Well, I tried," Kevin told Merla, "but your mother refuses to compromise. Another time then. Give me a kiss and I'll see you Friday night."

"I don't want to kiss you," Merla said.

"Sweetheart," Raven said softly. "You'll be coming back at your regular time and you can make the fudge with Papa Mac and Mrs. Reuben."

But the child knew from past experiences with her father that he was not a man of his word, that he would very likely not bring her back to her mother until the time he had first asked for and she screamed inside with disappointment. She looked at Adam with sad, hurt eyes and she blurted out to Kevin, "I want Adam to be my *only* daddy. I don't want you to be my daddy anymore."

Kevin looked as if he'd been struck and he looked at his daughter with blazing eyes. "I have to go now," he said stiffly, trying hard to hide his anger, "but I'll pick you up Friday afternoon."

He left then and Raven looked at his back with mounting fury. It was plain he intended to keep Merla for the time he had proposed. Well, Adam and she would just go to pick her up.

Merla came to her, got on Raven's lap and she held her. Adam smoothed her hair.

"We need to go now, love," Mrs. Reuben said. "Remember, you aren't feeling well and it's best that you lie down a while."

The child reluctantly agreed. They left after more soothing kisses and hugs and Merla said to Adam, "I do. I really *do* wish you were my only dad. Can't you be?"

"I'm your dad, too," Adam said, "and I love you so very much." He picked up the thin body and held her tightly. "But Kevin is your biological dad and that's the way it is."

When they had gone, Adam sat back down. "I'm forgetting something," he said. "I have to hitch a ride home with you. My car had to be taken to the shop; engine trouble. It won't be ready until sometime tomorrow. I'll get one of my guys to drop me by here."

"Sure thing and you can drive. Traffic was rough on the way over this morning."

He stood up and looked at her, his face wreathed in smiles. "Got a kiss for your old man?"

"How about a lot of kisses with a few hugs thrown in?"

"No way. I couldn't take it. My engine'll get revved up."

"Oh? I thought yesterday took care of that for a while."

"Did it for you? I know it didn't for me."

She shook her head. "What I think is we're gonna be on a honeymoon for the rest of our lives. You said you had something to tell me about Kevin."

"It could have waited. I just wanted to see you. Our intelligence says Kevin is seeing a lot of a city councilwoman and it seems to be getting serious. Kevin and Laverne Carr have been seeing each other, too. God only knows where that leads."

Late that afternoon when Raven came back from an interview, she saw a parking space on the street three blocks from her office and took it. It would save her a parking lot fee. So when she got off from work Adam was waiting for her downstairs and they set out for the place she'd parked. It was early December and the air was bright with Christmas songs and the Christmas spirit brought on long before time.

"How's the December dinner-dance coming along?" he asked. "It's nearly time. Are they working your fine brown can off?"

Raven laughed. "You've got it. Malcolm gets as excited as we do. He says it's his favorite event of the year."

Adam put his arm around her shoulder. "And you're my favorite everything."

"For which I'm grateful because you sure are mine."

It was not quitting time for most offices, so sidewalk traffic was light and they remarked on it. "You know," Raven said. "We've talked about a bodyguard for me, and I pretty much talked you out of it. Maybe it isn't going to be necessary. There's only the vial of blood since Tom died and we don't know when that was put there."

He looked at her sharply. "I don't want to take any chances. I've already spoken to a man I feel is right for the job. He's an ex-cop, unemployed right now. He'll be perfect."

"Adam, do me a favor. I like my freedom and we

ought to give this a chance to be over. With Tom's death it just might be. Let's wait and see. You know how I hate being watched. It's bad enough being watched by the hellhound...."

"Okay, we'll wait just a little longer, but if anything else happens... You saw Kevin's face today when you didn't want Merla to stay later with him. All that rage he couldn't hide. He wants the kid, Raven, and he'll do anything to get her. Our getting married was a surprise and it helped your case immensely. Now, if *he* gets married, it evens that playing field. Don't ever underestimate him, honey. He's a vicious guy."

"Tell me something I don't know."

One minute they were relaxed and talking, a block away from her car; then there was a loud roar of a speeding motorcycle engine and in a flash she saw it bearing down on her, its headlights hitting her face, blinding her.

"Raven, get out of the way!" Adam screamed as she moved swiftly and he pushed her so that she fell into the median strip.

"Oh my God!" she whimpered as she saw him fall too.

Then there was pandemonium as cars stopped and people tried to help both of them up, and to gawk. Soon there were two police cars and policemen with them.

"Are you hurt, ma'am?" a policeman asked. "And are you, sir?"

Raven laughed nervously. "I think my heavy down coat saved me a lot of grief," she said. "See about my husband, please." Her heart thundered painfully as she scrambled to her feet with the officer's help. Tears of rage stood in her eyes until she saw Adam begin to stand up with an officer's help.

"Why, Detective Steele," one officer said. "Take it easy now. Are you hurt? But then you might not know yet."

"Take care of my wife first," Adam said shortly, as he managed to stand, his head spinning.

"Honey, I'm okay, thanks to you," Raven told him. "But what about you?"

Before he could answer, a cop came swiftly to where they stood. "Well, we got the bastard," he growled. "He crashed into a brick wall trying to get away. He doesn't seem to be too badly hurt. We'll take him to a hospital and question him after they look him over. Detective, I was transferred to another team in your building a few days ago so you don't know me. I'm Sergeant Reeves and I'll take you both home and see that your car or cars get there too. You're sure you're all right now? Be still, both of you, so if you're not okay, we can take you to a hospital."

It was a miracle, but neither Raven nor Adam was badly hurt, only bruised. Heavy winter coats and scarves had done a major job of protecting them.

Sergeant Reeves took them home and stayed a short while to see if they really were okay. Merla's little face reflected deep anxiety and Mrs. Reuben hovered over them. "Hot baths in baking soda and Epsom salts are in order," she said. "I'll draw one for each one of you. It's a good thing I brought you that muscle balm. It's gotten me out of a painful pickle many a time."

Merla haunted them both as she stayed close, going into the bathroom with Raven and sitting on a bench by the tub as she soaked. Uncharacteristically, she was silent, frightened.

They let her stay up later than usual, so she was awake after they had had hot bowls of soup and when Sergeant Reeves had come back, his face grim.

"The guy who ran you down lied about who he is. He wasn't too badly hurt and he talked—at first all a bunch of damned lies," he said. "We found a slip of paper in his wallet, an old I.D. card in the secret pocket. It said he was an employee of McCloud Labs and it gave his real name: Cal Reams. Tomorrow I'll run the hell out of this one first thing."

Adam and Raven looked at each other, startled. "Still think you don't need a bodyguard?" he asked her.

Ricky took it hard. He had been sick with worry since his mother died. Was something even worse going to happen to his new mother and his dad? The boy felt choked with love and fear. Both Adam and Raven held him, soothed him.

Next day Cal Reams was silent, recalcitrant. And Kevin was virulent in his response, but his anger hurt his case, enshrouded him in even more suspicion. He was hauled in, questioned and every explosive lie or half lie he told buried him deeper and deeper. Finally he broke down and cried. "You can't blame a father for trying to get a kid he loves for his own. There are things I can do for my daughter my ex-wife could never do. I only want the best for Merla. I would swear that on a stack of Bibles."

Kevin denied everything, but the link was there and the woman had seen him furtively leaving Desi's apartment the night she was killed. The police were going to try hard to break Cal Reams down and they were experts. They had found in questioning that Reams had weak spots; they intended to hit him hard in every one.

Chapter 27

WMRY's annual December dinner-dance had been a rousing success from the beginning. For the fifth year it was held at The Gardens and Malcolm always pulled out all the stops to make it everything it could be. The parquet floors were polished to a brilliant shine, and large pots of red, white and pink poinsettias had been set about. Gaily colored balloons floated overhead and thousands of tiny white lights made it seem a fairyland. A delicate floral perfume permeated the air and rose lights made it all perfect.

Raven and Viveca had always played lead roles in the dinner-dance and this year was no exception. Even the hellhound couldn't altogether dim the ebullience Raven felt on this night. Now her heart soared with the news that Cal Reams was the culprit. And Kevin was behind this after all. It seemed that Cree had died because he knew too much about Tom *and* Kevin. Desi had died for the same reason. For a moment, Raven felt very sad. Cree had been here last year with Glenda. Tonight Raven and Adam had leaned on her to attend. She had agreed and had come with them.

The dance began at nine and would end at one. Now

as the revelers moved about the big restaurant and night club that they had to themselves tonight, Raven relaxed as she greeted strangers and those she knew. Cree would have insisted Glenda and she be happy. Adam came to her, gorgeous, she thought, in his tuxedo and burgundy cummerbund and carnation. She reached up and kissed his cheek. "Already I can't wait to get you home," she whispered.

"Be careful what you start," he told her. "I ignite fast around you, and I have plans for you when we leave here that will set your very soul on fire—from your scalp to the tips of your toes." He grinned as he hummed the melody to the country song, "I Want to Kiss You All Over." And she stood thrilling and laughing as she swatted his arm.

"You don't play fair," she told him. "I'm prisoner to what you tell me, and I glow for all the world to see. You keep it well under control."

"Ah, if only you could see my nether region, you'd know I have no control. I'm just putty in your hands."

Ken came to them. "I'm a little late, but I'm here. My dear, you look fabulous," he said to Raven.

Adam drew her to him. "She'd look fabulous in a gunnysack. My wife is a beautiful woman."

Ken's face was somber. "She is that, and I want to tell you I'm happy you got the devil who was stalking you. Two murders solved and I assume the hellhound goes to prison for life. Too bad D.C. doesn't have capital punishment."

Raven and Adam were both still somewhat bruised, but she had used Covermark to cover the few bruises that showed.

She felt she looked good in the ivory silk-and-wool dress that was fitted to her superb body with a long-sleeved off-the-shoulder bodice that displayed her cleavage. It was one of dress designer Roland's fabulous creations. With it she wore Rispa's gift of the amber-and-gold-beads necklace and Dosha's present of amber and gold drop earrings. Now, Rispa, Dosha and Mel came up and hugged Raven and Adam.

"You look wonderful tonight," Rispa said to Raven, "even better than usual and that has to be because the varmint's been caught. Thank God."

"Yes, thank God," Raven said. Rispa wore soft, draped pale gray silk jersey and Dosha was lovely in burgundy and pearls.

"Yes," Mel said to Raven, "you *are* looking well. I was worried about you when you had dinner with us, but that's all in the past now. Just swell up with my next grandchild. I can never wait for a new one."

Caitlin and Marty came up on that conversation. "If you had to walk them all night, you could wait," Marty said.

Mel scoffed. "Like I didn't walk you rascals all night more times than I care to count."

Carey came to them, with Viveca in tow. Mel gave her a low wolf whistle. "I think I feel a dance coming on," he said to Carey. "May I borrow your gorgeous wife?"

"Sure," Carey said, "if I can borrow yours."

And Raven teased them. "Now don't let him kidnap you, Viveca. Mel has an eye for the ladies. You look killer-good in that dress." And Viveca's backless black velvet gown and Austrian crystal jewelry fit her to perfection.

Rispa looked at her husband. "An eye for the ladies, huh? An *eye* is all he'd better have."

They all laughed as the two couples danced off.

The Steeles were all there except Damien who had a

prior engagement, Whit, who was on tour, Ashley who was hosting an affair at the Enchanted Farm and Annice who had a meeting in Baltimore.

Ken looked at Raven with his eyes narrowed. "I'd ask you to dance, Mrs. Steele, but your husband's look is fiercely possessive tonight and I'm not up to a duel right now. Later?"

"If I decide I can spare her," Adam teased.

Suddenly Ken's face lit up as he looked across the room at Allyson in scarlet chiffon and gold jewelry. "Lord!" he exclaimed, "talk about your metamorphosis. I'm going to check on this vision."

As he loped away, Raven and Adam laughed. "Allyson looks wonderful," Raven said, "totally unlike the usual ice princess." She felt a twinge of jealousy.

"Allyson can be quite warm and friendly," Adam said. Was he defending her? Raven wondered. She wondered too about the brief spell lately when Adam had been so preoccupied. He still wasn't altogether back to normal, but he was better.

"Adam," she said suddenly. "When will you tell me what's on your mind?" His expression changed and it was like a chill wind sweeping over him.

"As soon as I can put the pieces together."

"It's serious, isn't it?"

"Yes. It's serious."

"Honey, I love you so much. Please don't keep secrets from me. I'm strong. I can take it, whatever it is."

"I know you can, but you're human, too. You can only take so much. Listen love, we've just about got the monster off your back. And Kevin may be in jail before the week ends. We've got a lot to be happy about, you and I. Let's live it up. Dance?" He held out his arms and she went into them, snuggled her body close to his as her oriental perfume enveloped him.

Raven and Adam paused on the fringe of dancers. Someone spoke behind her, touched her shoulder. "Lady, you and Viveca should get an award for this one. Great party." Turning she welcomed Will Ryalls.

"Thank you." Raven thought he looked even better than usual in his tuxedo and blue cummerbund. She was going to be nosy. "Where's your date?"

He grinned broadly. "Couldn't make a choice. I'm up to my ears in women and I thought I'd bring a *couple*, but you probably wouldn't have liked that."

"It's your business. You're too young to settle down. Have fun. Play the field."

A bemused Adam listened before he said, "You've got school to finish."

"Yeah and I'm going back next fall."

"That's wonderful," Raven said and Adam agreed.

Dosha came back to them and Raven introduced her to Will. The four sat on cushioned chairs together and Will said, "I'd like to make my bid for the next dance with you."

"You're on," Dosha agreed.

There were two bands, Rich Curry and Curry's Circle, featuring his wife, Ellen, and Rafe Sampson. The second band was Nick Redmond's combo. Both were hot and Nick was famous. When they neared the bandstand Nick stopped what he was playing and went into "Passion's Fool."

In his dulcet baritone voice, Nick waved at them and began to croon:

> *Night after night we loved each other.*
> *For you I've broken every rule.*
> *Got no regrets, no shame, no teardrops,*
> *JUST CALL ME PASSION'S FOOL!*

Seeing Nick's wife, Janet, standing a little apart, Raven and Adam went to her. Dressed in off-the-shoulder heavy silk ecru crepe, she looked divinely happy.

"We don't see enough of you," Raven told her. "How's the bambino?"

"More precious every day." She laughed, reached into her small gold purse and brought out a couple of photos.

"What a doll!" Raven exclaimed. "You and Nick have got to come see us more often."

Janet nodded. "As much as I love teaching, Nick and I both felt I should stay home with the baby. So I have more time. Nick's busier than ever and he's on top now."

Raven reflected then that even though Janet was older than Nick, she knew of no couple that was happier.

Someone claimed Janet then for a dance.

By then Mel and Rispa danced near them and Mel gave Adam the A-okay sign, which Adam returned.

"Your parents are so wonderful and still so much in love," Raven told Adam. And she couldn't help asking wistfully, "Do you think we'll last like that?"

Adam's intake of breath was sharp and she felt his heart drumming. He seemed a bit choked. "I think we will." *Okay,* he told himself, *she's mostly out of the woods now. It's only a matter of time until we nab Kevin and it's over. He's not going to make a crazy move now with us on his back, so when am I going to tell her? She hasn't been truly happy in so long, but I have to tell her soon.* He moistened dry lips and held her so tightly she felt she'd break. His rock-solid body was turning her on and she wanted him so.

Right now he was helpless to explain anything so he held her and murmured. "It's true, you know. I want to kiss you all over. Go inside you and stay." He couldn't remember a time when he'd felt more like crying.

Papa Mac and Mrs. Reuben were late, but they came in happy. Mrs. Reuben wore garnet silk twill that flattered her beige skin and Papa Mac's tuxedo and garnet cummerbund were a match for her dress. It had been so long since Raven had seen him look happy the way he did these days. Mrs. Reuben was ecstatic with a new haircut of bangs and long, straight wisps across her forehead.

"Save a dance for me," Papa Mac said. "I'm all revved up and Rafe, Adam and I are going to give you all a thrill."

The chief of police tapped Adam on his shoulder and suddenly Adam's mood changed to a livelier one.

"Well, if you must, sir," Adam said laughing. "Remember we haven't been married too long."

The chief laughed heartily. "You'd have an exchange with my wife, but she's in Australia, globetrotting just now. Be kind to a lonely old man."

Raven smiled. "You don't really look lonely and you're certainly not old."

The chief pursed his lips. "Your wife's a keeper, son. Take first-class care of her. She knows how to make a man happy."

"I'll vouch for that," Adam said as the couple danced away.

Rich Curry and his group were onstage now and she knew the set would be long because Rafe Sampson was performing. The silver-haired, sixty-eight-year-old man blew a wild harmonica and crowds never wanted to let him go.

"You know," the chief said, "your husband is a really remarkable man. He could be chief one day, but I don't think he wants to be."

"He's crazy about community work," Raven said, "and he wants a lot of time to work with that."

"He's often told me commander is about as far up as he wants to go," the chief said. "Another thing, forgive me for being nosy, but he's often spoken of wanting to spend time with his family. God knows *I'm* away enough."

"Yes, he talks about that often. My husband is a wonderful man and I love him so very much."

The chief looked at her sharply. He was familiar with the trouble about the hellhound and he knew that with a few loose ends pulled tight, it would be over. Why were there tears in her voice?

"It must be a relief to be free of the monster who has been stalking you," he said and wondered if he should bring it up.

"Oh yes, but you've all been so helpful. You haven't made the demands on Adam you could have made and you've helped him to be largely free to stick with me. I really appreciate that."

"I could do no less. I have one son who's a lawyer in New York. My wife and I wanted more children, but it wasn't to be. I've often thought I'd like a son like Adam."

She smiled broadly then. "And I've always thought I'd like to have a husband like Adam. And presto, I have one."

She then danced with Adam's captain who was courtly and attentive. Like the chief, he told her how happy he was that the stalker had been caught. Then Ken and Allyson danced by close enough so that Raven could see that while Allyson was the soul of gaiety in her flaming chiffon, she looked far from happy and Adam had been unhappy. What was going on here?

She danced with Ken then and his eyes were questioning. "Why aren't you livelier?" he asked her. "You can put this horror behind you now. Has it gone so deep you can't quite get over it? Are you shell shocked, babe? If you need time off to recuperate from this, remember I've said all along you can take all the time you need. You were the one who wanted to keep on working. And Lord, what a fantastic job you've done."

"Thank you. Maybe later. Ken, thank you for everything."

"Hey, don't thank me. I'm your friend and I wanted to be a lot more. Well, what do you know. I can have you a little longer. It looks like the three harmonicas are hooking up to thrill us."

And indeed Adam, Papa Mac and Rafe Sampson had gathered around the microphone and were tuning up their harmonicas. Rafe led off with an absolutely wild riff that made the merrymakers gasp and laugh. Then it was Papa Mac's turn and he played sweetly with a world of soul, as if he played to a lover. But it was Adam who turned the house upside down with his riffs and trills that set the room on fire.

My God, Raven thought, *where is this coming from?* Because Adam was playing his heart out and he was looking directly at her. The men combined then on an oldie, "Old Black Magic," then Adam played solo, "Passion's Fool," and looked at Raven who wondered what he was trying to tell her. This was earth music, soul music and it was for her to respond with fever.

The crowd clung to the harmonica players, demanding two encores, before they let them go. The next dance set Raven found herself back in Adam's arms. "You're really good on that harmonica, you know," she told him. "But tonight you outdid yourself. What's going on?"

He hugged her close and she felt his heart beating fast. "More than you could ever guess," he said slowly and she thought he looked sad.

Should she mention it now? "In a very little while I can take the e.p.t. and the blood tests to see how your seeds're sprouting. Isn't that exciting?"

The shadow across his face deepened as he kissed her cheek. "Yeah, exciting."

Papa Mac claimed her for a dance and Adam teased him. "Be careful with her. That's precious cargo you're leading."

Papa Mac grinned. "That's the way I raised her. She's got herself a good man too."

Her cell phone rang and Papa Mac shook his head. "Don't they ever give you a break?"

The ring told her this was Ricky. "Hi Mom, I didn't really want to disturb you, but I wondered if you're having a good time."

"Ricky, it's ten-thirty. Is something wrong?"

"Nope. Everything seems right. I'm glad they caught that creep who was hassling you."

"Me too. But why are you still up?"

"Oh, I was in bed, but I got restless. I'm so glad I've got you for a mom. You're the best, Raven, and I love you."

His words went to her heart; he had come to be as special to her as Merla. "I love you," she said softly. "I'm so glad you came into my life, you and your dad."

"I think I'm gonna start calling you Mom all the time. Is that okay?"

"You bet it's okay. I'll love that."

"I looked in on Merla. She's dead to the world."

"Thanks. You go back to bed now. There's Rocky Road ice cream in the fridge. I got it today for you and Merla and forgot to tell you about it."

"Oh boy. I'm gonna latch on to that. Bye Mom. Love ya!"

Papa Mac had danced her to the sidelines to take the call. When she hung up, he held out his arms again for the rest of the dance. "Everything okay?"

"Super okay. Well, with Ricky anyway."

Papa Mac looked concerned. "Look baby girl, I don't

mean to pry but you and Adam both seem just a tad off to-night. The man scaring you half to death's been caught. We know he's connected to Kevin who I always detested. Your troubles ought to be about over. Why do I feel both of you are a little sad about something?"

"How perceptive you are," she murmured. "When I get to the bottom of it, I'll tell you what I know."

"Just always remember that you and Adam love each other as much or more than any couple I ever came across. Fight for something this precious."

"I intend to, but I've got to find out *how* to fight it."

Viveca got on the microphone then to announce that food was being served and Raven went over to join her. Malcolm was there, a splendid bear of a man in his tux-edo. "I told you ladies I'd do you proud. Did I live up to my word?"

Raven and Viveca hugged him and Viveca pinched his cheek. "Ah, but you're giving us a memorable time here. That food looks to die for."

Malcolm stood back and surveyed the long row of snowy damask-covered banquet tables groaning under silver platters of baked turkeys, glazed hams, roast beef, fried chicken and other meats. He pointed out the lamb roast, cut two small slices and served it on small plates with specially blended mustard and handed it to each one. And as they sampled the lamb, exclaiming over it, he poured them a little merlot in sparkling crystal glasses.

"Food fit for gods and goddesses," Viveca told him. "Ah, Malcolm. I love you. I've always loved you. Will you…?"

Viveca paused, grinning as Malcolm roared. "Now don't ask me to marry you, as much as I'd like to as fine as you look tonight. If my wife wasn't getting over flu, she'd be here. She loves these parties. And lady, have

mercy on my seven kids. How would my wife support
them if I married you?"

Malcolm and Viveca were deep in laughter then and Raven
drifted away from them and down the row of banquet tables.
What a spread, she thought. The taste of the delicious lamb
still lingered in her mouth. She'd take some home for Ricky
and Merla. Standing at the head of the tables, she surveyed
the food and the setting. Fine china, sparkling crystal and
gleaming silverware.

Tureens held green pea soup, oyster soup and New England clam chowder. There were lavish silver platters and
deep dishes of sliced meats, colorful macaroni and cheese,
scalloped and cheese-covered potatoes, raw, carved vegetables, huge salads—vegetable and potato—and fat, saucy
black and green olives stuffed with pimentos.

The desserts were almost enticing enough to make
you willing to undergo a minor heart attack. Malcolm's
special New Orleans Praline Cake took top honors. Big
and beautiful, it sat on its silver pedestal, but the smaller
desserts were no slouches. Lesser cakes, but not much
lesser, took honors too. Malcolm was famous for his
cakes. Pies of every description, but especially the pecan
dream pies, held their own in the food contest.

Ice cream of several flavors was there for those who
wanted it, but the night was cold and most people chose
the scrumptious eggnog, another Malcolm favorite and
unlike any eggnog Raven had ever tasted. There were
candies, too, pralines and fudge. The array seemed
endless.

Raven looked around for Adam and saw him earnestly
talking with Allyson when Ken walked up to the couple, said
something to Allyson and steered her toward the food.

Dosha spoke at Raven's elbow. "At last I catch up with

you. You've been a busy lady tonight, and this is all so beautiful. Thanks for inviting us."

"Thank *you* for coming. Dosha, you look wonderful, and so happy."

"No, you're the one who looks wonderful. You put the Venus de Milo to shame. Is it a Roland special design?"

"It is."

"I'm going to have to go to see that young man. Your necklace and earrings look beautiful on you, too and how I envy you that silk skin. You and the twins have the skin department sewed up."

"Oh," Raven scoffed. "I may be silk, but you're satin. You're going to make a beautiful July bride."

"If I don't have to do my ex-fiancé in before I can get to it."

Raven had talked with Dosha about her ex. "What's he up to now?"

"What *isn't* he up to? Daryl was born too handsome, too rich, too smart for his own good. His parents and his sisters spoiled him rotten. He seems worse since his time in prison, and he's mad with a world that's treated him specially all his life, and stopped for a little while."

Raven knew that Daryl Stoner was the scion of a filthy-rich real estate mogul, a friend of Tom Carr's, who'd made his fortune when land in D.C. was cheap. The mogul was a pillar of the community, along with his wife and four daughters, but Daryl was another matter. By the time he was thirty, he had set off in another direction, rubbed shoulders with the Cali Cartel and was knee deep in cocaine and illegal money—until he got caught. Everybody had been shocked.

His father's money and his own couldn't get him off and he went to prison for five years. Now he was free and pursuing Dosha with a frightening vengeance.

"What's the latest?" Raven asked.

"He won't take no from me for an answer. He's gotten to be a spoiled fool, if he wasn't always."

"He isn't threatening you, is he?"

"Overtly no, but he's certainly crowding me. I run into him far too often for it to be coincidence. Too many calls. He swears he won't take no for an answer."

"Are you afraid of him?"

"No, I'm not afraid of him, I'm just *sick* of him. His father had the nerve to call and tell me we should get married, that I'd be a stabilizing influence on him." Dosha laughed shortly. "I've got three big, hulking brothers, and he always had the good sense to be wary of them. I won't hesitate to call if I need them."

They served themselves and ate as they talked. Adam came up, smiled at his sister. "Spare my wife long enough for her to fix me a plate."

Dosha shook her head. "You're a big boy now, bro. Why don't you fix your own plate?"

"The food's better when she dishes it up."

Dosha laughed. "Mom may have raised you guys to be good husbands, but she spoiled you too."

Looking at him out of the corner of her eye, Raven wondered what the deep conversation with Allyson had been about. Now Allyson stood nearby still talking with Ken. And for the moment Adam seemed completely there with Raven who dished up and brought him his plate. He held his plate with one hand, then bent, lifted and kissed her hand as she flushed. It was such a small gesture, but it thrilled her.

"You two really have it bad," Dosha said. "I hope I'm this happy when I'm married."

"Wait'll we have our own little bambino," Raven told her. "You don't know what happiness is."

This time Dosha saw Adam's face go somber, just as Raven saw it, but it was quickly gone. And Dosha wondered what on earth this was all about.

It was during a lull in the party and a spell of the two bands playing popular Christmas tunes when Adam turned to Raven. "Let's get our coats and go out on the balcony for a bit of cold, fresh air. I want to kiss you and I don't want to embarrass you before all these people."

"Ah, you're sweet," she told him. "I'm for that, but this had better be good."

They collected their coats from the hat-check woman and in a few minutes were out on the balcony that had low lights. The moon was waning and it made Raven think of a recent night watching a full moon and making love until they were sated.

The cold air stung their faces. He took her in his arms and even with the thick coats between them he could feel their hearts thumping. His mouth on hers was hard and purposeful and his tongue sought and conquered the sweet hollows of her mouth, roughly taking possession until she was weak and half dizzy.

When he lifted his head he told her, "When we go back in, I've got one song request: 'Love Be Good To Me Tonight.'"

"Make it a long set," she murmured. "I'm in the same mood."

And in the shadows he stood still, watching and waiting. He had lived in the shadows all his life. *Bitch!* he tensed as he thought, *Enjoy what you have tonight because your time is almost over. You won't hurt anybody else the way you've hurt me. You've robbed me of everything I ever wanted and now you're going to pay. You took his life and I'm taking yours.*

Lord, it was cold out here, as cold as a winter grave, he thought, and he smiled as he thought too about Raven in her grave. He braced himself to slink back even deeper into the shadows, whispering to himself: "*Go on and be happy because in the next twenty-four hours there's gonna be a killing!*"

Chapter 28

At home that night, Adam turned to Raven. "Well, you and Viveca outdid yourself again. I said it earlier and I'll say it again, great show!"

Raven smiled and hugged him. "You promised me lots of action when we got home. We're here and I think I'll put on the nightgown I wore when I last seduced you big-time."

"Do that," he growled, grinning, "and you're in for more action than you can handle. Hey, I'd better check my messages. I've had my phone turned off so I could enjoy myself."

He got his cell phone from his jacket pocket and got his messages. The first one took his breath away. It was his doctor. "Adam, call me as soon as you can, no matter what the hour is. I've got good news. Bye."

Excited, he dialed the number and the doctor's sleepy voice came on. "I think you're going to be loving this, man. Your tests are *clear*. If you ever really did have cancer, it's in remission. Your PSA is registering top notch."

Adam's knees felt weak with relief. "I'm having a hard time taking this all in. You always said the tests were so borderline you weren't sure, and we were waiting it out for something to develop. Oh God, I'm thankful!"

"Yes, we both are. You're one of my favorite patients. Adam, tell me, I've been in this business a long time and I've had it happen a couple of times before, this remission business. Has something really good happened in your life lately? I know you've been under a tremendous strain with your wife being stalked. Has anything happened there?"

"We caught the guy and we think it's largely over. You think that's what happened to make this let up?"

"It surely could. We'll still have to watch and see, but this is the first time your PSA has been so low and no cancer cells at all are present. Please check with me again later this morning. There are several things we need to talk about."

"Will do."

There was no music, but Adam went to where Raven sat on the bed in her beautiful periwinkle seducing nightgown and pulled her to her feet as he whooped with pleasure. He danced her around the room.

"What on earth was that call about?""

"*I don't have it, baby*! The doctor thought I did. Early tests showed *possible* cancer, but it's *gone, gone, gone!*" He hugged her fiercely.

"That's why you've been so upset, so preoccupied?" she said slowly.

"Yeah, you'd better believe it. My doctor thinks catching that guy has everything to do with this remission. Oh, sweetheart." He couldn't hold her close enough.

"And I thought you had found you were in love with Allyson."

He laughed then. "No way. If I were going to be in love

with Allyson, I'd have fallen long ago. No, I think she's got her eye on someone. She's preoccupied, sort of dreamy. I hope so anyway, because she's a good egg. I had the doctor's reports sent to the office because I didn't want to worry you. You had so damned much on your shoulders. I told Allyson about it and she suffered along with me."

"I would have wanted to know. You needed me then." She kissed his face and held him, revelled in his tenderness mingled with strength and power.

"I had to protect you from further stress. Can you understand that?"

"Yes, I understand. That's you, but you were without me. Oh, my darling." She held his head to her bosom.

"But it's over for the time being anyway. The doctor says he's known few guys my age who have prostate trouble and those few didn't take care of themselves the way I do. But the stress about what you were going through was taking its toll."

They got champagne and Adam toasted them. "To us and our happiness, and a baby to seal it all, beginning some time back, but picking up speed tonight. Over the top, my angel. *Over the top!*"

They made love with a passion that transcended all the other times. Their heat was incendiary and incredibly sweet. For the first time since they'd known each other, they were free of fear. Nothing else but their love for each other mattered. Certainly not age. They were free to belong to each other and their children. And each exulted in that freedom.

Adam left for his office the next morning around eight-thirty. He had a meeting with the chief of police at ten. "I'll double back after the meeting which should be short just to get another kiss in. I'll be right in and right out."

Raven laughed gayly. "That could be a double entendré," she said. "Right in. Right out. That sure wasn't the case early this morning." She closed her eyes, remembering. "I love you," she said softly. "I'll always love you."

"And I adore you."

Chapter 29

After Adam had gone, Raven took a long, leisurely bath and put on blue sweats, slipped a matching sweatband on her head and did her Pilates exercises. It was Friday, but Ken had insisted that she and Viveca take the day off because they had worked so hard on the dinner-dance.

Pumping iron in their fitness room with the five-pound weights, she savored Adam's news and reveled in it. Happiness was a husband who was fine and not in love with Allyson. Merla and Ricky would call at lunchtime, so she was on her own. She had given Mrs. Reuben the day off. She couldn't wait for Adam to come home for a break. They hadn't been married long, so the hunger they felt for each other was fierce. These hot, intense feelings were new to her, but in her life she had enjoyed nothing more. Adam frequently said it would last; look at his parents. Maybe he was right. She hoped so.

Adam had taken a hot raisin bagel with cream cheese and Canadian bacon with him. She sat down on the high stool at the serving counter in the kitchen and ate the same. She thought she'd read a couple of reports on the

Tom Carr investigation. Special Investigations was mulling over whether or not to indict Allen Mills as Tom's accomplice.

And Cal Reams languished in jail, but had broken under police questioning. He had been close to Tom and to Kevin and had tried to kill Raven because they wanted him too. He said they agreed to pay him more money than he would ever see again. He swore that was the sole reason. And he swore he had not killed Cree and Desi but police said he was lying.

She was lost in thought when the doorbell rang. Looking out the door viewer, she saw Will and quickly opened the door.

"Hey!" she greeted him. "What brings you by?"

He grinned engagingly. "I remembered that you said some time back you'd give me a letter of recommendation if I ever needed one. Ken's agreed to give me one too. I just thought I'd talk to you about it. I was in the neighborhood and I parked my tin lizzy a couple of blocks away and walked over."

"Come in. Can I get you a bite of something?"

"No, no. I've eaten. Let me just tell you what I need from you."

And a few blocks away, Kevin McCloud sat in his sleek black Porsche and pondered his next move. Steele thought he had him sewed up tight, but he underestimated the power of high-powered lawyers, and Kevin had the best. People had killed and gotten away with it when they had men like these on their side and he sure as hell intended to give it his best shot.

Too bad about Tom; he should have been made of tougher stuff. He'd bet his bottom dollar *he*, Kevin, wouldn't have a heart attack. Steele knew and Raven knew that he and Tom were good friends, but they didn't know how deep the friendship went. Cree and Desi had found that out and both had paid the price. Kevin grinned sourly. Cal Reams was totally expendable. He hadn't succeeded in killing Raven, now that job still had to be done. With Steele connecting the dots, the detective was finding out that both Tom and Kevin were implicated in Desi and Cree's murders, and why.

And Raven would be a chief witness against him. Only, if he played his cards right, Raven would never testify. With Cree and Desi already dispensed with, there would be no case, no drum-tight case anyway. He had grown up knowing money talked. Soon his money would be shouting to the heavens.

He had his ducks almost in a row. He had a plan to ask Raven's forgiveness for the many things he'd done to her, throw her off balance and find a replacement for Carl Reams, someone smart enough to do the job. This time he wouldn't fail.

Will blinked a bit as he sat down. Raven switched on Beethoven's Fifth Symphony.

Will leaned back. "You sure like the heavy stuff."

"Oh, I find it soothing sometimes," she said, and wondered why she was nervous.

"If you say so. Good dance last night." He grinned.

"It *did* go well. About the recommendation—you're going back to school you say?"

"I'm changing schools. I'm going home, Raven, back to St. Louis and I plan to enroll at Washington University and study journalism. One day I'll be an investigative reporter like you—maybe."

His voice had gotten a bit slurred. "I'd like to talk with Adam too about criminal justice. Maybe I can combine the two. Is he around?"

"Well, he's coming back just a little later. Stick around and you can ask him then."

Will looked at his watch. "No idea just what time? I've got several things to do."

"No. Just that it'll be a little while."

Will relaxed then and drew a deep breath. His eyes narrowed and he leaned forward.

Suddenly she frowned. "Why are you looking at me like that?"

"Like *what*, mama?" He had switched to street slang.

"I'm not sure. What's the matter, Will?"

She was alarmed because Will's eyes had grown bitterly hostile and he looked at her as if he'd like to wring her neck. He said nothing, just stared.

"*Will*?"

He didn't answer.

"Will, what in the hell?…"

Then shock ran through her like jagged lightning as he laughed evilly and told her in that voice so similar to the one that had threatened her for so long. "*There's gonna be a killing.*" Breathy. Deep. Like one of the fiends Samuel Jackson portrayed. It was the voice that had tormented her at a distance since May. But it was here and now and she was nearly paralyzed with fear.

She tried to relax a bit. Will was great at teasing and she said in a shaky voice, "You *know* about all this. Did Ken tell you?"

"You don't get it, do you?" he growled. "No, you and your kind never get it. You're the first to die, then Ken.

Glen in Special Investigations. Everybody who's ever hurt me and killed my dad."

Her voice was steady now, puzzled. "You're not making sense. Who *is* your dad? I don't *know* your dad, Will, and I'd never hurt you. How could I hurt you or kill your dad?"

He said the name evenly and his voice was cracked and full of love. "*Tom Carr's my dad*, or *was* my dad before you and Ken and the goddamned Special Investigations bastards killed him. Now you're all going to die."

Tom Carr and Will Ryalls? But how—her mind boggled as the phone rang on the table near her. As she began to get up, he drew a .22 pistol from his inner jacket pocket and snarled, "Answer it and get rid of whoever it is fast. And don't play games with me."

It came to her in slow motion and her mind wasn't handling it well. A gun? And it was pointed levelly at her. His hand was steady. She had to find some way to let the person on the phone know she was in danger. Lord, let it be Adam calling.

"Hello," she said as steadily, as coolly as she could.

"Raven?" It was Adam as she'd hoped it would be.

"Yes, it's Raven McCloud. I can't talk right now. I'm very busy. I hope you understand." She held to the cold, clipped tone and he caught on, but she thought miserably, *He's too far away*.

"Where are you calling from? I'll try to call you back if I can," she said.

Adam's voice was sick then with concern and anger. *She's in danger*, every cell in his body screamed. "I'm on my way," he said. "I know what's going on. You hold on, baby, you *hear*? I'll be there very, very shortly."

With numb fingers, she hung up the phone and stood still. Will waved the gun. "At least you're smart in your last hours. Sit down. You're the kind who wants to know everything about everything. Well, I'm going to give you an earful."

His eyes were everywhere, but they always darted swiftly back to her. His voice was cold, without emotion as he spoke.

"I was raised without a father. My mother told me he was dead, that he died shortly after I was born. I was an only child and I found out she told my father I had died and she was keeping her sister's child. I look like my mother, not my dad, so he couldn't know. And God, the pain, the loneliness I suffered shouldn't happen to a dog. My mother did what she could, but she was bitter and she didn't answer my questions about my father, wouldn't talk about him at all, just that he had died. She didn't care a helluva lot for me.

"When I finished high school with great grades in spite of everything, I couldn't bear the loneliness anymore. I began college, but I dropped out and took a full-time job. I hired a private investigator and he traced my father to D.C. and found out who he was. It was the hardest thing I ever did, but I got in touch with him just over a year and a half ago and he accepted me as his son." His voice got warmer then, full of wonder. "He accepted me and he gave me money, urged me to go back to school.

"But his wife, Laverne, wanted no part of me and let me tell you, she ruled that house and him. She refused to let him put me in his will, so he set up a trust fund for me." His voice sounded choked then. "He told me he loved me, that I was the only son he'd ever had that he knew of.…"

The investigative reporter in her kicked in then as she questioned silently: *If he loved you so much, why did he never try to find you? Tom was a savvy man. He knew your mother hated him. Wouldn't he have had his doubts about whether you had died?*

Will was talking again. "My mother passed on a few months after I started college and you talk about being alone and *hurting*. Liquor and marijuana helped a lot, but even *that* couldn't kill the pain. Then I found him, and for the first time in my life I was happy."

He paused and looked at her more closely with red-dened eyes. "When the lies began about him stealing money from CCG he told me all about it, then there was the indictment. Yeah, months before, he told me about you and Ken, how Cree was betraying him after he'd tried to take him under his wing."

She wanted to fly at him, hurt him when he mentioned Cree's name. She was face to face with Cree's murderer—and soon now, *her* murderer. She fought down the rage she felt.

"And Desi Howe," she asked coldly. "Did *she* betray him too?"

He rocked back and forth. Apparently, he had changed his mind. "Why ask questions? You're not going to live long enough to sift the answers." He seemed to be enjoying himself.

Now she was silent because he was right. She *was* going to die. Adam could never get here in time. He'd said he knew what was going on, but he *couldn't* know. She plainly saw him then in her mind, saw his dear, earnest face and she sent him the message: *I love you. Oh God, I love you. Don't come trying to save me and get killed yourself. Please, Adam.*

Will continued to explain in a drained voice. "Cree was easy. He never suspected a thing. I made friends with him and he recommended me for the job at WMRY. I met you and I hated you on sight. It wasn't easy pretending the way I did, but I had a mission. You see, Laverne wouldn't let Dad hire me; she pitched such a hissy fit. He just gave me more money and said he'd work it all out later. He even hinted that he might leave her."

He paused, drew a deep breath and snorted. "Cree looked so surprised when I shot him and left him in his car right in the city. It was a clean job. I hated Cree for ratting on my old man and he was going to testify against him. He never dreamed I hated him. Cree laughed at me. He didn't believe I'd kill him up until I shot him." He paused again then before he continued. "Desi was a different kettle of fish. Suspicious as hell. She knew she was ratting and expected something bad to happen. That's why she wouldn't testify at first. She was set to testify against my dad *and* Kevin and Kevin wanted her killed at first, but Kevin got to her and she was scared of him. She should have kept on being scared.

"Then she *did* decide to testify and I had to do what I did. That one Dad asked me to do. He didn't ask me to kill Cree. I did that on my own, but he thanked me. He couldn't stand to see all he'd built up tumble. Dad was a very proud man, came up poor, made it in spades. He loved the life he lived and he wasn't about to let go of it. And I meant to do everything I could to help him. Before I found him, I wanted to die most of the time. He had saved my life; now I was going to save his. You and Ken and the damned Special Investigations Unit destroyed him. Oh, I know Ken had to give you the go ahead, but you *relished* your job.

"I used to look at you at the station and it was all I could do to keep from choking you every time I saw you, talked with you. And you and Ken were happy about what you were doing…. I slipped the blood into your bag. Cal Reams put the rose on your door."

Raven shook her head. "No, you're wrong. Tom was on the wrong track. Special Investigations had built a strong case against him for fraud, embezzlement and forgery, as well as bribery—"

"Shut up!" Will fairly screamed. "Whatever he did he *had* to do to make it. The news is full of bigger men who did worse things."

"You're right, and they went to prison and—"

His voice was ragged again with hatred. "My dad wasn't going to prison. He'd die first. Yeah, and he *did* die first, thanks to you and your damned buddies."

Raven sat thinking, he was wrong of course; Ken and Special Investigations were the ones who called the shots. She merely helped collect the evidence.

"*You killed him,*" he said again, his voice flat.

"He was responsible for killing two people in addition to the several million in money he stole from people who were helpless. Three children died because they couldn't get the treatment they needed."

"I have the honor of having killed the two hyenas who were set to testify against him and I'm proud of it. After killing you, I'll add two more notches to my belt: Kenneth Courtland and the guy in Special Investigations. If *I'm* killed after I complete that job, so be it. What in the hell do I have to live for now? I had nothing before I knew him. Now his money won't make up for his death.

"I called you, threatened and stalked you, helped kidnap your kid. By the way, that was your ex's idea. He warned me I'd better not hurt her one little bit and I didn't. He helped me find a guy from out of town to kidnap your kid so she could never identify us. I made the calls. I'm a great mimic. Kevin's a trip, but I've come to like the guy. He helped me find Cal to pull off the jobs, only Cal is a cretin. You should have been dead by now. If Kevin had his way you'd be dead and he'd have complete custody of his kid."

"She's *my* kid too."

"Kevin hates you and your husband, the detective. For what it's worth, I hate the both of you, too. I hate Laverne Carr, but I agree with something she often says—*an eye for an eye and a tooth for a tooth*. Now you're going to pay for taking my father's life."

He held the gun steady and she suddenly decided to fight to her death. *What choice did she have?* She thought she heard unfamiliar sounds somewhere in the vicinity of the basement, but it must have been wishful thinking.

Her wild movements took him by surprise and he reeled backward as she sprang up and came to his left. His gun sounded like a sharp blast and a bullet went into a mirror. Then she was all over him, butting his chin, her knee in his groin and he didn't have a chance to recover, but a second shot grazed her upper arm as Adam crashed through the basement door.

Will turned and his attention went in the direction of Adam coming at him, zigzagging, making him dizzy with trying to keep up with the action Adam had set in motion. But with a steadiness born of desperation, Will grabbed Raven and held on doggedly. "By God, she *dies!*" he snarled. "I don't give a damn if you kill me, but *she dies!*"

But Adam was level-headed with more purpose than he'd ever known. This monster held Adam's life in his hands—Raven, his wife. And he had only one chance to save her. His hands had never been so steady and his mark had never been so accurate as he fired at the target of Will's heart with God-given strength and precision. But there was a second shot, and another. It all happened so fast then that Raven couldn't possibly sort it out.

The gun dropped from Will's hand as he slumped and Adam kicked the gun away from him and told Raven to pick it up. She did as he told her. Will lay spread-eagled on his back as his eyes were slowly opening and fixing on some distant spot.

It was then that she saw with horror that Adam's shirt front was reddening with his blood. She screamed and went to him. She had to help him, but she also had to make absolutely certain that Will was dead. He could have another gun.

Police were rushing into the room from the basement and in seconds they had the scene under control. An ambulance crew ran in the front door as a policeman barked grimly, "Send for a second ambulance for the body. This clown won't be trying to kill anybody else."

Raven was on her knees by her husband's side, cradling his head in her arms, his blood soaking her sweats, and the blood from her own wound went unnoticed.

It was then that a policewoman came to her side. "You've been shot," she said, "and you're in a state of shock. We'll put you in the ambulance with Detective Steele. Can you stand up?"

"I *have* to stand up. I have to help him."

Adam was keenly aware at first of everything that went on around him. "Raven," he whispered.

"I'm right here, sweetheart," she said in a strong voice. "I'm not going anywhere." She huddled by him as she tried to keep it together. Adam needed her now.

It came so slowly; she was safe and Adam had heard someone say that the hellhound was dead. This time Raven's nightmare was really over, so he could relax. He tried to tell her that he loved her, but he couldn't talk; his tongue was too heavy. Then blackness enveloped him as he heard Raven cry his name and he lost all sense of time or place.

Adam awoke in a high, white hospital bed and at first he couldn't focus. He was coming back from a long way out. Then he saw her sitting by his bedside, holding his hand and she was crying.

"Hey!" he said in a croaked whisper. "Honey, please don't cry."

She could have been an angel for all he knew and he also knew he loved her. Why the hell was he swathed in bandages all over his upper body? He roused fairly rapidly, because he didn't have time to be out of commission.

"Adam," she whispered. "Sweetheart." She lifted his hand, kissed it, then held it to her face as her salty tears fell on his hand. "I love you. Oh, I love you."

"Love you too," he managed to get out as a doctor came into the room.

"Hey, there," the doctor said. "So you finally agreed to come back to us. Man, you've made a speedy come-around, for which I'm grateful."

"Couldn't stay away," Adam managed. "So much to come back to."

"I'll say you have," the doctor told them. "I'm going to examine you as soon as the nurse gets here. Someone told me to tell you your children are here, and other family members have spent the night camped out in the waiting room. Again, welcome back."

Raven sat by his bed, refused to leave his side. Her mind raced with thoughts about Adam and her, then simmered down to sweet reflections. "Dear God," she prayed, "please don't take him from us."

All doubts about the difference in their ages were swept away. He had risked his life to save her and she would have done the same for him. That was what mattered and nothing else. He was hers and she was his. Their children loved each other. And when he was fully awake, she had something precious to tell him, news she had gotten before the hellhound came calling.

Over the next day the doctor told Raven that Adam was making a miraculous recovery, but he didn't want him to talk much just yet. "One-half inch closer to his heart," the doctor had told her, "and he wouldn't be with us. He was lucky. God was with him."

And it was two more days before she could tell him her news.

"Can you stand a delightful, small shock?" she asked him.

"From you, yes."

"I have some news you're going to be delighted to hear."

"I know already from looking at you. You're glowing and so you're pregnant."

"Oh." She tapped his arm. "There's no way of surprising you. How would you know?"

"I said it, you're glowing. And I always told you I have potent seed. They were always headed straight to your womb. They couldn't miss. When did you know for certain?"

"The day you were shot. The doctor called me that morning right after you left. I had already taken the e.p.t., but I wanted to be sure, so I went in for a blood test and oh, I *am*."

"This calls for a prolonged kiss. Are you up to one? How's your arm?"

"Nothing hurts me now. Here's your kiss, lover." She stood up and leaned over him, brought her mouth to his and kissed him, her tongue going into the hollows of his mouth and he groaned. "I've got to get well in a hurry. You're making me hurt with wanting you."

Chapter 30

The Steeles were at the hospital every day—*all* of them, including Damien who had flown in from Nashville, and they teased Adam lovingly and relentlessly.

"Well, it really is true," Mel said, "you can't keep a good man down."

And Adam looked at his mother. "Mom, don't cry. It's over now and everything came out fine."

Rispa sniffed, "I'm crying because you two are having a baby and I'm so happy."

Adam just grinned from ear to ear.

Dosha got up and sat on the bed by her brother. "Ask me why I'm crying and I'll say it's because I love you so damned much, both of you."

Damien came to the bed. "You're tough, bro, and you'll pull through this in a hurry. How do you feel?"

Adam smiled crookedly. "Shot," he joked.

"Yeah," Damien came back. "You're too ornery *not* to make it."

Marty and Caitlin were there. Frank and Caroline. Whit. Ashley. Annice.

Looking at Marty and Caitlin, Adam teased them. "Next time bring the twins. We have to learn from them because who knows, we may have a set of our own."

Raven smiled. "Stop borrowing trouble. But then I really wouldn't mind."

Merla and Ricky were in school, but they had been there every afternoon and this was no exception.

"I was afraid you were gonna die," Merla confessed.

"Nah, I never thought so," Ricky offered. But he *had* been terrified, and the relief he felt was overwhelming.

The first day when the doctor said Adam could talk as much as he wanted to, Raven asked him how he had gotten to her in time.

Adam was silent for very long minutes, stringing it all together.

"When I called you," he said, "you let me know something was very wrong, but it was background info that made me know someone was there and *who*. You see, honey, when we found the old McCloud Labs I.D. card in Cal Reams' wallet, Allyson was on it in a shot. We got a search warrant and searched Cal's apartment and we found papers and an address book that Allyson brought back to the office and sifted through. Thanks to her thoroughness, this morning she found Will Ryalls' name with an asterisk beside it. She had been introduced to him at the dinner-dance. She had just called it to my attention and I called to tell you I'd be right home and don't let anybody in, certainly not Will Ryalls. But I was too late.

"I knew from your voice that something was horribly wrong and I guessed what it was. I told Allyson to call other policemen in and monitor the situation. And around the corner I saw Will's red Sting Ray parked and

God, I was sick. I crept into the house from the opposite side of where you were and came into the basement. I could hear music and I knew it would likely shield the sounds we made coming in. There were three other guys with me, ready for action. When I heard the shot, I was up the stairs and sneaking up on him. If I made a mistake, it was going to be all over for the both of us." His eyes narrowed as he flashed her a hungry look. "Hey, I could use another one of those special kisses."

She grinned. "As Merla says, we're always hugging and kissing on each other. Can't we ever get enough?"

"Uh-uh. We're good role models for love. Still think you're too old for me?"

"I think we're just perfect for each other. We go together like really good apple pie and ice cream."

A thought came to mind then that she really didn't want to talk about. "What happens to Kevin?"

"He's going up for a stretch. You said he told Desi that his lawyers would get him out of any trouble he got into. I'm betting he's wrong this time."

Kevin would be incarcerated long enough, she hoped, that she could raise Merla as the delightful person the child had always been.

Adam mended swiftly and went home in less than a week. It was a Saturday and the entire family was there. Such a joyous occasion, Adam thought, as he and Raven paused at the front door. "I want to carry you over the threshold," he told Raven as he kissed her cheek.

"Don't you dare." She laughed. "We've got to get you well again."

"I'm well enough for certain activities. And I'm always well enough to adore you."

"You're getting well for sure. All your freshness is coming back. But then that's one of the parts I love so much."

Then they were swamped by the other friends and neighbors. Raven thought as she touched her belly that it really
was a glorious life her baby would come into.

Epilogue

August of the following year

"Hold on now, sweetheart! Don't be nervous."

Raven couldn't help laughing. Adam was the one who was shot through with nerves. She had talked with her doctor who told her to hurry in because the baby would probably come at any minute. Raven's face lit in a beatific smile. The little rascal; he couldn't wait to get here. The doctor had thought it would be several more days, but her water had broken unexpectedly. And Adam had been all worried thumbs.

It was six-thirty A.M. Her bag had been packed and ready. Now they were on the highway, going to the hospital. "You're the one who's nervous, my love." She reached over and patted his knee to calm him, then let her hand lie on his knee and pressed lightly. "You drive," she said, "and I'm going to think about what's gone down these past months. I'm kind of old to be having a baby."

"Hush. We've put that part behind us."

"Yes. I know now it's how we come together and how

we love each other and we're superb at that. I'm not afraid of losing you any longer."

"And I'm not afraid of losing you. As for me, I'm stuck to you like glue. We've got us a baby to raise, along with Merla and Ricky."

She was silent then, watching the lush green scenery sweeping outside. D.C. was a beautiful city. There weren't many other cars out. As the miles flashed by, the past months flashed by and she remembered the bad as well as the truly wonderful.

Papa Mac and Mrs. Reuben were married now and lived part-time in the country at his house and part-time in D.C. at hers. Papa Mac often laughed and pinched himself. "I've got me a silver queen," he often chortled. "A regular fox." And Mrs. Reuben's eyes said she found him no less than a king.

Viveca and Carey just had their precious baby girl and Carey bragged that already they had a trunkful of photos. They had never been happier. Viveca enjoyed being a stay-at-home mom and planned to do volunteer work with children when her baby was two.

Raven started to say something and thought better of it. Let Adam focus on the road, but he looked at her reassuringly for brief moments as he drove.

She couldn't help grinning as she thought of Ken and Allyson linking together. He had given her a beautiful diamond and she didn't seem cold anymore. If it hadn't been for Allyson finding Will's name in Cal Reams's apartment, she, Raven wouldn't be alive. There was a lump in her throat because now she and Allyson were friends.

And Will Ryalls had died as he had lived, in bitter hatred. She couldn't help shuddering as it all came back.

Cal Reams was in prison for ten years for assault with attempt to kill and Kevin's fancy lawyers hadn't been able to get him off or, for that matter, get him less time. And Tom Carr's right-hand man, Allen Mills, had gone up for seven years for fraud, embezzlement and bribery. He had cried at his sentencing that Raven attended and it seemed that with Tom dead, the life had gone out of him.

It all brought her down to Kevin. *Kevin.* His bravado had informed the courtroom and the judge had gone especially hard on him. "Why a man like you with everything to revel in chooses a life of mayhem and murder, I'll never know."

When Kevin lifted his hand to protest, the judge and Kevin's lawyer shushed him.

"But I do know this," the judge continued. "I can protect this community from viciousness like yours. A man who would subject his daughter to what you subjected her to in having her kidnapped, well, Dr. McCloud, you degrade your title and your life."

The judge had given Kevin thirty years. "Because you killed those two people as surely as if you had pulled the trigger."

Kevin had cried like a baby, all the bravado was gone, and he had cursed his lawyers in court until the judge stopped him.

The Steeles were all doing wonderfully well. Adam and Raven's baby would be christened at the church near the Steeles, near Minden. And thinking of the Steeles made her think of Cree and a few acid tears gathered in her eyes. The baby would be named Adam Cree, but they would call the baby A.C. because Glenda's little boy was named Cree, Jr.

"Are you okay?" Adam asked.

"Never better. I was thinking of Cree."

"Funny, so was I. I guess we've gotten some closure now, but God, for a life like his to be wasted. Well, Glenda and we have got his baby son, Cree Jr., and our own little Adam Cree."

The red brick hospital came into view then and Adam breathed a huge sigh of relief as they pulled into the parking lot. At the hospital entrance, a wheelchair and attendants waited for them. Adam bent over and kissed her lightly on the mouth.

"They'll take you in," he said. "I'll park and be right there." He squeezed her hand. "Baby, this is another beginning for us that only leads to forever."

Dear Readers,

With all my heart I wish you the joy in reading that I had in writing Adam and Raven's story.

Love is so special to each and every one of us, so I wish it in full measure to you and yours. We deserve it, we treasure it and consider it the most valuable thing we know.

Your letters are always a delight to read and they warm my heart, so keep them coming. My Web site is www.francinecraft.com. I can also be contacted at francinecraft@yahoo.com.

The best of everything,

Francine

ABOUT THE AUTHOR

Francine Craft is the pen name of a Washington, D.C.-based writer who has enjoyed writing for many years. A native Mississippian, she has lived in New Orleans and found it one of the most fascinating places imaginable.

A veteran of many interesting jobs, Francine has been a research assistant for a large psychiatric organization, an elementary school teacher, a business school instructor and a federal government legal secretary.

She is constantly on the bestseller list for Amazon.com's multicultural romance writers and receives rave reviews from reviewers and readers. She is a member of Romance Writers of America.

Francine's hobbies are prodigious reading, photography and songwriting. She deeply enjoys time spent with friends.